# The Comédienne
by Wladyslaw S. Reymont
translated by Edmund Obecny

# For the Love
# of Children
by Wladyslaw S. Reymont
translated by Sergiej Nowikow

Riga : S. Novikov, 2017.

# ABOUT THIS BOOK

*The Comédienne* is a book by Wladyslaw S. Reymont. Wladyslaw S. Reymont is the 1924 laureate of the Nobel Prize in Literature. This is the story of a girl who comes to the capital to make a theater career. She meets corrupt, jealous, hysterical, and vulgar people lacking high principles and interests.

*For the Love of Children* is a curiously plotted work by Wladyslaw S.Reymont. The main storyline deals with the relations between a poor boy and a girl from a rich family. Besides, it is a striking depiction of different types of maternal love— cruel, self-sacrificing, patient. This is the first publication of the translation.

The latest version of the book can be found at the following locations:
www.amazon.co.uk/dp/1530484367
www.amazon.com/dp/1530484367

S. NOVIKOV

ISBN-10: 1530484367    ISBN-13: 978-1530484362

Other books from this series can be found at the following locations:

## Best of Polish Fairy Tales
www.amazon.com/dp/1517196353
Reading these fairy tales, you will enjoy the wisdom and life experience of many generations of Polish people that are behind them. The book includes more than 100 illustrations. None of these fairy tales has been previously published in this English translation.

## 52 Fairy Tales
www.amazon.com/dp/1530464714
The book contains 52 fairy tales for a sunny mood. You won't find the tales in other books since they were first compiled and translated into English in 2016. This compilation presents the FOLK VERSIONS of the tales.

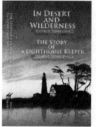

## The Story of a Lighthouse Keeper by Henryk Sienkiewicz
www.amazon.com/dp/1530494303
It is an overwhelming story of a retired elderly soldier who takes the job of a lighthouse keeper in the Caribbean Sea. Henryk Sienkiewicz is the 1905 laureate of the Nobel Prize in Literature.

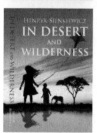

## In Desert and Wilderness
by Henryk Sienkiewicz
www.amazon.com/dp/1530248019
This is a novel by Henryk Sienkiewicz, his only work for children and teenagers. The book describes the wanderings of two children in Africa. It is a fascinating narrative full of adventure.

## Three Lamps and Other Polish Tales
www.amazon.com/dp/1517127998
This book comprises of 50 Polish folk fairy tales. These tales are radiant with the Polish people's vitality, filial love for one's parents, and the energy of kindness. This compilation presents the original folk versions of the tales.

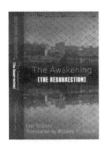

**The Awakening** by Leo Tolstoy
www.amazon.com/dp/1530465419
It tells the story of a nobleman
overburdened with the sin he has
committed. This sin concerns

a young peasant woman whom he seduced and then
left. He lives the ordinary life of a self-proud rich
man until he encounters his former lover.
The place where they see each other is the court,
and the girl is being accused. This is the translation by William E.
Smith, which is easy to read and understand. It is one of the best
translations of the work ever published.

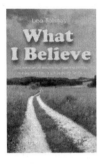

**What I Believe** by Leo Tolstoy
www.amazon.com/dp/1522841199
This edition of the book was banned
following its publication in Russia.
The author describes the changes

which happened to his mind. He also tells about
the long way he had covered before coming to his
ideas. The translation by Constantine Popoff
conveys the original meaning in brilliant detail.

# CONTENTS

# The Comédienne

## CHAPTER I

BUKOWIEC, a station on the Dombrowa railroad, lies in a beautiful spot. A winding line was cut among the beech and pine covered hills, and at the most level point, between a mighty hill towering above the woods wits bald and rocky summit, and a long narrow valley, glistening with pools and marshes, was placed the station. This two-story building of rough brick containing the quarters of the station-master and his assistant, a small wooden house at the side for the telegrapher and the minor employees, another similar one near the last switches for the watchman, three switch-houses at various points, and a freight-house were the only signs of human habitation.

Surrounding the station on all sides were the murmuring woods, while above, a strip of blue sky, slashed with gray clouds, extended like a wide-spreading roof.

The sun was veering toward the south and glowing ever brighter and warmer; the reddish slopes of the rocky hill, with its ragged summit gashed by spring freshets, were bathed in a flood of golden sunlight.

The calm of a spring afternoon diffused itself over all. The trees stood motionless without a murmur in their boughs. The sharp emerald leaves of the beeches drooped drowsily, as though lulled to sleep by the light, the warmth, and the silence. The twitter of birds sounded at rare intervals from the thickets, and only the cry of the water-fowls on the marshes and the somnolent hum of insects filled the air. Above the blue line of rails stretching in an endless chain of curves and zigzags, the warm air glowed with shifting hues of violet light.

Out of the office of the station-master came a short, squarely-built man with light, almost flaxen hair. He was dressed, or rather squeezed into a stylish surtout and held his hat in his hand while a workman helped him on with his overcoat.

The station-master stood before him, stroking his grayish beard with an automatic gesture and smiling in a friendly manner. He also was stocky, strongly-knit, and broad shouldered, and in his blue eyes, flashing jovially from beneath heavy eyebrows and a square forehead, there also gleamed determination and an unbending will. His straight nose, full lips, a certain contraction of the brows, and the sharp direct glance of his eyes, that seemed like a dagger-stroke—all these typified a violent nature.

"Good-bye, until to-morrow!" . . . said the blonde man merrily, extending his big hand in farewell.

"Good-bye! ... Oh come, let me hug you. To-morrow we'll celebrate the big event with a good drink."

"I am a little afraid of that to-morrow."

"Courage, my boy! Don't fear, I give you my word that everything will turn out all right. I'll tell Jenka all about it immediately. You will come to us to-morrow for dinner, propose to her, be accepted by her, in a month you will be married and we shall be neighbors . . . hey! I like you immensely, Mr. Andrew! I always dreamed of having such a son. Unfortunately I haven't any, but at least I'll have a son-in-law."

They kissed each other heartily; the younger jumped into a light mountain rig waiting near the platform and drove away at a swift pace along a narrow road leading through the wood. He glanced back, tipped his hat, sent a deeper bow to the windows of the second story, and disappeared in the shadow of the trees. After riding a little way, he sprang from the carriage, ordered the driver to go on, and continued his journey on foot by a short cut.

The station-master, as soon as his guest had vanished from sight, reëntered his office and busied himself with his official correspondence. He was highly satisfied that Grzesikiewicz had asked him for his daughter's hand and he had promised her to him in the certainty that she would agree.

Grzesikiewicz, although not handsome, was sensible and very rich. The woods among which stood the station and a few neighboring farmhouses were the property of his father. The elder Grzesikiewicz was primarily a peasant, who had transformed himself from an innkeeper into a trader and had made a fabulous fortune by the sale of timber and cattle-fodder.

Many people in the neighborhood still remembered that the old man used to be called Grzesik in his youth. They often ridiculed him for it, but no one upbraided him for changing his name, for he did not pose as an aristocrat, nor did he assume an overbearing air toward others because of his wealth.

He was a peasant, and in spite of all changes remained a peasant to the very core. His son received a thorough education and now helped his father. Two years ago he had made the acquaintance of the station-master's daughter after her return from the academy at Kielce and had fallen violently in love with her. His father offered no opposition, but told him plainly to go ahead and marry if he wanted.

Andrew met the girl quite often, became ever more deeply enamored of her, but never dared to speak to her of his love. She liked him, but at the same time her attitude was so frank and straightforward that his intended words of endearment and confessions of love always froze upon his lips before he had half uttered them. He felt that she belonged to a higher breed of women, inaccessible to such a "churl " as he often frankly called himself; but precisely because of his lowly origin he loved her all the more intensely.

Finally, he decided to speak to her father about it.

Orlowski received him with open arms, and in his arbitrary way, without consulting his daughter, at once gave him his word that all would be well. Grzesikiewicz was therefore thinking that Janina would not refuse him, that she must have already spoken of the matter with her father.

"Why not!" he whispered to himself. He was young, wealthy, and—well, he loved her so dearly. "In a month our marriage will take place," he added hurriedly and that thought filled him with such joy that he began to run swiftly through the woods, breaking branches off the trees, kicking the rotted stumps that were in his way, knocking off the heads of spring mushrooms, whistling and smiling. And he thought, too, how glad his mother would be to hear the news.

She was an old peasant woman, who with the exception of her dress had not changed in the least on account of her wealth. She thought of Janina as of a princess. Her one dream was to have for a daughter-in-law a real lady, an aristocrat whose beauty and high birth would dazzle her, for her husband and his money and the respect which the entire neighborhood showed him did not suffice her. She was always conscious of being a peasant and received all honors with a true peasant-like distrust.

"Andy!" she often said to her son. "Andy, I wish you would marry Miss Orlowska. That's what I call a real lady! When she looks at you, she makes you shudder with awe and wish to fall at her feet and beg some boon of her. . . . She must be very good for whenever she meets folks in the woods she greets them in God's name, chats with them, and pets the children . . . another would be incapable of that! Gentle birth will always out. I sent her a basket of mushrooms and when she met me she kissed my hand for it. And she is not lacking in wisdom. Ho! ho! she knows that I have a prize of a son. Andy, marry her. Hurry, and make hay while the sun shines!"

Andrew would usually laugh at his mother's prattle, kiss her hand, and promise her to settle at once everything according to her wishes.

"We will have a princess in our house and seat her in state in the parlor! Don't fear, Andy, I will not let her soil her hands with anything. I will wait upon her, serve her, hand her everything she needs; all she has to do is to read French books and play on the piano, for that is what a lady is for!" his mother would add.

And he was just as much of a peasant as she deep within himself; beneath the smooth veneer of the civilized and educated man seethed a primitive unbridled energy and the desire for a wife—a woman to rule him. This young Hercules, who, when he felt like it, could fling unaided into the wagon two-hundred pound sacks of wheat, and who often had to toil like a common laborer to quell with weariness the riotous tides that often rose in his healthy blood, unexhausted through dozens of generations—dreamed of Janina and was vanquished by her beauty and sweetness.

He now rushed along through the woods like a whirlwind and then flew across the fields, all green with the first vigorous shoots of the spring wheat, to tell his mother of the happiness awaiting him. He knew that he would find her in her favorite room whose walls were adorned with three rows of holy pictures in gilt frames—for that was the only luxury that she allowed herself.

The station-master, in the meanwhile, finished writing his official report, signed it, made an entry in his journal, placed it in an envelope, addressed it to "the Expeditor of the Station of Bukowiec," and called: "Anthony!"

A servant appeared at the door.

"Take this to the dispatcher!" ordered Orlowski.

The servant took the letter without a word and with the solemnest mien in the world laid it upon a table on the other side of the window. The station-master arose, stretched himself, took off his red cap, and walked over to that table; then he put on an ordinary cap with a red border and with the greatest gravity opened the letter that he had written a moment ago. He read it, wrote on the other side a few lines in reply, again signing his name, and then addressed it to the "Local Station-Master" and had Anthony deliver it to himself.

All the officials of the railway knew his mania and made merry at his expense. There was no expeditor in Bukowiec, hence he performed both functions,—that of station-master and dispatcher—but at two different tables.

As the station-master he was his own superior, so he often had moments of truly insane joy when, noticing some error in his accounts, or some omission in his duty as a dispatcher, he would indite a complaint against himself.

Everybody made fun of him, but he paid no attention and persisted in following his own way, saying in justification: "Order and system are the foundations of everything; if they are lacking, all else fails!"

Having finished his tasks, he locked all the drawers of his desk, glanced out on the platform, and went to his home. He entered not by way of the anteroom, but through the kitchen, for he had to know all that was going on. He peeped into the stove, gave the fire a jab with the poker, scolded the servant-girl because of some water spilled on the floor, and then proceeded to the dining-room.

"Where is Jenka?" he asked.

"Miss Janina will be here in a minute," answered Mrs. Krenska, a sort of housekeeper and *duenna* in one person, a pretty blonde with expressive features.

"What are you preparing for dinner?"

"The Director's favorite dish; chicken fricassee, sorrel soup, and cutlets—"

"Extravagance! By God, what extravagance! Soup and one kind of meat is enough even for a king! You will ruin me!"

"But Mr. Director ... I ordered this meal prepared especially for you, sir—"

"Bosh! You women have nothing in your heads but fricassees, sweets, and dainties. All that is bosh!"

"You judge us unfairly, sir; we generally economize more than men do."

"Aha! You economize so that you can later buy yourselves more fineries ... I know, you needn't tell me."

Mrs. Krenska did not answer, but began to set the table for dinner.

Just then, Janina entered. She was a girl of about twenty-two, tall, well-formed, and broad-shouldered. Her features were not very regular; she had black eyes, a straight forehead, a trifle too broad, dark eyebrows strongly accented, a Roman nose, and full glowing lips. Her eyes had a deep expression indicating an introspective nature; her lips were tightly drawn together in what seemed to be a semblance of dignity or hidden temper. Two deep lines clouded her clear forehead. Gorgeous, wavy blonde hair, with a reddish tinge, crowned her small round head. Her amber-gold complexion had the mellowness of a ripe peach. There was something strange about her voice: an alto that at times dropped into a deep baritone of almost masculine accents.

She bowed her head to her father and seated herself on the opposite side of the table.

"Grzesikiewicz was here to see me to-day," said Orlowski slowly serving the soup, for he always presided over the meals.

Janina glanced at him calmly.

"He asked me for your hand, Jenka."

"What did you tell him, Mr. Director?" quickly interposed Mrs. Krenska.

"That is our affair," he answered sternly. "Our affair ... I told him all would be well," he said, turning to Janina. "He will be here to-morrow for dinner and you can talk it over between yourselves."

"What's the use, father! Since you have told him that all would be well, you can receive him yourself to-morrow and tell him from me that everything is far from well. . . .

I do not wish to speak with him. To-morrow I will go to Kielce!"

"Bosh! If you were not a crazy fool, you would understand what an excellent husband he would make for you! Even though Grzesikiewicz is a peasant he's worth more to you than a prince, for he wants you . . . and he wants you because he's a fool. He could afford to take his pick of the best. ... You ought to be grateful to him for choosing you. He will propose to you to-morrow and in a month from now you will be Mrs. Grzesikiewicz."

"I will not be his wife! If he can get another, let him do so—"

"I swear to God that you will be Mrs. Grzesikiewicz!"

"No! I will not have him or anyone else! I will not marry!"

"Fool!" he retorted brutally. "You will marry because you need a roof over your head, food and dress, and someone to look after you. ... I don't intend to ruin myself completely for your sake . . . and when I am gone, what then?"

"I have my dower; I will get along without the aid of Grzesikiewicz or anyone like him. Aha, so your object in wanting to marry me is simply to provide for my support!" She regarded him defiantly.

"And what of it? For what else do women marry?"

"They marry for love and marry those whom they love."

"You're a fool, I tell you once again," he shouted vehemently, helping himself to another portion of chicken. "Love is nothing but this sauce, you can eat the chicken just as well without it; sauce is nothing but an invention, a freak and a modern fad!"

"No self-respecting woman sells herself to the first man that comes along merely because he is capable of supporting her!"

"You're a fool. They all do it, they all sell themselves. Love is childish prattle and nonsense. Don't irritate me."

"It is not a question of irritating you, father, or whether love is nonsense or not; it is a question of my future which you dispose of as though it belonged to you. Already at the time that Zielenkiewicz proposed to me. I told you that I do not intend to marry at all."

"Zielenkiewicz is merely Zielenkiewicz, but Grzesikiewicz is a very lord, and what I call a man! He is kind-hearted, wise—for did he not graduate from the academy at Dublany—and as strong as a bull. A fellow who can master the wildest horse and who, when he struck a peasant in the face the other day, knocked out six of his teeth with one blow—such a fellow is not good enough for you! I swear he is ideal, the highest of all ideals!"

"Yes, your ideal is an incomparable one; he'd make a good prize-fighter."

"You are as crazy as your mother was. Wait! Andrew will muzzle you and show you how such women are ruled. He will not spare the whip."

Janina violently shoved aside her chair, threw her spoon on the table, and left the room, slamming the door after her.

"Don't sit there gaping, but order the cutlets served for me," he shouted at Mrs. Krenska, who gazed after Janina with a sympathetic look.

She handed him the dish with a servile mien, whispering to him with a solicitous tone in her voice, "Mr. Director, you must not irritate yourself so, it is not good for your health."

"Such is my fate!" he drawled. "I can't even eat in peace, without having to listen to these everlasting squabbles." He then began to air at length his grievances and complaints over Janina's stubbornness, her wilful character, and his continual troubles with her.

Mrs. Krenska obsequiously pretended to agree with him, and occasionally emphasized some detail. She complained discreetly that she also had to bear a great deal because of Janina, sighed deeply, and wheedled him at every opportunity. She brought in the coffee and arrack and poured it for him herself. While doing so she fawned upon him, touched his hands and arms, as though accidentally, lowered her eyes, and kept up a continual flirtation, trying to awaken some spark in him.

Orlowski's anger slowly abated, and having drunk his coffee, he ejaculated, "Thank you! I swear to God that you alone understand me. ... You are a kind woman, Mrs. Krenska."

"Mr. Director, if I could only show you what I feel, what—" she faltered, dropping her eyes.

Orlowski pressed her hand and went to his own room for a nap.

Mrs. Krenska ordered the table cleared and afterwards, when she was alone, took up some sewing and sat near the window facing the station platform. Occasionally she would look up from her work and gaze at the woods, or at the long line of rails, but everything seemed deserted and silent. Finally, unable to sit still any longer, she arose and began to pace around the table with a soft, feline step, smiling and repeating to herself: "I will get him, I will get him! At last I will find a little rest in my life, my wanderings will come to an end!"

Scenes from the past floated before her memory: whole years of wandering with a company of provincial actors.

Krenska had abandoned the theater because she managed to catch a young fellow who married her. She lived with him for two whole years . . . two years which she recalled with bitterness. Her husband was insanely jealous and frequently beat her.

At last he died and she was free, but she had no longer any desire to return to the theater. She shuddered at the thought of resuming that eternal pilgrimage from town to town and the everlasting poverty of a provincial actor's life. Moreover, she realized that she was growing old and homely. So she sold all her household furnishings, received a pension from the management to which her husband had belonged, and for half a year played the rôle of a widow. She was very eager to marry a second time and sedulously spread her nets, but all in vain, for her own temperament stood in the way. With money in her pocket, there awakened in her again the former actress with her careless and sporty disposition and craving for pleasure and enjoyment. Being still seductive, she was surrounded by a swarm of various admirers with whom she squandered all she had, together with the reputation which she had succeeded in establishing for herself with the aid of her husband.

Krenska had no abilities of any kind, but she possessed a great deal of cleverness, so, instead of resigning herself to despair when the last of her admirers had forsaken her, she inserted an advertisement in the *Kielce Gazette* reading: "Middle-aged widow of a government official desires position as a housekeeper to widower, or as a social secretary."

She did not have to wait long for results. Her advertisement was answered in person by Orlowski, who was badly in need of a housekeeper, for Janina was still attending school and he could not himself manage the servants. Krenska seemed so quiet, humble, and full of grief over the loss of her husband that he did not ask her any questions, but engaged her immediately.

Orlowski was a widower who possessed a good salary, a few thousand dollars in cash, and an only daughter—an absent daughter whom he detested. Krenska at first tried to turn the heads of the station officials, but very soon sized up the situation and immediately began playing a new rôle whereby she perseveringly strove to attain the last act: Matrimony.

Orlowski became used to her. She knew how to make herself indispensable and always to show that indispensability so skillfully that it did not offend.

Moreover, the gray autumn days and the long wintry evenings brought her nearer to her goal, for Orlowski, who was fifty-eight years old and had rheumatism, was always a maniac, but during his rheumatic attacks he would become a raving maniac. She alone knew how to mollify and manage him with her inherent cleverness, sharpened by many years of theatrical experience.

There was only one obstacle in her way—Janina. Krenska realized that as long as Janina was at home she could accomplish nothing. She decided to wait—and waited patiently.

Orlowski loved his daughter with hatred, that is, he loved her because he hated her. He hated her because she was the daughter of his wife, whose memory he violently cursed—his wife, who after two years of conjugal life, left him, because she could no longer endure his tyranny and eccentricities. He brought legal action against her and tried to force her to return to him, but their separation became a permanent one. He raved with anger, but his relentlessness, unexampled stubbornness, and insane pride prevented him from begging his wife to return, which she might have done, for she was a good woman. Her only failing was an illness that baffled all the provincial doctors. She had the soul of a mimosa, so sensitive that every tear, pain, or grief would cast her into despair. Moreover she had an abnormal fear of thunderstorms, showers, frogs, dark rooms, unlucky numbers, and all loud sounds; so this husband of hers was killing her with his brutality.

Within a few years after their separation she died of nervous prostration, leaving Janina, who was then ten years old. Orlowski immediately took her away from his wife's family by force.

An additional reason for his hatred of Janina was because she happened to be a girl. With his wild and violent disposition he wanted a son on whom he could exercise not only his fists, but also his everyday humor. He had dreamed of a son and fancied that he would be a big and half-wild fellow, energetic and as strong as an oak.

He immediately sent Janina to a boarding-school, seeing her only once a year during her vacation. She spent the Christmas and Easter holidays at her aunt's home.

For these vacations, which were now in their third year, he would wait impatiently, for he was weary of being alone at his remote station. And as soon as Janina arrived hostilities between them would begin.

Janina grew up rapidly, and her mental and physical development were of the best, but having been conceived, born, and reared in an environment of continual hatred and quarrels and nursed with the tears and complaints of her mother at her father's brutality, she naturally disliked him and feared his scorn. This developed in her secretiveness and resentment. She rebelled against his despotism and niggardliness.

Janina inherited a few thousand rubles from her mother, and her father told her plainly that the interest on that sum would have to suffice her, for he did not intend to give her a single kopeck. She attended a first-class boarding-school, but after paying her fees and, later, her expenses at the academy she had so little left for her immediate needs that she had to continually think of how to make ends meet and to feel ashamed because of her worn shoes and dresses.

In a few years her classmates began to fear her, even the teachers often gave way to her, for she had her father's violent character and brooked no restraint. She never wept nor complained, but she was ever ready to avenge her wrongs with her fists, irrespective of what might happen to her. At the same time she was always one of the brightest scholars in her class.

All sincerely disliked her, but had to grant her supremacy. She herself became conscious of her superiority over the throng of her classmates, who treated her with aloofness, laughed at her shabby dresses and shoes, and barred her from all intimacy with them. Later she paid them back with unrelenting vengeance.

There were times when Orlowski was proud of Janina and warmly defended her before his friends, for the whole neighborhood was shocked at her tomboyish adventures. She would tramp through the woods late at night and in all kinds of weather, alone, like a young wild-boar separated from the herd. She was not a bit ashamed of climbing up trees for birds' nests, nor of riding astride in horseraces with the peasant lads on the pasturage. To avoid her father she would stay away from home for whole days at a time, dreaming of her return to school, while at school she would again dream of returning to the solitude of her home.

Such was Janina up to about the eighteenth year of her life when she graduated from high school and returned home for good. In her outward life she quieted down, but inwardly she became even more restless than before.

With her friend, Helen Walder, ideally beautiful and day dreaming of the emancipation of woman, she had parted. Helen went to Paris to study science. Janina had no desire to go, for she didn't feel the need of any knowledge of an abstract nature. She yearned for something that would exert a more potent influence upon her temperament—something that would absorb her whole being for all time.

Men, Janina avoided almost entirely, for they angered her with their impudence; the women bored her with their everlasting repetition of gossip, troubles, and intrigues. People in general seemed to keep aloof from her. All sorts of stories about her, more or less false, were circulated in the neighborhood.

She was a puzzle to all who knew her. Meanwhile, in her own soul she was waging a battle with her desires, to which she knew not how to give a definite form. She asked herself why she lived. She buried herself in books, but found no comfort there. She felt that she must find something that would absorb and thrill her entire being, felt that she would find it sooner or later, but in the meanwhile the agony of waiting almost drove her mad.

Zielenkiewicz, the owner of a heavily mortgaged village, proposed to her. Janina laughed outright at him and told him to his face that she did not intend to pay his debts with her dower.

She had reached her twenty-first year and was beginning to lose patience, when a commonplace occurrence decided her whole future.

In a nearby town an amateur theatrical was being arranged. Three one-act plays were selected and the parts had already been assigned, when there came a hitch: no one wanted to accept the rôle of Pawlowa in Blizinski's *The March Bachelor.*

The dramatic coach insisted on presenting this play, for he wanted to twit a certain neighbor with it, but none of the ladies would play the parts of Pawlowa or Eulalia.

Someone proposed that they request Janina Orlowska to take the part of Pawlowa, for they knew that she dared anything. She accepted it rather indifferently, and Mrs. Krenska, in whom memories of her histrionic past had suddenly awakened, induced Orlowski to announce that an amateur had also been found for the part of Eulalia.

The rehearsals lasted for about three months, for the cast of the players was changed several times—the usual fuss and confusion of provincial theaters where none of the ladies want to assume the part of an old, quarrelsome, or shady character, or that of a maid, but all wish to be heroines.

Krenska, whom Janina kept at a respectful distance from herself, never confiding anything to her nor asking her advice, found a good reason in the play for approaching her. She began to give her lessons in the art of acting, untiringly.

So absorbed did she become with her part, so deeply did she enter into the character, and so well did it fit her that she gave a very creditable presentation. She was every inch a peasant woman, a genuine Pawlowa, and received a clamorous ovation at the end of the play. This momentary triumph and the consciousness of her power filled her with a wild and unrestrained joy. It was with a feeling of intense regret that she saw the final curtain fall.

Krenska also created quite a furore. It was a rôle that she had often played with great success on the real stage. During the intermissions everyone was speaking only of her and of Janina.

"A comédienne! A born actress!" whispered the ladies, regarding Janina with a sort of contemptuous pity.

Orlowski, whom they thanked and congratulated for having so talented a daughter and companion, shrugged his shoulders. He was, however, satisfied, for he went behind the scenes, petted Janina, and kissed Krenska's hand.

"Good, good! . . . Nothing extraordinary, but at least I don't have to feel ashamed of you," was all the praise that he gave them.

After the performance Janina drew closer to Krenska and the latter, in a moment of weakness, betrayed the secret concerning her past life. She revealed to Janina a new realm, wondrous and alluring.

She listened with rapt attention to Krenska's accounts of the stage, her numerous appearances and triumphs, and the vivid life of an actor. As she related her experiences Krenska was herself carried away by enthusiasm and painted them in glowing colors; she no longer remembered the miseries of that life and held up only the brightest pictures to the gaze of the enraptured girl. She pulled out of her trunk faded and musty copies of rôles she had once impersonated, read them to Janina and played them, stirred by memories of the past.

All this fascinated the girl and awoke in her certain strong desires, but it did not, as yet, absorb her; it was not, as yet, that mysterious "something" for which she had been waiting so long.

She began to read with great interest the theatrical criticisms and the details about actors in the newspapers. Finally, whether actuated by ennui or by an instinctive impulse, she bought a complete set of Shakespeare's works and, forthwith, was lost! She found that "something" for which she had sought so long; she found her hero, her aim, her ideal—it was the theater. She devoured Shakespeare with all the inherent intensity of her nature.

It would be difficult to epitomize the violent upheaval that now took place in Janina's soul, the wild soaring of her imagination, and the enlargement and expansion of her whole being. There swarmed about her a vast throng of characters—evil, noble, base, petty, heroic, and struggling souls. There passed through her such tones and words, such overwhelming thoughts and emotions that she felt as though the whole universe was contained in her soul!

She became consumed with a desire for the theater and for unusual emotions. The winters seemed too warm for her, the snowfalls too light; the springs dragged along too slowly, the summers were too cool, the autumns too dry; all this she visioned in her imagination in far grander outlines. She wished to see the acme of beauty, the acme of evil, and every act magnified to titanic proportions.

Orlowski knew a little about her "disease," but he smiled at it in scorn.

"You comédienne!" he called her, scoffingly.

Krenska would add fuel to this fire, for she wished at any cost to see Janina leave home. She persuaded her of her talent and warmly praised the theatrical career.

Janina could not pluck up courage to take the decisive step. She feared those dark and vague presentiments and an unaccountable feeling of terror at times would seize upon her. She could not summon the necessary determination. A storm of some kind only could uproot her and carry her far away from home in the same way as it uprooted the trees and scattered them over the desolate fields. She was waiting now for some chance happening to cast her into the world. Krenska, in the meanwhile, kept her informed of the activities of the provincial theatrical companies. Janina made certain preparations and savings. Her father paid her regularly the interest on her inheritance and this enabled her in a year's time to lay aside about two hundred rubles.

Grzesikiewicz's proposal and her father's insistance on her marriage roused a stormy protest in her.

"No, no, no!" she repeated to herself, pacing excitedly up and down her room. "I will not marry!"

Janina had never contemplated matrimony seriously. At times the vision of a great, overwhelming love would gleam through her mind, and she would dream of it for a while; but of marriage she had never given a thought.

She even liked Grzesikiewicz, because he would never speak lightly to her about love, nor enact those amorous comedies to which other admirers had accustomed her. She liked him for the simplicity with which he would relate all that he had to suffer at school, how he was abused and humiliated as the son of a peasant and innkeeper and how he paid them back in peasant fashion—with his fists. He would smile while relating this to her, but there was in his smile a trace of sorrow.

She opened the door of her father's room and was about to tell him abruptly and decisively that there was no need of Grzesikiewicz's coming, but Orlowski was already enjoying his after-dinner nap, seated in a big arm-chair with his feet propped against the window-sill. The sun was shining straight into his face which was almost entirely bronzed from sunburn.

Janina withdrew.

"No, no, no! . . . Even though I have to run away from home, I will not marry!" she repeated to herself fiercely.

But immediately there followed this determination a feeling of womanly helplessness.

"I will go to my uncle's house. . . . Yes! . . . and from there I will go to the stage. No one can force me to stay here."

Thereupon, the blood would rush to her head with indignation and she would immediately gaze with courage into the future, determined to meet anything that might happen rather than submit.

She heard her father arise and then go to the window; she listened to the station bells, and to the jabbering of a few Jews who were boarding the train; she saw the red cap of her father, and the yellow striped cap of the telegrapher conversing through his window with some lady; she saw and heard all, but understood nothing, so absorbed was she in thought.

Krenska entered and in her habitual way began to circle around the table with quiet, cat-like motion before she spoke. Her face bore an expression of sympathy and there was tenderness in her voice.

"Miss Janina!"

The young woman glanced at her.

"No! I assure you that I will not!" she said with emphasis.

"Your father gave Grzesikiewicz his word of honor ... he will demand unquestioning obedience . . . what will come of it?"

"No! I will not marry! . . . My father can retract his word; he cannot compel me—"

"Yes . . . but there will be an awful rumpus, an awful rumpus!"

"I have stood so many, I can stand some more."

"I am afraid that this one will not end so smoothly. Your father has such a dreadful temper. ... I can't understand how you are able to bear as much as you do. ... If I were in your place, Miss Janina, I know what I should do . . . and do it now, immediately!"

"I am anxious to know . . . give me your advice."

"First of all, I would leave home to avoid all this trouble before it begins. I would go to Warsaw."

"Well, and what would you do next?" asked Janina with trembling voice.

"I would join some theater and let happen what will!"

"Yes, that's a good idea, but . . . but—"

And she broke off, for the old helplessness and fears reasserted themselves. She sat silent without answering Krenska.

Janina put on a jacket and felt hat and taking a stick wandered off into the woods.

She climbed to the top of that rocky hill from which spread out below her a wide view of the woods, the villages beyond them, and an endless expanse of fields. She sat gazing about her for a while, but the calm that reigned all around, contrasted with the feeling of unquiet and foreboding in her own soul, as before an impending storm, gave her no peace.

At dusk Janina returned home. She did not speak either to her father or to Krenska but immediately after supper went to her own room and sat reading George Sand's *Consuelo* until a late hour.

During the night she was perturbed with unquiet dreams from which she started up every now and then, perspiring heavily, and awoke fully before dawn, unable to sleep any longer. She lay upon her bed with wide open eyes, gazing fixedly at the ceiling on which flickered a patch of light reflected from the station lamp. A train went roaring by and she listened for a long while to its rhythmic rumbling and clatter that seemed like a whole choir of voices and tones streaming in through her window.

At the farther end of the room, steeped in a twilight full of pale gleams that flickered like severed rays from a light long since extinguished, she seemed to see apparitions and vague outlines of mysterious scenes, figures, and sounds. Her wearied brain peopled the room with the phantoms of hallucination. She beheld, as it were, a vast edifice with a long row of columns that seemed to emerge from the dusk and take shape.

In the morning she arose so worn out that she could scarcely stand on her feet.

She heard her father issuing orders for a sumptuous dinner and saw them making preparations. Krenska circled about her on tiptoe and smiled at her with a subtle, ironical smile that irritated Janina. She felt dazed with exhaustion and the storm that was brewing within her, and beheld everything with indifference, for her mind was continually dwelling on the impending battle with her father. She tried to read or occupy herself with something, but was too nervous.

She ran off to the woods, but immediately came back, for she knew not what to do there. A lethargy seemed to take hold of her and benumb her with an ever greater fear. Try as she would, Janina could not shake off this depressing mood.

She sat down at the piano and began mechanically to play scales, but the somnolent monotony of the tones only added to her nervousness. Later she played some of Chopin's Nocturnes, lingered over those mysterious tones that seemed like strains from another world, full of tears, pain, cries of anguish, and bleak despair; the radiance of cold moonlight nights, moans like the whisper of departing souls, the laughter of parting, the soft vibrations of subtle, sad life.

Suddenly, Janina stopped playing and burst into tears. She wept for a long time, not knowing why she wept—she who since her mother's death had not shed a single tear.

For the first time in her life—which up till now had been one continuous struggle, revolt, and protest—she felt overcome by distress. There awakened in her an irresistible longing to share her sorrows with someone, a longing to confide to some sympathetic heart those bewildered thoughts and feelings, that unexplainable misery and fear. She yearned for sympathy, feeling that her distress would be smaller, her anguish less violent, her tears not so bitter, if she could open her heart before some sincere woman friend.

Krenska summoned her to dinner, announcing that Grzesikiewicz was already waiting.

She wiped away the traces of tears from her eyes, arranged her hair—and went.

Grzesikiewicz kissed her hand and seated himself beside her at the table.

Orlowski was in a holiday humor and every now and then twitted Janina and hurled triumphant glances at her.

Grzesikiewicz was silent and uneasy; occasionally he would speak, but in such a low tone, Janina could scarcely hear what he said. Mrs. Krenska was plainly excited.

A gloomy atmosphere hung over them all. The dinner dragged wearily on. Orlowski at times became wrapt in thought, and would then knit his brows, angrily tug at his beard, and fling murderous glances at his daughter.

After dinner they went to the parlor. Black coffee and cognac were served. Orlowski quickly gulped down his coffee and left the room, kissing Janina on the forehead and growling some unintelligible remark as he departed.

They remained alone.

Janina kept looking out of the window. Grzesikiewicz, all flushed and flustered and unlike himself, began to say something, taking little swallows of coffee in between, until, finally, he drained it off at the gulp and shoved his cup and saucer aside so vigorously that they went tumbling over the table. She laughed at his violence and embarrassment.

"At a moment like this a man could swallow a lamp without noticing it," he remarked.

"That would be quite a feat," she answered, again bursting into empty laughter.

"Are you laughing at me?" he asked uneasily.

"No, only the idea of swallowing a lamp seemed comical."

They relapsed into silence. Janina fidgeted with the window-shade, while Grzesikiewicz tore at his gloves and impulsively bit his moustache; he was literally shaking with emotion.

"It is so hard for me, so awfully hard!" he began, raising his eyes to her entreatingly.

"Why?" she queried tersely and evasively.

"Well, because . . . because . . . For God's sake, I can't stand it any longer! No, I can't endure this torment any longer, so I'll come right out with it: I love you, Miss Janina, and beg you for your hand," he cried aloud, at once sighing with immense relief. But immediately he struck his forehead with his hand and, taking Janina's hand, began anew:

"I have loved you ever so long, but feared to tell you. And now I don't know how to express it as I would like to. . . . I love you and beg you to be my wife. . . . "

He kissed her hand fervently and gazed at her with his blue, honest eyes burning with blind love. His lips twitched nervously and a pallor overspread his features.

Janina arose from her chair and, looking straight into his eyes, answered slowly and quietly: "I do not love you."

All her nervousness had vanished.

Grzesikiewicz recoiled violently, as though someone had struck him, as though he did not understand. He said with a trembling voice:

"Miss Janina ... be my wife ... I love you!"

"I do not love you ... I cannot therefore marry you ... I will not marry at all!" she answered in the same cold tone, but at the last word her voice wavered with an accent of pity for him.

"God!" cried Grzesikiewicz, holding his hand to his head. "What does it mean? . . . You will not marry! ... You will not be my wife! . . . You do not love me!"

He threw himself impulsively on his knees before her, seized her hands, and, covering them with kisses, began, with what seemed almost tears of feverish terror, to entreat her fervently, humbly.

"You do not love me? . . . You will love me in time. I swear that I, my mother, and my father will be your slaves.

I will wait if you wish . . . Say that in a year, or two, or even five, you will love me. ... I will wait. . . . I swear to you that I will wait! But do not say no to me! For God's sake do not say that, for I shall go mad with despair! How can it be? You do not love me! . . . But I love *you* . . . we all love you ... we cannot live without you! . . . no. . . . Your father told me that . . . that . . . and now . . . God! I will go crazy! What are you doing to me! What are you doing to me!"

Springing up from the floor he fairly cried aloud with pain.

Mechanically he pulled off his gloves, tore them to pieces and flung them on the floor, buttoned up his coat to the topmost button, and struggling to control himself said: "Farewell, Miss Janina. But always . . . everywhere . . . forever . . . I will . . ." he whispered with great effort, bowed his head and went toward the door.

"Andrew!" she called after him forcibly.

Grzesikiewicz turned back from the door.

"Andrew," she said in a pleading voice, "I do not love you, but I respect you. ... I cannot marry you, I cannot . . . but I will always think of you as of a noble man. Surely you will understand that it would be a base thing for me to marry a man whom I do not love ... I know that you detest falsehood and hypocrisy—and so do I. Forgive me for hurting you, but I also suffer ... I also am not happy—oh no!"

"Janina—if you would only ... if you would only … "

She regarded him with such a sorrowful expression that he became silent. Then slowly he left the room.

Janina still sat there dazed, staring at the door through which he had gone, when Orlowski entered the room.

He had met Grzesikiewicz on the stairs and in his face had read what had happened.

Janina uttered a little cry of fear, so great a change had come over him. His face was ashen-gray, his eyes seemed to bulge from their sockets, his head swayed violently from side to side.

He seated himself near the table and with a quiet, smothered voice asked, "What did you tell Grzesikiewicz?"

"What I told you yesterday; that I do not love him and will not marry him!" she answered boldly, but she was startled at the seeming calm with which her father spoke.

"Why?" he queried sharply, as though he did not understand her.

"I told him that I do not love him and do not wish to marry at all. . . ."

"You are a fool! . . . a fool! . . . a fool!" he hissed at her through his tightly set teeth.

She regarded him calmly and all her old obstinacy returned.

"I said that you would marry him. I gave my word that you would marry him, and you *will* marry him!"

"I will not! ... no one is able to force me!" she answered sullenly, looking with steady gaze into her father's eyes.

"I will drag you to the altar. I will compel you! . . . You must! . . . " he cried hoarsely.

"No!"

"You will marry Grzesikiewicz, I tell you; I, your father, command you to do so! You will obey me immediately, or I will kill you!"

"Very well, kill me, if you want to, but I'll not obey you!"

"I will drive you out of this house!" he shouted.

"Very well!"

"I will disown you!"

"Very well!" she answered with growing determination. Janina felt that with each word her heart was hardening with greater resolve.

"I'll drive you out . . . do you hear? . . . and even though you die of hunger, I never want to hear of you again!"

"Very well!"

"Janina! I warn you, don't drive me to extremity. I beg you marry Grzesikiewicz, my daughter, my child! ... Isn't it for your good? You have no one but me in the world and I am old ... I will die . . . and you will remain alone without protection or support. . . . Janina, you have never loved me! . . . If you knew how unhappy I have been throughout my life, you would take pity on me!"

"No! . . . Never! . . . " she answered, unmoved even by his pleading.

"I ask you for the last time!" he shouted.

"For the last time I tell you no!" she flung back at him.

Orlowski hurled his chair to the floor with such force that it was shattered to pieces. He tore open the collar of his shirt, so violent was the paroxysm of fury that had seized him, and with the broken arm of the chair in his hand, he sprang at Janina to strike her, but the cold, almost scornful, expression of her face brought him to his senses.

"Get out of here!" he roared, pointing to the door, "get out! . . . Do you hear? I turn you out of my home forever! ... You will never again pass this threshold while I live, for I will kill you like a mad dog and throw you out of the door! ... I have no longer any daughter!"

"Very well, I will go . . ." she answered mechanically.

"I no longer have any daughter! Henceforth I don't want to know you or hear anything of you! ... Go and perish ... I will kill you! . . ." he shouted, rushing up and down the room like a madman.

His insane violence now burst out in full force. He rushed out of the house and from the window Janina saw him running toward the woods.

She sat silent, dumb, and as though turned to ice. She had expected everything, but never this. She burned with resentment but not a single tear clouded her eye. She gazed about her distractedly, for that hoarse cry still rang in her ears: "Get out of here! . . . get out!"

"I will go, I will go . . ." she whispered in a humble and broken voice through the tears that filled her heart, "I will go...."

"God, my God! why am I so unhappy?" she cried after a while.

Krenska, who had heard all, approached her. With feigned tears in her eyes she began to comfort her, but Janina gently pushed her away. It was not that which she needed; not that kind of comforting.

"My father has driven me out . . . I must leave . . . " she said, marveling at her own words.

"But that is preposterous! . . . Surely your father can be placated. . . . "

"No . . . I will not stay here any longer. I have enough of this torment . . . enough. . . ."

"Are you going to your aunt's house?"

Janina was sunk in thought for a moment, but suddenly her gloomy face brightened with a flash of determination.

"I will go and join the theater. The die is cast! . . ."

Krenska glanced at her sharply.

"Come, help me pack my trunk. I will leave on the next train."

"The next passenger train does not go to Kielce."

"It doesn't matter. I will go to Strzemieszyce, and from there, by the Viennese line to Warsaw. . . . "

"If I were you, Janina, I'd think it over. . . . Later you may regret it. . . . "

"What's done can't be undone! . . . "

And without paying any further attention to Krenska's remarks, Janina began to pack. Her lingerie, her dresses, her books and notes, and various trifles she carefully folded away into her school-day trunk, as though she were returning from her vacation.

At the end she bade farewell to Krenska indifferently. Outwardly she appeared calm and cool, while a slight tremor of her lips alone, and an inner tremor that she could not still, were the only traces of the storm.

She ordered her things carried downstairs, and, having still an hour's time, she went to the woods.

"Forever . . . " she said in a subdued tone, as though addressing the trees that seemed to bend toward her with a mournful murmur and rustling of their leaves.

"Forever! . . . " she whispered, gazing at the crimson gleams of the setting sun that filtered through the tangled branches of the beeches and shone upon the ground.

The woods seemed wrapt in a great silence, as though they were listening to her words of final farewell and dumbly wondering how one who had been born and reared in their midst, who had lived with their life, who had dreamed so many dreams in their embracing silence, could bid farewell.

The trees murmured mournfully. A sigh like a song of farewell and a sad reproach echoed through the wood. The ferns stirred with a gentle motion, the young hazel leaves fluttered restlessly, the pines rustled softly with their slender needles—the whole wood trembled and became alive with a prolonged moan. The song of the birds sounded in broken, startled little snatches, while over the sky, and over the earth carpeted with leaves and golden mosses and snowy valley-lilies, and through the whole verdant wood there flitted mysterious shadows, sounds and calls like the echo of sorrowful sobbing.

"Stay with me! . . . Stay!" the wood seemed to say.

The torrent roared noisily, swept away the broken boughs that impeded its course, circled and descended in a cloud of foam, a cascade of mist shining in the sun with all the colors of the rainbow; it went irresistibly onward, triumphantly, whispering: "Go! . . . Go!"

Then there followed a great silence, broken only by the hum of insects and the dull clatter of falling acorns.

"Forever! . . ." whispered Janina.

She arose and started back toward the station. She walked slowly, looking about her with fond, lingering gaze upon the trees, the woodpaths, and the hillsides.

Then she began to think of the new existence before her. There slowly arose in her soul a certain self-conscious power and increasing courage.

When she spied her father on the station platform, not so much as a tremor disturbed her. Already there loomed between them that new world which already lured her.

She even went to the station-master's office for a ticket. She stood before the window and asked for it in a loud voice. Orlowski (for he sold the tickets himself) raised his head with a violent start and something like a red shadow passed over his face, but he did not utter a word. He calmly handed her her change and stared at her coldly, stroking his beard.

On leaving, she turned her head and met his burning gaze. He started violently back from the window and swore aloud, while she went on, only somehow she went more slowly and her legs trembled under her. That gleam of his eyes, as though bloody with tears, struck deep into her heart.

The train arrived and she got on. From the window of the car she still kept gazing at the station. Krenska waved to her with a handkerchief from the house and pretended she was wiping away tears.

Orlowski, in a red cap and immaculately white gloves, paced up and down the platform with a stiff official air and did not glance even once in her direction.

The bell rang and the train pulled out.

The telegrapher was bowing his farewell to her, but she did not see him; she saw only how her father slowly turned about and entered the office.

"Forever! . . . " she whispered.

Orlowski came in for supper at the usual hour.

Krenska, in spite of her joy at Janina's departure, was uneasy; she glanced into his eyes with a feeling of fear, walked about even more silently than usual, and was humbler and smaller than ever before.

Orlowski seemed to be wrestling with himself, for he did not burst forth in curses and did not even mention Janina.

On the following day only he locked Janina's room and put the key away in his desk.

He did not sleep that night; his eyes were sunken and his face deathly pale. Krenska heard him walking up and down his room all night, but on the following day he was at work as usual.

At dinner Krenska plucked up courage to speak to him about something.

"Aha . . . I have still to settle with you!" he said.

Krenska grew pale. She began to speak to him about Janina, about her sympathy for her, how she had tried to dissuade her from leaving, how earnestly she had begged her.

"You're a fool!" he hurled at her. "She left because she wanted to. . . . Let her break her neck, if she wants to!"

Krenska began to commiserate his loneliness.

"A cur!" he snarled, spitting beside him in scorn. "You, madame, can leave to-day. I will pay you what is due you and then get out of this house as fast as you can go, or I swear to God I'll have my workmen throw you out! If I am to be alone I'll be entirely alone . . . without any guardians! A cur!"

Banging his glass against the table with such force that it flew into splinters, he went out.

# CHAPTER II

 THE little garden theater was beginning to awaken.

The curtain arose with a creaking sound and there appeared a barefooted and disheveled boy, clad only in a smock, who began to sweep the temple of art. The dust floated out in large clouds on the garden, settling on the red cloth coverings of the chairs and on the leaves of a few consumptive chestnut trees.

The waiters and servants of the restaurant began to put things to order under the large veranda. One could hear the clatter of washed glasses, the beating of rugs, the moving of chairs and the subdued whispers of the buffet-tender who arranged with a certain unction her rows of bottles, platters containing sandwiches, and huge bouquets *à la Makart*, resembling dried brooms. The glaring rays of the sun peered in at the sides of the garden and a throng of black sparrows swayed on the branches and perched on the chairs, clamoring for crumbs.

The clock over the buffet was slowly and solemnly striking the hour of ten, when a tall slim boy rushed in on the veranda; a torn cap was perched on the top of his touseled red hair, his freckled face wore a mischievous smile, and his nose was upturned. He ran straight to the buffet.

"Be careful, Wicek, or you'll lose your shoes!" . . . called the barmaid.

"I don't care; I'll get them remodeled!" he retorted jovially, gazing down at his shoes which clung miraculously to his feet despite the fact that they were minus both soles and tops.

"Please, miss, let me have a thimbleful of beer!" he cried bowing ostentatiously.

"Have you the price?" asked the barmaid, extending her palm.

"This evening, I'll pay you. I give you my word, I'll pay you for it without fail," he begged.

The barmaid merely shrugged her shoulders.

"O come on, let me have it, miss. ... I'll recommend you to the Shah of Persia. . . . Such a broad dame ought to have quite a pull with him. . . . "

The waiters burst out laughing, while the barmaid banged her metal tray against the counter.

"Wicek!" called someone from the entrance.

"At your service, Mr. Manager."

"Are they all here for the rehearsal?"

"Oh! They'll all be here without fail!" he answered, laughing roguishly.

"Did you notify them? . . . Did you go to them with the circular?"

"Yes, they all signed it."

"Did you take the play-bill to the director?"

"The director was still behind the scenes: he was lying in bed and gazing at his toes."

"You should have given it to his wife."

"But Mrs. Directress was in the midst of a tussle with her children; it was a little too noisy there."

"You will go with this letter to Comely Street. . . . Do you know where it is?"

"A few times over. 'She's quite a respectable dame,' as a certain man in the front row said of Miss Nicolette the other day."

"You will take this, wait for an answer, and come right back."

"But Mr. Manager, will I get something for going?"

"Didn't I give you something on account only last night?"

"Oh . . . only a copper! I spent it for beer and sardines, paid the balance of my rent, gave my shoemaker a deposit for a new pair of shoes, and now I'm dead broke!"

"You're a monkey! Here, take this. . . . "

"Blessed are the hands that dispense forty-cent pieces!" he cried with a comical grimace, shuffled his shoes, and ran out.

"Set the stage for the rehearsal!" called the manager, seating himself on the veranda.

The members of the company assembled slowly. They greeted each other in silence and scattered over the garden.

"Dobek," called the stage-manager to a tall man who was making straight for the buffet. "You guzzle from morn till night, and at the rehearsals I cannot hear a word you say. . . . Your prompting isn't worth a bean!"

"Mr. Manager, I had a bad dream that ran something like this: Night ... a well ... I stumbled and fell into it ... I was frozen stiff with fear ... I called for help ... no help was near ... splash!... and I was up to my neck in water. . . . Brr! ... I still feel so cold that nothing will warm me."

"Oh, hang your dreams! You drink from morn till night."

"That's because I can't drink like others: from night till morn. Brr! I feel so beastly chilled!"

"I'll order some hot tea for you—"

"Thank you, I'm quite well Mr. Topolski, and use herbs only when I'm sick. Must, the extracted juice, the constituent of rye, that's the only stuff that is worthy of the complete man that I have the honor to consider myself, Mr. Manager."

The director entered and Dobek went to the bar.

"Did you assign all the rôles of *Nitouche?*" the director asked.

"Not quite," answered Topolski, "those women . . . there are three candidates for Nitouche."

"Good morning, Mr. Director!" called one of the pillars of the theater, Majkowska, a handsome actress dressed in a light gown, a silken wrap, and a white hat with a big ostrich feather. She was all rosy from a good night's sleep and from an invisible layer of rouge. She had large, dark-blue eyes, full and car-mined lips, classical features, and a proud bearing. She played the principle rôles.

"Come here a minute, Mr. Director . . . there is a little matter I would like to speak to you about."

"Always at your service, madame. Perhaps you need some money?" ventured the director with a troubled mien.

"For the present . . . no. What will you have to drink, Mr. Director?"

"Ho! Ho! Somebody's blood is going to be shed!" he cried with a comical gesture.

"I asked what will you drink, Mr. Director?"

"Oh, I don't know. I'd take a glass of cognac, but . . . "

"You're afraid of your wife? She soes not appear in *Nitouche,* does she?"

"No, but . . . "

"Waiter! Two cognacs and sandwiches. . . . You will give the rôle of Nitouche to Nicolette, will you not, Mr. Director? Please do so, for I have a good reason for asking it. Remember, Mr. Cabinski, that I never ask for a thing in vain, and do this for me . . ."

"That's already the fourth candidate for the part! ... God! all that I have to stand because of these women!"

"Which of them wants this part?"

"Well, Kaczkowska, my wife, Mimi, and now, Nicolette...."

"Waiter! Two more cognacs," she called, rapping on the tray with her glass. "You will give the part to Nicolette, Mr. Director. I know for a certainty that she will not accept it, for with her wooden voice she could dance, but not sing. But you see, Mr. Director, this is the very reason for giving it to her."

"Well . . . not to mention my own wife, Mimi and Kaczkowska will tear off my head if I do!"

"You'll not lose much by that! I'll explain the matter to them. We will have a splendid farce, for you see that gentleman friend of hers will be present at to-day's rehearsal. Yesterday she boasted to him that you had her in mind when you announced in the papers that the rôle of Nitouche will be played by the beautiful and dashing Mme. X. X."

Cabinski began to laugh quietly.

"Only don't breathe a word about it. You'll see what will happen. Before him she will pretend to accept the part to show off. Halt will immediately begin to rehearse her and will make a fool of her before everyone. You will then take away her part and give it to whomever you like."

"You women are terrible in your malice."

"Bah, therein lies our strength."

They went out into the garden hall where several members of the company were already waiting for the rehearsal to begin. They sat about on chairs in little groups laughing, joking, telling tales, and complaining while the tuning of the orchestra furnished an accompaniment to the buzz of voices.

On the veranda an increasing number of guests was assembling and the hum of voices, the clatter of plates and the noisy shifting of chairs grew ever louder. The smoke of cigarettes ascended in clouds to the iron roof beams.

Janina Orlowska entered. She sat down at one of the tables and inquired of the waiter: "Can you tell me if the director of the theater has already arrived?"

"There he is!"

"Which one of them."

"What will you have, madame?"

"I beg your pardon, which of those gentlemen is Mr. Cabinski?"

"A seven! . . . four whiskies!" someone called to the waiter from a nearby table.

"Just a minute, just a minute!"

"Beer!" came another voice.

"Which of those gentlemen is the director?" patiently asked Janina for the second time.

"I will serve you in a minute, madam!" said the waiter bowing on all sides.

To Janina it seemed that they were all staring at her and that the waiters, as they passed with their hands full of beer-glasses and plates, cast such strange glances that she blushed in spite of herself.

Presently the waiter returned, bringing the coffee she had ordered.

"Do you wish to see the director, madame?"

"Yes."

"He is sitting there in the first row of seats. That short man in a white vest . . . there! Do you see him?"

"I do. Thank you!"

"Shall I tell him you wish to speak to him?"

"No. Anyway he seems to be busy."

"He is only chatting."

"And who are those gentlemen with whom he is talking?"

"They are also members of our company—actors."

She paid for the coffee, giving the waiter a ruble. He fumbled about a long time, as though looking for change, but, seeing that she was gazing in another direction, he bowed and thanked her.

Having finished her coffee, Janina went into the hall. She passed by the director and took a cursory look at him. All that she saw was a large, pale, anæmic face, covered with grayish splotches.

A few actors standing near him impressed her as handsome people. She noticed in their gestures, their smooth shaven faces, their easy, smiling airs something so superior to the men whom she had hitherto known, that she listened to their conversation with rapt attention.

The uncurtained stage, wrapt in darkness, drew her with its hidden mystery.

For the first time Janina saw the theater at close range and the actors off stage. The theater seemed to her like a Grecian temple and those people, whose profiles she had before her, and whose eloquent voices sounded in her ears, seemed like true priests of art.

She was regarding everything about her with interest, when she suddenly noticed that the waiter who had served her was whispering something to the director and pointing to her with a slight gesture.

There ran through Janina a tremor of fear, strange and depressing. She did not look up again, but felt that someone was approaching, that someone's glances were resting on her head and encircling her figure.

She was still at a loss how to begin and what to say, but felt that she must speak.

She arose when she noticed Cabinski standing before her.

"I am Mr. Cabinski, the director."

She stood there unable to utter a word.

"You deigned to ask for me, madame?" he queried with a courteous bow, signifying that he was ready to listen to her.

"Yes . . . if you please . . . Mr. Director. I wished to ask you . . . perhaps you could," she stuttered, unable for the moment to find the right words to express what she wished to say.

"Pray rest a little, madame, and calm your self. Is it something very important?" he whispered, bending toward her and at the same time winking significantly to the actors who were looking on.

"Oh, it is very important!" she answered, meeting his gaze. "I wish to ask you, Mr. Director, if you would accept me as a member of your company."

This last sentence she uttered quickly as though fearing that her courage and voice might fail her ere it was spoken.

"Ah! . . . is that all? . . . You wish to be engaged, miss?" He stiffened suddenly, studying her with a critical gaze.

"I journeyed here especially for that purpose. You will not refuse me, Mr. Director, will you?"

"With whom did you appear before?"

"Pardon me, but I don't quite understand."

"With what company? . . . Where?"

"I have never before appeared in the theater. I came here straight from the country for the express purpose of joining it."

"You have never appeared before? . . . Then, I have no place for you! " and he turned to go.

Janina was seized with a desperate fear that her quest would fail, so with courage and a tone of strong entreaty in her voice she began to speak hurriedly:

"Mr. Director! I journeyed here especially to join your company. I love the theater so ardently that I cannot live without it! . . . Do not refuse me! I do not know anyone here in Warsaw. I came to you because I had read so much about you in the papers. I feel that I could play ... I have memorized so many rôles! ... You will see, Mr. Director ... if you only let me appear . . . you will see!"

Cabinski was silent.

"Or perhaps you would prefer to have me call to-morrow? ... I can wait a few days, if you wish," she added, seeing that he did not answer, but was observing her intently.

Her voice trembled with entreaty; it modulated with ease and there was so much originality and warmth in her tone that Cabinski listened to her with pleasure.

"Now I have no time, but after the rehearsal we can discuss the matter more thoroughly," he said.

She wanted impulsively to press his hand and thank him for the promise, but her courage failed her, for she noticed that an increasing number of people were curiously observing them.

"Hey there, Cabinski!"

"Man alive!"

"Director! What's that ... a rendezvous? In broad daylight, before the eyes of all, and scarcely three flights away from Pepa?"

Such were the bantering remarks hurled at him from every direction after his parting with Janina.

"Who is the charmer?"

"Director, it's rather careless to carry on such an affair right there in the limelight."

"Ha! ha! now we've got you! . . . You posed as a flawless crystal, my muddy amber!" called one of the company, a fleshless individual with habitually contorted lips that seemed to spew gall and malice.

"Go to the devil, my dear! This is the first time I saw her," retorted Cabinski.

"A pretty woman! What does she want?"

"A novice of some kind . . . she's seeking an engagement."

"Take her, Director. There are never too many pretty women on the stage."

"The director has enough of those calves."

"Don't fear, Wladek, they do not encumber the budget, for Cabinski has a custom of failing to pay his actors, particularly the young and pretty ladies."

Thereat they all began laughing.

"Treat us to a whiskey, Director, and I will tell you something," Glas began anew.

"Well, what is it?"

"That the manager will treat us to another. ... "

"My funny sir, your belly grows at the expense of your wit . . . you are beginning to prate like a fool," remarked Wladek.

"Only for fools . . ." Glas maliciously thrust back at Wladek and retired behind the scenes.

"John!" came the voice of the director's wife from the veranda.

Cabinski went out to meet her.

She was a tall, stout woman with a face that still retained traces of great beauty, now carefully preserved with paint; she had coarse features, large eyes, narrow lips, and a very low forehead. Her dress was of an exaggerated youthful style and color, so that from afar she gave the impression of being a young woman.

She was very proud of her director-husband, of her dramatic talent, and of her children, of which she had four. In real life she was fond of playing the rôle of a matron occupied only with her home and the upbringing of her children, while in truth she was nothing but a comédienne, both in life and behind the scenes. On the stage she impersonated dramatic mothers and all the elder, unhappy women, never understanding her parts, but acting them, nevertheless, with fervor and pathos.

She was a terror to her servants, to her own children, and to young actresses whom she suspected of possessing talents. She had a shrewish temper which she masked before others with an exaggerated calm and feigned weakness.

"Good morning, gentlemen!" . . . she called, leaning with a careless attitude on her husband's arm.

The company thronged around her, Majkowska greeting her with an effusive kiss.

"How charming Madame Directress looks to-day," remarked Glas.

"Your vision must have improved, for the directress always looks charming!" interposed Wladek.

"How is your health? . . . Yesterday's performance must have taxed your strength."

"You played superbly! . . . We all stood behind the scenes in rapt attention."

"The critics were all weeping. I saw Zarski wiping his eyes with his handkerchief."

"After sneezing . . . he has a bad catarrh," called someone from the side.

"The public was fascinated and swept off its feet in the third act . . . they arose in their chairs."

"That's because they wanted to run away from such a treat," came the mocking voice again.

"How many bouquets did you receive, Madame Directress?"

"Ask the director, he paid the bill."

"Ah, Mr. Counselor, you are unbearable to-day!" cried the directress in a sweet voice, although almost pale with rage, for all the actors were growing red in the face in their effort to keep from laughing.

"It's intended as a kindness. . . . All the rest of them are saying pretty things, let me say something sensible."

"You are an impertinent man, Mr. Counselor! . . . How can you say such things? . . .

Moreover, what do I care about the theater! If I played well, I owe it to my husband; if I played badly it's the fault of the director for forcing me to appear continually in new rôles! If I had my way, I would lock myself up with my children and confine myself to domestic affairs. . . . My God! art is such a big thing and we are all, compared with it, so small, so small that I tremble with fear before each new performance!" she declaimed.

"Please let me have a word with you in private," called Majkowska.

"Do you see? . . . there is not even time to talk of art!" she sighed deeply and departed.

"An old scarecrow!"

"An everlasting cow! . . . She thinks she is an artist!"

"Yesterday she bellowed terribly."

"She flung herself around the stage as though she had St. Vitus' dance!"

"Hush! . . . according to her that is realism!"

On the veranda Majkowska was concluding her conversation with Mrs. Cabinska.

"Will you give me your word of honor, Madame Directress?"

"Of course, I'll see to it right away."

"It must be done. Nicolette has made herself impossible in this company. Why, she even dares to criticize your own playing! Yesterday I saw her making disparaging remarks to that editor," Majkowska whispered.

"What! she dares to meddle with me?"

"I never indulge in gossip, nor do I want to sow hatred, but—"

"What did she say? ... in the presence of the editor, did you say? Ah, the vile coquette!"

Majkowska smothered a smile, but hastily replied, "No, I'll not tell you ... I do not like to repeat gossip!"

"Well, I'll pay her back for it! ... Wait, we'll teach her a lesson! " hissed the directress.

"Dobek, prompter! . . . get into your box!"

"Ladies and gentlemen, the rehearsal commences!"

"To the stage! to the stage!" was the cry that went up all over the hall as the actors hurried behind the scenes.

"Mr. Director!" called Majkowska, "you can give the rôle to Nicolette . . . your wife agrees to it."

"Very well, my dears, very well. . . ."

He went out on the veranda where Nicolette was already seated with a young gentleman, very fastidiously dressed.

"We request your presence at the rehearsal, Miss Nicolette.. . . "

"What are you rehearsing?" asked Nicolette.

*"Nitouche* . . . why, don't you know that you are to appear in the title rôle? ... I have already advertised it in the papers."

Kazckowska, who had at that moment entered and was looking at them, hastily covered her face with her parasol, so as not to burst out laughing at the comical look of embarrassment on Nicolette's face.

"I am too indisposed at present to take part in the rehearsal," she said, scrutinizing Cabiniski and Kaczkowska.

Evidently she suspected some ruse, but Cabinski, with the solemnest mien in the world, handed her the rôle.

"Here is your part, madame. . . . We begin immediately," he said, going away.

"But Mr. Director! my dear Director, I pray you, go on with the rehearsal without me! . . . I have such a headache that I doubt I could sing," she pleaded.

"It can't be done. We begin immediately."

"Oh, please do sing, Miss Nicolette! I'm crazy to hear you sing!" begged the squire.

"Director!"

"What is it, my soprano?"

And the directress appeared, pointing to Janina who was standing behind the scenes.

"A novice," answered Cabinski.

"Are you going to engage her?"

"Yes, we need chorus girls. The sisters from Prague have left, for they made nothing but scandals."

"She looks rather homely," opined Mrs. Cabinska.

"But she has a very scenic face! . . . and also a very nice, though strange voice."

Janina did not lose a word of this conversation, carried on in an undertone; she had also heard the chorus of praise that went up on the directress's appearance, and later, the chorus of derision. She gazed with a bewildered look on that whole company.

"Clear the stage! clear the stage!"

Those standing on the stage hastily moved back behind the scenes, for at the moment the entire chorus rushed out in a gallop: a throng of women, chiefly young women, but with painted faces, faded and blighted by their feverish life. There were blondes and brunettes, small and tall, thin and stout— a motley gathering from all spheres of life. There were among them the faces of madonnas with defiant glances, and the smooth, round faces, expressionless and unintelligent, of peasant girls. And all were boredly cynical, or, at least, appeared so.

They began to sing.

"Halt! Start over again!" roared the director of the orchestra, an individual with a big red face and huge mutton-chop whiskers.

The chorus retired and came back again with heavy step, carrying on a sort of collective can-canade, but every minute there was heard the sharp bang of the conductor's baton against his desk and the hoarse yell—"Halt! Start over again!" And swinging his baton he would mutter under his nose, "You cattle!"

The chorus rehearsal dragged on interminably. The actors, scattered about in the seats, yawned wearily and those who took part in the evening's performance paced up and down behind the scenes, indifferently waiting for their turn to rehearse.

In the men's dressing-room Wicek was shining the shoes of the stage-manager and giving him a hasty account of his mission to Comely Street.

"Did you deliver the letter? . . . Have you an answer?"

"I should smile!" and he handed Topolski a long pink envelope.

"Wicek! . . . If you squeal a word of this to anyone, you clown, you know what awaits you!"

"That's stale news! . . . The lady said just that, too. Only she added a ruble to her warning."

"Maurice!" called Majkowska sharply, appearing at the door of the dressing-room.

"Wait a minute. ... I can't go with only one shoe shined, can I!"

"Why didn't you have the maid shine them?"

"The maid is always at your service and I can't get a single thing from her."

"Well, go and hire another."

"All right, but it will be for myself alone."

"Nicolette, to the stage!"

"Call her!" cried Cabinski from the stage to those sitting around in the chairs.

"Come, Maurice," whispered Majkowska. "It'll be worth seeing."

"Nicolette, to the stage!" cried those in the chairs.

"In a moment! Here I am . . . " and Nicolette, with a sandwich in her mouth and a box of candy under her arm, rushed for the stage entrance with such violence that the floor creaked under her steps.

"What the devil do you mean by appearing so late! This is a rehearsal ... we are all waiting," angrily muttered the conductor of the orchestra.

"I am not the only one you are waiting for," she retorted.

"Precisely, we are waiting only for you, madame, and you know we have not come here to argue. . . . On with the rehearsal!"

"But I have not yet learned a single line. Let Kaczkowska sing . . . that is a part for her!"

"The part was given to you, wasn't it? . . . Well, then there's no use arguing! Let us begin—"

"Oh, director! Can't we postpone it till this afternoon? Just now, it . . ."

"Begin!"

"Try it, Miss Nicolette . . . that part is well adapted to your voice. ... I myself asked the director to give it to you," encouraged Mrs. Cabinska with a friendly smile.

Nicolette listened, scanning the faces of the whole company, but they were all immobile. Only the young gentleman smiled amorously at her from the chairs.

The conductor raised his baton, the orchestra began to play, and the prompter gave her the first words of her part.

Nicolette, who was noted for never being able to learn her rôle, now tripped up in the very first line and sang it as falsely as possible.

They began over again; it went a little better, but "Halt," as they called the conductor, intentionally skipped a measure, causing her to make an awful mess of it.

A chorus of laughter arose on the stage.

"A musical cow!"

"To the ballet with such a voice and such an ear!"

Nicolette, on the verge of tears, approached Cabinski.

"I told you that I could not sing just now. ... I had not even time to glance at my part."

"Aha, so you cannot, madame? . . . Please hand me the rôle! . . . Kaczkowska will sing it."

"I *can* sing, but just now I am unable to . . . I don't want to flunk!"

"To turn the heads of gentlemen, to make intrigues, to slander others before the press reporters, to go gallivanting all about town . . . for that you have time!" hissed Mrs. Cabinska.

"Oh, go and mind your children . . . but don't you dare to meddle with my affairs."

"Director! She insults me, *that* . . . "

"Hand me the part," ordered Cabinski. "You can sing in the chorus, madame, since you are unable to sing a rôle."

"Oh no! . . . Just for that I am going to sing it! ... I don't care a snap for these vile intrigues!"

"Who are you saying that to?" cried Cabinska, jumping up from her chair.

"Well, to you, if you like."

"You are dismissed from the company!" interposed Cabinski.

"Oh, go to the devil, all of you!" shouted Nicolette throwing the rôle into Cabinski's face. "It's known long ago that in your company there is no place for a respectable woman!"

"Get out of here, you adventuress!"

Cabinska sprang at her, but halfway across she stopped short and burst into tears.

"On the right there is a sofa ... it will be more comfortable for you to faint on, Madame Directress!" called someone from the chairs.

The company smiled with set faces.

"Pepa! . . . my wife! . . . calm yourself. . . . For God's sake can't we ever do any thing without these continual rumpuses!"

"Am I the cause of it?"

"I'm not blaming you . . . but you could at least calm yourself . . . there's no reason for you acting this way!"

"So that is the kind of husband and father you are! . . . that is the kind of director!" she shouted in fury.

"Hold out only one hour, and you'll go straight to heaven, you martyr!" someone called to Cabinski.

"Sir," queried a spectator, holding up one of the actors by the button of his coat. "Sir, are they playing something new?"

"First of all, that is a button from my coat which you have pulled off!" cried the actor, "and that, my dear sir, is the first act of a moving farce entitled *Behind the Scenes;* it is given each day with great success."

The stage became deserted. The orchestra was tuning its instruments; "Halt" went for a drink of beer, and the company scattered about the garden. Cabinski, holding his head with both hands, paced up and down the stage like a madman, complaining half in anger, half in commiseration, for his wife was still quietly continuing her spasms.

"Oh what people! What people! What scandals!"

Janina, startled by the brutality of the spectacle she had just witnessed, retreated behind the farthermost scene. She felt that it was now impossible to speak with the director.

"So these are artists! . . . this is the theater!" she was thinking.

The rehearsal, after a short intermission, began anew—with Kaczkowska as the titular heroine.

Majkowska was in a splendid humor, being so successfully rid of her rival.

The director, after his wife's departure, rubbed his hands in glee and motioned to Topolski. They went out to the buffet for a drink. Without a doubt he must have made something on his break with Nicolette.

Stanislawski, the oldest member of the company, walked up and down the dressing-room, spitting with disgust and muttering to Mirowska, who was sitting on a chair with her feet curled up under her.

"Scandals . . . nothing but scandals! . . . how can we expect to have any success! . . ."

Mirowska nodded her assent, smiling faintly and keeping steadily on with the crocheting of a handkerchief.

After the rehearsal Janina boldly approached Cabinski.

"Mr. Director—" she began.

"Ah, it is you, miss? . . . I will accept you. Come to-morrow before the performance, and we will talk it over. I have not the time now."

"Thank you ever so much, sir!" she answered overjoyed.

"Have you any kind of a voice?"

"A voice?"

"Do you sing?"

"At home I used to sing a little . . . but I do not think I have a stage voice . . . however, I . . ."

"Only come a little earlier and we shall try you out. ... I shall speak to the musical director."

# CHAPTER III

 THE Lazienki Park in Warsaw was athrob with the breath of spring. The roses bloomed and the jasmines diffused their heavy odor through the park. It was so quiet and lovely there, that Janina sat for a few hours near the lake, forgetting everything.

The swans with spreading wings, like white cloudlets, floated over the azure bosom of the water; the marble statues glowed with immaculate whiteness; the fresh and luxuriant foliage was like a vast sea of emerald steeped in golden sunlight; the red blossoms of the chestnut trees floated down on the ground, the waters and the lawns, and flickered like rosy sparks among the shadows of the trees.

The noisy hum of the city reached here in a subdued echo and lost itself among the bushes.

Janina had come here straight from the theater. What she had seen disquieted her; she felt within herself a dull pain of disillusionment and hesitation.

She did not wish to remember anything, but only kept repeating to herself, "I'm in the theater! ... I'm in the theater!"

There passed before her mind the figures of her future companions. Instinctively she felt that in those faces there was nothing friendly, only, envy and hypocrisy.

Presently she proceeded to her hotel at which she had stopped on the advice of her fellow-travelers, on the train to Warsaw. It was a cheap affair on the outskirts of the city and frequented chiefly by petty farm officials and the actors of small provincial theaters.

She was given a small room on the third floor, with a window looking out upon the red roofs of the old city, extending in crooked and irregular lines. It was such an ugly view that, on returning from Lazienki, with her eyes and soul still full of the green of the verdure and the golden sunlight, she immediately pulled down the shades and began to unpack her trunk.

She had not yet had time to think of her father. The city, the hubbub and bustle which engulfed her immediately upon her arrival at the station, the weariness caused by the journey and by the last moments at Bukowiec, and afterwards those feverish hours at the theater, the rehearsal, the park, the waiting for evening and her own coming rehearsal—all this had so completely absorbed her that she forgot almost entirely about home.

She dressed carefully, for she wished to appear at her best.

When she arrived at the garden-theater the lights were already turned on and the public was beginning to assemble. She went boldly behind the scenes. The stage hands were arranging the decorations; of the company, no one was as yet present.

In the dressing-rooms the gaslights flared brightly. The costumer was preparing gaudy costumes, and the make-up man sat whistling and combing a wig with long, bright tresses.

In the ladies' dressing-room an old woman was standing under the gaslight, sewing something.

Janina explored all the corners, examining everything, emboldened by the fact that no one paid the slightest attention to her. The walls behind the huge canvas decorations were dirty, with their plaster broken off, and covered with sticky dampness. The floors, the moldings, the shabby furniture and decorations, that seemed to her like beggarly rags, were thick with dust and filth. The odor of mastic, cosmetics, and burnt hair, floating over the stage, nauseated her.

She viewed the canvas scenes of what were supposed to be magnificient castles, the chambers of the kings of operetta, gorgeous landscapes—and beheld at close view a cheap smear of colors which could satisfy only the grossest of senses and then only from a distance. In the storeroom she saw cardboard crowns; the satin robes were poor imitations, the velvets were cheap taffeta, the ermines were painted cambric, the gold was gilded paper, the armor was of cardboard, the swords and daggers of wood.

She gazed at that future kingdom of hers as though wishing to convince herself of its worthiness. And, though it was sham, tinsel, lies, and comedy she tried to see above it all something infinitely higher—art.

The stage was not yet set, and was only dimly lighted. Janina crossed it a few times with the stately stride of a heroine, then again, with the light, graceful airiness of an ingénue, or with the quick feverish step of a woman who carries with her death and destruction; and with each new impersonation, her face assumed the appropriate expression, her eyes glowed with the flame of the Eumenides, with storm, desire, conflict, or, kindling with the mood of love, longing, anxiety they shone like stars on a spring night.

She passed through these various transformations unconsciously, impelled by the memory of the plays and rôles she had read, and so great was her abstraction, that she forgot about everything and paid no attention to the stagehands, who were moving about her.

"My Al used to act the same way . . . the same way!" said a quiet voice from behind the scenes near the ladies' dressing-room.

Janina paused in confusion. She saw standing there a middle-aged woman of medium height, with a withered face and stern demeanor.

"You have joined our company, miss?" she inquired with a sharp energetic voice, piercing Janina with her round, owl-like eyes.

"Not quite. ... I am about to have a trial with the musical director. Ah, yes, Mr. Cabinski even said that it was to take place before the performance! . . . " she cried, recalling what he had told her.

"Aha! with that drunkard . . . "

Janina glanced at her, surprised.

"Have you set your heart on being with us, miss?"

"In the theater? . . . yes! ... I journeyed here for that very purpose."

"From whence?" asked the elderly woman abruptly.

"From home," answered Janina, but more quietly and with a certain hesitation.

"Ah ... I see . . . you are entirely new to the profession! . . . Well, well! that is curious! . . . "

"Why? . . . why should it be so strange for one who loves the theater to try to join it? . . ."

"Oh, that's what all of them say! . . . while in truth, each of them runs away either from something ... or for something. . . ."

Janina was conscious of an accent of hidden malice in her voice. "Do you know, madam, how soon the musical director will arrive?" she asked.

"I don't!" snapped back the elderly woman, and walked away.

Janina moved back a little, for just then the workmen were spreading a huge waxed canvas over the stage. She was gazing at this absent-mindedly, when the elderly woman reappeared and addressed her in a milder tone, "I will give you a piece of advice, miss. . . . It is necessary for you to win over the musical director."

"But how am I to do it?"

"Have you money?"

"I have, but . . . "

"If you will listen to me, I will advise you."

"Certainly."

"You must get him a little drunk, then the rehearsal will come off splendidly."

Janina glanced at her in amazement.

"Ha! ha!" laughed the other quietly. " Ha! ha! she is a real moon-calf!"

After a moment she whispered, "Let us go to the dressing-room. I will enlighten you a little . . . "

She pulled Janina after her, and afterwards, busying herself with pinning a dress on a mannikin, she remarked, "We must get acquainted."

"Tell me, madam, how about that musical director?" asked Janina.

"It's necessary to buy him some cognac. Yes!" she added after a moment, "Cognac, beer, and sandwiches will, perhaps, be sufficient."

"How much would that cost?"

"I think that for three rubles you can give him a decent treat. Let me have the money and I will order everything for you. I had better go right away."

Janina gave her the money.

Sowinska left and in about a quarter of an hour returned, breathless.

"Well, everything is settled! Come along, miss, the director is waiting."

Behind the restaurant hall there was a room with a piano. "Halt," flushed and sleepy, was already waiting there.

"Cabinski spoke to me about you, miss!" he began. "What can you sing? . . . Whew! how warm I feel! . . . Perhaps you will raise the window?" he said, turning to Sowinska.

Janina felt disturbed by his hoarse voice and his inflamed, drunken face, but she sat down to the piano, wondering what she should select to sing.

"Ah! you also play, miss? . . " he queried in great surprise.

"Yes," she answered, and began playing the introduction to some song, without seeing the signs that Sowinska was making to her.

"Please sing something for me," he said, "I want to hear only your voice. ... Or perhaps you could sing some solo part? "

"Mr. Director ... I feel that I have a calling for the drama, or even for the comedy, but never for the opera."

"But we are not talking about the opera . . ."

"About what, then?"

"About this . . . the operetta!" he cried, striking his knee. "Sing, Miss! ... I have only a little time and I am burning up with this heat."

She began to sing a song of Tosti's. The director listened, but at the same time gazed at Sowinska and pointed to his parched lips.

When Janina had ended, he cried, "Very well ... we will accept you ... I must hurry out, for I'm roasting."

"Perhaps you will have a drink of something with us, Mr. Director? . . . " she queried timidly, understanding the signs that Sowinska gave her.

He pretended to excuse himself, but in the end remained.

Sowinska ordered the waiter to bring half a bottle of cognac, three beers and some sandwiches, and, having drained her own glass, she hastily left them, saying that she had forgotten something in the dressing-room.

"Halt" shoved his chair nearer to Janina's.

"Hm! . . . you have a voice, miss ... a very nice voice . . . " he said and laid his big red paw upon her knee, while with the other he began to pour some brandy into his beer.

She moved back a little, disgusted.

"You can put on a bold front on the stage. . . . I will help you . . ." he added, draining his glass at one gulp.

"If you will be so kind, Mr. Director . . . " Janina said, drawing away from him.

"I will see to it ... I will take care of you!"

And suddenly he took her about the waist and drew her to him.

Janina shoved him back with such force that he fell sprawling upon the table, and then ran to the door, ready to cry out.

"Whew! . . . wait a minute . . . you're a fool! . . . stay! . . . I wanted to take care of you, help you, but since you're such a blooming fool, go and hang yourself! ... "

He drank the rest of his cognac and left.

On the veranda sat Cabinski with the stage-manager.

"Has she any kind of a voice?" he inquired of "Halt," for he had seen Janina entering the room. "A soprano?"

"Ho, ho! something unheard of . . . almost an alto!"

Janina sat for about an hour in that room, unable to control the indignation and rage that shook her. There were lucid moments when she would spring up as though ready to rush out and away from those people, but immediately she would sink down again with a moan.

"Where will I go?" she asked herself, and then added with a sudden determination. "No, I will stay! ... I will bear all, if it is necessary ... I must! ... I must!"

Janina became set in her stubborn determination. She collected within herself all her powers for impending battle with misfortune, with obstacles, with the whole evil and hostile world—and for a moment, she saw herself on some dizzying height where was fame and the intoxication of triumph.

Presently Sowinska came in.

"Thank you, for your advice . . . and for leaving me with a pig! . . . " the girl exclaimed, half weeping.

"I was in a hurry ... he did not eat you, did he? . . . He's a good man. . . . "

"Then leave your daughter alone with that good man!" retorted Janina harshly.

"My daughter is not an actress," answered Sowinska.

"Oh! ... It doesn't matter . . . It's only a lesson for me," she whispered, turning away.

She met Cabinski and, approaching him, asked, "Will you accept me, Mr. Director?"

"You may consider yourself engaged," he answered. "As for your salary we shall speak of that another day."

"What am I to play? ... I should like to take the part of Clara in *The Iron Master*."

Cabinski glanced at her sharply and covered his mouth with his hand so as not to burst out laughing.

"Just a moment . . . just a moment . . . you must first acquaint yourself with the stage. In the meanwhile, you will appear with the chorus. Halt told me that you know how to play the piano and read notes. To-morrow I will give you some scores of the operettas we play and you can learn the chorus parts."

Janina went to the dressing-room and had scarcely opened the door, when someone pushed her back, slammed the door in her face and called out angrily "Upstairs with you! that is where the chorus girls belong! "

She set her teeth and went upstairs.

The dressing-room of the chorus was a long, narrow and low apartment. Rows of unshaded gaslights burned above long bare, board tables extending along the walls on three sides of the room. The walls were covered with unbeveled and unpainted boards which were scribbled all over with names, dates jokes and caricatures, done in charcoal or rouge paint. On the bare wall hung a whole string of dresses and costumes.

About twenty women sat undressed before mirrors of various shapes, and before each one there burned candles.

Janina spying an unoccupied chair, near the door, sat down and began to look about her.

"I beg your pardon, but that is my seat!" called a stout brunette.

Janina stood aside.

"Did you come to see someone? . . ." asked the same chorus-girl, rubbing her face with vaseline before applying powder.

"No. I came to the dressing-room. I am one of the company," answered Janina rather loudly.

"Oh, you are?"

A few heads raised themselves above the tables and a few pairs of eyes were centered upon Janina.

Janina told the brunette her name.

"Girls! . . . this new one calls herself Orlowska. Get acquainted with her!" called the brunette.

A few of those sitting nearest her stretched out their hands in greeting and then proceeded with their make-up.

"Louise, loan me some powder."

"Go buy it!"

"Say Sowinska!" called down one of the girls through the open door to the lower dressing-room, "I met that same guy . . . you know! . . . I was walking along Nowy Swiat."

"Tell it to the marines! Who would fall for such a scarecrow as you!" put in another.

"I've bought a new suit . . . look!" cried a small, very pretty blonde.

"You mean *he* bought it for you!"

"Goodness, no! ... I bought it from my own savings."

"Persian lamb! . . . oh! . . . Do you think we'll believe you?. . . Come now, you bought it out of that fellow's savings, didn't you?"

"It's pure lily! . . . The waist is low-cut with a yoke of cream-colored embroidery, the skirt is plain with a shirred hem, the hat is trimmed with violets," another girl was recounting, as she slipped her ballet skirts over her head.

"Listen there, you lily-colored kid . . . give me back that ruble that you owe me. . . ."

"After the play when I get it I'll give it back to you, honest!"

"Ha! ha! Cabinski will give it to you, like fun ... "

"I tell you, my dear, I'm getting desperate. . . . He coughed a little . . . but I thought nothing of it . . . until yesterday, when I looked down his little throat I saw . . . white spots ... I ran for the doctor ... he examined him and said: diphtheria! I sat by him all night, rubbed his throat every hour ... he couldn't say a word, only showed me with his little finger how it hurt . . . and the tears streamed down his face so pitifully that I thought I'd die of grief ... I left the janitress with him, for I must make some money ... I left my cloak to cover him with . . . but all, all that is not enough! . . ." a slim and pretty actress with a face worn by suffering and poverty was telling her neighbor in a subdued voice, while she curled her hair, carmined her pale lips, and with the pencil gave a defiant touch to her eyes dimmed by tears and sleepiness.

"Helen! your mother asked about you to-day . . . "

"Surely, not about me . . . my mother died long ago."

"Don't tell me that! Majkowska knows you and your mother well and saw you together on Marshalkowska Street the other day."

"Majkowska ought to buy herself a pair of glasses, if she's so blind as that ... I was going downtown with the housekeeper."

The other girls began to laugh at her. The one who had denied her mother blew out her candle and left in irritation.

"She's ashamed of her own mother. That's true, but such a mother! . . . "

"A plain peasant woman. She compromises her before everybody. ... At least, she could refrain from making a show before other people!"

"How so? Can a girl be ashamed of her mother? . . . " cried Janina, who had been sitting in silence, until those last words stirred her to indignation.

"You are a newcomer, so you don't know anything," several answered her at once.

"May I come in? . . ." called a masculine voice from without.

"You can't! you can't!" chorused the girls energetically.

"Zielinska! your editor has come."

A tall, stout chorus girl, rustling her skirts, passed out of the room.

"Shepska! take a look out after them."

Shepska went out, but came back immediately.

"They've gone downstairs."

The stage bell rang violently.

"To the stage!" called the stage-director at the door. "We begin immediately!"

There arose an indescribable hubbub. All the girls began to talk and shout at the same time; they ran about, tore away hairpins and curling irons from one another, powdered themselves, quarreled over trifles, blew out candles, hastily closed their dressing-cases and rushed down the stairs in crowds, for the second bell had already sounded.

Janina descended last of all and stood behind the scenes. The performance began. They were playing some kind of half fairy-like operetta. Janina could hardly recognize those people or that theater—everything had undergone such a magical transformation and taken on a new beauty under the influence of powder, paint, and light! . . .

The music, with the quiet caressing tones of the flute, floated through the silence and stole into Janina's soul, lulling it sweetly . . . and later, a dance of some kind, soft, voluptuous, and intoxicating, enveloped her with its charm, lured and rocked her on the waves of rhythm and held her in an ecstatic lethargy.

She felt herself drawn ever farther into a confused whirl of lights, tones and colors. Her impulsive and sensuous nature, struggling hitherto with the drab commonplace of everyday events and people, was fascinated. It was almost as she had visioned it in her soul; full of lights, music, thrilling accents, ecstatic swoons, strong colors, and stormy and overpowering emotions, breaking with the force of thunderbolts.

The suffocating odor of powder dust floated about her like a cloud, while from the crowded hall there flowed a stream of hot breaths and desiring glances that broke against the stage like a magnetic wave, drowning in forgetfulness all that was not song, music, and pleasure.

When the act ended and a storm of applause broke loose, she was on the verge of fainting. She bent her head and eagerly drank in those murmurs resembling lightning flashes and, like them blinding the soul. She breathed in those cries of the delighted public with her full breath and with all the might of her soul that craved for fame. She closed her eyes, so that that impression, that picture might last longer.

The enchanting vision had dissolved. Over the stage moved men in their shirt sleeves and without vests; they were changing the scenes, arranging the furniture, fastening the props. She saw the grimy necks, the dirty and ugly faces, the coarse and hardened hands and the heavy forms.

She went out on the stage and through a slit in the curtain gazed out on the dim hall packed full of people. She saw hundreds of young faces, women's faces, smiling and still stirred by the music, while their owners fanned themselves; the men in their black evening clothes formed dark spots scattered at regular intervals, upon the light background of feminine toilettes.

Janina felt a strange disappointment as she realized that the faces of the public were very much like those of Grzesikiewicz, her father, her home acquaintances, the principal of her boarding school, the professors at the academy and the telegrapher at Bukowiec. For the moment, it seemed to her that that was a sheer impossibility. How so? . . . She, of course, knew what to think about those others, whom long ago she had classified as fools, light-heads, drunkards, gossipers, silly geese and house-hens; small and shallow souls, a band of common eaters-of-bread, sunk in the shallow morass of material existence. And these people that filled the theater and doled out applause, and whom she had once thought of as demi-gods—were they the same as those others? Janina asked herself, that, wonderingly.

"Madame!" said a voice beside her.

She tore her face away from the curtain. At her side stood a handsome, elegantly dressed young man who was holding his hand to his hat, smiling in a conventional manner.

"Just let me look a moment . . ." he said.

Janina moved away a bit.

He glanced through the slit in the curtain and relinquished her place to her.

"Pardon me, pardon me for disturbing you . . ." he said.

"Oh, I've looked all I wanted to, sir . . ." she answered.

"Not a very interesting sight, is it? . . ." he queried. "The most authentic Philistia; trade-mongers and shoemakers. . . . Perhaps you think, madame, that they come to hear, and admire the play? Oh, no! . . . they come here to display their new clothes, have supper, and kill time. . . . "

"Well then, who does come for the play itself?" she asked.

"In this place, no one. . . . At the Grand Theater and at the Varieties . . . there, perhaps, you may yet find a group, a very small group who love art and who come for the sake of art alone. I have often touched upon that matter in the papers."

"Mr. Editor, let me have a cigarette!" called an actor from behind the scenes.

"At your service." He handed the actor a silver cigarette-case.

Janina, moving away, gazed with admiration at the writer, delighted with the opportunity of observing such a man at close range.

How many times in the country while listening to the everlasting conversations about farming, politics, rainy and clear weather, she had dreamed of this other world, of people who would discourse to her of ideals, art, humanity, progress and poetry, and who impersonated in themselves all those ideals.

"You must not be very long in this company for I have not had the pleasure of seeing you before . . . "

"I was engaged only to-day."

"Have you appeared elsewhere before?"

"No, never on the real stage. ... I took part only in amateur theatricals."

"That is the way nearly all dramatic talent develops. I know... I happen to know . . . Modrzejewska herself often mentioned that fact to me," he remarked, with a condescending smile.

"Mr. Editor ... do your duty!" called Kaczkowska, extending her hands.

The editor buttoned her gloves, kissed each of her hands a few times, received a slap on the shoulder in reward and retreated to the curtain where Janina was standing.

"So this is your first appearance in the theater? . . . " he asked. "No doubt it's a case of the family opposing . . . inflexible determination on your part . . . the isolation and dullness of the countryside . . . your first appearance as an amateur . . . stage fright . . . success . . . the recognition of the divine spark within yourself . . . your dreams of the real stage . . . tears . . . sleepless nights ... a struggle with an adverse environment . . . finally, consent . . . or perhaps a secret escape in the night . . . fear . . . anxiety . . . going the rounds of the directors . . . seeking an engagement . . . ecstasy . . . art . . . godliness!" he spoke rapidly, telegraphically.

"You have almost guessed it, Mr. Editor . . . it was the same with me," said Janina.

"You see, mademoiselle, I knew so from the first. It's intuition that's all! I'll take care of you, upon my word! . . . I'll insert a little item about you in our next issue. Later, give a few details under a sensational headline, next, a longer article about the new star on the horizon of dramatic art," he sped on. . . . "You will sweep them off their feet . . . the directors will tear you away from each other, and in about a year or two . . . you will be in the Grand Theater at Warsaw! . . . "

"But, Mr. Editor, no one knows me; no one, as yet, knows whether I have talent . . . "

"You have talent, my word! My intuition tells me that. . . . Do not believe the testimony of the senses, mademoiselle, hold yourself aloof from all reasoning, throw to the dogs all calculations, but do not fail to believe intuition! . . . "

"Come here, editor . . . hurry!" called someone to him.

"Au revoir! au revoir!" he said, throwing a kiss to Janina and touching the brim of his hat as he disappeared.

Janina arose from her seat, but that same intuition which he had advised her to heed, told her not to take his words seriously. He seemed to her a light-headed individual given to hasty judgments. That promise of notices and articles in the papers and his extravagant praises of her talent seemed to her merely insincere twaddle. Even his face, gestures, and manner of speaking reminded her of a certain notorious braggart living in the vicinity of Bukowiec.

The second act of the play commenced.

Janina looked on, but it did not carry her away as the first had done.

"How do you like our theater? . . . " asked the brunette chorus girl, whom she had met in the dressing-room.

"Very well!" answered Janina.

"Bah! the theater is like a plague; when it infects anyone, you might as well say amen! . . . " whispered the brunette, her voice hard.

Behind the scenes, in the almost dark passages between the decorations there was a great number of people. The actors stood in the passages and certain pairs were crouched in the darkness; whispers and discreet laughs sounded on all sides.

The stage-director, an old, bald man without a collar and dressed only in a vest, with a scenario in one hand and a bell in the other, ran up and down at the back.

"To the stage! You enter immediately, madame! . . . enter! . . ." h e cried all perspired and flushed, and ran on again, gathered from the dressing-rooms those who were needed on the stage, and at the appropriate moment whispered "Enter!"

Janina saw how the actors suddenly interrupted their conversations, left each other in the midst of some sentence, stood down half-empty glasses, and rushed for the entrances, waiting for their turn, immovable and silent or nervously whispering the words of their rôles, and entering into their characters; she saw the quivering of lips and eyelids, the trembling of legs, the sudden paleness beneath the layer of paint, and the feverish glances of stage fright ...

"Enter!" sounded a voice like the crack of a whip.

Almost everyone started violently, hastily assumed the required facial expression, crossed himself a few times and went on.

Each time the stage door opened a thrill went through Janina at that wave of strange fire, that streamed toward her from the public.

She began again to lose herself in the play. That mysterious gloom, those garish hues and forms, emerging from the shadows and suddenly flooded with light, the strains of invisible music, the echo of singing, the sound of subdued footfalls and strange whispers in the darkness, the feverish rapture of the public, the glowing eyes, the excitement, the thundering applause, like a far-away storm, streams of dazzling light alternating with darkness, the throng of people, the pathetic ring of words, tragic cries, heart-rending sobs, moans, weeping, a whole melodrama, pompously and noisily acted—all this filled Janina with a fervor different from the one she had felt in the first act, the fervor of energy and action. She went through the playing with all the actors, suffered together with those paper heroes and heroines, feared with them and loved with them; she felt their nervousness before entering the stage, trembled with emotion in the pathetic moments of the play, while certain words and cries sent so strange and painful a tremor through her that they brought the tears to her eyes and a faint cry to her lips.

An increasing number of people from the audience began to come behind the scenes. Boxes of candy, bouquets, and single flowers circulated freely from hand to hand. Beer, whisky, and cognac were drunk and cakes were snatched from a huge tray. Gusts of laughter broke out here and there, jokes exploded like fireworks in the air. Some of the chorus girls had dressed and were going out into the garden.

Janina saw actors in their negligee only, parading up and down before their dressing-rooms; women, in white petticoats with naked shoulders and with half of their stage make-up removed, were strolling about the stage and peeping through the curtain at the public. On noticing some stranger, they would retreat uttering little shrieks, smiling coquettishly, and darting significant glances.

Waiters from the restaurant, maids, and stage hands went flying about like hunting hounds.

"Sowinska!"

"Tailor!"

"Costumer!"

"A pair of pants and a cape!"

"A cane for the stage and a letter!"

"Wicek! run to the director and tell him that it is time for him to dress for the last act!"

"Set the stage!"

"Wicek! send me some rouge, beer, and sandwiches! . . . " called one actress across the stage.

In the dressing-rooms reigned chaos, forced and hurried changing of dress, feverish make-up with cosmetics that were almost melting from the heat, and quarrels. . . .

"If you pass before me again on the stage, sir, I'll kick your shins, as I live!"

"Go kick your dog! My part calls for that . . . here, read it!"

"You intentionally hide me from view!"

"What did I tell you!" said another. "I merely popped out and immediately there arose a murmur of applause."

"It was only the wind and that fellow thinks it was applause," answered another voice.

"There was a murmur of disgust, because you bungled your part."

"How the deuce can one keep from bungling when Dobek prompts like a consumptive nag?"

"Speak yourself, and I will then stop . . . we'll see what a fool you'll make of yourself!

... I put word after word into his ear as with a shovel and . . . nothing doing! . . . I shout out so loudly that Halt kicks at the stage for silence . . . but that fellow still stands there like a dummy!" retorted Dobek.

"I always know my part; you trip me up intentionally."

"Tailor! a belt, a sword and a hat . . . hurry!"

" . . . Mary! if you tell me to go, there will go with me night and suffering, loneliness and tears ... Mary! do you not hear me?

. . . It is the voice of the heart that loves you . . . the voice. . . " repeated Wladek, pacing up and down the dressing-room with his rôle and gesticulating wildly, deaf to all that was going on about him.

"Hey there, Wladek . . . put on the soft pedal. . . . You'll have enough opportunity to roar and groan on the stage until our ears are sore," called someone.

"Gentlemen! haven't you perhaps seen Peter?" inquired an actress, poking her head through the door.

"Gentlemen, see if Peter isn't sitting somewhere under the table," mocked someone.

"Milady . . . Peter went upstairs with a very pretty little dame."

"Murder him, madame! he's unfaithful!"

Such were the remarks, punctuated with laughter, that greeted her.

The actress vanished and from the other side of the stage one could hear her asking everyone, "Have you seen Peter?"

"She will go crazy some day from jealousy over him! . . ." remarked someone.

"A respectable woman!"

"But that doesn't prevent her from being a fool."

"How are you, Editor!"

"Oh, it's the editor, is it! . . . that means we'll have beer and cigarettes."

"And here comes the counselor! . . ."

"Good evening Counselor!"

"What news at the box office?"

"Fine! . . . The theater is sold out, for I saw Gold smoking a cigar."

"Praised be the gods! The advances on our salaries will be larger."

"How do you do, Bolek! . . . Don't come in here, or you will melt like butter ... we have a little Africa here to-day ... "

"We'll cool ourselves immediately, for I've ordered the beer . . . "

"To the stage, everybody! . . . The people to the stage! The priests to the stage! The soldiers to the stage!" shouted the stage-director, rushing from one dressing-room to the other.

After a moment, all had vanished.

It was well after ten o'clock, the next morning at her hotel when Janina awoke, worn-out completely; for the moment, she could not understand, where she was.

She no longer felt any of yesterday's feverish raptures, but rather a quiet gladness that she was already in the theater. At moments, the bright tone of her mood was overcast by some shadow, some presentiment, or unconscious memory from the past; it was the glimmering of something unpleasant which, although it quickly vanished, left traces of uneasiness.

She hastily drank her tea and was about to go out, when someone gently rapped at the door.

"Come in!" she called.

There entered an old Jewish woman, neatly dressed, with a big box under her arm.

"Good morning, miss!"

"Good morning," she answered, surprised by the visit.

"Perhaps you will buy something, miss? ... I have good, cheap wares. Perhaps you need some jewelry? Perhaps some gloves or hairpins,—they are pure silver. I have all kinds of articles at different prices and all are genuine Parisian goods!. . . " she chattered on rapidly, spreading the contents of her box on the table, while her little black eyes with heavy red lids, like the eyes of a hawk, wandered about the room and took stock of everything.

Janina kept silent.

"It won't harm you to look at them . . . " insisted the Jewess. "I have cheap things and pretty things! Perhaps you will have some ribbons, or laces, or stockings? ... or will you have some of these silk handkerchiefs? . . . "

Janina began to examine the collection spread out on the table and selected a few yards of some ribbon.

"Perhaps your mother will also buy something? . . . " ventured the Jewess, looking at her intently.

"I am alone."

"Alone?" she drawled, with an inquisitive contraction of her eyebrows.

"Yes, but I don't intend to live here," explained Janina, as though justifying herself.

"Perhaps I might recommend a boarding house to you? ... I know a certain widow who . . . "

"Very well," interrupted the girl, "you might find me a room with some private family on Nowy Swiat, near the theater . . . "

"You belong to the theater, miss?" . . . ah! . . ."

"Yes."

"Perhaps you need something else? ... I have beautiful things for the theater."

"No, I have all I want."

"I will sell them cheap ... as I'm an honest woman . . . cheap! They are just what you want for the theater."

"I don't need anything."

"May I die, if they are not dirt cheap! . . . These are such hard times."

She replaced all her wares in the box and drew closer to Janina.

"Perhaps you will give me a chance to make something?. . . "

"I won't buy anything else, for I don't need it!" answered Jane, growing impatient.

"I don't mean that!"

The old woman began to whisper hurriedly—"I know nice young men ... do you understand, miss? . . . rich young men ! . . .

That is not my business, but they asked me to . . . They'll come to see you themselves . . . Nice, rich, young men."

"What? . . . What?" cried Janina.

"Why are you so excited, Miss?"

"Get out of here, or I'll call the servant!" shouted Janina.

"Goodness, what a temper! . . . I knew at least ten ladies, who were the same as you in the beginning and afterwards they were ready to kiss my hands, if only I would introduce them to some gentleman . . . "

She did not finish, for Janina opened the door, and pushed her out.

At the theater she met Sowinska on the veranda, and immediately, in the politest manner, asked her if she did not know of some room she could rent with a private family.

"Ah, that just fits in fine! . . . If you wish, there is a room in our house that you may have. We can let you have it cheap, together with your meals. It is a very nice room on the lower floor, with windows facing the south, and a separate entrance from the hall."

They agreed on the price and Janina said she would pay her a month's rent in advance.

"So that all's settled!" said Sowinska. "You will find our house very quiet, for my daughter has no children. . . . Come, I will show you the room."

"Not until after the rehearsal; and if you haven't the time to wait, leave me the address and I will find the place myself."

Sowinska gave her the address and went away.

Janina was handed her notes and took part in the rehearsal, singing from them.

Kaczkowska wanted Halt to accompany her at the piano.

"Give me a rest, madame! I have no time!" he answered.

"If you wish, madame, I will accompany you, providing it is from notes . . . " proposed Janina.

Kaczkowska drew her eagerly away to the room with the piano and kept her busy for about an hour; but the whole company at once became interested in this chorus girl who could play the piano.

Afterward Cabinska spoke with Janina a long time, and requested her to come to her home the following day after the rehearsal.

Janina went straight from the theater to Sowinska's house to look at her room.

# CHAPTER IV

"THE Management has the honor of requesting the presence of the lady and gentleman artists of the Company, as also the members of the orchestra and the choruses, at a tea and social to be held at the home of the Director on the 6th of this month, after the performance. The Director of the Society of Dramatic Artists. (Signed) John, the Anointed, Cabinski.

"Well, what do you say, Pepa? . . . Will this do? . . . " the Director asked his wife after he had read aloud the invitation.

"Teddy! be quiet, I can't hear what father is reading."

"Mamma, Eddy took my roll!"

"Papa, Teddy called me a jackass!"

"Silence! By God! with those children . . . Quiet them, Pepa."

"If you give me a penny, pa, I'll be quiet."

"And me too, me too!—"

Cabinski held the whip on his knee under the table and waited; as soon as the children had advanced near enough, he sprang up and began to belabor them.

There arose a squealing and screeching; the door flew open and the junior directors went sliding down the banisters to the accompaniment of howls.

Cabinski calmly proceeded to read over again the invitation.

"At what time do you wish to invite them?"

"After the performance."

"You'll have to ask some of the reporters. But that must be done personally."

"I haven't time."

"Ask someone from the chorus to write the invitations for you."

"Bah! And let them make stupid mistakes? Perhaps you will write them for me, Pepa? . . . You have a neat hand."

"No, it's not proper that I, the wife of the director, should write to strange men. I told that . . . what is the name of the girl whom you engaged for the chorus? . . . "

"Orlowska."

"Yes . . . I told her to come here to-day. I like her. Kaczkowska told me that she plays the piano excellently, so the thought struck me that . . . "

"Well then, let her write the invitations; if she plays the piano, she must also know how to write."

"Not only that, but I think that she could teach Jadzia how to play . . . "

"Do you know, that's not at all a bad idea! . . . We might include that in her future salary."

"How much are you paying her?" she asked, lighting a cigarette.

"I have not yet agreed upon a price . . . but I will pay her as much as I pay the others," he answered with a strange smile.

"Which means that . . . "

"That I'll pay her a great, a great deal . . . in the future.'

"Ha! ha! ha!"

Both began to laugh, and then became silent.

"John, what do you propose for the supper?"

"I don't know as yet . . . I'll talk it over at the restaurant. We'll arrange it somehow ..."

Cabinski proceeded to make a clean copy of the invitation, while Pepa sat in a rocking-chair, puffing away at her cigarette.

"John! . . . Haven't you noticed anything peculiar about Majkowska's acting, recently?"

"No, nothing ... if she performs a little spasmodically, that's merely her style."

"A little! . . . Why, she goes into epileptic fits! The editor told me the papers are calling attention to it."

"For God's sake, Pepa! Do you want to drive away our best actress? You ousted Nicolette, who had a gallery of her own."

"Well, and you had a great liking for her too; I happen to know something about that."

"And I could tell you something about that editor of yours . . . "

"What business is that of yours! . . . Do I interfere when you go prowling about backrooms with chorus girls?"

"But neither do I ask you what you do! . . . So what's the use of quarreling about it? . . . Only I will not let you touch Majkowska! With you it's merely a question of intrigue, while with me it's one of existence. You know right well that there is not another such pair of heroic actors as Mela Majkowska and

Topolski, anywhere in the provinces, and perhaps not even at the Warsaw Theater. To tell the truth, they are the sole props of our company! You want to oust Mela, do you? ... I tell you she has the sympathy of the whole public, the press praises her . . . and she has real talent! . . . "

"And I? ... " she asked threateningly, facing him.

"You? ... You also have talent, but" . . . he added softly, "but . . . "

"There are no 'buts' about it! You are an absolute idiot. . . . You have no conception whatever about acting, or plays, or artists. You are yourself a great artist, oh, such a great artist! Do you remember how you played the part of Francis in *The Robbers?* . . . Do you? ... If you don't, I'll tell you . . . You played it like a shoemaker, like a circus clown! . . . "

Cabinski sprang up as though someone had struck him with a whip.

"That's a lie! The famous Krolikowski played it in the same way; they advised me to imitate him, and I did . . . "

"Krolikowski played like you? . . . You're a fool, my artist!"

"Pepa, you had better keep quiet, or I'll tell you what you are!"

"O tell me, please do tell me!" she cried out in a rage.

"Nothing great, nor even anything small, my dear."

"Tell me plainly what you mean . . ."

"Well then, I'll tell you that you are not a Modrzejewska," laughed Cabinski.

"Silence, you clown! . . . " she yelled throwing her lighted cigarette at him.

"Wait, wait, you backstairs prima donna," he hissed, growing pale with rage.

Cabinski in his dressing gown, torn at the elbows, in his night clothes and slippers, began to pace up and down the room, while Pepa, just as she had arisen from sleep, unwashed, with yesterday's stage make-up still adorning her face, and her hair all disheveled, whirled around in circles, her white and soiled petticoat rustling.

They stared at each other with furious and threatening glances. Their old competitive enmity burst out in full force. They hated each other as artists because they mutually and irresistibly envied each other their talents and success with the public.

"I played poorly, did I? . . . I played like a circus clown? . . ." he shouted.

He seized a glass from one of the racks and hurled it to the floor.

Quickly Pepa intercepted him and screened the dishes with her body.

"Get out of the way!" he growled threateningly, clenching his fists.

"These are mine!" she cried and threw the whole heap of dishes at his feet with such force that they broke into little bits.

"You cow!"

"You fool!"

"Please ma'am, let me have the money for breakfast," said the maid, at that instant entering.

"Let my husband give it to you!" answered Cabinska, and with a proud stride, went into the next room, slamming the door after her.

"Let me have the money, sir. It's late and the children are crying!"

He laid a ruble on the table, brushed his top hat with his sleeve and departed.

The nurse took a pitcher and a basket for rolls and went out.

The Cabinskis had no more time to think of their household than of their children, and cared for nothing, absorbed entirely by the theater, their rôles, and their struggle for success.

The canvas walls of the stage scenes and decorations representing elegant salons and interiors sufficed them entirely; there they breathed more freely and felt better. In the same way a canvas scene depicting some wild landscape with a castle on the summit of a chocolate-colored hill and a wood painted below sufficed them as a substitute for real fields and woods. The smell of mastic, cosmetics, and perfume were to them the sweetest odors. They merely came home to sleep, their real home, where they lived habitually, was on the stage and behind the scenes.

Cabinski had been in the theater some twenty years, playing continually, and still, he desired each new rôle for himself and envied others.

Pepa never took account of anything, but listened only to her momentary instinct and sometimes to her husband. She doted on the melodrama, on strained and nerve-thrilling situations; she liked a sweeping gesture, an exalted tone of voice, and glaring novelties. Her pathos was often of the exaggerated variety, but she played with fervor. A certain play, or some accent or word would move her so deeply that even after leaving the stage she would still shed real tears behind the scenes.

She knew her parts better than anyone else, for she would memorize them with mechanical precision. For her children she cared about as much as for her old dresses: she bore them—and left them to the care of her husband and the nurse.

Immediately after Cabinski's departure Pepa called through the door, "Nurse, come here!"

The nurse had just returned with the coffee and the boys whom she had dragged in from the yard with difficulty.

She served the breakfast to the children and promised: "Eddy ... you will get a pair of new shoes . . . papa will buy them for you. Teddy will get a new suit and Jadzia a dress . . . Drink your coffee, dears!"

She patted their heads, handed them the rolls and wiped their faces with maternal solicitude. She loved them and fussed over them as though they were her own children.

"Nurse!" shouted Cabinska, sticking her head through the door.

"Yes, I hear you."

"Where is Tony?"

"She's gone to the laundry."

"You will go, nurse, for my dress to Sowinska on Widok Street. Do you know where it is? . . ."

"Of course, I know! . . . That skinny woman who's as cross as a chained dog. . . ."

"Go right away."

"Mamma! ... let us also go with nurse . . . " begged the children, for they feared their mother.

"You will take the children along with you, nurse."

"Of course, that's understood ... I wouldn't leave them here alone!"

She dressed the children, put on a sort of woolen dress with broad red and white stripes, covered her head with a kerchief, and went out with them.

Cabinska dressed and was about to go out, when the bell rang. A small, rather corpulent and very active gentleman pushed his way in. It was the counselor.

His face was carefully shaven, he wore gold-rimmed glasses on his small nose, and a smile, that seemed glued there, on his thin lips.

"May I come in? . . . Will Madame Directress permit it? . . . Only for a minute, for I must be right off again! . . . " he recited rapidly.

"Of course, the esteemed counselor is always welcome. . . . " called Cabinska, appearing.

"Good morning! Pray let me kiss your little hand. . . . You look charming to-day. I merely dropped in here on my way . . . "

"Please be seated."

The counselor sat down, wiped his glasses with his handkerchief, smoothed his very sparse, but ungrayed black hair, hastily crossed his legs, and blinked a few times with neuralgic eyes.

"I read in to-day's *Messenger* a very flattering mention about you, Madame Directress."

"It's unmerited, for I don't know how that rôle ought to be played."

"You played it beautifully, wonderfully!"

"Oh, you're a naughty flatterer, Mr. Counselor! . . . " she chided.

"I speak nothing but the truth, the unadulterated truth, my word of honor!"

"Please ma'am it is already noon," interrupted the nurse, who had returned.

"You are bound for the theater, Madame Directress?"

"Yes, I'll drop in to see the rehearsal, and then take a walk about town."

"Then we will go together, agreed? . . ." asked the counselor. "On the way we shall settle a little piece of business."

Cabinska glanced at him uneasily. He was again blinking his eyes, crossing his feet, and adjusting his glasses which had a habit of continually slipping off.

"No doubt he wants that money, . . ." thought Cabinska, as they were going down the stairs.

The counselor, in the meanwhile, was smiling and chirping away in honeyed tones.

This strange individual would show up at the garden-theater at the very first performance and vanish after the last, until the following spring. He freely loaned money which was never returned to him. He would give suppers, bring gifts of candy to the actresses, take the young novices under his wing and was always reputed to be in love with some actress platonically. Immediately upon his first appearance, Cabinski had borrowed one hundred rubles from him—and before all those present he had intentionally forced him to accept as security his wife's bracelet with the object of convincing them that he had no money.

They entered the theater and quietly took their seats, for the rehearsal was already in full swing and Kaczkowska with Topolski were just in the midst of a capital love scene.

The counselor listened, bowed on all sides with a smile and whispered to the directress: "Love is a splendid thing ... on the stage!"

"Even in life it is not bad," she remarked.

"True love is very rare in life, so I prefer it on the stage, for here I can enjoy it every day," he spoke hurriedly, and his eyelids began to blink again.

"You have been disillusioned, Counselor?"

"Oh no, by no means! . . . How are you, Piesh!"

"Well, sated with food, and bored," replied a tall actor with a handsome, thoughtful face, extending his hand.

"Will you smoke some Egyptian cigarettes?"

"I will, if you will let me have some," he answered coolly.

"Mrs. Piesh is as well and as jealous as ever, eh? . . . " inquired the counselor, handing him a cigarette.

"Just as you are always in a good humor . . . Both are diseases."

"So you consider humor a disease, eh?" asked the counselor.

"I hold that a normal man ought to be indifferent and care for nothing."

"How long have you been riding that hobbyhorse?"

"Truth is usually learned late."

"How long will you stick to that truth?"

"Perhaps forever, if I can find nothing better."

"Piesh, to the stage!" came the voice of the stage-director.

The actor arose stiffly, and with a quick, automatic step, went behind the scenes.

"A curious, a very curious fellow!" whispered the counselor.

"Yes, but very tiresome with his everlasting truths, ideals, and other foolish haberdashery!" cried a young actor dressed like a doll in a light suit, a pink-striped shirt and yellow calf-skin pumps.

"Ah, Wawrzecki! ... You must have again slain some innocent beauty, for your face is as radiant as the sun . . . "

"It's easy for you to joke, Mr. Counselor! . . ." he defended himself with a knowing smile, advancing his shapely foot. He posed gracefully, raised his hand, and flashed his jeweled rings, for the directress was gazing at him through half-closed eyes.

"Well then, in your estimation who is not tiresome, eh? . . . Come now, confess my boy!"

"The counselor, for he has humor and a good heart; the director when he pays; the public when it applauds us; pretty and kind women, the spring, if it is warm; people, when they are happy—all that is beautiful pleasant and smiling; while tiresome things are all those that are ugly: cares, tears, suffering, poverty, old age and cold. . . . "

"Who is that young lady over there?" inquired the counselor, pointing to Janina who was listening attentively to the rehearsal.

"A novice."

"She has an engaging expression. Her face shows good breeding and intelligence. Do you know who she is? . . . "

"Wicek!" called Cabinska to the boy who was playing about the garden, "go and ask that lady, standing near the box, to come here."

Wicek ran over to Janina circled about her, glanced into her eyes and said: "The old woman over there wishes to see you."

"What old woman? . . . Who? . . . " she asked, unable to understand him.

"Cabinska, Mrs. Pepa, the directress, of course! . . . "

Janina approached slowly, while the counselor observed her intently.

"Please have a seat, mademoiselle. This is our dear counselor, the patron of our theater," spoke Cabinska, introducing him.

"I beg your pardon!" cried the counselor, grasping her hand and turning the palm to the light.

"Don't be afraid, Miss Orlowska! . . . The counselor has an innocent mania of fortune telling," cried Cabinska merrily, peering over the shoulder of the counselor into the palm he was examining.

"Ho! ho! a strange one, a strange one!" whispered the old man.

He took from his pocket a small magnifying-glass and through it examined minutely the lines of the palm, the fingernails, the finger joints, and the entire hand.

"Ladies and gentlemen! We tell fortunes here from the hands, the feet, and something else besides! . . . Here we predict the future, and dispense talent, virtue, and money in the future. Admission only five copecks, only five copecks! . . . for the poorer people only ten groszy! Please step in, ladies and gentlemen, please step in!" cried Wawrzecki, excellently imitating the voice of the show criers on Ujazdowski Square.

The actors and actresses surrounded the trio on all sides.

"Tell us something, Mr. Counselor!"

"Will she marry soon?"

"When will she eclipse Modrzejewska?"

"Will she get a rich hubby?"

"How many suitors has she had in the past?"

The counselor did not answer, but quietly continued to examine both of Janina's palms.

She heard those derisive remarks, but was unable to move, for that strange man actually held her pinned to her seat. She felt herself burning with anger, yet could not move her hands which he held.

Finally, the counselor released her and said to those surrounding them: "For once you might refrain from your clownishness, for sometimes it is not so foolish as it is inhuman. I beg your pardon, mademoiselle, for having exposed you to their rudeness; ... I greatly beg your pardon, but I simply could not resist examining your hands; that is my weakness. . . . "

He kissed her hand ostentatiously and turned to the surprised Cabinska: "Come, let us go, Mrs. Directress!"

Janina was consumed with such curiosity, that, in spite of all those spectators, she asked quietly: "Will you not tell me anything Mr. Counselor?"

The counselor gazed about him, and then bent toward Janina and whispered very quietly: "Now, I cannot ... In two weeks, when I return, I will tell you all."

"Oh come, Counselor!" cried Cabinska, "Oh, I almost forgot! . . . Will it be possible for you to come to see me after the rehearsal Miss Orlowska?" she asked, turning to Janina.

"Certainly, I'll come," answered Janina, resuming her seat.

"Where shall we go, Madame Directress?" asked the counselor. He seemed less jovial, and wrapt in thought.

"I suppose we might go to my pastry shop."

Cabinska did not question him, and only after they had seated themselves at the pastry shop, where she regularly spent a few hours each day, drinking chocolate, smoking cigarettes, and gazing at the street crowds, did she venture to ask him with a pretended indifference: "What did you notice in that hussy's hands, Mr. Counselor?"

The counselor shifted impatiently, put his binoculars upon his nose, and called to the waiter, "Black coffee and very light chocolate!"

Then he turned to Cabinska. "You see, that is a secret ... to be sure, one that means little, but nevertheless, not my own to disclose."

Cabinska insisted, for merely to say: "a secret," throws all women out of balance; but he told her nothing, only remarking abruptly, "I am leaving town, Mrs. Directress."

"Where are you going?" she inquired, greatly surprised.

"I must . . ." he said, "I will return in two weeks. Before I go, I would like to settle our . . . "

Cabinska frowned and waited to hear what he would say further.

"For you see, it might happen that I would return only in the fall when you will no longer be in Warsaw."

"I surmised long ago that you were an old usurer," Cabinska was thinking, tinkling her glass with a spoon.

"Some fruit cakes!" he called to the waiter and then, turning to her again, continued . . . "And that is why I wish to return to you, dear lady, your bracelet."

"But we have not yet the money. Our success is continually being interrupted . . . we have so many old payments to meet..."

"Oh, don't bother about the money. Imagine that I am giving you this for your name day as a small token of friendship. . . will you? " he asked, slipping the bracelet upon her plump wrist.

"Oh, Counselor, Counselor! if I did not love my John so much, I would . . . " she cried, overjoyed at regaining her bracelet without any obligations. She squeezed his hands so heartily and beamed upon him with her joyous gaze so closely, that he felt her breath upon his cheeks.

He gently pushed her aside, biting his lips.

"Ah, Counselor, you are an ideal man!"

"Oh, let us drop that! ... You can invite me to be a godfather to your next child."

"Oh, you're a rogue, Mr. Counselor! . . . What's that? . . . you already want to depart?"

"My train leaves in two hours. Goodbye!"

He paid the bill at the buffet and hurried away, sending her a smile through the window.

Cabinska still sat there, gazing out upon the street.

"Is it possible that he loves me?" she thought to herself, sipping her cooled chocolate.

She pulled some rôle out of her pocket, read a few lines, and again gazed out upon the street.

The dilapidated hacks, pulled by lean horses, dragged along lazily; the tramways rumbled by; along the sidewalks people threaded like a long, immovable ribbon.

The clock chimed three. Cabinska arose and started for home, walking slowly until she spied the editor walking with Nicolette and the calm horizon of her mind suddenly became clouded.

"He, with Nicolette? . . . with that . . . base intriguer?"

Already from a distance she scorched them with the gaze of a Gorgon.

At the corner of Warecka Street, Nicolette suddenly disappeared and the editor approached her with a beaming countenance.

"Good morning! . . ." he cried, extending his hand.

Pepa measured him coolly and turned her face away.

"What sort of nonsense is this, Pepa?" he asked, quietly.

"Oh, you are unspeakably mean!" she retorted.

"A comedy of some kind again? . . ." he queried.

"You dare to speak to me in that way?"

"Well . . . I'll quit then and merely say: good-day!" he snapped back angrily, bowed stiffly and, before she could bethink herself, jumped into a hack and drove away.

Cabinska was petrified with indignation.

Cabinska, on returning home whipped the children, scolded the nurse, and locked herself in her room.

She heard her husband enter, ask for her, and knock at her door; when dinner was served, she did not come out, but paced angrily up and down her room.

Soon thereafter, Janina arrived. Cabinska greeted her cordially in her boudoir, becoming suddenly unrecognizably hospitable.

Janina left alone, began to explore that boudoir with curiosity, for, although the entire house looked like a junk shop, or a railroad waiting-room of the third class, filled with packs, valises and trunks, this one room possessed an almost, luxurious air. It had two windows opening upon the garden, the walls were decorated with a paper resembling brocatelle, and cupids were painted on the ceiling. The grotesquely carved furniture was upholstered with crimson silk striped with gold. A cream-colored rug in imitation of antique Italian covered the floor. A set of Shakespeare, bound in gilded morocco lay on a lacquered table painted in Chinese designs.

Janina did not pay much attention to all this, for she was entirely absorbed by the wreaths hanging on the walls which bore such inscriptions as these: "To our companion on the occasion of her birthday," "To a distinguished artist," "From the grateful public," "To the Directress—from the Company," "From the admirers of your talent." The laurel branches and palm leaves were yellow and shrunken from age and hung there covered with dust and cobwebs. The broad white, yellow, and red ribbons streamed down the walls like separate colors of the rainbow with their gold-stamped letters proclaiming glories that had long since passed into oblivion. Those inscriptions and withered wreaths gave the room the appearance of a mortuary chapel.

Janina was looking through an album, when Cabinska quietly entered. Her face wore an expression of suffering and melancholy; she dropped down heavily into a chair, sighed deeply and whispered, "Pardon me for letting you bore yourself here."

"Oh I didn't feel a bit bored!"

"This is my sanctuary. Here I lock myself up when life becomes unbearable. I come here to recall a happy past and to dream of that which will never more return …" she added, indicating the rôles and the wreaths hanging on the walls.

"Are you ill, Madame Directress? . . . perhaps I am intruding, and solitude is the best medicine." Janina spoke with sincere sympathy.

"Oh, please stay! ... It affords me real relief to speak with a person who is, as yet, a stranger to this world of falsehood and vanity!" she said with emphasis, as though reciting a rôle.

"I don't know whether I am worthy of your confidence," answered Janina modestly.

"Oh, my artistic intuition never deceives me! ... I pray you sit nearer to me! So you have never before been in the theater, mademoiselle?"

"No."

"How I envy you! . . . Ah, if I could begin over again, I would not know all this bitterness and disappointment! Do you love the theater?"

"I have sacrificed almost everything for it."

"Oh, the fate of artists is a sad one! One must sacrifice all; peace, domestic happiness, love, family, and friends—and for what? . . . for that which they write about us; for such wreaths that last only a few days; for the handclaps of the tiresome throng. . . . Oh, beware the provinces, mademoiselle! . . . Look at me . . . Do you see those wreaths? . . . They are splendid and withered, are they not? And yet, not so long ago I played at Lwow. . . . "

She paused for a moment as though fascinated by the memory of those days.

"The stages of the whole world were open to me. The director of the *Comédie Française* came purposely to see me and offer me an engagement. . . . "

"You possess also a mastery of French, madame?"

"Do not interrupt me. I was paid a salary of several thousand rubles; the papers could not find words strong enough to praise my acting; I was pelted with flowers and bracelets set with diamonds! (She unconsciously adjusted her cheap bracelet.) Counts and princes courted my favors. . . . Then came a great misfortune which changed everything; I fell in love . . . Yes, do not wonder at that! I loved, as deeply as it is possible to love, the most beautiful and best man in the whole world. ... He was a nobleman, a prince and heir to a large estate. We were about to be married. I cannot tell you how happy we were! ... Then ... like a bolt from the blue sky ... his family, the old prince, a tyrannical magnate without a heart parted us. ... He took him away and wanted to pay me a hundred thousand guldens or even a million, if only I would renounce my beloved. I threw the money at his feet and showed him the door. He avenged himself cruelly. He spread the most dishonorable calumnies about me, bribed the press, and persecuted me at every step, the base wretch! ... I had to leave Lwow and my life took an entirely different turn . . . a different turn . . . "

Cabinska paced up and down the room, tears in her eyes, love in her smile, a sad bitterness upon her lips, a tragic mask of resignation upon her face, forsaken, violent grief in her voice.

She acted the tale with such mastery that Janina believed everything.

"If you knew how sincerely I sympathize with you, madame! . . . What a dreadful fate!"

"That is already past! . . . " answered Cabinska, dropping into her chair.

She herself had come almost to believe in those stories, retold with numerous variations a hundred times over to all those who were willing to listen. Sometimes, on ending her account, moved by the picture of that fancied misfortune, she would actually suffer.

Cabinska had acted the parts of so many unfortunate and betrayed women that she had already lost all memory of the bounds of her own individuality; her own emotions became merged and identified in ever greater degree with the characters which she impersonated, and thus it happened that her fanciful tales were not downright lies.

After a long silence, Cabinska asked in a calm voice, "You live at Mrs. Sowinska's, mademoiselle?"

"Not yet," answered Janina, "I have already rented the room, but they have to renovate it. In the meanwhile, I am living at the hotel."

"Kaczkowska and Halt told me that you play the piano very well."

"A little bit."

"I wanted to ask you, if you would not teach my Yadzia? . . . She is a very bright girl and has a good ear for music."

"With real pleasure. My knowledge is rather limited, but I can teach your daughter the rudiments of music. . . . Only, I don't know whether I will have enough time. ..."

"Oh, certainly! And as to your fee, we shall include that in your salary."

"Very well. ... Is your daughter already started?"

"Excellently. You can convince yourself immediately. . . . Nurse, bring Yadzia here!" called Cabinska.

They passed into the next room in which stood the director's bed, a few packs and baskets, and an old rattle-box of a piano.

Janina heard Yadzia play and agreed that she would give her lessons regularly between two and three o'clock in the afternoon, when her parents were not at home.

"When are you to make your first appearance at the theater?" asked Cabinska.

"To-day, in the *Gypsy Baron.*"

"Have you a costume?"

"Miss Falkowska promised to loan me one."

"Come with me. . . . Perhaps I'll find something for you. . . ."

They went into the room where the children slept with the nurse. Cabinska pulled out of a package a fairly well-preserved costume and gave it to Janina.

"You see, mademoiselle, we furnish the costumes, but since the members of the company prefer to have their own, because ours, of course, cannot be so very elegant, ours often lie here unused. ... I will loan you this one."

"I also will have my own."

"That is best."

They took leave of each other very cordially and the nurse carried Janina's costume after her to the hotel.

With such passionate eagerness did Janina anticipate her first appearance on the stage, that she arrived at the theater when there was hardly anyone as yet behind the scenes. The chorus girls assembled slowly and dressed even more slowly. Conversation, laughter, subdued whisperings went on as usual, but she heard nothing, so preoccupied was she with her dressing.

They all began to help her, laughing because she did not even have powder or rouge.

"What, you never powdered yourself?" they chorused.

"No . . . What for? ..." she answered simply.

"We'll have to make her a face, for she's too pale," remarked one of them.

They rubbed her face with a layer of white cosmetic, shaded this with rouge, carmined her lips, underscored her eyes with a little pencil dipped in black pigment, and curled and pinned her hair. She was passed on from hand to hand and given a thousand advices and warnings.

"On entering the stage look straight at the public, so that you don't trip."

"And before you enter, see that you cross yourself."

"Always enter with your right foot foremost."

"Now you look fine! . . . but do you want to appear on the stage in short skirts without wearing tights?"

"I haven't any! . . . "

All began to laugh at her embarrassed look.

"I will loan you a pair," cried Zielinska. "I think they'll fit you." They treated her with undisguised favor, for they had heard that she was to teach Cabinska's daughter and that Pepa had loaned her a costume.

Janina, looking in the mirror, hardly recognized herself. It seemed as though she wore a mask, only slightly resembling her own face and with that strange expression that all the chorus girls wore.

She went downstairs to Sowinska.

"My dear madame, tell me truly, how do I look?" she begged, all excited and flushed.

Sowinska scrutinized her from all sides and, with her finger, spread the rouge more thoroughly on her cheeks.

"Who gave you that costume?" she asked.

"Madame Directress loaned it to me."

"Oh! something must have melted her to-day!"

"She told me such sad stories. . . . "

"The actress! ... if she only played that way on the stage there would be no better in the world."

"You must be joking, madame! . . . She told me about Lwow and her past."

"She's a liar, that old hag! She was then the sweetheart of some hussar and made such scandals that they turned her out of the theater. What was she at the Lwow theater? ... a chorus girl only. Ho! ho! those are old tricks. . . . We all know them here long since!"

"Tell me how I look?" asked Janina at length.

"Beautiful. . . . I'll wager they'll all be chasing after you!"

An increasing nervousness seized Janina. She walked up and down the stage, peered through the hole in the curtain, viewed herself in all the mirrors, and then tried to sit still and wait, but could not endure it. The feverish excitement and nervousness attendant upon a first appearance shook her as with the ague. She could not stand or sit still for a single moment.

It seemed as though she did not see the people, the preparations that were going on about her, the lights, or even the stage itself, but only had in her brain the reflection of a confused and moving mass of eyes and faces. At each moment she would gaze with terror at the audience and feel as though her heart were ceasing to beat.

When the bell rang for the second time, she hurried off the stage and took her place in the chorus that was already assembled behind the scenes; while waiting for the moment to enter, she unconsciously crossed herself, and her whole body trembled so violently that one of the chorus girls, noticing her confusion, took her by the arm.

"Enter!" shouted the stage-director. The throng carried her along with it and pushed her to the front of the stage.

The sudden silence and magnified glare of light restored her senses somewhat, and after leaving the stage she stood behind one of the scenes and completely regained her composure.

On her second entrance she felt only a slight tremor. She sang, heard the music, and gazed straight at the public. She was also emboldened by seeing the editor sitting in the front row and encouraging her with a friendly smile. She kept looking at him and after that she was able to distinguish with increasing clearness individual faces in the audience.

In some scene in which the chorus promenaded about the back of the stage, while a comic dialogue was going on at the front, Janina's companions indulged in whispered conversations.

"Brona, look! Your fellow is there in the third row toward the left."

"Oh look! Dasha is in the theater . . . goodness, how she is dolled up. ..."

"Siwinska! fasten my hooks, for I feel my skirt is falling down."

"Lou! your wig is coming off."

"Look to your own shags!"

"I'm going to Marceline with someone to-morrow . . . perhaps you will go with us, Zielinska?"

"Look at the eyes that student is making at me!"

"I don't care a snap for penniless plugs."

"But what merry chaps they are!"

"No, thank you! They have nothing but whiskey and sardines. That's a treat, only for those of the street."

"Hush! Cabinska is sitting in that box."

"My gracious, what a maidenly make-up she has to-day!"

"Quiet, we sing!"

Behind the scenes stood a great variety of people: waitresses, stage-hands, restaurant boys, and actors waiting for their cues to enter—all these were gazing on the stage.

Cabinska's nurse, with the two eldest children, was sitting near the proscenium under the ropes of the curtain.

Wawrzecki from behind the scenes was violently beckoning to Mimi who was just then singing a duet with Wladek. In the pauses, the actress would spitefully stick out her tongue at him.

"Give me the key to the house ... I forgot my shoes, and I need them right away!" he whispered.

"It's in my skirt pocket in the dressing-room," she answered, backing away toward the center of the stage with a broad musical phrase on her lips.

"Halt" was banging the desk with his baton, for Wladek was cutting short his tones and continually wavering. The threatening anger of the orchestra director only made him all the more nervous, and his singing was growing steadily worse.

"The damned Hun is purposely trying to trip me!" he muttered angrily under his breath, embracing the singing Mimi in the love scene.

"For God's sake don't squeeze me so hard!" panted Mimi, at the same time smiling at him rapturously.

"For I adore you with the frenzy of love . . . for I adore you!" sang Wladek with fiery intonation.

"Are you crazy? I will be all black and blue and ... "

She suddenly broke off, for Wladek had finished his song and the applause came roaring like an avalanche, so she pulled him by the hand and they walked to the front of the stage to bow to the audience.

During the intermission Janina observed the editor standing in the center aisle, conversing with some stout, blond man.

"Can you tell me, sir, with what paper that editor is connected?" Janina asked the stage- director, who was supervising the arrangement of the scenery for the next act.

"With no paper, probably. He's merely a theatrical critic."

"He told me himself that . . . "

"Ha, ha!" laughed the stage-director, "I see you're green!"

"But he is sitting in the chairs reserved for the press," persisted Janina stating what she thought was a convincing argument.

"What of that? There are more of his kind there. Do you see that light blonde? He alone is a real writer and the rest are merely migratory birds. God alone knows what their occupation is . . . but since they hobnob with everybody, talk a lot, have money from somewhere, and occupy the foremost places everywhere, no one even bothers asking who they are."

"Ah, you look so fascinating, so fascinating," cried the editor at that instant rushing in upon the stage and already from a distance extending his hands to her. "A veritable portrait by Greuze! Only a little more courage and everything will go smoothly. I will insert an item to-morrow about your first appearance on the stage."

"Thank you," she answered coolly, without looking at him.

The editor turned about and made off for the actors' dressing-room.

"Good evening, gentlemen!" he called entering.

"How are things going in the hall? Were you at the box office? . . . "

"Nearly all the seats are sold out."

"How is the play taking?"

"Well, very well! ... I see, Mr. Director that you have replenished the chorus: that charming, new blonde attracts all eyes. . . . "

"Good, good. . . . Hurry there, give me my belly!"

"Mr. Director, please let me have an order for two rubles. I must immediately send for my boots," begged some actor, hastily pulling on his costume.

"After the performance!" answered Cabinski, holding the pillow to his stomach, "tie it fast, Andy!"

They wrapt him about with long strips like a mummy.

"Mr. Director, I need my boots on the stage. . . . I cannot play without them!"

"Go to the devil, my dear sir, and don't disturb me now. . . . Ring!" he called to the stage-director.

Cabinski, whenever he played, created a big confusion in the dressing-room. He always suffered from stage fright, so he would try to overcome it by shouting, scolding, and quarreling over every trifle.

The costumer, the tailor, the property man all had to hustle about him and continually remind him lest he forget something. Despite the fact that he always commenced dressing early, he was always late. Only on the stage did he recover his equanimity.

Now it was the same; his cane had been mislaid and he rushed about, wildly shouting: "My cane! Who took my cane! . . . My cane! Damn it! I must go right on!"

"You snort like an elephant in the dressing-room, but on the stage you buzz as quietly as a fly," slowly remarked Stanislawski, who hated all noises.

"If you don't like to hear it, go out into the hall."

"I'll stay right here, and I want quiet. No one can dress in peace with you around."

"Podesta, to the stage!" called the stage-director.

Cabinski ran out, grabbed a cane out of somebody's hand, tied a black handkerchief about his neck and rushed on the stage.

Stanislawski departed behind the scenes, all the others dispersed, and the dressing-room became deserted, only the tailor remaining to gather up the costumes scattered over the floor and tables and take them to the storeroom.

In the dressing-room of the leading ladies of the caste such a storm had broken loose that Cabinski, who was just leaving the stage, went there to pour oil on the troubled waters.

As he entered, Kaczkowska threw herself at him from one side and Mimi from the other; both grasped him by the hands and each sought to out-shout the other.

"If you allow such things to happen, Director, I will leave the company! . . . "

"It's a scandal, Director! . . . everybody saw it. . . . I will not stay in her company another hour!"

"Director! she . . ."

"Now don't lie!"

"It's insulting!"

"It's base and ridiculous!"

"For God's sake! what's all this about?" cried Cabinski in desperation.

"I will tell you how it happened, Director...."

"It is I who ought to tell, for she is a liar!"

"Now my dears, please be quiet or I swear I'll go right out."

"It was this way. I received a bouquet, for it was most plainly intended for me, and this . . . lady, who happened to be standing nearer, cut me off and took my bouquet. . . . And, instead of giving it to me, to whom it belonged, she brazenly bowed and kept it for herself!" cried Kaczkowska amid tears and bursts of anger.

At that Mimi began to cry.

"Mimi, you will blur the paint under your eyes!" called someone.

Mimi immediately stopped crying.

"What do you ladies want me to do?" asked Cabinski, when he found an opportunity to speak.

"Tell her to give me back that bouquet and apologize."

"I can, but with my fist . . . " retorted Mimi. "You can ask the chorus, Director . . . they all saw."

"The chorus from the fourth act!" called Cabinski behind the scenes.

There entered a throng of women and men already half-undressed, and among them Janina.

"Well, let us arrange a judgment of Solomon!"

An increasing number of onlookers began to crowd into the dressing-room and derisive remarks, aimed at the generally disliked Kaczkowska, flew about.

"Who saw to whom the bouquet was given?" asked Cabinski.

"We weren't taking notice," all replied, unwilling to incur the disfavor of either of the contestants. Only Janina who detested injustice, finally said: "The bouquet was given to Miss Zarzecka. I stood beside her and saw distinctly."

"What does that calf want here? She came from the street and thinks she can interfere in what's none of her business!" cried Kaczkowska.

Janina advanced, her voice hoarse with anger.

"You have no right to insult me, madame!" she cried. "Do you hear! I haven't ever let anyone insult me, nor will I!"

A strange silence suddenly fell, for all were impressed by the dignity and force of Janina's words. She glared at Kaczkowska with glowing eyes and then turned on her heel and left the room.

Cabinski had fled to the box office after hastily divesting himself of his costume.

"Whew! she's a sound nut, that new one."

"Kaczkowska will never forgive her that . . . "

"What can she do? . . . Miss Orlowska has the backing of the management."

Mimi, immediately after the play, went to the dressing-room of the chorus where she found Janina still agitated.

"How good you are!" cried the actress effusively.

"What I did was right . . . that's all," Janina replied.

"Take a trip with us to Bielany, won't you?" begged Mimi.

"When? . . . And who are going?"

"We're going within the next few days. There will be Wawrzecki, I, a certain author, a very jolly chap, whose play we are to present, Majkowska, Topolski and you. You must come with us!"

After lengthy persuasions and kisses, which Janina received indifferently, she finally agreed to accompany them.

They waited for Wawrzecki and afterwards all went together to a pastry shop for tea, taking with them also Topolski, who there composed a circular addressed to the whole company requesting them to appear without fail at the morrow's rehearsal, punctually at ten o'clock.

# CHAPTER V

FOR Cabinski all days on which there was a performance were important days, but only three days were extraordinary: Christmas Eve, Easter Day, and . . . the name day of his wife which fell on the 19th of July, sacred to St. Vincent de Paul. On those three days the director and his wife would hold a reception on a grand scale.

Cabinski the miser would vanish, and in his place would appear Cabinski the munificent, dispensing hospitality after the ancient custom of the Polish nobility, while certain deeply hidden hereditary cells of lavishness opened up in his ego. The guests were received and fêted generously and no expense was spared. And, if later, as a result of this, advances on salaries were smaller for a month or so, their deferment more frequent, and the director's complaints of a deficit more numerous, hardly anyone minded, for all enjoyed themselves to the utmost, particularly on the name day of the directress.

Cabinska's Christian name was Vincentine, but none bothered their heads about why her husband called her "Pepa," for nobody was interested to that extent.

In accordance with the announcement of Topolski, the company assembled punctually for the rehearsal. They were to play *The Martyr* by D'Ennery, in which the title rôle, one of the showiest and most lachrymose in her repertory, was invariably acted each year by the directress. She played it really well, putting into it her entire store of tears and vocal lamentations, and had the deep satisfaction of thrilling the public.

Those name day performances were usually a real benefit for all kinds of novices, for the caste was purposely made up of the poorest players so that the acting of Pepa might thereby shine forth more effectively.

Cabinska went direct to the stage without speaking to anyone and during the entire rehearsal wore on her face an expression of tender emotion and absorption. At the end of the rehearsal the entire company gathered about her and

Topolski came forward. Cabinska modestly lowered her eyes and, pretending to be surprised, waited.

"Allow me, esteemed Directress to extend to you in the name of your fellow-actors and actresses their most cordial felicitations on the occasion of your name day and to wish you with all our hearts that you may continue to remain for a long time the ornament of our stage and a blessing to your husband and children. In grateful appreciation of your artistic services and your companionship, the company begs you, my dear madame, to accept this humble token of our affection which is only a poor return for your goodness and kind-heartedness."

Topolski ended and handed her an open case in which was a set of sapphire gems bought from the contributions of the whole company. He kissed her hand and stepped aside.

Then all began to approach Cabinska separately; the men kissed her hands, while the women threw themselves on her neck with protestations of friendship and good wishes.

Wladek, who had been the first to pay his tribute at hand-kissing, drew Topolski aside behind the scenes.

"Spit out the dregs of that congratulatory tommyrot, or you'll poison yourself with such a big dose of hypocrisy."

"But it won't poison her."

"Bah! the sapphires cost one hundred and twenty rubles; for so much money she can listen a whole week."

"Thank you, thank you with my whole heart! You put me to shame my dear comrades, for in truth I do not know what I have done to merit so much kindness," said Cabinska with emotion. Really, the sapphires were very pretty.

The director smiled, rubbed his hands, and invited all to his home after the performance.

The directress singled out for a particularly effusive kiss Janina who, led by sympathy, had brought her a lovely bouquet of roses, explaining that she had not contributed to the fund for the general gift as it was collected before her advent into the company.

Cabinska would not part with Janina and took her along with her to dinner.

"Truly, they must be very good people and must love you," said Janina at the table.

"Once a year will not ruin them," answered Cabinska merrily.

Together they went to the pastry shop so as not to interfere with the preparations that were being made for the evening reception. She sat there relating to Janina the history of her past name day celebrations with a tender pathos which could not, however, disguise a certain feeling of bitterness and uneasiness over the fact that the editor had not even sent her a card of greeting.

The performance was a real ovation. From the public she received a mass of flowers, while the editor sent her a big basket of them together with an imposing bracelet.

That overwhelmed her. As soon as he appeared behind the scenes, she drew him into the darkest corner and kissed him with fiery passion.

The Cabinski home presented an unusual appearance. In the first room, in the middle of a huge rug that completely covered the dirty floor, was a circular stand bearing a fan-shaped palm, while two mirrors with marble consoles stood in the corners. Heavy, cherry-colored, velvet portières were draped over the windows and the doors. A clump of azaleas and rhododendrons between the windows formed an oasis of gorgeous greenery, accentuating the beautiful lines of a yellowish plaster statue of Venus de Milo which stood on a pedestal draped with purple cloth.

The piano at the further end of the room, decked with a garland of artificial flowers, bore upon it a huge golden tray stacked with visiting cards. Four little tables with little blue chairs surrounding them were placed in the most brilliantly lighted parts of the room. The tarnished and chipped gilded frames of the mirrors were skillfully masked with red muslin, pinned artistically with flowers. The torn wall paper was covered with pictures. The whole salon presented so elegant and artistic an appearance, that Cabinska, on returning from the theater stood amazed and cried out enthusiastically: "A splendid scene! . . . John you are a master-decorator!"

"Heavens! . . . it's as beautiful as in a comedy!" added the nurse, crossing the salon on tiptoe.

The second and larger room which ordinarily served the purpose of a store room, crammed with scenic odds and ends, had now been transformed into a dining room and dazzled with its restaurant-like splendor: the whiteness of its table covers, its polished trays, its bouquets of flowers, its mass of burnished dishes, and its formality.

Cabinska hardly had time to dress herself in a stately lily-colored gown in which her faded complexion, ruined by cosmetics, took on a youthful expression and freshness, when the company began thronging in. The ladies retired to Cabinska's room adjoining the boudoir, while the gentlemen left their street attire in the kitchen divided in two by a French wall painted in the style of Louis XV, which had been brought from the stage.

Wicek, in theatrical livery that consisted of boots with yellow, cardboard tops, a blue spencer a few sizes too big for him, decked with red cord and a mass of gold buttons, helped the actors to lay aside their wraps with a grave and stiff mien, like a real groom from an English comedy; but his roguish disposition could not long endure the mood.

"What a monkey the director has made of me, eh? My own mother wouldn't know me in these duds. No doubt I'll have to pay for it all by going without supper or absolution!" he whispered, smiling.

The ladies all in gala array, rouged and charming, began to fill the room with a stiff and icy atmosphere, sitting about immovable and shy.

Janina arrived rather late, for she had a long distance to come from her hotel, and wished to dress carefully. She greeted everyone, and her eyes wandered with a look of surprise over the room, struck by the tone of solemnity that reigned over all.

Dressed in a cream-colored silk gown shading off into heliotrope, with gentians in her hair and corsage, tall and lithe, with her rosy complexion and reddish-golden hair, she looked very original and beautiful. She possessed a great deal of grace and natural distinction, and moved about with ease, as though accustomed to the atmosphere of the salon, while the rest of the company felt unnatural and constrained by the theatrical elegance of their surroundings. They walked about, conversed and smiled, as though they were on the stage, playing some very difficult rôle that demanded continual attention. One could see that the very carpet under their feet restrained them, that they sat down with a certain fear on the silk-lined chairs, that they seemed to be merely passing through the room, afraid to touch any of the objects about them.

It was a festive reception with wine served by the restaurant waiters, and with trays of cakes and liqueurs circulating about in ponderous bottles. This only added to the restraint of the ladies. They knew not how to eat or drink gracefully, they feared to stain their dresses and the furniture and feared also to serve as the butt of ridicule for a few gentlemen who were not at all impressed with this sham elegance, and were gazing at them and making spiteful remarks.

Majkowska, who to-day presented a truly stately appearance in her light yellow dress with a border of roses, with her black, almost ebony hair, olive complexion, and classically beautiful face—a typical Veronese—took Janina by the arm and gracefully promenaded about the salon with her, casting proud glances at those about them.

On the other hand, her mother, whom some mischievous person had seated on a little tabouret, was undergoing agonies. She had in one hand a glassful of wine, in the other a tart and a cake in her lap. She drank the wine and was at a loss what to do with the glass. She gazed pleadingly at her daughter, grew red in the face, and finally asked Zielinska, who was sitting near her: "My dear lady, what shall I do with this glass?"

"Stand it under the chair."

The old woman did as she was advised. Everyone began to laugh at her, so she picked it up again and held it in her hand.

Old Mrs. Niedzielska, the mother of Wladek and the owner of a house on Piwna Street, who was always honored by the Cabinskis, sat under the shade of the palm grove with Kaczkowska, and continually followed her son with her eyes.

The men in the dining room were, meanwhile, storming the buffet.

"Where do you get your everlasting humor, Glas?" asked Razowiec, who, although he was the gloomiest actor in the company, played the parts of the merriest rakes and the funniest uncles.

"That is a public secret. I do not worry, and I have a good digestion," answered Glas.

"You have precisely that which I am lacking. ... Do you know I tried the recipe which you recommended, but got no results . . . nothing will help me any more. I feel certain that I shall not outlive this winter for if my stomach does not pain me it is my back, if it isn't my back then it's my heart, or else this dreadful pain passes into my neck and racks my spine as with an iron rod."

"Imagination! Drink a cognac to me. . . . Don't think of your illness and you'll be well."

"You laugh, but I tell you truly that I can no longer sleep for whole nights at a time. . . ."

"Imagination, I tell you! Drink a cognac to me!"

"It is easy for those who have never suffered to ridicule."

"I have suffered, my God, I have suffered. . . . Drink a cognac to me! I once ate in the restaurant 'Under the Star' such a cutlet that I lay in bed a whole week after it and writhed like an eel with pain."

They retired to the further end of the buffet near the window and continued their conversation. The one complained and lamented, the other ceaselessly laughed, saying every minute, "Drink a cognac to me!"

"Maurice," called Majkowska in a whisper, lifting the portières.

Topolski bent over toward her and she murmured into his ear: "I love you! ... do you know? ..." and she passed on, conversing with Janina.

Throughout the salon formed small groups of people conversing.

Cabinski kept running about continually, inviting the guests to drink, pouring out the liquors for them, and kissing everybody.

Pepa sat in the salon with the editor and Kotlicki, who was one of the steady patrons of the theater. She was relating something in a lively and jovial tone, for the editor would every now and then burst out in a discreet laugh, while Kotlicki would contort into a smile, his long equine face, and gather about him his coat-tails. All that was known about him was that he was rich and ennuied.

Kotlicki listened patiently enough, but, at last, bending toward Cabinska, he asked in a wooden, expressionless voice, "When does the culminating act of to-day's performance begin—the supper?"

"Immediately ... we are waiting only for the owner of the house to arrive."

"No doubt the rent for the last quarter must be unpaid, if you show her so much consideration," he whispered ironically.

"You always see everything in the worst light!" she answered, throwing a flower at him.

"To-day I merely see that the directress is fascinating, that Majkowska has the mien of a lioness, and that the lady who is walking with her . . . but who is she?"

"A newly engaged chorus girl."

"Well, I see that yonder aspirant to the dramatic art is beautiful by virtue of her originality and alone possesses more distinction than all the rest of them taken together. Furthermore, I see that Mimi to-day resembles a freshly baked roll, white and round and rosy; that Rosinska has the face of a black poodle who has fallen into a bin of flour and not yet succeeded in shaking it off, and that her Sophie looks like a freshly washed and combed little greyhound. Kaczkowska looks like a frying pan covered with melted butter; Mrs. Piesh like a hen seeking her strayed chicks; and Mrs. Glas like a calf enveloped in a rainbow. Where the dickens did she get all those colors she wears?"

"You are a merciless mocker!"

"You can make me relent, Directress, by hurrying the supper . . ." he answered and became silent.

The directress began telling in detail about a new joke that Majkowska had played on Topolski. Kotlicki, listening to it, frowned impatiently.

"It is too bad that there is not a law which would compel you ladies to pierce your tongues instead of your ears," he said derisively, enveloping himself in a cloud of cigar smoke and observing Janina who was still promenading with Majkowska.

Both beamed with satisfaction, realizing the attention they attracted. Janina's eyes were joyous, and her crimson lips smiled charmingly revealing her pearly teeth.

Wladek was engaged in some lengthy conversation with his mother and also followed Janina with his eyes. Meeting the glances of Kotlicki he turned away.

Shortly they were joined by Sophie Rosinska, a fourteen-year old typical actor's child with the long, thin mouth of a greyhound, a pale complexion, and the large eyes of a madonna. Her short, curled hair shook with every motion of her head and her thin, narrow lips fairly bit with their spitefulness as she related something to Majkowska in her lively voice.

"Sophie!" energetically called Mrs. Rosinska.

Sophie left them and sat down beside her mother, gloomy and sulky.

"I constantly keep telling you not to have anything to do with Majkowska!" whispered Rosinska, adjusting the curls on her daughter's head.

"Don't bother me with your nonsense. Mamma! ... I'm sick and tired of listening to it! I like Miss Mela because she isn't a scarecrow like those others," saucily prattled Sophie and smiled with childish naïveté at Niedzielska, who was looking at her.

"Wait till we get home. I'll fix you!"

"All right, all right . . . we'll see about that, Mother!"

Mrs. Rosinska turned to Stanislawski, who sat beside her all the while and chatted without drinking anything. She began to make remarks about Majkowska, with whom she was always on a war footing, for they had almost the same repertory and Majkowska had, in addition, talent, youth, and beauty, none of which Rosinska possessed. Rosinska hated all young women, for in each she now saw a rival and a thief stealing her rôles and her favor with the public.

Lately she had become intimate with Stanislawski for she felt that something similar was happening to him. He never spoke to her about it, nor ever complained, but now, when he bent toward her his thin, waxen face all seamed with wrinkles as fine as hairs, his yellowish eyes glowed gloomily.

"Did you notice how Cabinska played to-day?" she asked him.

"Did I notice?" answered Stanislawski, "I see that every day. I know long ago what they are . . . long ago! What is Cabinski himself? ... A clown and tightrope walker who in our days would not even have been permitted to play the part of a lackey! . . . And Wladek! he's an artist, is he? . . . A beast who makes a public house of the stage! ... He plays only for his mistresses! His noblemen are shoemakers and barbers, while his barbers and shoemakers are loafers from the water front. . . What do they introduce on the stage? . . . Hooligans, the street, slang and mud. . . . And what is Glas? ... A drunkard in life, which is a minor consideration, but it is not permissible for a true artist to wander about taverns with the most disgusting hoodlums; it is not permissible for a true artist to introduce on the stage the hiccoughs of a drunkard and vulgar brutality. . . . Take Ziolkowski's *The Master and the Apprentice* for instance: there you have a type, a finished type of a drunkard presented in broad and classical outlines; there is gesture and pose and mimicry, but there is also nobility. What does Glas make of that rôle? ... He makes a filthy, repulsive, drunken shoemaker of the lowest order. That is their art! . . . And Piesh? . . . Piesh is also not much better, although he bears the stamp of a good artist ... but his acting is a miserable and an everlasting botch; he has a humor on the stage, like that of fighting dogs, but not human and noble . . . and not ours! . . . "

He became silent a moment and rubbed his eyes with his long skinny hand with thin, knotty fingers.

"And Krzykiewicz? . . . and Wawrzecki? . . . and Razowiec? . . . perhaps they are artists, eh? ... Artists! . . . Do you remember Kalacinski? . . . He was an artist! Or Krzensinski, Stobinski, Felek, and Chelchowski? . . . Those were artists who could bring down the house! . . . What are our actors compared with them? . . ." he asked encompassing with an inimical glance the company about them. "What is this band of shoemakers, tailors, paper hangers, barbers? . . . Comedians, ragamuffins, and clowns! . . . Bah! art is going to the dogs. In a few more years when we are gone, they will make of the stage a barroom, a circus, or a storage warehouse.

"Do you hear? . . . they give me half-sheet rôles of old men and old nincompoops, to me! . . . do you hear? . . . to me, who for forty years have upheld the entire classical repertory—to me! Oh! oh!" he hissed quietly tearing his finger nails convulsively. "Topolski! . . . Topolski alone has a talent, but what does he do with it? . . . A bandit, a Singalese, who goes into epileptic fits on the stage, who is ready to put a barn on the stage if those new authors require it. They call that realism, while in truth it is nothing but roguery! ... "

"And the women? . . . you forget the women, sir! . . . Who plays the parts of sweethearts and heroines? . . . Who is in the chorus? . . . scrub-women and barmaids, who have made of the theater a screen for their licentiousness. But that's nothing . . . the directors want that; what do they care if these women possess neither talent, intelligence nor beauty! . . . They give them the most important rôles. They act the parts of heroines and look like chambermaids or like those who walk the streets! . . . But what do the directors care as long as the business keeps going and the box office is sold out . . . that's all they care about!" She spoke rapidly and the blood rushed to her face so violently that she became all red, in spite of the thick layer of powder and cream.

The stage-director, who was once the celebrated hero of a few theaters, and old Mirowska who was still retained only as a favor because of her old age and brilliant past completed the camp of the veterans of the old actors' guard, who had fought in other times, and looked upon the present with gloomy eyes. They stood beneath the bridge of a sinking ship, hence no one even heard their cries of despair.

Kotlicki beckoned to Wladek and made room for him beside himself.

Wladek in passing Janina cast a glance of fiery passion at her, and then sat down near Kotlicki, rubbing his knee which bothered him whenever he sat for any length of time.

"Rheumatism is already there, eh? . . . while fame and money are still far away! . . ." Kotlicki began mockingly.

"Oh, the deuce take fame! . . . Money I wouldn't mind having . . . "

"Do you think you will ever get it?"

"I will . . . my faith in that is unfailing! At times it seems to me as though I already felt it in my pocket."

"That's true. Your mother owns a house."

"And six children and a pile of debts as high as the chimney! . . . No, not that! ... I will get the money elsewhere . . . "

"In the meanwhile, according to your old custom you borrow it wherever you can, eh?" Kotlicki mocked on.

"Oh, don't fear. I'll return yours this month yet, without fail."

"I will wait even until the reappearance of the comet of 1812; it will pass this way again in about a year. . . . "

"Don't mock me. . . . You'd not hurt people as much with a club as you do with your cynicism."

"That's my weapon!" answered Kotlicki, contracting his brows.

"Perhaps, before long, I shall marry and then I will pay up all my debts. . . . "

Kotlicki turned violently towards him, glanced straight into his eyes and began to laugh with his quiet, neighing voice, screwing his face into a grimace.

"That is the finest piece of invention that I have ever heard!"

"No, I seriously intend to marry and have already selected something: a brownstone house and a girl of twenty, a light blonde, plump, graceful and resolute. . . . If my mother helps me, I shall marry before this season is over."

"And what of the theater?"

"I will organize a company of my own." Kotlicki laughed again.

"Your mother is too sensible and I am sure that she will not let herself be caught on that hook, my dear! . . . Why are you ogling that beauty in the cream-colored dress so persistently, eh?"

"Oh she's a cocoanut of a woman!"

"Yes, but that cocoanut is too hard for your weak teeth. You won't crack it, and you're likely to lose a tooth in trying. . . ."

"Do you know what the savages do? . . . When they haven't a knife or a stone handy, they light a fire, put the cocoanut in it, and the heat bursts it open . . . "

"And when there is no fire to be had, what then? ... You don't answer me, my clever chap? . . . Then I'll tell you: when there is no fire to be had, they content themselves with gazing on the cocoanut, consoling themselves with the thought that someone else will show them how to do it."

Their conversation was interrupted by the entrance of the owner of the house. A confused murmur arose from those assembled. Cabinska went forward to greet her with extended hand and the mien of resplendent majesty.

"It is a pleasure to meet you! . . a real pleasure!" she announced with a faint smile, condescendingly extending her hand to the persons whom Cabinska introduced to her. She sought to appear coldly indifferent, while in reality she had been dying from curiosity ever since the morning to view these noted women about whom she had heard so much.

Cabinski approached her smiling, with wine and cakes in his hand, but Pepa was already inviting all to sit down to supper.

The landlady excused herself for being late, but her thin voice was drowned amid the hubbub of the guests seating themselves at the table. She was given an honorary place between Pepa, Majkowska, and the editor. Kotlicki seated himself at the end of the table alongside of Janina, while Wladek wedged himself in between Janina and Zielinska

After a toast pronounced by the editor in honor of the celebrant, conversation burst forth like a cascade and with unrestrained flow filled the entire room. All began to talk at the same time, to laugh and to joke. Inebriation began to envelop all brains in a rosy mist of merriment and to weave joy around all hearts.

In the middle of the supper the doorbell rang violently.

"Who can that be?" asked Cabinska. "Nurse, go and open the door!"

The nurse was busy about a side table where the children were eating; she went immediately to open the door.

"Who came?" inquired Cabinska.

"Oh, nobody! Only that unchristened little goldfish!" she answered scornfully.

Those sitting nearest burst out laughing.

"Ah, yes. Our dear and invaluable Gold!" Gold entered and bowed to the company, tugging at his sparse, yellow little beard.

"How are you, goldfish?"

"Hey there, Treasurer! Oh pearl of treasurers, come over to us."

The treasurer bowed, paying no attention to the jibes that were hurled at him.

"Mrs. Directress will pardon me for coming late, but my family lives in the Jewish quarter and I really had to stay with them till the end of the Sabbath," he explained to Cabinska.

"Have a seat, sir. If you can't eat, you're at least allowed to drink," invited Cabinski, making room for Gold alongside himself.

Gold located himself carefully and began to eat. When the company had forgotten him a bit, he ventured to address them:

"I have brought you the latest news, for I see no one knows it, as yet. . . . "

He took a newspaper from his side pocket and began to read aloud: "Miss Snilowska, the noted and talented artist of the provincial theaters, playing under the pseudonym of 'Nicolette' has received permission to make her début in the Warsaw Theater. She will make her first appearance next Tuesday in Sardou's *Odette*. We hope that the management, in engaging Miss Snilowska, has added a very valuable acquisition to the stage."

He folded away the paper and calmly continued to eat. The company was struck dumb with amazement.

"Nicolette on the Warsaw stage! . . . Nicolette making her début! . . . Nicoette! . . . " they whispered with subdued voices.

Everybody began to look at Majkowska and Pepa, but both were silent.

Majkowska's face wore a scornful expression while Pepa, unable to conceal the anger that raged within her, tore distractedly at the lace on her sleeves.

"No doubt she is now blessing that intrigue that caused her to leave us, for it helped instead of harming her," said someone.

"Or else it was her talent that helped her!" intentionally added Kotlicki.

"Talent?" cried Cabinska, "Nicolette and talent! Ha! ha! ha! Why she could not even play a chambermaid on our stage!"

"Nevertheless in the Warsaw Theater she will play the second-best roles," interposed Kotlicki.

"The Warsaw Theater! The Warsaw Theater! That is a still poorer show than ours!" added Glas.

"Ho! ho! what do the Warsaw Theater and its actors amount to! . . . Nothing great, to be sure!" shouted Krzykiewicz, all flushed with drinking as he filled the landlady's glass with wine.

"Only pay us such salaries as their actors get, and you will see who we are!" called Piesh.

"That's true! Piesh is right. Who can think only of art when his rent is in arrears? "

"That's a falsehood! That would mean that you could make an artist of any swineherd whom you fed," called Stanislawski across the table.

"Poverty is a fire that burns rubbish, but the true metal only comes out of it all the purer," quickly said Topolski.

"Nonsense! It comes out not purer, but only more sooty, and afterwards the rust devours it all the more quickly. A bottle is worth something not because it may have once contained the choicest Tokay, but because it's now full of brandy!" stammered Glas in a drunken voice.

"The Warsaw Theater! My God! with the exception of two or three persons it's full of the scum of the profession which the provinces no longer could stand."

"Just let the press give us the support it gives them, let it insert half a column daily about us and round up the public for us each day as it does for them! . . . "

"Well, what then? . . . Even at that you'd remain nothing but Wawrzecki!" sneered Kotlicki.

"Yes, but the public would come and see that Wawrzecki is not a bit worse and perhaps a great deal better actor than those patented celebrities."

"Let me speak!" whimpered Glas, vainly trying to rise from his chair and steady himself.

"The public! . . . the public is a flock of sheep which runs where it is driven by the shepherds."

"Don't say that, Topolski . . . "

"Don't try to deny it, Kotlicki! I tell you that the public is a pack of fools, but its leaders are even greater fools!"

"Let me speak," mumbled Glas in a voice that was already growing inaudible, while he leaned on the table and gazed at the candles with hazy eyes.

"Glas, go to sleep, for you're drunk," said Topolski sharply.

"I am drunk? ... I am drunk? . . ." stuttered Glas, his face as ruddy as the dawn.

The wine and liquors circulated more freely, and the guests began shifting their seats.

Wladek seated himself between Majkowska and the landlady, embarking on a flirtation with the latter. Mimi, growing exhilarated, approached Kaczkowska, with whom she had already exchanged glances and friendly words across the table. They now sat close together, holding each other about the waist like the sincerest friends.

Janina, who had been answering Kotlicki only in brief sentences, preoccupied with what she saw and heard about her glanced at him with an amazed and questioning look.

"You are surprised?" he asked.

"Yes, for not so long ago they were so angry at one another."

"Bosh! that was only a little comedy, played fairly well in their momentary mood . . . "

"A comedy? . . . and I thought that ..."

"That they would begin to pull each other's hair, no doubt ... for even that sometimes happens behind the stage between the best of friends and actors. From what planet have you dropped down that these people surprise you so greatly? . . . "

"I came from the country where one hears hardly anything about artists, only about the theater itself," she answered straightforwardly.

"Ah, in that case, I beg your pardon. . . . Now I understand your amazement and I will presume to enlighten you that all those quarrels, rumpuses, intrigues, envies, and even fights are nothing but nerves, nerves, nerves! They vibrate in all of these people at the slightest touch, like the strings of an old piano. Their tears, their angers, and their hatreds are all momentary, and their loves last about a week, at the longest. It is the comedy of life of nervous individuals, acted a hundredfold better than that which they present on the stage, for it is played instinctively. I might describe it thus: all women in the theater are hysterical, and the men, whether great or small, are neurasthenics. Here you will find everything but real human beings. Have you been long in the theater?"

"This is my first month."

"No wonder that everything amazes you; but in a month or so you'll no longer see anything surprising; everything will then appear to you natural and commonplace."

"In other words, you infer that I also will become a subject to hysteria," she gaily added.

"Yes. I give you my word that I am speaking with absolute sincerity. You think you can live with impunity in this environment without becoming like all the rest of them; while I tell you that that is a natural necessity. Suppose we expatiate on that a bit . . . will you allow me?"

"Certainly."

"In the country you must know the woods. . . . Now please recall to your mind the woodsmen. Have they not in themselves something of that wood which they are continually chopping? They become stiff and stalwart, gloomy and indifferent. And what of the butcher? Does not a man who is continually occupied in killing, who breathes in the odor of raw meat and steaming blood, in time become stamped with the same characteristics as those beasts which he has slain? He does, and I would say that he is himself a beast. And what of the peasant? Do you know the village well?"

Janina nodded.

"Imagine for a moment the green fields in springtime, golden in the summer, russet-gray and mournful in the autumn, white and hard like a desert in the winter. Now behold the peasant as he is from his birth until his death . . . the average, normal peasant. The peasant boy is like a wild, unbridled colt, like the irresistible urge of the spring.

In the prime of his manhood he is like the summer, a physical potentate, hard as the earth baked by the July sun, gray as his fallows and pastures, slow as the ripening of the grain. Autumn corresponds entirely to the old age of the peasant—that desperate, ugly old age with its bleared eyes and earthy complexion, like the ground beneath the plow; it lacks strength and goes about in beggars' garments like the earth that has been reft of the bulk of its fruits with only a few dried and yellow stalks sticking out here and there in the potato fields; the peasant is already slowly returning to the earth from whence he sprung, the earth which itself becomes dumb and silent after the harvest and lies there in the pale autumn sunlight, quiet, passive, and drowsy. . . . Afterwards comes winter: the peasant in his white coffin, in his new boots and clean shirt, lies down to rest in that earth which has, like him, arrayed itself in a white shroud of snow and fallen to sleep—that earth whose life he was a part of, which he unconsciously loved, and with which he dies together, as cold and hard as those ice-covered furrows that nourished him. . . ."

Kotlicki meditated a moment and then continued: "And yet you think that you can remain in the theater without becoming a hysterical type? That's impossible! This phantom life, this daily portrayal of new characters, feelings and thoughts upon that shifting plane of impressions, amid artificial stimulants—this must metamorphose every human being, demolish his former personality and recast or rather disintegrate his soul so that you can put almost any stamp upon it. You must become a chameleon; on the stage, for art's sake, in life, from necessity."

"In other words, one must degenerate to become an artist," added Janina.

"Well, what of that? . . . Even though you fall, others will surely reach the goal and convince themselves that it wasn't worth reaching—that it isn't worth striving for, nor shedding a single tear, nor bearing a single pang ... for everything is illusion, illusion, illusion. . . ."

They became silent. Janina felt a sudden chill depression. That former fear of the unknown, experienced at Bukowiec, now took possession of her.

Kotlicki leaned with one elbow on the table and looked absently into the crystal carafes containing the arrack. He poured out and drank glass after glass. The conversation with Janina had wearied him; he continued to speak to her, but felt vexed at himself for having said so much. His yellow face, covered with freckles and short reddish hair, hard and seamed with deep lines, resembled a horse's face as it was reflected in the red glass of the carafe.

Gazing at Janina he saw so much strength and inner health, so many desires, dreams, and hopes, that he muttered to himself in a hollow, dissatisfied tone: "What for? . . . What for? . . . "

Then he gulped down another glass of wine and became absorbed in the general conversation. Voices sounded harshly, faces were red, and eyes glowed through a mist of alcoholic intoxication, while many lips were already mumbling indistinctly and incoherently. All were talking at once, arguing heatedly and quarreling volubly, unceremoniously swearing, shouting or laughing.

The candles, almost burnt out, were replaced by new ones. Gray dawn, filtering in through the reed shades in thin streaks, dimmed the glare of the lights.

The guests rose from the table and scattered about the adjoining rooms. Cabinska, followed by a few ladies, repaired to the boudoir for tea. In the first room a few tables were arranged and a game of cards commenced.

Only Gold still sat at the festal board and ate, relating something to Glas, who was now quite drunk.

"They are poor people. . . . My sister is a widow with six children; I help her as much as I can, but that doesn't amount to much. . . . And, in the meanwhile, the children are growing up and need ever more . . . " Gold was saying.

"Then cheat us more, you dog's face! . . ."

"The elder is about to take up a medical course, the next in age is a store clerk and the rest of them are such small and weak and sickly tots that it pains one to look at them! ..."

"Then drown them, like puppies! . . . Drown them and be done with it!" mumbled Glas.

"You are very drunk . . . " whispered Gold scornfully, "you have no idea what children are! . . . "

"Get married and you'll have kids of your own . . ." stuttered Glas.

"I can't ... I must first see that these are provided for," replied Gold quietly grasping a cup of tea in both hands and sipping it in little gulps, "I must first make men of them . . . " he added, his eyes glowing.

All around there was a hum of voices as in a beehive when the swarm of young bees is ready to fly out into the world. The hidden desires, envies, feuds, and troubles broke out irresistibly. The talking grew louder, people were denounced without pardon, slandered without mercy, reviled and derided without pity. Those assembled there had now become their natural selves: no one masked himself any longer nor confined himself within the bounds of one rôle.

All played a thousand different rôles. The hidden comedy of souls now found its stage, its audience, and its actors, often very talented ones.

Janina exhilarated by the wine, conversed with Wawrzecki about the theater. Afterwards she strayed about the rooms, watched the men playing cards, and listened to a variety of conversations and arguments.

Janina roused herself from her meditations, for Kotlicki stood before her with a cup of tea in his hand and with his sharp ennuied voice began to speak: "You are observing the company, mademoiselle? Truly, what remarkable energy there is in all their actions, what strong souls they now appear to be!"

"Your malice also has strength . . . " she replied slowly.

'And is wasted on slander and ridicule, you wished to add, didn't you?"

"Almost so."

"We shall see, we shall see . . ." he said slowly, standing his cup upon the table and then, taking leave of Janina he left quietly.

In the anteroom where the sleepy Wicek handed him his overcoat, he heard the monotonous whispering of the children's voices behind the screen. He raised the curtain and saw Cabinski's four little boys kneeling in their nightgowns and repeating their prayers after the nurse.

A small night-lamp, glowing before a holy picture above the nurse's bed, faintly illumined that group of children and the old, gray-haired woman, who humbly bowed to the ground, struck her breast with her hand and whispered in a tearful voice: " O Lamb of God, who purgest the sins of the world!"

The children repeated the words after her with drowsy voices and beat their breasts with their little hands.

Kotlicki withdrew quietly and without a smile. Only when he had reached the stairs, he whispered: "Well, well! We shall see, we shall see. . . . "

Janina started for the boudoir, but Niedzielska stopped her and drew her into a conversation; later Wladek joined them.

The company began to break up.

"Do you live far away?" Niedzielska asked Janina.

"On Podwal Street, but in a week at most I am moving to Widok Street."

"Ah, that's good, for we live on Piwna Street, so we can go together. . . . "

They left immediately. Niedzielska took Janina by the arm, while Wladek walked alongside, a little angry because he had to accompany his mother; he swore to himself, while aloud he made melancholy remarks about the weather.

The streets were deserted and silent. Dawn was already illumining the dark depths of the horizon and the outlines of the houses became distinct. The gas lamps extended like an endless golden chain with their links of pale flames diffusing a mist of light upon the dew-covered sidewalks and the gray walls of the houses. The fresh brisk breeze of a July morning swept down the streets with a strange charm and tranquility. The houses stood silent, still wrapt in slumber.

Arrived at her hotel Niedzielska kissed Janina with a sudden friendliness and they parted.

# CHAPTER VI

"WILL you find it comfortable here?"

"I think so. It is quiet and light.. . . Who lived here before me?"

"Miss Nicolette. She is now at the Warsaw Theater . . . That's a good omen."

"No, not entirely. They are likely not to engage her. . . . "

"Oh, they'll engage her all right. . . . Miss Zarnecka is clever," said Mme. Anna, the daughter of Sowinska into whose home Janina had just moved.

She was twenty-four years old, neither homely nor pretty with an indefinite color of hair and eyes, but with a very definite slenderness and bad temper.

She conducted a dressmaking establishment under the name of Mme. Anna and although she made her living on actresses and very often received free tickets to the theater, she never went there and hated artists. There were often scenes over this with her mother, but old Sowinska,would not so much as listen to any suggestion that she should abandon the theater. She had become so deeply rooted there that she could not tear herself away, although Mme. Anna would turn almost yellow from shame over the fact that her mother was a theatrical seamstress. She was disgustingly stingy, ignorant, pitiless, and jealous.

Mme. Anna examined Janina's wardrobe with ill-concealed malice.

"All that will have to be made over, for it smells of the country," she decreed.

Janina began to protest a little, maintaining that the same styles could often be seen in the streets.

"Yes, but who wears them, please take notice of that: shopwomen or shoemakers' wives; a self-respecting woman will not wear such rags!" Mme. Anna scornfully persisted.

"Well then, have them made over. I can pay you immediately for the work and also a full month's rent in advance."

"Oh, there's no hurry. You'll need to buy a few costumes."

"I'll have enough left for that."

Janina paid thirty rubles for her room.

"I am already settled for good," she later said to the old woman who dropped in to see her.

"Bosh, it won't be for long! In two months you'll be moving again. An actor's life is a gypsy life, from wagon to wagon, from town to town. . . . "

"Perhaps at some time I'll be able to settle down permanently," said Janina.

Sowinska smiled gloomily. "That is the way one thinks in the beginning, but afterwards . . . afterwards it ends in eternal wandering. ... You become worn-out like a rag and die on a hotel bed."

"Not all end in that way," answered Janina gaily, paying little attention.

"What are you laughing at? . . . It's not at all funny!" cried Sowinska.

"Am I laughing? ... I merely said that not all end in that way."

"All ought to end in that way, every one of them!" Sowinska shouted angrily and left.

Janina could not understand either her violent anger, or her last words.

. . . . . . .

The days sped on. Janina absorbed the theater into herself ever more deeply. She attended the rehearsals regularly, afterwards went to give lessons for two hours to Cabinska's daughter, and later would go home for dinner, prepare her wardrobe for the performance, and at about eight in the evening start off again for the theater.

On the days when no operettas were played and the choruses were free, she went to the Summer Theater and there, squeezed high up in the gallery, spent entire evenings dreaming. She devoured with her eyes the actresses, their gestures, costumes, mimicry, and voices. She followed the action of the plays so closely that later she could re-create them in her mind with detailed accuracy and often, after returning from the theater, she would light the candles, stand before the large mirror, and repeat the acting which she had seen, observing intently every quiver of her facial expression and trying out every conceivable pose. But she was seldom satisfied with herself.

106

The plays which she saw left her cold and bored. She was not stirred by the bourgeois dramas with their eternal conventional conflicts and flirtations. She repeated the banal lines of these plays apathetically and in the midst of some scene would stop and go to bed.

She asked Cabinski to give her a rôle in the cast of a new play, but he put her off with nothing.

"I am keeping you in mind, but first you must familiarize yourself with the stage. . . . When we present some melodrama or folk play you will get a bigger rôle . . . " was all he said.

In the meanwhile they were playing only operettas, for they filled the theater.

Janina smiled in reply to Cabinski's vague promises, although torn by impatience. But she had already learned to control her feelings and to wear a mask of smiling indifference. She consoled herself with the thought that sooner or later she would have done with the chorus and that the moment must at last arrive when she would appear in a real rôle.

She had already become saturated with the atmosphere in which she lived. And that public, so strange and capricious, which some accused of ignorance, of a total lack of taste and higher desires, and others of indifference, but to which all paid homage and before which they all cringed and trembled, begging its favors—that public even filled Janina with anger. There was something strange in her attitude. She would dress very fastidiously for the stage, merely for the purpose of attracting attention to herself; she would adopt the most graceful poses, but whenever she felt the gaze of the multitude it would send a depressing shudder through her.

"Shoemakers!" she would whisper scornfully, thereafter remaining in the shadow.

In the dressing-room chorus girls passively submitted to Janina, for they feared her, knowing that she had intimate and continual relations with the management. They were likewise impressed by the fact that Wladek followed her continually and that Kotlicki, who formerly used to come behind the scenes only occasionally, now sat there daily throughout the whole performance and conversed with Janina with his hat off. She was surrounded by a sort of invisible aura of unconscious respect, for although many surmises were made about her on account of Kotlicki, no one ever dared insinuate anything to her face.

At first, Janina inclined toward the leading actresses of the company and wanted to enter upon a more intimate acquaintance with them, but they discouraged her, for whenever she began to speak to them about the theater or about art, they would become silent, or else commence to tell her about their own triumphs.

Stanislawski and the stage-director were Janina's sincere friends. Many times during the rehearsals they would go upstairs to the deserted dressing-rooms or to the storeroom under the stage, and there tell stories of the theater and the actors of their day—an epoch that was already dead. They would conjure up before her eyes great figures, great souls, and great passions almost like those she had dreamed of.

How much advice they gave her concerning enunciations, classical pose, and the best manner of reciting her lines! She listened with interest, but when she tried to play the fragment of some rôle according to their instructions, she found she could not do it, and they would then appear so stiff, pathetic and unnatural that she began to treat them with an indulgent pity.

With Mme. Anna, Janina lived on a footing of cool politeness. With Sowinska she was a little more intimate, for the old woman fawned upon her as a tenant who regularly paid her rent in advance. Sowinska was coarse and violent. There were certain days that she would eat nothing, nor even go to the theater, but would sit locked in her room, crying, or at moments swearing extraordinarily.

After such days she seemed even more energetic and would indulge with greater zest in behind-the-stage intrigues. She would walk among the audience and speak quietly with the young men who hung about the theater. She would bring the actresses invitations to suppers, bouquets, candy, and letters and would seek with a genuine zeal to induce the stubborn ones to yield to the advances made to them. She accompanied the girls as a chaperon to carousals and knew just when to find an important reason for leaving. At such times there would gleam under her mask of kindhearted and wrinkled old age an expression of cruel glee.

Janina overheard once how the old woman spoke to Shepska, who had joined the theater after being seduced by a member of the chorus.

"Listen to me, madame! . . . What does your lover give you? A home on Brewery Street and sardines with tea for breakfast, dinner and supper. . . . It's a shame to waste yourself on such a poor fool! Don't you know that you could live as comfortably as you wish and laugh at Cabinski! Why should you have scruples! ... A person profits by life only as he enjoys it! . . . A young and pretty girl ought not waste herself on a penniless nobody. . . . Perhaps you think you will the sooner get a rôle by remaining where you are? . . . Oho! when pears grow on a pine tree! Only those are given rôles who have someone backing them."

Usually she accomplished her purpose, and though often offered costly presents, seldom accepted anything.

"I don't want them. If I advise anyone, it's because I wish them well," she would answer briefly.

Janina who had learned enough of the more intimate phases of life behind the scenes, regarded Sowinska with a certain awe. She knew that it was not for gain that the old woman shoved the younger ones into the mire of degradation, but for some hidden reason. At times, she feared her, unable to endure the enigmatic look with which Sowinska scrutinized her face. She felt instinctively that Sowinska seemed to be waiting for something or watching for some opportunity.

On one of those lachrymose days of Sowinska's Janina, who was just starting for the theater, dropped in to see her.

Entering the room she stood amazed. Sowinska was kneeling beside an open trunk, while on the bed, the table and the chairs were spread the parts of some theatrical costume and on the floor were lying stacks of faded copies of rôles. Sowinska was holding in her hand the photograph of a young man with a strange face, long and so thin that all the cheek bones could be seen distinctly protruding through the skin. He had an abnormally high forehead with wide temples and a huge head. Large eyes gazed out of the pale face like the sunken hollows in a dead man's skull.

Sowinska turned to the girl with the photograph in her hands and in a voice trembling with anguish, whispered: "Look, this is my son . . . and these are my sacred relics!"

"Was he an artist?"

"An artist? ... I should say so, but not like those monkeys of Cabinski's. How he played! The papers wrote about him. He was in Plock and I went to see him. When he appeared in *The Robbers* the whole theater shook with applause and cries of admiration. I sat behind the scenes and when I heard his voice and saw him I was so overcome with emotion that I thought I would die for very joy!

"I loved him so dearly that I would have let myself be torn to shreds for him! ... He was an artist, an artist! He never owned a penny and poverty often devoured him like a dog, but I tried to help him as much as I could. I slaved for him and lived on nothing but tea and bread to save something for him."

She ceased speaking while tears flowed softly down her faded, pale face.

Janina, after a long silence, asked quietly: "Where is your son now?"

"Where?" she answered, rising from the floor. "Where? . . . He is dead! He shot himself."

She began to breathe heavily.

"My whole life has been like that!" she began again. "His father was a tailor and I kept a shop. In the beginning all went well for we had plenty of money and a decent home. My husband worked for a circus and shortly a performer caught his eye and he followed her into the world when the circus moved on."

She sighed heavily.

"I merely set my teeth tightly together. I toiled like a galley slave to gain a mere living for myself and daughter, but I was stricken by an epidemic. When I came out of it, everything went to the dogs, for my shop was sold to cover my debts. I was practically turned out into the street without a penny. An unspeakable rage seized me. I borrowed money wherever I could and together with my child went to seek my husband. I found him living with a shopkeeper in such comfort that he had forgotten all about us. I took him by the neck and brought him back with us to Warsaw. ... He staid with me a whole year, bestowed another child upon me, and ran away again. My daughter grew up, we took home sewing, and managed to make a living somehow.

"Then after some years they brought back my husband— stone-blind. I gave him a nook in my home, for my children desired it. God was at least merciful enough to take him away.

"Later, I married off my daughter to a peasant. One day about two years ago, I was present at my daughter's name day party to which a few relatives and friends had been invited. In the midst of it they brought me a telegram from Suwalki asking me to come immediately, for my son was very ill."

She paused for a moment, gazed blankly about the room and in a low voice, filled with despair whispered on, lifting her pale face to Janina's:

"He was already dead. . . . They were waiting for me to bury him. . . . "

"Later they told me that he had fallen in love with a chorus girl and killed himself for her! They showed her to me. She was the vilest sort. And that was why he killed himself. . . .

"When I caught her in the street, I would have killed her, killed her like a mad dog to avenge my wrong and anguish! . . . " Sowinska shouted aloud, clenching her fists.

"Such is my life, such! I curse it every day, but cannot forget . . . all that still burns here in my bosom ... I am in the theater, for it always seems to me that he will return, that he is already dressing and will immediately appear on the stage . . .

"My God, God! . . . Ah, it was not he that was to blame, but she . . . you girls tear to pieces a mother's heart ... I would trample you all underfoot like so many worms, into the mud, into poverty, so that you might agonize as I do ... so that you might suffer, suffer, suffer. . . . "

She ceased, breathing heavily. Her yellow waxen face glared with wild hatred. Her wrinkles twitched and her pale bitten lips seethed.

Janina had been standing all the while eagerly absorbing her every word and gesture. The overwhelming reality of Sowinska's grief, so simple and strong, had called forth a responsive chord in her own heart.

She was standing in the street, wondering where she should go, when a voice behind her said: "Good morning, Miss Orlowska!"

She turned about quickly. Mrs. Niedzielska, Wladek's mother, was standing before her with a smile on her aged, simple face.

Janina greeted her hastily.

"I was about to take a walk," she said.

"Perhaps you will drop into my house for a minute? . . . " begged Niedzielska quietly. "I am so much alone that often for whole days I don't see anyone except Anna and the janitor."

She hobbled slowly along.

"Certainly, I still have a little time before the performance," answered Janina.

"You're not in the theater very long, are you?"

"Only three weeks."

"I could tell that right away!"

"How?"

"I can't exactly explain. I watched you at Cabinska's party and immediately knew that you were a newcomer. I even mentioned it to Wladek . . . "

"Please make yourself at home. . . . I'll be with you in a minute. Niedzielska played hostess quite grandly, once they were arrived at her home.

Janina, left alone, observed with curiosity the old-fashioned mahogany table covered with an embroidered net doily which stood before a huge lounge upholstered with black horsehair; the chairs, upholstered with the same material, had lyre-shaped backs. A yellow polished dresser was filled with grotesque porcelain, greenish pitchers, colored bric-a-brac, wineglasses with monograms, and flower-painted teacups standing on high legs. A clock under a bell glass, old, faded steel engravings of the Empire period, a lamp with a green shade on a separate table, a few pots with miserable flowers on the window sill and two cages with canaries constituted the entire furnishings.

"Let us have a drink of coffee . . . "  said Niedzielska, reëntering.

She took from the dresser two showy cups and placed them on the table. Then she went to the kitchen and brought in the coffee, already poured into two chipped bowls, and a plate with a few stale cakes.

"O goodness, I forgot that I had already set the cups on the table . . . well, it doesn't matter. We can drink the coffee just as well out of these, can't we? . . . "  she said, at once adding, "dear me, I forgot the sugar! Do you like your coffee sweet, mademoiselle?"

The old woman left the room and through the door Janina could hear her taking sugar out of a glass bowl. She brought in on a little saucer two lumps.

"Please have some in your coffee. . . . You see at my age I can't have anything sweet," she said, drinking audibly.

Finally, after perhaps half an hour, in which her hostess chattered interminably and Janina listened with increasing weariness, the girl got up to go, and at the very door she met Wladek.

"Visiting my mother!" he exclaimed.

"Certainly. There's nothing wrong in that," she answered, smiling at his confusion.

"Heavens! No doubt she's been telling you what a scoundrel I am. I beg your pardon for having had to listen."

"Oh, it didn't offend me in the least."

"It only made you laugh, I know. The whole theater is laughing at my expense, for all the ladies have already been here."

"Your mother loves you," Janina spoke seriously.

"That love is beginning to choke me like a bone in my throat!" he answered sourly and wanted to add something else, but Janina bowed silently and passed on.

Wladek did not have the courage to follow her and went upstairs.

"What is happening in my own home?" she thought as she walked toward the theater. "What is my father doing? . . . "

And she suddenly felt within herself a glimmer of sympathy for that tyrant. She saw now how lonely he must be among strangers who ridiculed his eccentricities.

During the whole performance, the vision of her father constantly recurred in her memory. She asked herself what it was that had made him so cruel, and why he hated her?

Kotlicki brought her a bouquet of roses. She received it coolly, without even glancing at him.

"I see that you are out of sorts to-day," he said, taking her hand.

She pulled it away.

Majkowska, who was just then passing, whispered, pointing to Rosinska: "What a scarecrow! What conventional acting! She is incapable of producing even a single accent of true feeling!"

Behind Janina some gentleman in a high hat was pressing the hands of one of the chorus girls.

"Things are turning out fine, for to-morrow, there will be no rehearsal and we can go to Bielany in the afternoon. Wait for us at your home, we will drop in and take you along with us," whispered Mimi.

"I also am going on that outing," said Kotlicki, "you are going too, aren't you?"

"Probably . . . but if I couldn't go it would be just as great a success."

"In that case I wouldn't go either."

He bent so closely over Janina that she felt his breath upon her face.

"I don't understand you," she said, moving away from him.

"I am going along only for your sake," he whispered in a still quieter tone.

"For my sake? . . . " she queried, glancing at him sharply, and stirred by a sudden aversion.

"Yes . . . surely you must have guessed by now that I love you," said Kotlicki, drawing together his lips which were trembling and looking at her pleadingly.

"There they say the same, only they play a little better!" she remarked scornfully, pointing to the stage.

Kotlicki drew himself erect, a sullen shadow passed over his equine face, his eyes gleaming threateningly.

"I will convince you! . . . "

"Very well, but to-morrow at Bielany, not now," Janina coolly extended her hand in farewell and left for the dressing-room.

Kotlicki gazed after her covetously, biting his lips.

"A comédienne!" he finally whispered, leaving the theater.

# CHAPTER VII

JANINA awoke at about half-past ten in the morning. Sowinska had just brought in her breakfast.

"Was anyone here to see me?. . . " she asked.

Sowinska nodded her head and handed Janina a letter.

"About an hour ago a ruddy fellow delivered it and asked me to give it to you."

Janina nervously tore open the envelope and immediately recognized the handwriting of Grzesikiewicz:—

"MY DEAR MISS ORLOWSKA:

"I have purposely come to Warsaw to see you on a very important matter. If you will kindly deign to be home at eleven o'clock I shall be there at that hour. Please pardon my boldness. Allow me to kiss your hands and remain

Your humble servant,
GRZESIKIEWICZ."

"What's going to happen? . . . " thought Janina, dressing hastily. "What kind of important matter can it be that he writes of? Concerning my father? . . . Can it be that he is ill and longing for me? . . . Oh no! No!"

She quickly drank her tea, tidied her room and patiently awaited Grzesikiewicz's visit. The thought of seeing at last some one of her own people from Bukowiec even filled her with a certain joy.

"Perhaps he will propose to me again?" Janina thought to herself. And she saw his big weather-beaten face, bronzed by the sun, and those blue eyes gazing so mildly from beneath his shock of flaxen hair. She remembered too, his embarrassed shyness.

"A good, honest man!" she said to herself, walking up and down the room; but then the thought occurred to her that his visit was likely to spoil her intended trip to Bielany, and her enthusiasm began to cool. She determined she would speak to him briefly.

"I wonder what he wants of me?" Janina asked herself uneasily, assuming the most impossible things.

"My father must be very sick and wants me to come to him," she answered herself.

She stood in the center of the room almost dazed, with fear that she must return to Bukowiec.

"No, it is impossible! . . . I couldn't stand it there a single week . . . and moreover, he drove me away from home forever . . . "

A chaotic conflict between hate, sorrow, and a quiet, scarcely perceptible feeling of homesickness began to rage in Janina's heart.

The bell rang in the anteroom.

Janina sat down and waited quietly. She heard the door opening, the voices of Grzesikiewicz and Sowinska, and the sound of an overcoat being hung up.

"May I come in?" asked a voice outside.

"Please do," she whispered, choking with trepidation as she arose from her chair.

Grzesikiewicz entered. His face was even more sunburnt than usual and his blue eyes seemed bluer. He walked stiffly and erectly like a petrified block of meat squeezed into a tight surtout with difficulty. He almost threw his hat upon a basket standing near the door and, kissing Janina's hand, said quickly: "Good morning . . . "

He straightened himself, scanned her face with his eyes and sat down heavily in a chair.

"I had a hard time finding you . . ." he began, and suddenly broke off. Then, as if to bolster up his courage, he attempted to shove aside a chair that interfered with his actions but pushed it so hard that it fell over.

He sprang up, all red in the face, and began to apologize.

Janina smiled, so vividly did that impulsive action remind her of their last talk and that unfortunate proposal. And for a moment it seemed to her that it was now that he was to propose and that they were sitting in the quiet parlor at Bukowiec. She could not explain to herself the impression that he made on her with that honest face, worn by suffering, and with those bright blue eyes which seemed to bring with them echoes of those beloved fields and woods, those quiet glens, that golden sunlight and the free and bounteous life of nature. For one fleeting moment her mind dwelt on all this, but at the same time there awoke memories of all her sufferings and her banishment.

She handed him a box of cigarettes and said in an easy tone, breaking the somewhat prolonged silence: "You give proof of no small courage and . . . kindness by visiting me after all that has happened. . . . "

"Do you remember what I told you the last time," he answered, subduing and softening his voice, "that I would never and always! ... That I would never cease and would always continue to love you!"

Janina moved impatiently, for his deeply sincere accent pained her.

"I beg your pardon ... if it makes you angry, I will not say another word about myself . . ." he said with resignation.

"What is the news from home?" she asked, raising her eyes to his.

"How can I tell you? . . . It's something that beggars all description. You would not know your father; he has become an impossible autocrat in his official duties, and outside of them he goes hunting, visits his neighbors, whistles to himself . . . but has become so thin and worn that it is hard to recognize him. Worry is eating him away like a canker."

"Why? . . . What is there for my father to worry about?"

"My God! How can you ask such a question? Are you joking, or haven't you a spark of feeling in you? . . . Why is he worrying? . . . Because you are away . . . because he, like all of us, is dying with longing for you! . . . "

"And what about Krenska? . . . " Janina asked with apparent calmness, although stirred deeply by what he had told her.

"What has Krenska to do with this? . . . He threw her out the very next day after your departure, afterwards received a few days' official leave from his duties and left Bukowiec. ... In about a week he returned so woebegone and haggard that we scarcely recognized him. Even strangers are crying over him, but you had no pity on him and went forth into the world . . . and what kind of world, besides? . . . "

Janina sprang up violently from her chair.

"Yes, you may be angry with me if you will, but I love you, I love you too well, and we all love you too well to be denied the right to speak what we feel. Have me thrown out of here if you will, and I'll not complain, but I'll wait for you at the street door or meet you anywhere else and keep telling you that your father is dying without you and that he is growing sicker and weaker every day! My mother came across him not so long ago in the woods: he was lying in some bushes and crying like a child. You are killing him. Both of you are killing each other with your pride and unrelenting stubbornness. You are the best woman in the world and I feel that you will not leave him alone, that you will return and give up theatrical life. . . . Aren't you ashamed of associating with such a band of scoundrels? . . . How can you possibly exhibit yourself on the stage! . . . "

He broke off and breathing heavily, wiped his eyes with his handkerchief. Never before had he said so much at one time.

Janina sat with bowed head, her face as pale as a sheet, her lips set tightly and her heart filled with a storm of rebellion and suffering.

That sharp voice which she had just heard had in it such a tearful, deep and soul-stirring expression and those words: "Your father is suffering . . . your father is crying . . . your father is longing for you!" penetrated her with so sharp a grief and harried her so painfully, that at moments she wanted to spring up and go to him as quickly as she could; but then again, memories of the past would flood her brain and she would become cool and hardened. Finally she recalled the theater and became entirely indifferent.

"No! He has driven me away forever. ... I am alone in the world and will remain alone. I could not live without the theater!" Janina said to herself and there arose in her again that mad desire for theatrical conquest.

Grzesikiewicz also became silent, his eyes clouding mistily. He devoured her with his eyes, and had a great desire to fall on his knees before her, kiss her hands and feet and the hem of her dress and beg her to listen to him . . . Then again, when he remembered the whole tragedy of the situation, he felt like springing up from his chair and smashing everything that came in his way; or again such a violent grief would convulse him that he could have cried aloud in sheer despair.

He sat and gazed at that beloved face, now pale and worn, on which the feverish night life of the theater had already left its imprint, and he felt that he would give his very life for her, if she would only go back.

Janina finally bent on him eyes that were glowing with irrevocable determination.

"You must know how my father hates me; you must also know that, when I refused to marry you, he drove me out of his

118

house forever ... he almost cursed me and drove me out . . . " she repeated with bitterness. "I left because I had to, but I will never return. I will not exchange the freedom of the theater for slavery at home. Things happened as they did because they had to. My father told me at that time that he had no longer a daughter, and I now answer that I have no longer a father. We have parted and will never be reunited again. I am entirely able to shift for myself, and art will suffice me for everything."

"So you will not return?" asked Grzesikiewicz, for that was all he understood of her words.

"No! I have no home and I will not forsake the theater!" replied Janina in a calm voice, regarding him coolly, but her pale lips trembled a little and her bosom throbbed violently, convulsed by the conflict within.

"You will kill him ... he loves you so ... he will not outlive such a blow. . . ." said Grzesikiewicz gently.

"No, Andrew, my father does not love me. A person whom you love you do not torment for whole years at a time and then drive away from home like the worst. . . . Even a dog does not turn its young ones out . . . even an animal never does what was done to me!"

"I have seen and know how bitterly he regrets those reckless words and how hard it is for him to live without you. I swear that you will make him happy by returning! That you will restore him to life!"

"Did he tell you that he desired me to return to Bukowiec? Perhaps he has given you a letter for me? Please tell me the whole truth!" she spoke rapidly.

Grzesikiewicz hesitated in confusion and became even sadder.

"No. He neither said anything about it, nor gave me a letter for you," he answered, lowering his voice.

"So that is how much he loves me and how greatly he longs to see me? Ha! ha! ha!" she laughed harshly.

"Don't you know him yet? He will die of thirst rather than beg a glass of water. When I was leaving and told him where I was going, he did not say a word, but looked at me in such a way and gripped my hand so firmly that I understood him entirely. ..."

"No, you did not understand him at all. My father is not at all concerned about me; he is only concerned over the fact that the whole neighborhood must be speaking about my departure and my joining the theater. . . . Surely, Krenska must have left no stone unturned. . . . He is concerned only about the gossip that is circulating. He feels disgraced through me. He would like to see me broken and begging forgiveness at his feet. That is what he is anxious about!"

"You do not know him! Such hearts . . ."

Janina hastily interrupted him: "Let us not speak of hearts where on one side they do not at all enter into the question, where they are entirely lacking and there is only an insane . . . "

"So then? . . . " he asked rising, for he was choking with a spasm of anger.

The bell in the hall rang sharply, evidently pulled violently by someone.

"I will never return," said Janina with final determination.

"Janina . . . have mercy . . . "

"I do not understand that word," she answered with emphasis, "and I repeat: never! unless it be . . . after I am dead."

"Don't say that, for . . . "

He did not finish for the door suddenly swung wide open and Mimi with Wawrzecki came rushing in.

"Well, are you coming? Hurry and dress yourself, for we start immediately! ... Ah, I beg your pardon, I did not know you had a visitor," cried Mimi, observing Grzesikiewicz who took his hat, bowed automatically, and, without looking at anyone, whispered.

"Good-bye."

And without more ado he left.

Janina sprang up as though she wished to detain him, but Kotlicki and Topolski were just then entering and greeted her jocularly. After them came some third person.

"What sort of broad gentleman was that? As I live, it is the first time that I saw such a mass of meat in a surtout!" cried that third comer.

"This is Mr. Glogowski. In a week we are to present his play and in a month he will be famous throughout Europe!" said Wawrzecki, introducing him.

"And in three months my fame will reach Mars with all its appurtenances! ... If you are going to bluff, at least let it be a good bluff," laughed Glogowski.

Janina greeted them all, and in a subdued voice answered Mimi who was asking her about Grzesikiewicz: "An old friend of mine and former neighbor, a very honest man . . ."

"He must be flushed with money, that youth ... he looks it!" exclaimed Glogowski.

"Yes, he is wealthy. His family owns the largest sheep-growing ranch in Congressional Poland . . . "

"A shepherd! ... he rather looks as though he were a keeper of elephants! . . ." jested Wawrzecki.

Kotlicki only smiled and discreetly observed Janina.

"Something must have happened here . . . for her voice shows she is deeply moved," he thought. "Perhaps that was her former lover? . . . "

"Come, hurry, for Mela is waiting downstairs in a hack," cried Mimi impatiently.

Janina dressed hastily and they all went out together.

They rode to the bank of the Wisla and from there took a boat to Bielany.

All were in a springtime humor, except Janina. She sat gloomily rapt in thought.

Kotlicki chatted jovially, Wawrzecki jested with Glogowski and the women took part in the merriment, but Janina hardly heard a thing that was being said. She was still pondering her conversation with Grzesikiewicz and the heavy feeling it had left in her heart.

"Is anything troubling you?" Kotlicki asked with anxiety in his voice.

"Me? Oh nothing! ... I was just musing upon human misery," she answered.

"It is not worth thinking of anything that is not pleasure, full of life and youth . . . "

"Don't complete that nonsense. It is just as if you were to eat off the butter on a piece of bread and then muse over your dry crust that you did a foolish thing after all," interposed Glogowski, "I see you do not like to eat, only to lick at things."

"My dear sir, I have the honor of knowing that ever since I was a schoolboy," Kotlicki retorted sarcastically.

"That isn't the point; the point is that you advocate downright silly things. For instance indulgence, while you have had ample opportunity to prove upon yourself the sad results of that jolly theory."

"Both in life and in literature you are always paradoxical."

"I'll wager you have weak lungs, arthritis, neurasthenia and . . . "

"Count up to twenty."

They began to argue vehemently and then to quarrel.

The boat had passed the railroad bridge and the vast calm of the open country enveloped them on all sides. The sun was shining brightly, but a chill dampness arose from the murky waters of the river. The small waves, saturated with light, like serpents with gleaming scales, splashed about in the sunlight. The long sand dunes resembled water giants, basking in the sun with yellow upturned bellies. A string of scows floated before them; the pilot in a small cockleshell boat rowed on in front and every now and then would raise his voice in a cry which echoed across the water and reached them in a confused medley of tones. A few boatmen plied their oars with automatic motion and their sad song was wafted to the party and floated above their heads. Afterwards a growing silence began to spread around them.

The mild verdure of the shores, the sunlit trail of the waters gleaming with the sheeny softness of satin, the gentle rocking of the boat, the rhythmical stroke of the oars unconsciously imposed a silence upon everybody.

"I will not return!" thought Janina, automatically repeating those words, while she gazed upon the blue expanse of waters and pursued with her eyes the waves that fled swiftly on before her, "I will not return!"

She felt that loneliness was embracing her with ever wider arms and surrounding her soul with an emptiness into which she gazed defiantly. Her sorrow, the thought of her father and Grzesikiewicz, all her former acquaintances and her whole past seemed to be flowing on far behind her so that she saw them dimly in the distant gray mist and only the faint echo of an entreaty or of weeping seemed to reach her now and then.

No! she would not have the strength to turn back and swim against that current that was bearing her onward. Nevertheless, she felt that tears were dropping upon her heart and burning it with bitterness.

They disembarked at the landing-stage at Bielany and began to wind their way up the hill.

Janina walked ahead of the company with Kotlicki who did not leave her for a moment.

"You owe me a reply," he said after a while, assuming a tender expression.

"I answered you yesterday, and to-day you owe me an explanation," she said harshly, for now, after that recent conversation with Grzesikiewicz and all that it had cost her, she felt an almost physical aversion and hatred toward Kotlicki; he struck her as repulsive and brazen.

"An explanation? . . . Can one explain love or analyze a feeling? . . ." he began, uneasily biting his thin lips. He did not like the tone of her voice.

"Let us be sincere, for what you told me is . . ." she cried impulsively.

"Is sincerity itself."

"No, it is only a comedy!" Janina retorted sharply and felt a great desire to strike him in the face.

"You offend me! One can believe a person's feelings without sharing them," he said in a quieter tone so that those who followed them would not hear.

"Now please listen to what I have to say! I want to tell you that your comedy not only wearies me, but is beginning to anger me. I am still too little a hysterical actress and too much a normal woman to take pleasure in such acting. I was never taught by my mother, the secret code of a woman's conduct toward a man, nor did they warn me of man's falsehood and baseness. I observed that quickly enough for myself, and see it every day behind the scenes. You think that to every woman who is in the theater you can boldly talk about your love as though it were some trifle, in the hope that perhaps she will swallow your bait! Actresses are so playful and so silly, aren't they?" she said with stinging scorn. "Would you dare to tell me the same, if I were at home? No, you wouldn't dare tell me you loved me, if you didn't, for there, I would be a woman in your eyes, while here I am only an actress; for there, I would have behind me a father, mother, brothers or some convention which would prohibit you from many things. But here, you don't hesitate. And why? Because here I am alone and an actress, that is a woman to whom you can with impunity tell lies, whom you can with impunity possess and then cast off and go your way without the slightest fear of losing your reputation. Oh, you can be sure, Mr. Kotlicki, that I will not become your mistress, nor any other man's if I do not love him! I have already thought much, too much, about the matter to be deceived by fine phrases!" She spoke rapidly, and her sharp words fell like blows.

He trembled with impatience and gazed on her in amazement. He did not know her, and had not assumed for a moment that he would find an actress who would tell him such things to his face. He gazed at her through half-closed eyes, and stammered ever more frequently, so immensely did he like her for her courage. She fascinated him by her strength of character and honesty, for by those words she had spoken, by her face which faithfully reflected all her inner feelings, and by the sincere tones of her voice he began to perceive that she was an honest and uncommon girl; and in addition she was so beautiful!

"The whip was rawhide with leaden weights at the end of it. You beat with a womanly fury both the guilty and the innocent," said Kotlicki, and seeing that Janina did not answer he added after a while, "Is this not enough for you? If it would be possible during that entire flagellation to kiss your hands, I beg you to continue . . . "

"Kotlicki! ... Wait a minute there and help us carry the baskets! . . . " called Wawrzecki.

The men carried the baskets with the provisions, while the whole company walked along the steep river bank, seeking a convenient spot for a camping ground.

All about them the lonely wood rustled softly with its young oak leaves and juniper bushes. They halted under a grove of verdant oaks. Behind them was the woodland solitude while beneath them the Wisla gleamed in the sunlight and murmured with its blue waves breaking against the shore.

After the preliminary drinks and sandwiches all became lively.

"Well, now let us drink the health of the initiators of the outing!" cried Glogowski, filling the glasses.

"Let us rather drink to the success of your new play," cried several voices.

"No, that will not help it any ... it will turn out a fiasco anyway . . . "

"Perhaps Topolski will now reveal to us his secret plan," said Kotlicki who was calmly stretched out on his plaid beside Janina.

"Let that rest! After we have had plenty to eat and still more to drink will be time enough. Perhaps the ladies will untie those packages," cried Wawrzecki.

Napkins were spread out on the grass and a variety of dainties was brought forward and set upon them amid laughter.

"That's nice, but where is the tea?" exclaimed Janina.

Kotlicki jumped up.

"The tea is here and also the samovar, only you, sir, will have to go for some water. We shall go together for it to the Wisla!" cried Majkowska, shaking the charcoal out of a pitcher.

Kotlicki frowned a bit, but went along with her. In a few minutes the samovar was started, Glogowski proving himself a real master.

"That is my specialty!" he shouted blowing at the fire like a pair of bellows. "And I must tell you ladies that very often, more often than I like, I lack coal. It is then that my inventive genius comes to the fore: I stoke the fire with papers or, if that is also missing, I pluck a board from the floor and, willy nilly, the tea is produced."

"You must lead a very diversified life!" remarked Topolski with a laugh.

"A trifle! Just a trifle . . . but I won't say that I relish it."

"I proclaim to all in general and to everyone in particular that the tea is beginning to boil! . . . Now, ladies, assume the rôles of Hebes!" called Glogowski.

Janina poured out the tea for all of them before sitting down near Mimi.

"I am organizing a dramatic society," began Topolski.

"I will tell you the only way to do it: you engage a few score of the theatrical tribe by promising them high salaries and give them small advances; you look for a lady treasurer who is wise enough to have a bond and naïve enough to deposit it; with it you buy the necessary accessories, have them sent on account and you are ready either to begin, or to break up. And in two months you can repeat the same prescription until you get results," jested Wawrzecki.

"Wawrzecki, quit your confounded nonsense!" cried the irritated Topolski, drinking one glass of brandy after another. "That kind of company any idiot can organize, any Cabinski. I don't want a band of players who will scatter to the four winds as soon as some one lures them with the promise of a big advance, but a strong organization with a well-defined plan, an organization as solid as a stonewall!"

"You often broke up companies yourself and yet you think you can manage actors? ..." persisted Wawrzecki.

"I am sure of it. Listen all! This is how I would go about it: condition one—about five thousand rubles to begin with; I fish out of all the companies their best forces, thirty persons at most; I pay them moderately but honestly; I assure dividends . . . "

"Come now, you had better give up dreaming about dividends!" growled Kotlicki.

"There will be a dividend! there must be!" cried Topolski with growing enthusiasm. "I select my plays: a series of typical and classical things; these will be the walls and foundations of my edifice; furthermore, all the more important novelties and all the folkplays, but away with operetta, away with clownishness, away with the circus, away with everything that is not true art! I want to have a theater and not a puppet show! artists are not clowns!" he cried in an ever louder voice.

Topolski began to cough so violently that all the veins in his neck swelled like whipcords. He coughed for a long time, then took a drink of brandy and began talking again, but in a quieter and slower voice, without looking at anyone, or seeing anything beyond this dream of his whole life, which he related in short and tangled sentences.

Kotlicki, who was not stirred even for a moment by that speech full of inspiration as well as illogicality, remarked: "You are a little late. Antoine in Paris has long ago put into practice what you propose; those are his ideas . . . "

"No, those are my ideas, my dreams; for twenty years already I am carrying them within me!" cried Topolski, growing suddenly livid as though struck by lightning, and gazing in a dazed way at Kotlicki.

"What of that, when others have already partially realized those dreams and given them their name . . . "

"Thieves! they have stolen my idea! they have stolen my idea!" shouted Topolski and fell over half-senseless on the grass, covering his face with his hands, sobbing convulsively and stammering in a drunken voice: "They have stolen my idea! . . . Help! they have stolen my idea!" And he continued to roll about on the grass, sobbing like a grieved child.

"Not because of the fact that that idea is already known do I see the impossibility of realizing such a project," began Glogowski calmly, "but because our public has not yet reached the point where it is ready for such a theater and does not feel the need of such a stage. In the meanwhile, give them the farce full of acrobatic stunts and leg-shows, a half-naked ballet, cancan howling, a little, cheap kitchen sentimentality, a heap of empty phrases on the subject of virtue, morality, the family, duty, love, and . . . "

"Count up to twenty . . . " laughed Kotlicki.

"Just as is the public, so are its theaters; one is worth as much as the other!" remarked Majkowska.

"He who wants to rule the multitude and rule over it, must flatter it and do that which the multitude wants; he must give it that which it needs; he must first be its slave so that he may later become its master," said Kotlicki slowly and with unction.

"I will say: no! I neither want to cringe to the mob, nor be its master; I prefer to go my own way alone . . ." answered Glogowski emphatically.

"A splendid standpoint! From it you can laugh at everyone to your heart's content."

"Miss Janina, please let me have some tea!" cried the already irritated Glogowski, springing up violently, throwing his hat at a tree and feverishly rumpling his sparse hair.

"You are ever a fiery radical of native breed," said Kotlicki with a good-natured irony.

"And you are a poor fish, a seal, a whale . . ."

"Count up to twenty!"

"Those are fine arguments, indeed! . . . Here is a much better one," cried Wawrzecki, handing Glogowski his cane.

Glogowski calmed himself, gazed around a moment and began drinking his tea.

Majkowska was listening silently, while Mimi, stretched out on Wawrzecki's overcoat, was fast asleep.

Janina was serving tea to all and did not lose a word of that conversation. She had already forgotten about Grzesikiewicz, about her father, and about her talk with Kotlicki, and was entirely engrossed by the questions that were now being discussed, while Topolski's dreams fascinated her by their fantasies. Such general discussions on art and artistic subjects absorbed her entirely.

"What about your dramatic society?" she asked Topolski who was just raising his head.

"It will be ... it must be formed!" answered Topolski.

"I warrant you it will be," interposed Kotlicki, "not the kind that Topolski desires but that which will be the best within the bounds of possibility. It will even be possible to introduce certain improvements by way of variety and attraction, but we shall leave the reformation of the theater to someone else; for that you would need hundreds of thousands of rubles and you would have to start it in Paris."

"The reformation of the theater will not originate with the managers, and as for dramatic creativity, what is it really? . . . The seeking of something in the dark, a doglike scenting about, an aimless straying, or the antics of a flea. A genius must arrive to revolutionize the modern theater; I already have a feeling that one is coming . . ." asserted Glogowski.

"How is that? . . . Aren't the existing masterpieces of the drama sufficient for creating an ideal theater?" queried Janina.

"No . . . those masterpieces belong to the past; we need other works. For us those masterpieces are a very important archeology," answered Glogowski.

"So in your estimation Shakespeare is antiquated?"

"Sh! let us not speak of him; he is the whole universe; we can merely contemplate him, but never understand him . . . "

"And Schiller?"

"A Utopian and classic: an echo of the Encyclopedists and the French Revolution. He represents nobility, order, German doctrinarianism and pathetic and wearisome declamation."

"And Goethe?" ventured Janina, who had developed a great liking for Glogowski's paradoxical definitions.

"That means only *Faust*, but *Faust* is so complicated a machine that since the death of the inventor no one knows how to wind it or start it going. The commentators push its wheels, take it apart, clean it, and dust it, but the machine will not go and already is beginning to rust a little. . . . Moreover, it is a furious aristocracy. That Mr. Faust is first of all not the ideal type of man, but an experimenter; he is nothing but the brain of one of those learned rabbis who spend their whole lives on pondering whether it is proper to enter the synagogue with the right or the left foot first; he is a vivisector, who, after breaking the heart of Margaret in the process of his experimentation, and fearing the threat of imprisonment, and being unable by virtue of his shortsightedness to see anything beyond his study and his retorts, makes a sport of complaining and laments that life is base and knowledge is worthless. In truth, it requires a great deal of genuinely German arrogance to maintain when you have a catarrh that everybody else has it or ought to have it."

"I prefer such merry works to your wise plays," whispered Kotlicki.

"Oh, and what of Shelley and Byron?" begged Janina, whose interest was fully aroused.

"I prefer foolishness even when it presumes to speak rather than when it seeks to create something," Glogowski hastily flung back at Kotlicki.

"Aha, Byron! . . . Byron is a steam engine producing a rebellious energy; a lord who was dissatisfied in England and dissatisfied in Venice with Suiciolla, for although he had a warm climate and money he was bored. He is a rebel-individualist, a strong, passionate monster; a lord who is always seething with fury and using all the forces of his wonderful talent to spite his enemies. He slapped England's face with masterpieces. He is a mighty protestant out of boredom and in his own personal interest."

"And Shelley?"

"Shelley again, is a divine lingo for the public of Saturn; he is the poet of the elements and not for us mortals."

Glogowski became silent and went to pour himself some tea.

"We are still listening; at least, I am waiting with impatience for you to continue your very interesting exposition," exclaimed Janina.

"Very well, but I am going to skip over a great many immortals so as to finish sooner."

"You can continue on the condition that you'll do so without tinkling the bells and beating the tambourine."

"Kotlicki, keep quiet! You are a miserable philistine, a typical representative of your base species and you are denied a voice when human beings are speaking!"

"Gentlemen, please quit your arguing, for I can't sleep," pitifully pleaded Mimi.

"Yes, yes, it isn't at all amusing!" added Majkowska with a mighty yawn.

Wawrzecki began again to fill the glasses. Glogowski moved close to Janina and began enthusiastically to expound to her his theory.

"Ibsen makes a strange impression on me; he foreshadows someone mightier than himself who is yet to come; he is like the light of dawn before the rising sun. And as regards the newest, over-praised and over-advertised Germans:

Suderman and Company they are merely a loud prating about small things; much ado about nothing.

They wish to convince the world for instance that it is unnecessary to wear suspenders with your trousers, because you can sometimes wear them without suspenders."

"So we have finally got to the point where there are no more left to dispose of," interposed Kotlicki. "One got a whack over the head, another a jab in the ribs, a third a very polite kick and so forth . . ."

"No, my dear sir, *I* still remain!" rejoined Glogowski, with a comical bow.

"We demolished vast edifices for the sake of a soap bubble."

"Perhaps, but since even in soap bubbles the sun is reflected . . ."

"Therefore, let us have another drink of brandy!" exclaimed Topolski, who had been silent up till now.

"Throw out all that argumentation to the dogs! . . . Let us drink and quit thinking!" chimed in Wawrzecki.

"That last statement is an epitome of yourself, Wawrzecki!" remarked Glogowski.

"Let us drink and love one another!" proposed Kotlicki, rousing himself and tinkling his glass against the bottle.

"To that I will agree, as I am Glogowski, I will agree, for love alone is the soul of the world!"

"Wait a minute, I will sing you something about love," cried Wawrzecki, and he proceeded to drone an amorous ditty.

"Bravo Wawrzecki!" cried the entire company and with that they all abandoned themselves to pure merriment, ceased arguing and babbled any nonsense that came to their lips.

"Most esteemed ladies and gentlemen! the sky is beginning to cloud and on earth the bottles are all empty. Let us beat a retreat!" finally suggested Wawrzecki.

"But how?" chorused a few voices.

"We will go on foot, for it is not more than a mile to Warsaw."

"We'll hire some husky fellow to carry the baskets for us. I'll go and see if I can find someone," said Wawrzecki, and he went off in the direction of a monastery.

Before he returned all were ready for the homeward journey. The general mood of gayety had even risen, for Mimi was dancing a waltz with Glogowski on the greensward.

Topolski was so drunk that he continually kept talking to himself and quarreling with Majkowska. Kotlicki smiled and kept close to Janina who had become very sportive and merry. She smiled at him and conversed with him, hardly remembering his recent proposal. He was sure that the impression of it had merely glided over her soul and sunk away in forgetfulness.

They walked in disordered groups as is usual after an outing. Janina was weaving a wreath of oak leaves, while Kotlicki was helping her and amusing her with piquant remarks. She listened to him, but when they entered into a bigger and real wood where the ground was covered with dense underbrush, she suddenly became grave, gazed at the trees with such great joy, touched their trunks and branches with such tenderness, her lips and eyes glowed with such rapture, that Kotlicki asked her, pointing to the trees: "No doubt they must be good friends of yours?"

"Yes indeed, good and sincere friends and not comedians!" she replied with a light irony in her voice.

"You have a very vengeful memory. You neither believe, nor forgive. I desire only one thing: to be able to convince you . . . "

"Then marry me!" she exclaimed quickly, turning towards him.

"I beg for your hand!" he murmured in the same tone.

They glanced straight into each other's eyes and both suddenly became gloomy. Janina knitted her brows and began unconsciously to tear her unfinished wreath with her teeth, while Kotlicki bowed his head and became silent.

"Come, let us hurry, we shall be late for the performance!" called someone, and they hastened to catch up with the rest of the company.

"So to-morrow there is to be a read rehearsal of my play?" Glogowski was asking Topolski.

"To be exact, it will be only a reading of the play itself, for Dobek has not yet finished writing out the rôles," answered Topolski.

"Great Scott! and when do you expect to present it?"

"Don't fear, the Philistines will hiss and hoot you soon enough, without your hurrying!" Kotlicki twitted him.

"We shall present it in a week from next Tuesday ... at least I would have it so," replied Topolski.

"Or, strictly speaking, there will remain for rehearsals and for the learning of the rôles only four days. No one will know his part, no one will be able to master it even passably in so short a time. That's nothing short of murder, cold-blooded murder!" cried Glogowski.

"You'll treat Dobek to a few whiskeys and he will safely pull the play through for you," suggested Wawrzecki.

"Yes, he will shout for everybody. ... As the matter stands, it is best to announce that there will take place merely a reading of the play."

"You needn't worry about me, I'll learn my rôle," Majkowska assured him.

"And I also," added Janina.

"I know the ladies always know their parts but the men... "

"The men will play their parts well without having to learn them," remarked Wawrzecki. "Don't you know that Glas never studies his rôles! A few rehearsals familiarize him with the situations of the play and the prompter does the rest."

"That's why he plays so splendidly!" sneered Glogowski.

"What do you want? He's a good actor and not at all a bad comedian."

"Yes, because he always knows how to improvise some nonsense with which to cover up his bungling."

"Please give me an entirely serious answer. Were those last words of yours only a joke or were they an expression of your wishes and a condition?" Kotlicki again whispered to Janina as a certain idea entered into his head.

"Every variety is good, providing it is not wearisome. Have you heard that before?" answered Janina impatiently.

"Thank you! I will remember it. . . . But do you know this: patience is the first condition of success."

Kotlicki glanced at her quizzically, bowed to her with his head, and retired among the rest of the company. He possessed a brazen self-confidence and decided, at all events, to wait.

Kotlicki was not one of those whom a woman can drive away from herself with scorn or even with insults. He accepted everything and carefully stored it away in his memory for a future reckoning. He was a man who had a contempt for women, who told people what he thought to their very faces, and who always craved women and love. He ignored the fact that he was ugly, for he knew he was rich enough to buy any woman that he might desire. He belonged to that category of men—which is ready for anything.

He now walked along smiling at some thought that was in his mind, and striking with his cane the weeds that were in his path.

It grew dark and the rain began to fall in large drops.

"We will get drenched like chickens!" laughed Mimi, opening her parasol.

"Miss Janina, my umbrella is at your service," called Glogowski.

"Thank you very much, but as far as I am able, I do not use any protection against the rain; I just dote on getting wet in the rain."

"You have the instincts of . . ." he broke off suddenly and pressed his hand to his mouth with a comical gesture.

"Finish what you began to say . . . please do . . ."

"You have the instincts of fish and geese. ... I am curious to know how they have developed in you."

Janina smiled, for she remembered her old autumn and winter tramps through the woods in the greatest storms and rainfalls, and she answered merrily: "I like such things. I am used from my childhood to endure rains and rough weather ... I am simply wild about storms."

"My, what fiery blood! It must be something atavistic."

"It's merely a habit or an inner need which has grown to the proportions of a passion."

Glogowski offered his arm to Janina; she accepted and began to relate to him in an easy, friendly tone the various adventures she had experienced on her excursions in the country. She felt as unrestrained in his company as though she had known him from childhood. At moments she would even forget that this was the first time in her life that she had met him. She was won over to him by his bright and happy face and by the somewhat mild sincerity of his character; she felt in him a brotherly and honest soul.

Glogowski listened to her, answered her questions, and observed her with curiosity. Finally, choosing an appropriate moment, he said frankly: "May the deuce take me, but you are an interesting woman, a very interesting one! I will tell you something; just now a certain thought struck me and I offer it to you hot from the griddle, only don't think it strange. I detest conventionality, social hypocrisy, the affectation of actresses, etc., count up to twenty! . . . and that is just what I fail, as yet, to see in you. Oho! I immediately noticed that you were free from all that. Frankly, I like you as a certain type that one meets very rarely. It is interesting, interesting!" he repeated, almost to himself. "We might become friends!" he cried delightedly, speaking his thoughts aloud, "For, although women always disappoint me, because sooner or later the female of the species crops out in every one of them, still, a new experiment might be worth something. . . . "

"Frankness in return for frankness," said Janina, laughing at the lightning-like swiftness with which he formed determinations. "You also are an interesting specimen."

"Well, then, we agree! Let us shake and be good friends!" he exclaimed, extending his hand.

"But I haven't yet finished what I wanted to say: I must tell you that I do without confidants and friends entirely. That smacks of sentimentality and is not very safe."

"Bosh! Friendship is worth more than love. I see it's beginning to pour in earnest. It is the dogs crying over rejected friendship. I shall have the opportunity of meeting you more often, shall I not? For you have within you something . . . something like a piece of a certain kind of soul that one comes across very rarely."

"I am at the theater every day for rehearsals and almost every day at the performances."

"Oh the deuce take it, that won't do at all! If I attended on you for only once a week, it would give rise to so much gossip, twaddle, surmises,"

"Oh I don't care what people say about me!" Janina laughed with an easy air.

"Ho! ho! I see you are of the fighting variety ... a regular gamecock! I like a person who treats with scant ceremony that old rag called public opinion."

"I think that as long as I have nothing to reproach myself with, I can listen calmly to what they say about me."

"Pride, a capital pride!"

"Why don't you bring out your play in the Warsaw Theater?"

"Because they did not want to produce it. That, you see, is a very elegant and highly perfumed establishment and only for a very delicate and subtly feeling public, while my play does not smell a bit of the salon; at the most, it smells of the fields, a little of the woods and a trifle of the peasant's hut. There they want, not truth, but flirtation, conventionality bluffing, etc., count up to twenty. Moreover, I had no backing, and they already have their patented play manufacturers."

"I thought it was only necessary to write something good and they would immediately produce it—"

"Great Scott! No! . . . quite the reverse is true. Just look how much I must bear before even such as Cabinski presents my play! ... Now raise that to the fourth power and only then will you have some conception of the joys of a beginning comedy writer, who, in addition, does not know how to secure patronage for his plays."

They became silent. The rain fell incessantly and was already forming big puddles of water along the road. Glogowski gazed gloomily at the city whose towers appeared outlined upon the misty horizon.

"A base city!" he grumbled angrily. "For three years I have vainly been trying to conquer it. I am struggling and killing myself, and yet, not even a dog knows me."

"If you keep on telling them that they are base knaves and fools you will never conquer them."

"I will. They will not love me, to be sure, but they will have to reckon with me, they must! However, such citadels are most easily stormed by actors, singers, and dancers. They make a clean sweep of everything with only one appearance."

"But their triumph is only for a day. After they have left the stage all trace of them is lost like that of a stone cast into the water!" said Janina with a certain bitterness, gazing fixedly at the ever nearer appearing, crowded walls of Warsaw. Only at that moment did she realize that the fame of which she dreamed was merely the fame of a day.

"It seems to me that you have an appetite for the same thing that I have," remarked Glogowski.

"I have!" she answered with emphasis and her voice resounded with the explosive force of something that had been long pent up.

"I have!" she repeated, but this time in a much quieter tone and without enthusiasm. The light died away in Janina's eyes and they strayed aimlessly over those heights of the city in the distance, without understanding anything, for she was perturbed by the thought of that ephemeral fame, for she remembered the faded wreaths of Cabinska and the bygone fame of Stanislawski, for she was thinking with growing bitterness of those thousands of famous actors who were dead and whose names even were forgotten. Janina felt a distressing conflict of feelings in her breast. She leaned more heavily on Glogowski's arm and walked on without saying another word.

At Zakroczymska Street they took a hack; Kotlicki jumped in and went along with them, forming a party of three. Janina eyed him angrily, but he pretended he did not notice it and gazed at her with his everlasting smile. Glogowski and Kotlicki accompanied her to her home. She had only enough time left to rush into the house, change her dress, take the things she needed and immediately start off again for the theater.

Because of the rain a few of the other chorus girls were also late. Cabinski, expecting an empty house on account of the weather, was irritated and rushed up and down the stage, shouting to all those who were entering: "I see you girls are getting lazy. It is already past eight o'clock and not one of you is yet dressed."

"We have been attending vespers at the Church of St. Charles of Borromeus," explained Zielinska.

"Don't try to fool me with vespers! The deuce with vespers! Tend to that which gives you your bread!"

"You provide us so generously with it, Mr. Director!" angrily retorted Louise.

"What, I don't pay you? What else do you live on?"

"What do we live on? . . . Certainly not your absurd and merely promised salaries!"

"Oh, and you are also late?" he cried to Janina who was just entering.

"I appear only in the third act, so I still have plenty of time."

"Wicek! go run and get Miss Rosinska. Where is Sophie? Hurry up and begin! May the devil take you all!" shouted Cabinski growing exasperated.

He peered through the slit in the curtain.

"The theater is already filled, by God, and not a soul is, as yet, in the dressing-rooms! Afterwards they complain that I don't pay them! Gentlemen! for God's sake, hurry and get dressed and begin!"

"Right away, as soon as we finish this game."

A few undressed actors with their make-up half-completed were playing a game of poker. Stanislawski alone sat in a corner of the dressing-room before his mirror and was making up his face. Already for the third time he was rubbing off the paint with a towel and making up anew. He gymnasticated his mouth, contracted his brows in anger, puckered his forehead and cast all sorts of glances.

He was rehearsing a character and with each change of his physiognomy, he mumbled beneath his breath the corresponding parts of his rôle, only now and then tossing in the direction of the card players a ten-copeck piece and two words: "A four . . . ten coppers!"

"The public is starting a rumpus! It's time to ring and begin!" pleaded Cabinski.

"Don't disturb us, Director. Let them wait. ... A trump! . . . Shell out the coin!"

"A jack . . . you pay!"

"A queen of hearts . . . hand over five shekles!"

"All's ready! Stake something on Desdemona, Director," cried one of the players, shuffling and stacking the cards.

"She will betray me!" hissed Cabinski.

"Doesn't she betray you anyway?"

"Ring!" shouted Cabinski to the stage-director, hearing a stamping of feet in the hall.

For a few minutes nothing was heard but the rustling of cards, falling with lightning-like rapidity upon the table.

"Four aces . . . you're done for!"

"Shell out!"

"A jack!"

"A five . . . that's good. I'll at least make something."

"A queen of hearts."

"Have some consideration for the ladies!" persisted Cabinski.

"A queen of spades. Shell out!"

"Enough of that! Hurry and dress yourselves! The audience is already beginning to howl."

"If that amuses them, why interfere?"

"You'll change your minds about it, if they leave the theater and demand their money back!" cried Cabinski, rushing out in utter desperation.

The actors threw down their cards and all began to dress themselves in feverish haste and to complete their make-up.

"What do we play first?"

"*The Vow.*"

"Stanislawski!"

"You can ring, I am coming!" called Stanislawski, as he slowly made his way to the stage.

"Hurry! or they'll wreck the theater!" cried Cabinski in the doorway.

They were giving a so-called "dramatic bouquet," or "as you like it," that is: a comic sketch, a one-act operetta, a scene from a drama and a solo dance. Almost the entire company took part in the performance.

Janina sat behind the scenes and watched the stage, waiting for her turn. She felt greatly overwrought by the happenings of that entire day. She closed her eyes and became rapt in a quiet meditation of the words of Grzesikiewicz, who had again recurred to her memory, but suddenly, she started with a shudder, for behind his face she saw emerging the satyr-like face of Kotlicki with its mocking smile; then, there passed before her mind a vision of Glogowski with his large head and kindly look. She rubbed her eyes as though to drive those visions away from her, but that smile of Kotlicki would not leave her memory.

"What a disgusting poodle that Rosinska is!" whispered Majkowska, standing before Janina.

Janina roused herself and looked up at Majkowska with a certain dissatisfaction. What interest did all that have for her at the present moment? And she already began to feel vexed and impatient at that eternal battle of all with everybody. She wasn't a bit concerned about Rosinska, whose acting was, in reality, impossible, and nauseatingly sentimental.

"Cabinski would do well to keep her off the stage," continued Majkowska without heeding Janina's silence, but she broke off quickly, for there approached them just then Sophie, Rosinska's daughter, who was to dance a solo *pas* with a shawl.

She stood beside Majkowska, all dressed for the dance. In that costume she looked like a girl of twelve; her figure was undeveloped, her face was thin and mobile, while her gray eyes and cynically contorted, carmined lips wore the expression of an experienced courtesan. She watched the acting of her mother, hissing between her teeth with dissatisfaction. Finally, she bent over toward Majkowska and whispered so that Janina could not hear her: "Just look how that old woman is playing!"

"Who? Your mother?"

"Yes. Just look at the eyes she is making at that fellow in the high hat! Hopping about like an old turkey hen, too!

Gee whiz, how she has dolled herself up! She's bent on making herself look young and doesn't even know how to make up her face decently. I am ashamed of her. She thinks that all are such fools that they will not notice her artificial beauty. Ha! ha! She can't fool me, for one. When she dresses, she locks herself up so as not to let me see how she pads and pieces herself together, ha! ha!" she laughed with an almost hostile expression. "Those men are such simps that they believe everything they see. . . . She buys everything for herself and I can't even beg money for a parasol from her."

"Sophie, who ever heard of speaking that way about one's mother!" Majkowska reproved her.

"Oh slush! a mother isn't anything so great! In about four years I can become a mother myself, a few times, if I want to; but I'm not so foolish as all that ... no kids for mine, not on your life! I'd have to be some fool!'

"You are a nasty and silly kid! I'm going to tell your mother immediately . . . " indignantly whispered Majkowska, walking away.

"She's a silly fool herself, even though she is an actress of standing." Sophie hurled after her, pouting her lips spitefully.

"Stop that! You're preventing me from hearing what is being said on the stage."

"You won't lose much, Miss Janina! The old woman has a voice like a cracked pot," continued Sophie unabashed.

Janina made an impatient motion.

"And if you only knew how she lies to me! At Lublin there came to our house a certain gentleman named Kulasiewicz, whom I called 'Kulas' for he never even brought me any candy. She spanked me for it and told me that he was my father. . . . Ha! ha! ha! I know what kind of 'fathers' they are. . . . At Lublin, there was Kulas, at Lodz, Kaminski and now, she has two of them. . . . She tries to hide the fact, and thinks that I envy her. I'd have to be some fool for that! Such penniless jiggers you can pick up anywhere by the bushel . . . "

"Stop that, Sophie, you are a wicked girl!" whispered Janina, boiling with indignation at the cynicism of that actor's child.

"What's wrong in what I say? Isn't it true?" she answered with a wonderful accent of true innocence.

"You ask me what's wrong! Where will you find another child who says such horrid things about her mother?"

"Well, why is she such a fool? All of the other actresses have lovers who at least have money, while she . . . look at what she's got! I also would be better off if she were wiser. . . . Believe me, when I grow up, I'll not be such a fool as she! . . . "

Janina staggered back, staring at her in amazement, but Sophie did not understand that and, bending more closely over her, whispered significantly: "Have you already got someone, Miss Janina?"

She hurried away immediately, for the curtain had already descended and her dance was to begin right away in the *entr'acte.*

Janina shuddered as though something unclean had touched her. A cold chill passed through her and a blush of shame and humiliation covered her face.

"What filth!" she whispered to herself; Sophie, unconscious of her was all smiling and radiant on the stage.

Sophie's long thin mouth like that of a greyhound merely flashed now and then in the wild tempo of the waltz she was performing. She danced with such temperament and skill that a storm of applause greeted her. Someone even threw her a bouquet. She picked it up and, retreating from the stage, smiled coquettishly like a veteran actress, sniffing in with distended nostrils those signs of the public's satisfaction.

"Miss Janina," she cried behind the scenes. "Look, I got a bouquet! Now Cabinski must give me a raise. They came especially to see me dance . . . Do you hear how they are recalling me!" and she leaped out upon the open stage to bow to the public.

"Your stage prating isn't worth a fig!" she said to the actresses. "If it weren't for the dance the theater would be empty." And she pirouetted on tiptoe, laughed triumphantly and went off to her dressing-room.

The company had begun to play an act of a very lachrymose drama entitled *The Daughter of Fabricius.* Topolski appeared in the rôle of Fabricius and Majkowska impersonated his daughter. They played entirely well although Topolski was still so drunk that he didn't know where he was, but he nevertheless acted so perfectly that no one was aware of it. Only Stanislawski stood behind the scenes and laughed aloud at his automatic motions and the blank expression of his eyes. Majkowska was upholding Topolski every now and then, for he would have fallen on the stage.

"Mirowska! come here and see how they are acting!" called Stanislawski to the old actress who was to-day apathetically disposed, his eyes glowing with feverish animosity.

"That is my rôle! I ought to be playing it. Look what he has made of it, the drunken beast!" he hissed between his tightly set teeth. And when, applause, that was in spite of everything, merited, broke out, Stanislawski became pale with rage and grasped at one of the scenes to keep from falling over, so great an envy was choking him.

"Cattle! Cattle!" he whispered hoarsely, shaking his fist threateningly at the public. Then he went to look for the stage-director but being unable to find him, came back. He continued to walk about excited and angry, scarcely able to stand on his feet.

"My daughter! . . . My beloved child! so you do not spurn your aged father? ... You press to your pure heart your criminal father? . . . You do not flee from his tears and kisses?" came floating from the stage Topolski's ardent whisper and struck the old actor so forcibly that he stood still, thrilled by the acting, forgot entirely about his envy, repeated those words in a whisper and put into those quiet accents of fatherly love so much feeling and tears, so much blood and inspiration and appeared at the same time so funny standing in the dim light behind the scenes with hands pathetically outstretched into empty space, with head bent forward and eyes fixed upon the rope of the curtain, that Wicek, who saw him, ran to the dressing-room crying: "Gentlemen, come and see Stanislawski showing something new behind the scenes."

They all rushed in a crowd to view the sight and, seeing him still standing in the same pathetic pose, burst out laughing in unison.

"Ha! ha! a South American monkey!"

"That is an African mammoth, that has lived for a hundred years, devoured human beings, devoured paper, devoured rôles, devoured fame until it died from indigestion," cried Wawrzecki, imitating the voice and speech of a provincial showman.

Stanislawski suddenly roused himself, glanced in back of him and encountering the derisive gazes that were centered on him, trembled, and sadly dropped his head upon his breast.

Janina who had witnessed this entire scene and who in the moments of the old actor's ecstasy had not even dared to move a finger for fear of disturbing him, could no longer restrain herself when she saw tears in his eyes and that whole band of cattle jeering at him. She walked up to Stanislawski and kissed his hand with involuntary respect.

"My child! my child!" he whispered feebly turning his head to hide the tears that were streaming from his eyes ever more profusely. He pressed her hand tightly and went out.

A storm of wild sorrow, pain, and hatred shook Stanislawski so violently that he could scarcely descend the stairs. He went out into the hall, encompassed the stage and the public with a gaze of unspeakable sadness and walked across the veranda toward the street, but turned about abruptly and remained.

"He would make a very venerable guardian!" cried someone to Janina after Stanislawski's departure.

"He might organize a new company and play lovers together with her!" added another voice.

"Jackals! Jackals!" cried Janina aloud, staring defiantly at them. And she had a great desire to spit in the eyes of all those cowards, so violent a wave of hatred surged through her and so base and cruel did they all appear to her. She restrained herself however, and resumed her seat, but for a long time could not calm herself.

When Janina went on the stage with the chorus, she was still trembling and agitated and the first person she saw in the audience was Grzesikiewicz who sat in the front row of seats. Their eyes met; he made a motion as though he wanted to leave, while she stood amazed for one brief instant in the center of the stage, but immediately collected herself, for she also spied Kotlicki sitting not far away and closely observing Grzesikiewicz and further on Niedzielska who was standing near the stalls and smiling at her in a friendly manner.

Janina did not look at Grzesikiewicz, but she felt his eyes upon her and that began to add to her agitation and excitement. She remembered that she had on short skirts and a peculiar shame filled her at the thought that she was standing before him in these gaudy, theatrical togs. It is impossible to describe what took place within her. Never before had she felt like this. In her stage appearances she usually gazed at the public with an expression of aloofness as on a foolish and slavish throng, but to-day it seemed to her as though she were standing in the front part of a huge cage like some animal on exhibition, while that audience had come to view her and amuse itself with her antics. For the first time she saw that smile which was not on any particular face, but which, nevertheless, hov- vered over all faces and seemed to fill the theater; it was a smile of indulgent and unconscious irony, a smile of crushing superiority that is seen on the faces of older people when they watch the playing of children. She felt it everywhere.

Afterwards Janina saw only the eyes of Grzesikiewicz immovably fixed upon her. She violently tore herself away from that gaze and looked in another direction, but saw, nevertheless, how Grzesikiewicz got up and left the theater. To be sure, she was not waiting for him, nor did she expect to see him again, yet his departure touched her painfully. She gazed as though with a certain feeling of disappointment at the empty seat which he had occupied just a moment ago and then she retreated with the chorus to the back of the stage.

Glas stood before the very box of the prompter and quietly and significantly began to knock with his foot to Dobek for he was to sing some solo part of which, as was his usual custom, he did not know a single word. Halt signaled to him with his baton and Glas with a comically attuned face began to sing some remembered word and strain his ears for a cue from Dobek, but Dobek was silent.

Halt rapped at his desk energetically, but Glas kept on singing one and the same thing over and over again, whispering pleadingly to Dobek in the pauses: "Prompt! Prompt!"

The chorus, scattered at the back of the stage, began to be confused by the situation, while behind the scenes someone began to recite aloud to Glas, the words of the unfortunate song, but Glas, all perspiring and red with anger and emotion kept on singing, in a circle: "You are mine, oh lovely Rose!" without hearing anything, or knowing what was going on about him.

"Prompt!" he whispered once more in despair, for already the orchestra and a part of the audience had noticed what was happening and was laughing at him. He kicked Dobek in the face and suddenly stood mute and motionless, gazing with a blank expression at the public, for Dobek, having received a kick in the teeth, grabbed Glas by the leg and held him tightly.

"Do you see, my boy! Next time don't try to get frisky!" whispered the prompter, holding Glas so tightly by the leg that he could not move. "You are done for! You tried to fix Dobek, now Dobek has fixed you! Now we are even!"

The situation was saved by Halt and Kaczkowska who began to sing the following number. Dobek let go Glas's leg, retreated as deeply as he could into his box and calmly continued to prompt from memory, smiling good-naturedly at Cabinski, who was shaking his fist threateningly at him from behind the scenes.

Janina had not yet succeeded in making out what was happening at the front of the stage, for she saw Grzesikiewicz returning with a large bouquet in his hand. He resumed his former seat and only when the chorus again appeared on the proscenium did he rise, walk over to the orchestra and throw the flowers at Janina's feet. Then he turned about calmly, passed through the hall and vanished, without caring that he had called forth a sensation in the theater.

The girl automatically picked up the flowers and retreated to the back of the stage behind her companions, feeling the eyes of the whole audience centered upon her.

"Is there a 'soul' in it?" whispered Zieliaska, pointing to the bouquet.

"Look in the center of the flowers, perhaps you will find something among them," another one of the chorus girls whispered to her.

Janina did not look, but felt a deep gratitude toward Grzesikiewicz for those flowers. After the curtain fell she left the stage without paying any attention to the violent quarrel that broke out between Glas and Dobek.

Glas was jumping with rage, while Dobek was slowly putting on his overcoat and calmly and tauntingly answering: "An eye for an eye. Sweet is vengeance to the human heart."

He had revenged himself for the trick that Glas had played on him on the foregoing day when he had got Dobek drunk and together with Wladek made him up as a negro. Dobek as soon as he had sobered a bit had calmly gone straight from the saloon to the theater without knowing what had happened to his physiognomy. They had a roaring good time behind the scenes, but Dobek swore vengeance and kept his word, threatening in addition that he would yet get square with Wladek.

Cabinski, irritated by what had happened on the stage, said all kinds of things to Glas, but the latter did not answer him, so deeply humiliated was he by his breakdown on the stage.

Janina all dressed in her street attire, was only waiting for Sowinska to go home with her, when Wladek sidled up to her and softly asked:

144

"Will you allow me to accompany you? . . ."

"I am going with Sowinska and besides you live in another part of the city," answered J anina.

"Sowinska has just requested me to tell you that she will not return for an hour. She is at the director's house."

"Well then, let us go."

"Perhaps your bouquet is in the way, let me carry it for you . . ." he said, extending his hand to take the flowers.

"Oh no, thank you. . . ." answered Janina.

"It must be very precious! . . ." he said, emphasizing his words with a laugh.

"I don't know how much it costs," she answered coldly, showing no disposition to converse with him.

Wladek laughed, then he spoke about his mother and finally said: "Perhaps you will come to see us? My mother is ill and for a few days she has not left her bed."

"Your mother is ill? Why, I saw her in the theater to-day."

"Is that possible!" he cried in real confusion. "I give you my word that I was certain she was ill ... for my mother told me that for a few days she has not risen from her bed. . . .

"My mother is trying some scheme on me . . ." he finally added with a frown.

Old Niedzielska was merely continually and persistently spying on him and always had to know with whom he was carrying on a romance, for she constantly trembled at the thought that Wladek might marry some actress.

He took leave of Janina with an attitude of exaggerated respect at the very door of her house and told her that he must go to see, his mother to convince himself about her illness.

As soon as Janina had entered the house, Wladek went to the theater and, meeting Sowinska, held a long and secret conversation with her. The old woman eyed him derisively and promised him her support.

Then he hurried away to Krzykiewicz's house for a game of cards, for they would often arrange such card-playing evenings now at this, now at another actor's home, to which they would invite many of their friends from the public. Janina, having entered her room, placed her flowers in a vase with water and, retiring to sleep, gazed once more at the roses and tenderly whispered: "How good he is!"

# CHAPTER VIII

"PLEASE miss, here's the circular!" cried Wicek, entering Janina's room.

"What is the news? . . . "

"The reading of that new play, or something like that!" he replied prying about the room.

Janina signed her name to the circular in which the stage-manager summoned the entire company to appear at noon for the reading of Glogowski's play *The Churls*.

"A fine bouquet!" exclaimed Wicek, eyeing the flowers standing in the vase. "You might still melt it. . . . "

"Speak like a human being!" said Janina, handing back the signed paper.

"That means I could still sell that bouquet for you."

"But who sells such bouquets and who buys them? . . . "

"Pardon me, miss, but I see you are still green! Some ladies as soon as they receive flowers, sell them to the old woman who peddles flowers in the evening at the theater. I could get a ruble easy for that. If you would give it to me . . . "

"You can't have it. . . . But here's something else for you."

Wicek humbly kissed Janina's hand, overjoyed with the ruble she gave him.

After Wicek's departure Janina changed the water in the vase with the flowers and was just standing it on the table when Sowinska entered with her breakfast.

Sowinska was to-day all radiant: her gray, owlish eyes were beaming with unaccustomed friendliness.

The old woman stood the coffee on the table and, pointing to the bouquet, remarked with a smile:

"What beautiful flowers! Are they from that gentleman who was here yesterday?"

"Yes," came the curt reply.

"I know someone who would be very pleased to send you the same kind every day. . . . " Sowinska spoke in a tone of pretended indifference, as she tidied the room.

"Flowers?" asked Janina.

"Well . . . and something more, if it were accepted."

"That person would have to be quite a fool."

"Don't you know that love makes fools of everyone?"

"That may be," answered Janina curtly.

"Don't you surmise who it is?"

"I'm not at all curious."

"Yet, you know him very well."

"Thank you, but I don't need any information."

"Don't get angry. . . . What is there wrong in it? ..." slowly drawled Sowinska.

"Ah, so it is you who presume to tell me that? ..."

"Yes I, and you know that I wish you as well as I wish my own daughter."

"You wish me as well as your own daughter?" slowly repeated Janina, looking straight into the other's face.

Sowinska dropped her eyes and silently left the room, but behind the door she paused and shook her fist threateningly.

"You saint! Wait!" she hissed.

When Janina reached the theater she found only Piesh, Topolski, and Glogowski present.

Glogowski approached her with a smile, extending his hand.

"Good morning. I was thinking about you yesterday; you must unfailingly thank me for that. . . . "

"I do thank you! But I'm curious to know . . ."

"I assure you I didn't think ill about you. ... I didn't think about you as others of my sex would think about such beautiful women as you, no! May I croak if I did! I thought ... 'Where does your strength come from?'"

"No doubt from the same source as weakness comes from; it's inherent," answered Janina seating herself.

"You must have some nice little dogma and with your mind fixed on that you go forward. That dogma has reddish-yellow hair, a yearly income of about ten thousand rubles, he wears binoculars and . . . " jested Topolski.

"And . . . forget the rest of it! It's always time enough for nonsense, that never grows old," Glogowski interrupted Topolski.

"You'll also drink with us, won't you, Miss Janina?"

"Thank you! I don't drink."

"But you must . . . if it be only to moisten your lips. It is the beginning of the funeral celebration over my play," joked Glogowski.

"Exaggeration!" mumbled Piesh.

"Well, we shall see! Come on, Mr. Piesh, Mr. Topolski, let's have another," cried Glogowski, pouring out the cognac.

He smiled and joked continually, led the arriving actors to the buffet and seemed very lively, but one could see that under his forced gayety there was a hidden anxiety and doubt regarding the success of his play.

On the veranda a noisy little revel had begun, where Glogowski was treating everybody, but the humors of all those present seemed to be partially dampened by the drizzling weather. Cabinski every now and then gazed up at the sky, took off his top hat and scratched his head with dissatisfaction. Pepa walked about as glum as an autumn day . . . Majkowska glared at Topolski with fiery eyes and seemed to have a great desire to create a scene, for her lips were pale and her eyes red, either from crying or sleeplessness. Glas also stalked about like a poisoned man after yesterday's fiasco and failed to utter a single one of his usual jokes. Razowiec was examining his tongue in a mirror and lamenting to Mrs. Piesh. Even Wawrzecki was not "in the proper situation," as he chose to describe his indisposition.

"It is half-past twelve. . . . Come, let's begin to read the play," said Topolski, the stage-manager.

A table was pushed out into the center of the stage, chairs were placed around it and Topolski, armed with a pencil, began to read.

Glogowski did not sit down, but kept walking about in big circles and every time he passed Janina he would whisper some remark at which she laughed quietly, while he continued to pace about, rumple his hair, throw his hat into the air and smoke one cigarette after another, all the time, however, listening attentively to the reading.

Outside the rain continued to drizzle and the water dripped monotonously down the drainpipes. The drab, dull daylight streamed in upon the stage. Glas amused himself by throwing cigarette butts at Dobek's nose, while Wladek gently blew at the head of the dozing Mirowska. From the dressing-room came the buzz of a saw cutting wood and the hammering of nails—it was the stage mechanician preparing his props for the evening performance.

"Mr. Glogowski, we shall have to cut out a little here," remarked Topolski occasionally.

"Go ahead!" Glogowski would reply, continuing his promenade.

The whispers grew louder.

"Kaminska will you go downtown with me? I want to buy some material for a dress."

"All right, we shall look over some autumn capes while we're at it."

"What is that going to be? ... an insertion?" Rosinska asked Mrs. Piesh who was busily crocheting something.

"Yes, do you see what a nice design it is? I got a sample from the directress."

Again there followed a moment of complete silence in which was heard nothing but the even voice of the stage-manager, the dripping of the rain and the buzz of the saw in the dressing-room.

"Let me have a cigarette," said Wawrzecki turning to Wladek. "Did you win anything at cards yesterday?"

"I lost, as usual, just as I was on the point of making a big haul of three hundred rubles. Some luck, eh? . . . A certain plan has occurred to my mind! . . . " Wladek leaned over toward Wawrzecki and began to whisper secretly into his ear.

"What have you done about your living quarters?" Krzykiewicz asked Glas, handing him a cigarette.

"Oh, nothing, I'm still living in the same place."

"Are you paying your rent?"

"Not yet, but soon!" answered the comedian, winking one of his eyes.

"Listen Glas! I heard that Cabinski is buying a house on Leszno Street."

"What are you trying to tell me! By Gad, I'd immediately move into it to make up for the salary he owes me. Where would he get the money?"

"Ciepieszewski saw him with the agents who have the house for sale."

"Nurse!" called Cabinska.

The nurse hastily entered carrying a letter under her apron.

"It wasn't I, it was Felka who broke that looking-glass. She threw a champagne bottle aiming at the chandelier, but struck the mirror instead. Bang! and immediately thirty rubles were added to the bill. That fat guy of hers merely frowned," one of the chorus girls was relating.

"Don't lie! I was not drunk and I remember exactly who broke it," retorted Felka.

"You remember do you? Do you also remember how you jumped off the table and then took off your shoes and . . . ha! ha! ha! ha!"

"Be quiet there!" sharply called Topolski to the chorus girls.

They subdued their voices, but Mimi began almost aloud to tell Kaczkowska about a new style of hat she had seen on Long Street.

"If it goes on that way much longer, I won't be able to stand it! The landlord has ordered me to move. Yesterday I pawned almost the last rag, for I had to buy my Johnnie some wine. The poor little fellow is convalescing so slowly. He already wants to get out of bed and is getting restless and peevish. If Ciepieszewski doesn't engage me and pay me in advance, the landlord will throw me out into the street," whispered Wolska to one of her companions of the chorus.

"But are you sure Ciepieszewski is organizing a company?" asked her listener.

"He is, undoubtedly. I am to see him in a few days to sign a contract."

"So you're not going to stay with Cabinski?"

"No, he doesn't want to pay the overdue salary he owes me."

Thirty years were written plainly on Wolska's wearied face on which worry had left its deep marks. The thick layer of powder and rouge could not coneal those wrinkles, nor the unrest that glowed in her eyes. She had a six-year-old son who had been ill since the spring. She defended him desperately, at the expense of starving herself.

"Counselor! Welcome to our company!" cried Glas, spying the old man, who for a few weeks had not been seen in the theater.

The counselor entered and began greeting everybody. The reading of the play was interrupted, for all sprang up from their seats.

"Good morning! Good morning! Am I interrupting you?"

"No, no!" chorused the actors.

"Have a seat, Counselor. We shall listen together," cried Cabinska.

"Ah, young master! my regards to you!" called the counselor to Glogowski.

"An old idiot!" growled Glogowski, nodding his head and hiding behind the scenes, for he was already exasperated at those continual interruptions and conversations.

"Silence! For goodness' sake, this is getting to be like a real synagogue!" cried the irritated Topolski and began to read on.

But no one listened any longer. The directress left with the counselor and, one by one, the others quietly slipped out after her. The rain began to pour heavily and beat so noisy a tattoo upon the tin roof of the theater that it drowned out all other sounds. It became so dark, that Topolski could not see to read.

The entire company removed to the men's dressing-room. It was lighter and warmer there, so they began to chat.

Janina stood together with Glogowski in the doorway and was saying something in an enthusiastic voice about the theater when Rosinska interrupted her with derision: "Goodness, you seem to be obsessed by the theater! . . . Well, well, I would never have believed such a thing possible had I not heard it. . . ."

"Why, it's simple enough; the theater holds everything that I desire."

"I, on the other hand, only begin to live outside of the theater."

"Then why don't you abandon the stage?"

"If I only could break away. I'd not stay here another hour!" she answered with bitterness.

"That's merely talk! Each one of us could break away from the theater, if we only would," said Wolska quietly. "For me this life is harder than for any of you and I know that if I forsook the stage my lot would be much better, but whenever I think that I shall have to quit the stage some day, so great a fear besets me that it seems as though I should die without it."

"The theater is a slow poisoning, a dying by inches each day!" complained Razowiec.

"Don't you whine, for your sickness comes not from the theater, but from your stomach," remarked Wawrzecki.

"That continual dying and poisoning is, nevertheless, a kind of ecstasy!" began Janina anew.

"Oh, a splendid ecstasy! If you want to call hunger, continual envy, and the inability to live otherwise, an ecstasy!" sneered Rosinska.

"Happy are they who have not fallen a prey to that disease, or escaped it in time," added Razowiec.

"But isn't it better to live and suffer and die in that way, as long as you have art as your goal. A thousand times would I prefer to live that way than to be my husband's servant, the slave of my children, and a household chattel!" exclaimed Janina with a passionate outburst.

Wladek began to declaim with a comical pathos:

"Oh priestess, most elect!
To thee, in this temple of art,
High altars I'll erect!

"Please forgive me that," continued Wladek. "I myself say that outside of art there is nothing! If it were not for the theater. . . "

"You would have become a cobbler!" interposed Glas.

"Only a very young and a very naïve woman can talk like that," spitefully exclaimed Kaczkowska.

"Or one who does not yet know what Cabinski's salary tastes like," added Rosinska.

"Oh, thou art worthy of pity! You have enthusiasm . . . poverty will rob you of it; you have inspiration . . . poverty will rob you of it; you have youth, talent, and beauty . . . poverty will rob you of it all!" declaimed Piesh in the stern tones of an oracle.

"No, all that is nothing! . . . But such a company, such artists, such plays as these will ruin everything. And if you are able to endure such a hell then you will become a great artist!" whispered Stanislawski sourly.

"A master has proclaimed it, so bow your heads, oh multitude, and say that it must be so!" jeered Wawrzecki.

"Fool! . . . " snarled Stanislawski.

"Mummy!" retorted Wawrzecki.

"I'll tell you how I began my career," said Wladek. "I was in the fourth grade at school when I saw Rossi in *Hamlet* and from that moment the theater claimed me entirely! I pilfered cash from my father to buy tragedies and attended the theater. I spent whole days and nights in learning rôles, and dreamed that I would conquer the whole world . . ."

"And you're nothing but a tyro in Cabinski's company," jeered Dobek.

"I learned that Richter had come to Warsaw and intended to open a school of dramatic art," continued Wladek. "I went to see him, for I felt that I had talent and wished to learn. He lived on St. John's Street. I came to his house and rang the bell. He opened the door himself, let me in and then locked it. I began to perspire with fear and didn't know how to begin. I stood first on one foot and then on the other. He was calmly washing a saucepan. Then, he poured some oil into an oil-stove, took off his coat, put on a house-jacket and began to peel potatoes.

"After a long silence, seeing that I would not get him to respond in that way, I began to stammer something about my calling, my love of art, my desire to learn and so forth. . . . He continued to peel his potatoes. Finally, I asked him to give me lessons. He glanced at me and grumbled: 'How old are you, my boy?' I stood there dumbfounded like a mummy and he continued to question: 'Did you come with your mother?' Tears began to fill my eyes, while he spoke again: 'Your father will give you a walloping, and they'll expel you from school.' I felt so distressed and humiliated that I could not utter a word 'Recite some verse for me, young man,' he said quietly, all the while systematically peeling his potatoes."

"So your inclination to roar on the stage harks away back to those days, eh?" jeered Glas.

"Glas, don't interrupt me. . . . Ha! thought I, I'll have to show him! And although I was all trembling with emotion I assumed a tragic pose and began to recite. . . . I writhed, shouted, burst out in a fit of passion like Othello, seethed with hatred, like a samovar and finally finished, all covered with perspiration. 'Some more,' said Richter, continually peeling the potatoes, while not a single muscle of his face betrayed what he thought of it all. I thought that everything was going fine, so I selected 'Hagar.' I despaired like Niobe, cursed like Lear, pleaded, threatened, and ended up, all exhausted and breathless. He said: 'Still more!' He stopped peeling the potatoes and began to chop meat. Enraptured by the tone of encouragement I selected from Slowacki's *Mazeppa* that prison-scene from the fourth act and recited the whole of it. I put into it so much feeling and force that I became hoarse; my hair stood on end, I trembled, forgot my surroundings, inspiration carried me away, fire blazed from me as from a stove, my voice melted in tears. Tragedy swept me off my feet, the room began to dance about me, a colored mist swam before my eyes, my breath was beginning to fail, I began to grow weak and to choke with emotion, and I seemed about to faint . . . when he sneezed and began to wipe tears from his eyes with his coat-sleeve. I stopped reciting. He laid down the onion that he was slicing, put a pitcher into my hand and calmly said to me: 'Go and bring me some water.' I brought it. He spilled the potatoes into it, stood them on the oil-stove and lit the wick. I timidly asked him whether I could come to take lessons from him. 'Yes, come,' he answered, 'you can sweep the floor and carry water for me. Do you know how to speak Chinese?' 'No,' I answered,

153

not knowing what he was driving at. 'Well, then learn it and come back to me and we shall then speak about the theater!'... I shall never forget that moment as long as I live."

"Don't get mawkish over it, for Glogowski won't treat you to any more beer anyway," remarked Glas.

"Say what you will, but it is art alone that makes life worth something," persisted Wladek.

"And didn't you see Richter again?" asked Janina curiously.

"How could he ... he hasn't learned Chinese yet," interposed Glas.

"No, I didn't go to see him; and moreover, when they expelled me from school I immediately ran away from home and joined Krzyzanowski's company," answered Wladek.

"You were with Krzyzanowski?" asked someone.

"For a whole year I walked with him, his wife, his son, the immortal Leo and one other actress. I say that I 'walked' because in those days we seldom used other means of locomotion. Very often there was nothing to eat, but I could act and declaim as much as I liked. I had an enormous repertoire. With a cast of four persons we presented Shakespeare and Schiller, most wonderfully made over for our own use by Krzyzanowski, who besides that had a great many plays of his own with double or quadruple titles."

While the rain continued interminably, they drew together in a still closer circle and chatted. Suddenly their conversation was interrupted by loud cries from the stage.

"Quiet! what is that?" asked everybody. "Aha! Majkowska versus Topolski in a scene of free love."

Janina went out to see what was happening. On the almost totally dark stage the heroic pair were engaged in a quarrel.

"Where were you?" cried Majkowska, springing at Topolski with clenched fists.

"Let me alone, Mela."

"Where were you all last night?"

"I tell you, please go away. ... If you are ill, go home."

"You were playing cards again, weren't you? And I haven't even enough money for a dress! I couldn't even buy myself a supper last night!"

"Why didn't you want the money when you could have had it?"

"Oh, yes, you'd want me to have money so that you could gamble it away. You would even help me to get the money for that purpose ... you base scoundrel!"

She sprang at him with nervous fury. Her beautiful, statuesque face glowed with rage. She grasped his arm, pinched him and shook him, without herself knowing what she was doing.

Topolski, losing his patience, struck her violently away from him.

Majkowska with almost a roar—so little did her voice seem to have in it anything human—and with spasmodic laughter, and crying, and tragic wringing of hands, fell on her knees before him.

"Maurice, my soul's beloved, forgive me! . . . Light of my life! Ha! ha! ha! you damned scoundrel, you! . . . My dearest, my dearest, forgive me! . . . "

She groveled to his feet, grasped his hands and began rapturously to kiss them.

Topolski stood there gloomily. He felt ashamed of his own anger, so he merely chewed his cigarette and whispered quietly: "Come, get up from the floor and stop playing that comedy. . . . Have you no shame! ... In a minute you will have everybody in here looking at you."

Majkowska's mother, an old woman, resembling a witch, came running up to her and tried to raise her from the floor.

"Mela, my daughter!" she cried.

"Mother, take that crazy woman away from here; she is continually creating scandals," said Topolski and went out into the hall.

"My dear daughter! Do you see! I told you and begged you not to go with such a poor fool! . . . See what your love has brought you to, my Mela! Come, get up, my child!"

"Go to the devil, mother!" cried Majkowska, pushing away her mother.

Then she sprang up from the floor and began to pace rapidly up and down the stage. In this violent motion she must have spent the rest of her anger, for she began to hum and smile to herself and afterwards called to Janina in the most natural voice: "Perhaps you will take a walk with me? . . . "

"Very well, it has even stopped raining . . . " answered the younger woman, glancing at her face.

"I have a fine lover, haven't I? . . . Did you see what was going on?"

"I saw and cannot yet calm my indignation."

"Oh, nonsense!"

"How can you stand such a thing?"

"I love him too much to pay attention to such trifles."

Janina began to laugh nervously, and said: "Such things are to be seen only in the operetta . . . well, and behind the scenes."

"Bah, I will avenge myself for it!"

"You will avenge yourself? I'm very curious to know how. . . . "

"I will marry him ... I will make him marry me!"

"So that will be your vengeance?" inquired Janina in amazement.

"There couldn't be a better one. Oh, I'll make his life warm for him! . . . Come, I have to buy some chocolate."

"You didn't have money for supper?" cried Janina involuntarily.

"Ha! ha! ha! How naïve you still are! You saw the gentlemen who sends me bouquets and yet, you think that I have no money! Where were you brought up?"

Suddenly, she changed the tone of her voice and asked Janina inquisitively: "Tell me, have you also someone? . . . "

"I have art!" answered Janina gravely, not even offended by her question.

"You are either very ambitious or very wise ... I did not know you before. . . . " said Majkowska and began to listen more attentively.

"Ambitious . . . perhaps, for I have only one object in belonging to the theater and that is art."

"Come, don't try to play a farce with me! Ha! ha! Art, as an aim of life! That is a theme for a fine couplet, but it is an old trick."

"That depends on the person in question."

Majkowska became silent and began gloomily to ponder.

"It was hard to catch up with you!" called someone behind them.

"Oh, what brings you here, Counselor? So you are off duty?" spitefully whispered Majkowska, for she knew that the counselor always attended Cabinska.

"I want to change my mistress. ... I am seeking a new position."

"In my service the duties are very exacting."

"Oh, in that case, thank you! I am already too old ... I know someone who would be more considerate for my age." And he bowed to Janina with studied courtesy.

"Will you come with us, Counselor?" asked Majkowska.

"Certainly, but you must permit me to lead the way, ladies."

"Very well, we'll agree to whatever you suggest."

"I propose that we have breakfast at 'Versailles.'"

"I must return to the theater," said Janina.

"They've not yet finished reading the play."

"They'll finish it without you. Come, let us go," urged Majkowska.

They walked slowly, for the rain had stopped entirely and the July sun was drying the mud in the streets. The counselor wiggled about, gazed into Janina's eyes and smiled significantly; he bowed to acquaintances he met on the way and before the younger ones he assumed the pose of a conquerer.

The "Versailles Restaurant" was empty. They seated themselves near the balcony and the counselor ordered a very choice breakfast.

It was after three o'clock when they returned to the theater. The rehearsal of the day's performance was in full swing. Cabinski was about to grumble at them for coming late, but Majkowska gave him such a crushing look that he merely frowned and walked away.

Her mother approached her with a letter. Majkowska read it, immediately scribbled a few words in reply and handed them to the old woman.

"Deliver this right away, mother," she said.

"Mela, but suppose I don't find him in?" asked her mother.

"Then wait, but do not give it to anyone else but him! Here's something for your trouble, mother . . . " and tapping her throat with her fingers after the custom of drinkers she gave her a forty—copeck piece.

The greenish eyes of the old woman gleamed with gratitude and she hurried away with the message.

Janina looked for Glogowski, but he had already left, so she went out into the hall to the counselor who had returned with them, for she remembered that he had promised to tell her what he had read in her palm.

"Mr. Counselor, you owe me something," she began, sitting down beside him.

"I? . . . I? . . . Upon my word I don't remember that I owe you anything."

"You promised to tell me what you had read in my palm not so long ago."

"Yes, but not here. Come, we had better go to the dressing-room so that it won't attract anyone's attention."

They went to the dressing-room of the chorus.

The counselor spent quite a while examining both her hands very minutely and finally said with some embarrassment: "Upon my word, this is the first time that I see such strange hands!"

"Oh, please tell me everything!"

"I can't. . . . And I don't know whether it's true."

"It makes no difference whether it is true or not, you must tell me by all means, my dear Counselor!" coaxed Janina.

"A mental disorder of some kind, it seems. . . . Of course I don't know and I don't believe it. I tell you only what I see, but . . . but . . ."

"And what of the theater?" Janina asked.

"You will be famous . . . you will be very famous!" he whispered hurriedly without looking at her.

"That isn't true; you didn't see that there!" she exclaimed, reading the falsehood in his eyes.

"My word! my word of honor all that is written there! You will achieve fame, but through so much suffering, through so many tears. . . . Beware of dreaming!"

And he kissed her hand.

The noisy buzz of voices merged with tones of music broke the stillness in which both of them had become rapt.

For a little while Janina sat alone, after her companion withdrew, torn by dim forebodings.

"You are going to be very famous! Beware of dreaming!" she kept repeating to herself.

That evening the counselor sent to Janina a bouquet, a box of candy, and a letter inviting her to supper at the "Idyl," mentioning that Topolski and Majkowska were also to be there.

She read it and, not knowing what to do, asked Sowinska.

"Sell the bouquet, eat the candy, and go to the supper."

"So that is your advice? . . . " asked Janina.

Sowinska scornfully shrugged her shoulders.

Janina angrily threw the bouquet in a corner, distributed the candy among the chorus girls, and after the performance went straight home, highly indignant at the counselor whom she had looked upon as a very serious and honest man.

On the next day at the rehearsal Majkowska remarked tauntingly to Janina: "You are an immaculate romanticist."

"No, only I respect myself," answered Janina.

"Get thee to a nunnery!" declaimed Majkowska.

In the afternoon Janina went as usual to Cabinska's home to give Yadzia her piano lesson, but she could not forget that scornful shrug of Sowinska's shoulders and Majkowska's words.

She finished the lesson and then sat for a long time playing Chopin's *Nocturnes*, finding in their melancholy strains a balm for her own sorrows.

"Miss Janina . . . My husband has left a rôle here for you!" called Cabinska from the other room.

Janina closed the piano and began to peruse the rôle. It consisted of a few words from Glogowski's new play and did not satisfy her in the least, for it was nothing but a short little episode. Nevertheless, this was to be her first real appearance in the drama.

The play had been postponed until the following Thursday and rehearsals of it were to be held every afternoon, for Glogowski had earnestly requested that and generously treated the entire cast each day to get them to learn their rôles well.

A few days after receiving her first rôle Janina's first month at Sowinska's expired. The old woman reminded her of it in the morning, asking for the money as soon as possible.

Janina gave her ten rubles, solemnly promising to pay the balance in a few days. She had only a few rubles left of her entire capital. She thought in astonishment how she had spent the two hundred rubles which she had brought with her from Bukowiec.

"What am I going to do?" Janina asked herself, determining as soon as possible to ask Cabinski for her overdue salary.

She did so at the very next rehearsal.

"I haven't the money!" cried Cabinski at once. "Moreover, I never pay beginners in my company for the first month. It's strange that no one informed you about that. Others are already here a whole season and they don't bother me about their salaries."

Janina listened in consternation and finally said frankly: "Mr. Director, in a week's time I will not have a penny left to live on."

"And that old . . . counselor . . . can't he give it to you? . . . Surely, everyone knows that ..."

"Oh, Mr. Diréctor!" whispered Janina, blushing deeply.

"A pretty deceiver!" he muttered with a cynical twist of his lips.

Janina forcibly suppressed her indignation and said: "In the meantime I need ten rubles, for I must buy myself a costume for the new play."

"Ten rubles! Ha! ha! ha! That's great! Even Majkowska does not ask for so much at one time! Ten rubles! what delightful simplicity!" Cabinski laughed heartily and then, turning to go, he said: "Remind me of it this evening and I will give you an order to the treasurer."

That evening Janina received one ruble.

Janina knew that the chorus girls even after the most profitable performance received only fifty copecks on account and usually only two gold pieces or forty groszy. Only now, did she recall those sad and worn faces of the elder actresses. There were revealed to her now many things that she had never seen before, or seeing them, had never understood. Her own want opened wide her eyes to the poverty that oppressed everyone in the theater and those hidden daily struggles with it that they often disguised under a glittering veil of gayety.

That daily standing before the treasurer's window and fairly begging for money, which she was now compelled to do, cast a shadow over Janina's soul and filled her with bitterness. It made her all the more eager to get a larger rôle so that she might get out of that hated chorus, but Cabinski steadily put her off.

Kotlicki hovered about Janina incessantly, but did not renew his proposal and seemed to be waiting his chance.

Wladek was the most companionable of all in regard to Janina and told everyone that she visited his mother. Niedzielska continually spied on Wladek, for she already suspected him of liking Janina.

The girl received Wladek's attentions with the same indifference that she received Kotlicki's, with the same indifference that she received the bouquets and candy which the counselor sent her every day. None of these three silent admirers interested her in the least and she kept them at a respectable distance from herself by her coolness.

The other actresses ridiculed Janina's inflexibility, but in their hearts they sincerely envied her. She ignored their spiteful remarks, for she knew that to answer them would be merely to invite a greater avalanche of ridicule.

Janina liked only Glogowski, who because of the coming presentation of his play would spend whole days at the theater. He openly singled her out as an object of his special regard from among all the women, spoke only with her on weighty subjects and treated her alone as a human being. She felt highly flattered and grateful. She liked him especially because he never mentioned love to her, nor boasted. Often they would go together for walks in Lazienki Park. Janina associated with him on a footing of sincere friendship.

After the final rehearsal of *The Churls*, Glogowski and Janina left the theater together. He seemed to be more gloomy than usual. He was racked with anxiety over his play that was to be given that evening, yet he laughed aloud.

"Suppose we take a ride to the Botanical Gardens. Do you agree?" he suggested.

Janina assented and they started off.

They found an unoccupied seat near one of the pools, under a huge plane tree and for a time sat there in silence.

The garden was fairly empty. A few persons seated here and there upon the benches appeared like shadows in the sultry air. The last roses of summer gleamed with their bright hues through the foliage of the low-hanging branches; the stocks in the central flower-bed diffused a heavy fragrance. The birds twittered only at rare intervals with somnolent voices. The trees stood motionless as though listening to the sunlit tranquility of that August day. Only now and then some leaf or withered twig would float down in a spiral line upon the lawns. The golden splashes of sunlight filtering through the branches formed a shifting mosaic upon the grass and gleamed like strips of pale platinum.

"Let the devil take it all!" Glogowski occasionally flung out into the silence and distractedly rumpled his hair.

Janina merely glanced at him, loath to mar with words the silence that enveloped her—that calm of nature lulled to sleep by the excessive warmth. She also was lulled by some unknown tenderness that had no connection with any particular thing, but seemed to float down out of space, from the blue sky, from the transparent whiteness of the slowly sailing clouds from the deep verdure of the trees.

"For goodness' sake, say something, or I'll go crazy, or get hydrophobia! . . ." he suddenly exclaimed.

Janina burst out laughing, "Well, let us talk about this evening, if about nothing else," ventured the girl.

"Do you want to drive me crazy altogether? May the deuce take me, but I fear I won't endure till this evening!"

"But haven't you told me that this is not your first play, so. . ."

"Yes, but at the presentation of each new one the ague always shakes me, for always at the last moment I see that I have written rubbish, tommyrot, cheap trash . . ."

"I don't pretend to be a judge, but I liked the play immensely. It is so frank."

"What? Do you mean that seriously?" he cried.

"Of course."

"For you see, I told myself that if this play fails, I shall . . . "

"Will you give up writing?"

"No, but I shall vanish from the horizon for a few months and write another one. I will write a second, a third ... I will write until I produce a perfectly good one! I must!"

"Tell me, do you think Majkowska will make a good *Antka* in my play?" he suddenly asked.

"It seems to me that that rôle is well-suited to her."

"Maurice also will play his part well, but the rest of them are a miserable lot and the staging terrible. It's bound to turn out a fiasco!"

"Mimi knows nothing about the peasants and her imitation of their dialect is ludicrous," remarked Janina.

"I heard her and it pained me to listen! Do you know the peasants? Ah, Great Scott!" he cried impulsively. "Why don't you act that rôle? . . . "

"Because they didn't give it to me."

"Why didn't you tell me about that sooner? May the deuce take me, but even if I had to smash up the whole theater I would have forced them to give you that rôle!"

"The director gave me the part of Phillip's wife."

"That's merely a super, an episode ... it could have been given to anyone. I feel that Mimi is going to chatter like a soubrette from an operetta. See what you have caused me! By glory, what a mess! If you think that life is a charming operetta, you are greatly mistaken!"

"I already happen to know something about that ..." answered Janina with a bitter smile.

"So far you don't know anything . . . you will learn it only later on. But after all women usually have an easier time of it. We men have to fight hard to grasp our share and have to pay dearly. God knows how dearly."

"Don't you think the women pay anything?"

"It's this way: women, and particularly those on the stage, owe the minimum part of their success to their talents or themselves; the maximum part to their lovers who support them and the rest to the gallantry of those men who hope to be able to support them some day."

Janina answered nothing, for there flashed before her mind a picture of Majkowska with Topolski in back of her, Mimi with Wawrzecki, Kaczkowska with one of the journalists and so on through almost all of them.

"Don't be angry with me. I merely stated a fact that came to my mind."

"No. I'm not angry. I admit you're entirely right."

"With you, it will not be that way, I feel it. Come, let us go now!" he suddenly cried, jumping up from the bench.

"I will say something more . . . " said Glogowski when they were already walking down the shaded paths on their way back, "I will repeat what I said on the day that I first met you at Bielany; let us be friends! . . .

It's no use trying to deny it, man is a gregarious beast: he always needs someone near him so that his lot on this earth may be half-way bearable . . . Man does not stand alone; he must lean against and link up with others, go together with them and feel together with them to be able to accomplish anything. To be sure, one kindred soul suffices. Let us be friends!"

"All right," said Janina, "but I will lay down one condition."

"Quick, for God's sake! For perhaps I will not accept it!"

"It is this: give me your word of honor that you will never, never speak to me about love, and that you will not fall in love with me. You can even confide in me, if you wish, all your love affairs and disappointments."

"Agreed, all along the line! I seal that with my solemn word of honor!" cried Glogowski.

They gravely pressed each others' hands.

"This is a union of pure souls with ideal aims!" he laughed, winking his eyes. "Something makes me feel so merry now that I could take my own head in my hands and kiss it heartily."

"It is a premonition of the triumph of your *Churls*."

"Don't remind me of that. I know what awaits me. But I must now bid farewell to you."

"Aren't you going to escort me home?"

"No ... Oh well, all right, but I warn you I will talk to you about . . . love!" he cried gayly.

"Well, in that case, good-by! May God preserve you from such falsehoods."

"Your ears must have surfeited on that rubbish, if the very mention of it nauseates you. . . . "

"Go now if you wish ... I will tell you about it some other time. . . . "

Glogowski leaped into a hack and drove away in haste toward Comely Street and Janina went home.

She tried on the peasant costume which Mme. Anna was making for her appearance and thought with a smile of the alliance that she had formed with Glogowski.

At the theater it was evident that a première was to be given. All the members of the company appeared earlier, dressed and made up more carefully than usual and only Krzykiewicz, as was his custom, paraded about the dressing-room and the stage half-dressed with his rouge pot in his hand.

Stanislawski, who when he played, usually came about two hours before the performance, was already dressed and only now and then added an extra touch to his make-up.

Wawrzecki, with his rôle in his hand paced up and down the dressing-room rehearsing in an undertone.

The stage-director ran about more swiftly than usual and in the ladies' dressing-room livelier quarrels were going on. Everyone was more nervous to-day. The prompter supervised the stage arrangements and watched the public that was beginning to fill the hall. The chorus girls, who were to act as supers, were already dressed in their peasant costumes and straggled all about the stage.

"Dobek!" called Majkowska. "My dear fellow, only support me well! ... I know my part, but in the second act slip me the words of that monologue a little louder."

Dobek nodded his head and had not yet returned to his post when Glas accosted him.

"Dobek! Will you have a drink of whisky, eh? Perhaps you'd like a sandwich?" he asked the prompter in a solicitous tone.

"To the sandwich add a beer," answered Dobek, smiling blissfully.

"My good fellow, don't fail me! I really know my part to-day, but I'm likely to get stuck here and there . . . "

"Well, well! only don't lie down yourself and you can be sure I won't let you perish."

And in this way, every other minute some actor or actress would approach Dobek, who solemnly promised to "uphold" them all.

"Dobek! I need only the first words of each line . . . remember!" reminded Topolski at the very last.

Glogowski strayed about the stage, himself set up the interior of the peasants' hut, gave instructions to the actors and uneasily scanned the first row of seats occupied by the representatives of the press.

"It will be warm for me to-morrow!" he whispered to himself, and began to walk about feverishly, for he was unable to stand or sit still in one spot. Finally, he went out into the garden-hall, stood leaning against a chestnut tree and watched with beating heart the first act of his play which had just begun.

The audience sat coldly and quietly listening. An oppressive silence filled the hall. Glogowski saw hundreds of eyes and immovable heads, he even saw the restaurant waiters standing on chairs beneath the veranda, watching the stage. The voices of the actors resounded distinctly, floating out to that dark, densely packed mass of people.

Glogowski sat down in the darkest corner behind the scenes on a heap of decorations, covered his face with his hands and listened.

Scene followed scene, and still that same ominous silence reigned. Glogowski was unable to sit there quietly! He heard the baritone voice of Topolski, the soprano of Majkowska and the somewhat hoarse voice of Glas, but it was not that which he wished to hear. Not that! He bit his fingers so violently that tears came to his eyes from the pain.

The first act ended.

A few lukewarm handclaps broke out here and there and died away again in the general silence.

Glogowski sprang up and with craning neck and feverishly gleaming eyes waited, but he heard only the thump of the falling curtain and the buzz of voices suddenly rising in the hall.

During the intermission he again observed the public. Their faces wore a strange expression. The members of the press frowned, and whispered something among themselves, while certain of them made notes.

"I feel cold!" whispered Glogowski to himself, shaking as though with an icy chill. And he began to stray distractedly all about the theater.

"I congratulate you!" said Kotlicki, pressing Glogowski's hand. "The play is too severe and brutal, but it is something new!"

"Which means neither fish nor flesh!" answered Glogowski with a forced smile.

"We'll see how it will be further on. . . . The public is surprised to see a folk play without dances. . . . "

"What the devil do they want! It is not a ballet!" muttered Glogowski impatiently.

"But you know they dote on songs and dances."

"Then let them go to a vaudeville show!" retorted Glogowski. And he walked away.

After the second act the applause was louder and more prolonged.

In the dressing-rooms the humor of the actors began to rise to its usual level.

Cabinski had already twice sent Wicek to the box office to find out how things were going there. Gold's first reply was: "Good," and his second: "Sold out."

Glogowski continued to torment himself, but now in a different way, for having heard the applause for which he had so feverishly waited, he had calmed himself a bit and sat behind the scenes watching the play. Now he became pale with anger, kicked his hat with his foot and hissed with impatience, for he could no longer endure what he saw. Out of his peasant characters, which were in every inch true to life, they were making banal figures of the sentimental melodrama, puppets dressed in folk costumes. The playing of the men actors was at least to some extent bearable, but the women, with the exception of Majkowska and Mirowska, who acted the part of an old beggar woman, played abominably. Instead of speaking their parts, they rattled them off in a singsong voice, and overemphasized hatred, love, and laughter. Everything was done so mechanically, artifically, and thoughtlessly, without a grain of truth or sincerity that Glogowski fairly choked with despair. It was merely a masquerade.

"Sharper! More energetically!" he whispered, stamping his foot, but no one paid any attention to his exhortations.

Suddenly, a smile flitted over his lips, for he saw Janina entering the stage. She caught that smile and that saved her, for her voice had died in her breast. She was trembling from stage fright so that she did not see the stage, nor the actors, nor the public; it seemed to her that she was engulfed in a sea of light. When she saw that friendly smile she immediately recovered her calm and courage.

Janina was merely to grasp a broom, take her drunken husband by the collar, shout a few lines of imprecation and complaint and then drag him out forcibly through the door. She did all this a trifle too violently, but with such realism that she gave the impression of an infuriated peasant woman.

Glogowski went to Janina. She stood on the stairs leading to the dressing-room; her eyes beamed with a certain deep satisfaction.

"Very good! . . . that was a real peasant woman. You have a temperament and a voice and those are two first-rate endowments!" said Glogowski, and tip-toed back to his seat.

"Perhaps we ought to give an encore of that scene?" whispered Cabinski into his ear.

"Dry up and go to the devil!" answered Glogowski in the same quiet whisper and felt a great desire to strike Cabinski. But just then, a new thought occurred to his mind, for he saw the nurse standing nearby.

"Nurse!" he called to her.

The nurse unwillingly approached Glogowski.

"Tell me, nurse, what do you think of that comedy?" he asked her curiously.

"The title is very unpolitic . . . 'churls'! Everyone knows that peasants are not nobles, but to call them by such a scornful name for the amusement of others is a downright sin!"

"Well, that is of minor importance . . . but do you think those characters resemble real peasants?"

"Yes, you have hit upon the real thing Peasants are just like that, only they don't dress so elegantly, nor are they so refined in their bearing and speech. But pardon me, sir, if I say one thing; what's the use of it all? Present, if you wish, nobles, Jews, or any other kind of ragamuffins, but to make a laughing-stock and a comedy of honest tillers of the soil is a downright shame! God is like to punish you for such frivolity! A husbandman is a husbandman ... beware of trifling with him!" she added in conclusion and continued to gaze at the stage with an ever greater severity and almost with tears of indignation in her eyes.

Glogowski had no time to wonder at her attitude for just then the third act ended amid thunderous applause and calls for the author, but he did not go out to bow.

A few journalists came to shake hands with him and praise his play. He listened to them indifferently, for already his mind was occupied with a plan for remaking that play. Now first did he see in detail its various inconsistencies and the things that were lacking, and immediately completed them in his mind, added new scenes, changed about situations and was so absorbed with his task that he no longer paid any attention to how they were playing the fourth act.

Again applause filled the entire hall and the unanimous cry of: "Author! Author!"

"They're calling for you, go out to them," someone whispered into Glogowski's ear.

"The deuce I will! Go to the devil, sweet brother!"

Majkowska and Topolski were also being recalled.

Majkowska, all breathless, ran up to Glogowski.

"Mr. Glogowski! come, hurry!" she cried, taking him by the hand.

"Let me alone!" he growled threateningly.

Majkowska left him and Glogowski sat there and continued to think. Neither the applause, nor the demands for his appearance nor the success of his play interested him·any longer, for he was sorely worried by the knowledge that his play was entirely bad. He saw its defects ever more plainly and the knowledge that another one of his efforts had proved vain made him writhe with pain. With helpless rage he listened to the public applauding the rude and characteristically comic episodes which were merely the background upon which the souls of his *Churls* had to be outlined, while the theme and thesis of the play itself passed without making any impression.

"Mr. Glogowski I want you to go out after the fifth act if they call for you," Janina said to him decisively.

"But please consider, who is calling for me! Don't you see that it is the gallery? Don't you see the smiles of derision upon the faces of the press and the public in the first rows of seats? I tell you the play is bad, abominable and rotten! Wait and see what they will write about it to-morrow."

"What will happen to-morrow we shall see to-morrow. To-day there is success and your splendid play."

"Splendid!" he cried painfully. "If you could see the plan of it that I have here in my head, if you could see how splendid and complete it is here, you would know that what they are playing is merely a poor rag and a fragment."

Immediately afterwards Cabinski, Topolski, and Kotlicki approached Glogowski and urged him to appear before the public, but still he resisted. Only at the end of the play when the entire audience was wildly applauding and calling for the author, Glogowski went out on the stage with Majkowska, bowed ostentatiously, smoothed his shock of hair and clumsily retreated behind the scenes.

"If the play had dances, songs, and music, I wager it would run to the end of the season," said Cabinski.

"Dry up, or drink yourself to death, but do not tell me such nonsense," shouted Glogowski. "The next thing you know, the restaurant-keeper will come running in here and begin to berate me because for the same reasons he sold less beer and whiskey; a public that must listen and laughs seldom prefers hot tea."

"But my dear sir, nobody writes plays for himself, he writes them for other human beings."

"Yes, for human beings, but not for Zulus," retorted Glogowski.

Kotlicki again approached Glogowski and spoke to him for a long while. Glogowski frowned and said: "First of all, I haven't the money for it, for it would cost a great deal and, in the second place, I am not at all anxious to be 'one of our well-known and celebrated,' for that is a prostitution of one's talent!"

"I can be of service to you with my funds, if you wish. ... I presume that our old ties of companionship at school . . . "

"Let us drop that! . . . " Glogowski violently interrupted him. "But that has given me a certain idea . . . Suppose we arrange a little supper, but only for a few persons, eh?"

"Good! we will draw up a list right away; Mr. and Mrs. Cabinski, Majkowska and Topolski, Mimi and Wawrzecki and Glas, as an entertainer, of course. Whom else shall we include?"

Kotlicki wished to suggest Janina, but was restrained from saying so openly.

"Aha! I know . . . Miss Orlowska . . . the *Filipka* of my play! Did you see how superbly she acted the part?"

"Indeed, she played it well . . . " answered Kotlicki, glancing suspiciously at Glogowski, for he thought that he also had designs upon Janina.

"Go and invite them. I will come right away."

Kotlicki went out into the restaurant garden, while Glogowski hurried upstairs to the chorus dressing-room and called through the door: "Miss Orlowska!"

Janina peered out.

"Please hurry and get dressed for the whole crowd of us is going out for supper and you can't refuse."

About a half hour later they were all sitting in a room of one of the large restaurants on Nowy Swiat.

The whiskey and lunch were attacked energetically for the nervous strain of the last few hours had sharpened everybody's appetite. They spoke little, but drank a great deal.

Janina did not wish to drink, but Glogowski begged her and cried out: "You must drink and that settles it. You must drink, if only to celebrate such an honorable burial as we have held today."

She drank one glass on trial, but afterwards was forced to drink others; moreover, she felt that it helped her, for she had not yet rid herself of stage nervousness and was trembling about the fate of the play.

After various courses had been served, the waiters placed on the table a whole battery of bottles full of wines and liqueurs.

"Now we'll have something to fight with!" cried Glas jovially, tinkling a bottle with his knife.

"You will fall a victim to your own triumph, if you continue to attack with the same fervor," laughed Wawrzecki.

"You people can talk, while we drink!" called Kotlicki, raising his glass. "Here's to the health of our author!"

"May you choke, you Zulu!" growled Glogowski, rising and touching glasses with everybody.

"May he live long and write a new masterpiece each year!" cried Cabinski, already quite tipsy.

"You, Director, also create masterpieces almost every year, yet no one upbraids you for it," jested Glas.

"With the help of God and man, gentlemen, yes, yes!" answered Cabinski.

Mimi burst out laughing and all joined her.

"Come let me hug you! For once you do not lie!" cried Glas.

Pepa almost died laughing.

"Here's to the health of Mr. and Mrs. Director!" called Wawrzecki.

"May they live long and with the help of God and man create more masterpieces!"

Here's to the health of the whole company!"

"And now let us drink to the public."

"Permit me to interrupt you a moment. Since I alone here represent the public, therefore render homage to me. Approach me with respect and drink to me. You may even kiss me and ask me for some favor. I will consider your request and bestow whatever I am able to!" cried Kotlicki gleefully.

He took a glass from the table, stood before a mirror and waited.

"Can you beat that for conceit! I will be the first to undergo the ordeal!" cried Glogowski, and with brimming glass, already a bit wobbly on his pins he approached Kotlicki.

"Most esteemed and gracious lady! I give you plays written with my heart's blood; only understand and value them justly!" he declaimed with mock pathos, kissing Kotlicki's face.

"If you, oh master, will write them for me, if you will not offend me with brutalities, if you will reckon with me and write for me alone so that I can enjoy and entertain myself, then I will give you success!"

"First I will kick you and may you croak!" hissed Glogowski bitterly.

Cabinski approached next.

"Most esteemed public! You are the sun, you are beauty, you are omnipotence, you are wisdom, you are the highest judge! Yours are these children of Melpomene and for you do they live, play, and sing! Tell me, oh mighty lady, why are you not kind to us? I entreat you, oh enlightened one, give us each day a full theater!"

"My dear! Have a little money when you come to Warsaw, have a large repertoire, a select company, beautiful choruses and give those plays which I like and your treasury will be bursting with gold."

"Esteemed public!" cried Glas, with a comical pathos, kissing Kotlicki's beard.

"Speak!" said Kotlicki.

"Esteemed female! Give me some money and then have your head shaved, a yellow jacket put on you and green paper pasted about you and we will see that you are sent where you belong."

"I can't promise you money, but I assure you, you'll get . . . delirium tremens, my son . . ." answered Kotlicki!

"Topolski, it's your turn!"

"Give me a rest! I have enough of your puppet shows."

Cabinska also did not wish to take part in the amusement, but Mimi bowed comically and stroked Kotlicki's face.

"My dear! my precious public!" she entreated in caressing tones. "Keep Wladek from continually falling in love with some new charmer and ... see, I could make use of a bracelet, then a green suit for the fall, some furs for the winter and ... see that the director pays me my salary."

"You will get what you wish, for you desired it sincerely, and here is the address."

He handed her his visiting card.

"Fine! Bravo!" cried the company.

"Miss Majkowska may now approach, for I promise her a great deal in advance," announced Kotlicki.

"You are an old deceiver, dear public! You promise continually, but you never give me what you promise!" said Mela.

"I will give you . . . in a year from now a début at the Warsaw Theater and surely engage you."

Majkowska shrugged her shoulders indifferently and sat down.

"Miss Orlowska!"

Janina arose; she felt a trifle dizzy but at the same time she was so jolly and the game appeared so comical to her, that she approached Kotlicki and called out in an entreating tone: "I desire only one thing: to be able to play. I ask only to be given rôles."

"We shall speak about that with the director and you will get them."

"Let us quit that, for it is getting wearisome, Kotlicki! Come over here, we are starting the second round of drinks."

They began to drink in earnest. The room became full of buzzing voices and cigarette smoke. Each of the assembled company argued and persuaded separately, and everyone shouted nonsense.

Majkowska leaned with her elbows upon the table and, beating time with a knife against a bottle of champagne, sang gayly.

The directress argued loudly with Mimi. Topolski was silent and drank to himself alone. Wawrzecki was relating various funny anecdotes to Janina, while Glogowski, Glas, and Kotlicki were engaged in a controversy about the public.

Janina laughed and bickered with Wawrzecki, but already the wine had taken such an effect upon her that she hardly knew what she was doing. The room whirled around with her and the candles elongated themselves to the size of torches.

Once she would feel a mad desire to dance, then again to launch bottles like ducks into the large mirrors which appeared to be water to her; or again, she tried hard to understand what Glogowski was just then saying. Glogowski, all flushed and tipsy, with disheveled hair and with his necktie on his back, was shouting, waving his hands, striking his fist against Glas's stomach instead of the table.

Glogowski shouted on: "To the dogs with the public's judgment! I tell you the play is bad! And if the audience applauded it and you now praise it, that is the best proof that I am right. There were a thousand of you; it is so hard for a thousand people to agree upon the truth. The individual alone is a thinking man, but the multitude is an ignorant herd that knows nothing."

"The multitude is a great man, proclaims an old proverb," whispered Kotlicki sententiously.

"It proclaims nonsense! The multitude is nothing but a big noise, a big illusion, a big hallucination," retorted Glogowski.

"Master, you seem to be devilishly sure of yourself."

"Dilettante, I merely know myself."

"By ginger! so many crazes in such a weak box!" whispered Glas, feeling Glogowski's chest.

"Genius does not abide in meat. A fat man is merely a fat animal. A lofty soul abhors fat. A healthy stomach and normality denote merely the average mortal and the average mortal is nothing but a boor."

"And such paradoxes are merely chaff."

"For asses and *pseudo-intelligents a.*"

"*Dixit*, brother! The Rhenish speaks through your lips."

"Begin all over again!" interrupted Glas, grabbing them both around the neck.

"If it is to drink, good; if it is to talk, I'll say good night!" yelled Kotlicki.

"Then let us drink!"

"Wawrzecki, dog's face! Get Mimi and another girl and we'll arrange a little chorus."

They immediately got together and intoned a gay song. Only Glogowski did not sing, for he leaned against Cabinski and fell fast asleep and Janina's head was so heavy that she could not utter a single tone.

The singing continued with increasing gayety, while Janina felt an irresistible drowsiness overpowering her, felt herself reeling from her chair.

Later she was half-conscious of someone supporting her, covering her, leading her and felt that she was riding in a hack. She felt something near her which she could not make out, felt a hot breath on her face, and arms stealing about her waist; she heard the rumble of wheels and with difficulty distinguished a voice whispering into her ear:—"I love you, I love you!" but she could not understand what it all meant.

Suddenly she trembled, for she felt hot kisses upon her mouth. She sprang up violently and recovered her senses.

Kotlicki was sitting beside her, holding her about the waist and kissing her. She wanted to shove him away from her, but her hands dropped heavily to her side; she wanted to scream out loud, but had no strength left; drowsiness overpowered her again and threw her into a lethargy, as it were.

Finally, the hack stopped and the sudden silence awakened her. She saw that she was standing on the sidewalk and that Kotlicki was ringing the doorbell of some house.

"God! God!" she whispered in bewilderment, unable to understand where she was.

Only then did Janina realize everything in a flash when Kotlicki drew close to her and whispered sweetly: "Come!"

She tore herself away from him with the force of great fear. He tried to put his arm about her again but she shoved him back with such violence that he went hurtling against the wall and then she ran as though bereft of her senses, for it seemed to her that he was pursuing, that he was already catching up with her and ready to seize her. Her heart beat like a trip hammer and her face burned with shame and terror.

"God! God!" she breathed, running ever faster.

The streets were deserted and she was frightened by the sound of her own footsteps, by the hacks that she met at the street corners, by the shadows that fell from the house walls and by that awful stony silence of the sleeping city in which there seemed to tremble sounds of weeping, sobs, and some horrible, dissolute laughter and drunken cries that made her shudder. She paused in the shadow of a doorway, looked about her in terror, and gradually remembered all that had happened: the play, the supper, how she had drunk, the singing and how someone was again forcing her to drink; and amid all those confused fragments of her memory there appeared the long equine face of Kotlicki, the ride in the hack, and his kisses!

"The vile wretch! The vile wretch!" she whispered to herself, recovering herself entirely; and she clenched her fists until the nails dug into her flesh, so violent a wave of anger and hatred surged through her. She was choking with tears of helplessness and such humiliation that she sobbed spasmodically as she returned home.

It was already dawning.

Sowinska opened the door for her and grumbled in irritation: "You should have come home earlier, instead of waking people at this hour of the night."

Janina did not answer, bowing her head as under a blow.

"The base wretches! The base wretches!" That was the one cry that arose in her heart, filled with rebellion and hatred.

Janina no longer felt the shame and the humiliation, but only a boundless rage. She ran about the room as though she were mad, unknowingly ripped her waist and, unable to control her fury, fell exhausted upon her bed with her clothes on.

Her sleep was one dreadful torment. She sprang up every minute with a cry as though to run away, then again, she raised her hand as though with a glass full of wine and shouted through her sleep: *Vive!* She would begin to sing or to cry every now and then with her feverish lips: "The base wretches! The base wretches!"

# CHAPTER IX

IN a few days after the première of *The Churls*, which remained upon the bill, but attracted ever smaller audiences, Glogowski came to Janina's home.

"What is the matter with you...?" she exclaimed, extending her hand in friendly greeting.

"Nothing. . . . Well, I improved my play a little. Did you read the criticisms?"

"Some of them."

"I have brought all the reviews," said Glogowski. "I'll read them."

He began to read.

One of the important weeklies maintained that *The Churls* was a very good, original, and superbly realistic play; that with Glogowski there had, at last, appeared a real dramatist who had let a current of fresh air into the stagnant and anæmic atmosphere of our dramatic creativity, and had given us real people and real life. The only cause for regret was that the staging of the play was beneath criticism and the acting of it, with one or two exceptions, scandalous.

The reviewer of one of the most estimable dailies for two whole days rambled on in a special supplement about the history of the theater in France and about German actors, he discussed theatrical novelties and after every two paragraphs or so would remark in parenthesis: "I saw him at the *Odéon*," "I heard this at the *Burg Theater*," "I admired such acting in London," etc. Then he adduced various theatrical anecdotes, praised actors who had died half a century ago, harked back to the past of the stage, spoke in several paragraphs about the red rags of radicalism that had begun to appear on the stage, praised with paternal indulgence the actors appearing in *The Churls*, flattered Cabinski and wound up by saying that he would probably give his opinion of the play itself only after the author had written another one, for this one was merely to be forgiven a novice.

A third reviewer contended that the play was not at all bad and would even be excellent, if the author had chosen to honor theatrical traditions and added music and dances to it.

A fourth took a diametrically opposite viewpoint, maintaining that the play was positively worthless, that it was rubbish, but that the author possessed at least the one merit that he had avoided the cut and dried formulas by failing to introduce the usual songs and dances which always lower the value of folk plays.

In the fifth review a "specialist" on garden-theaters wrote about a hundred paragraphs somewhat to this effect: "*The Churls* by Mr. Glogowski—hm! … not a bad thing … it would even be entirely good . . . but . . . although, considering again … at any rate … one must have the courage to tell the truth. … At all events … be that as it may … (with a little qualifying phrase) the author has a talent. The play is … hm ... let us see, how can we define it? About two months ago I wrote something about it, so I refer those that are interested to my former article. … They played it excellently,"—and he enumerated the entire cast, placing beside the name of each actress a sugary epithet, and an ingratiating remark, a polite description, a melancholy equivocation and an empty phrase.

"What do you call all that?" inquired Janina.

"A libretto for an operetta. Entitle it *Theatrical Criticisms* and set it to music and you will have such a show that the whole nation will flock to it as to a church festival."

"And what answer did you give to all that?"

"I? . . . Nothing, of course! I merely turned my back on them and, since I have a splendid plan for a new play, I shall immediately start working on it. I have received a job as a dramatic coach at Radomsk and I shall go there for a half year. I am only waiting for the final notification."

"Is it absolutely necessary for you to go?"

"Yes, I must! Dramatic coaching is my only means of support. For two months I have been without any occupation and now I am penniless. I presented the play at my own expense, paid my respects to the public, had a good time at Warsaw and now it is time to quit! It is time to ring down the curtain so that I may prepare for another farce. Good-bye, Miss Janina. Before I leave, I'll drop in here or at the theater."

He shook hands with her, exclaimed, "May the deuce take me!" and hurried away.

Janina was sad. She had become so accustomed to Glogowski, to his eccentricities, paradoxes, and to that rough and ready manner which was merely a screen for his shyness and hypersensitive delicacy that regret filled her at the thought that she was now to remain alone.

She had no more money left and was living solely on what she received at the theater. Janina dared not admit it to herself, but with each new request for money she would be reminded of her home and of those times when it was unnecessary for her to think of anything, for she had all she needed. She felt deeply humiliated by this almost daily begging for a few meager copecks, but there was no way out of it, unless it was the one that she constantly read in the gray eyes of Sowinska and saw exemplified in the life of her companions.

Almost each evening Janina would stroll on Theater Place. If she was in a great hurry, she would only pass through the place, get a glimpse of the Grand Theater and return home again, but if she had plenty of time she would find a seat on the square or on a bench near the tramcar station and from there gaze at the rows of columns, at the lofty profile of the theater's façade and lose herself in dreaming. She somehow felt that those walls drew her irresistibly to them. She experienced moments of deep delight when passing under the colonnade, or when in the calm of a bright night she viewed the long gray mass of the edifice. That huge stone giant seemed to speak to her and she would listen to the whispers, the echoes, and the sounds that floated from it. Spread out before her in the dim twilight and visible to her soul alone, there would pass before her imagination the scenes that were acted there not long ago.

An additional reason for losing herself in dreams was to dull the pinch of poverty, that had become more acute, for the second half of the theatrical season, from a financial standpoint, was a great deal worse than the first. The attendance was increasingly smaller because of the continual rains and the cold evenings and, of course, the pay of the actors was proportionately smaller.

It often happened that Cabinski in the middle of a performance would take the cash box and make away with it under the pretext that he was ill, leaving only a few rubles to be divided among the company and, if he was caught before he made his escape, he would almost cry.

And if he led anyone by the arm in a friendly manner to the box office it was a prearranged sign for Gold, who was to say that there was no money to be had. If he did not lead a person in this manner, the treasurer would assume a worried look and complain: "I haven't even enough to pay the gas bills and where am I going to get the money for the rent? Why, there isn't enough to pay running expenses."

"Let him have at least something. Perhaps we can put off the payment of some bill to-day . . ." Cabinski would pretend to intercede.

He would then leave an order for the payment of the money and walk away. But it almost always so happened that Gold did not have the sum for which the order was made out. The amount paid was always short, even if it were only by a few copecks. The actors called him all sorts of names, but each took what was offered.

Gold pretended to be insulted and usually appealed to the directress, who would always sit in the box office whenever she was not taking part in the play. Cabinska would then sharply reproach the actors and loudly praise the honesty of Gold, who with the small salary that he received helped his sister, in addition to supporting himself. Gold would beam with joy at the remembrance of his sister; his eyes would flash with tenderness and at such moments he would fervently promise to pay the missing amount on the following day without fail; but he never paid.

The performances were rattled off to get through with them, for the general disorder caused by Cabinski's overthieveries was growing ever greater and, moreover, the nearness of the departure for Warsaw, the debts in which all were swamped, the approach of winter and the worry over securing new engagements did not put anyone in a mood for playing.

And all the while Cabinski, kissed everyone and promised to pay, but never did so. He knew how to arrange matters so skillfully and acted so excellently the part of a man worried about the welfare of everyone that Janina feeling his troubles and believing him, often lacked the courage to remind him of the money he owed her. Moreover, she knew that between the director and his wife there went on a continual battle over expenses and that the nurse often bought various things for the children out of her own sayings, while Cabinska would sit twice as long at the pastry shop to avoid hearing the complaints.

Slowly, but in an ever narrowing circle, poverty hemmed Janina in and clouded her face with ceaseless worry.

Janina suffered all the more in her present condition because she was unable to seclude herself from other people as she used to do at Bukowiec after every quarrel with her father. She could not rave with the gales and calm herself inwardly by sheer physical exhaustion. She tramped about the city but everywhere she met too many people. She would have gladly confided to Glogowski all that troubled her, but had not the courage to do so, for she was restrained by pride. Glogowski seemed to guess her condition, or at least her worries, and would often remind her that she ought to tell him everything . . . everything. But she did not do so.

She stayed at home as little as possible, and whenever she entered the house she tried to do it so quietly that no one might hear her. It was not the possibility that she might find herself thrown out into the street on the morrow that frightened her, but the fact that Mme. Anna or Sowinska might say to her curtly: "Pay what you owe me."

But that moment finally arrived. While eating her dinner Janina knew the inevitable had come. She caught just one glance of Mme. Anna's eyes while she was serving the soup and in them read everything.

After the meal, which to Janina had been torture, Mme. Anna followed her immediately and, in the most unconcerned manner, began to relate something about a fantastic customer. Then, suddenly, as though she had remembered something, she said: "Oh yes, I almost forgot! Perhaps you will let me have that half-month's rent, for I must pay the landlord to-day."

"I haven't the money to-day . . . " she wanted to add something else, but her voice failed her.

"What do you mean? Please give me what you owe me! I hope you don't think that I can feed anyone free of charge . . . just for fun, or for the sake of having them as an ornament in my home! A fine ornament indeed, that stays up all night and comes home only in the wee hours of the morning!"

"You needn't fear that I won't pay you!" cried Janina suddenly aroused.

"I need the money right away!"

"You will have it ... in an hour!" answered Janina, making some sudden determination; she glanced with such scorn at Mme. Anna that the latter left without a word, slamming the door after her.

From her companions Janina had heard something about the pawnshop and she immediately went there to pawn her gold bracelet, the only one that she possessed.

On returning home she immediately paid Mme. Anna, who was surprised, but not very polite.

Having done that Janina added: "I will have my meals at the restaurant; I don't want to trouble you."

"Just as you like. If things here don't suit you, you are free to do as you please!" whispered the deeply humiliated Mme. Anna.

By that one act Janina incurred the enmity of the whole house.

"I will sell everything I possess . . . even to the last button!" she said to herself with bitter resolve.

And Janina calculated that for one half of what she had been paying Mme. Anna she could get all the food that she needed. Wolska directed her to a cheap lunch-room and she went there for her dinners; when she had not money enough for that, a roll with a sardine had to suffice her for the entire day.

But one day the theater was closed, for there were only twenty rubles in the treasury; on the following day the performance was postponed because of a heavy downpour. Janina, like everyone else, did not receive a single copeck from Cabinski and during those two days had absolutely nothing to eat.

This first hunger which she could not appease because she had nothing to appease it with had a fearful effect upon her. She felt within herself a strange and unceasing pain.

"Starvation! Starvation!" Janina whispered to herself in terror.

Hitherto she had known it by its name only. Now she wondered at that sensation of hunger within her. It seemed strange to her that she felt like eating and hadn't the money even to buy herself a roll!

"Is it possible that I have nothing to eat?" Janina asked herself.

From the kitchen there was wafted to her the smell of frying meat. She shut the door tightly for that smell nauseated her.

Janina remembered with a strange emotion that the majority of great artists in various ages also suffered poverty and hunger. The thought consoled her for a while. She felt as though she were anointed with the first pang of martyrdom for art's sake.

She smiled in the mirror with a melancholy look at her yellowish and worn face. She tried to read to rid herself, as it were, of her own personality, but she could not, for she constantly felt that growing hunger.

She gazed out of the window at the long yard surrounded on all sides by the high windows of the adjoining houses, but she saw how in a few houses people were sitting down to the table and saw the workmen in the yard also eating their dinner from small clay pots. She quickly drew back from the window for she felt hunger like a steel hand with sharp claws tearing her even more violently.

"Everybody is eating!" Janina said to herself as though this was the first time that she had taken note of that fact.

Later she lay down and slept until the evening without going either to the rehearsal or to Cabinska's home, but she felt even weaker upon awaking and had a painful dizziness in her head, while that keen and constant sapping sensation within herself tormented her so that she wept.

In the evening in the dressing-room a boisterous gayety possessed Janina; she laughed continually, joked and made fun of her companions quarreled over some trifle with Mimi and then flirted from the stage with the occupants of the front row of seats.

When the counselor appeared behind the scenes right after the first act with a box of candy, Janina greeted him joyously and pressed his hand so tightly that the old man became confused. Afterwards she sat down in some dark corner, waiting for the stage- director to cry: "Enter!" When the darkness and silence enveloped her, she broke into convulsive sobbing.

After the performance Janina received a quadruple payment on account—two whole rubles. Cabinski gave them to her himself in secret so that the others might not see it.

Janina went out for supper on the veranda and became intoxicated with one glass of whiskey so that she herself requested Wladek to escort her home.

From that evening Wladek followed her like a shadow and began openly to show her his love, paying no attention to the fact that his mother was asking everybody in the theater about him and constantly tracking both him and Janina.

One day Glogowski came rushing into Janina's home and cried out already from the doorway: "Well, I have come back again to my Zulus! . . . "

He flung his hat on a trunk, sat on the bed and began to roll a cigarette.

Janina gazed at him calmly and thought how strange it was that the coming of this friend who had interested her so deeply in the past should now leave her so indifferent.

"So you do not weep with joy at seeing me again, eh? Ha! I'll have to resign myself to it. No doubt the dogs alone will weep over me! May the deuce take me! But don't you happen to know what is the matter with Kotlicki? He does not come to the theater any more and I can't find him anywhere. He must have journeyed somewhere."

"I have not seen him since the night of that supper," answered Janina slowly.

"There must be some reason for his disappearance! Probably some adventure, some love affair, some . . . But why should I bother about such a green monkey, eh? Isn't that true?"

"Indeed it is!" whispered Janina, turning her face toward the window.

"Oh! and what does that mean?" he cried, glancing sharply into her eyes. "Goodness, how you have changed! Sunken and glassy eyes, yellowish complexion, sharpened features. . . . What does it all mean?" he asked in a quieter tone.

Suddenly he struck his hand to his forehead and began to run up and down the room like a maniac.

"What an idiot I am. What a monster! Here I am parading about Warsaw, while here real, artistic poverty has quartered itself in earnest! Miss Janina," he cried, taking her hand and looking steadily into her eyes, "Miss Janina! I want you to tell me everything as at confession. May the deuce take me, but you must tell me!"

Janina was silent; but seeing his honest face and hearing that sympathetic voice whose accents had a strange way of gripping one's heart, she suddenly felt overcome by feeling, and tears stood in her eyes. She could not speak for emotion.

"Well, well, there's no use crying, for I shall depart anyway," he said jokingly to hide his own emotion. "Now, just listen to me . . . but without any protests or loud opposition, for I detest parliamentarism! I see you are in poverty and theatrical poverty in the bargain. . . . Well, I happen to know what it's like. Now, for goodness' sake, stop blushing. Poverty that is honestly acquired is not anything to be ashamed of! It's nothing but an ordinary smallpox which all people who are worth anything in this world have to pass through. Ho! ho! I have been playing blind-man's buff with troubles since many a year! Well, I shall end what I am saying in a gallop. Let us do this . . . "

He turned around, took from his pocket-book thirty rubles, that is, all the money that had been sent him for his journey, placed it under Janina's pillow and returned to his former seat.

"'Now we are agreed, are we not, my cousin . . .' said Louis XI after beheading the Duke of Anjou. I will accept no appeal and if you dare to . . . "

He grasped his hat and extending his hand, said softly: "Good-bye, Miss Janina."

With a desperate motion, Janina hastily barred the door with her body.

"No, no! Do not humiliate me! I am unfortunate enough as it is," she whispered, firmly holding his hand.

"There you have a woman's philosophy! May the deuce take me, but that which I did is as natural as the fact that I will some day blow out my brains and that you will become a great actress!"

Janina began to expostulate with him, and finally to urge him to take back his money, saying that she did not need it, that she would not accept it, and showing a deep aversion to being helped.

Glogowski became gloomy and said roughly: "What! May the deuce take me, but of the two of us I certainly am not the fool! But no! I refuse to get provoked about it. I shall sit down calmly and talk it over with you seriously. I don't want you to get angry at me over such an empty thing as money. You don't want to take it, although you need it, and why? Because a false shame deters you, because you have been taught that such simple human things as helping one another lowers one's pride. Such conceptions are already becoming putrid. To the museum with them! Those are foolish and evil prejudices. May the deuce take me, but it requires a European brain and hysterical subtlety to hesitate to accept money from a human being like yourself when you are in need. Why and to what purpose do you think the human herd unites itself into some form of society? Is it mutually to devour and rob one another or mutually to help one another? I know you will tell me that it is otherwise, but I answer you that that is precisely why we have so much evil in this world. And once we recognize a thing as evil we ought to shun it. Man ought to do good. That is his duty. To do good is the wisest mathematics. But Great Scott! What's the use of my making so much ado about it!" he cried in irritation.

He continued to speak for a long while yet, scoffed, swore occasionally, shouted: "May the deuce take me," and raged fiercely, but in his voice there was so much sincere and deep friendliness, such heartfelt kindness, that Janina, although she was not at all convinced, accepted his proffered aid with a grateful handclasp only because she did not wish to offend him by refusing.

"Well, that is what I like! And now . . . good-bye!" he said, arising to go.

"Good-bye! I wish to thank you once more and I am so very grateful and obligated to you . . . " murmured Janina.

"If you only knew how much kindness people have shown me! I would like to repay only one hundredth part of it to others. I will add yet that we shall no doubt meet each other in the spring."

"Where?" asked Janina.

"Bah! I don't know! but that it will be in the theater of that I am sure, for I have determined to join the theater in the spring, if only for a half year so that I may gain a better knowledge of the stage."

"Oh, that's an excellent idea!"

"Now we are even with one another, as my father used to say after he had massaged my hide so that it shone as though freshly tanned. I leave you my address and say nothing, only remind you that you are to tell me everything by letter . . . everything! Do you give me your word?"

"I give you my word!" Janina answered gravely.

"I trust your word as though it were that of a man, although with women a word of honor is usually an empty word only, which they make use of, but never fulfill. Good-bye!"

Glogowski pressed both her hands firmly, raised them a little as though he were eager to kiss them, but quickly dropped them again, glanced into her eyes, laughed a trifle unnaturally—and departed.

Janina sat thinking for a long time about him. She felt so deep a gratitude toward him and felt so cheered and strengthened by her talk with him that she regretted she did not know on what train Glogowski was leaving, for she had a desire to see him once more.

Then again, there arose in her something that protested loudly against the aid he had given her, something that saw in that kindness an insult.

"Alms!" Janina whispered bitterly and felt a burning pain of humiliation.

"Can't I live alone, can't I get along by my own unaided strength, can't I be sufficient unto myself? Must I continually lean on someone for support? Must there always be someone watching over me? The others know how to help themselves, why can't I?" she asked herself.

Janina pondered over this, but a moment later she went to the pawnshop to redeem her bracelet and on the way bought herself an inexpensive autumn hat.

Life dragged on for her slowly, sluggishly, and wearily.

Janina was sustained only by the hope, or rather by a deep faith that all this would change radically and soon, and in this longing anticipation she began to pay ever more attention to Wladek. She knew that he loved her. She listened almost daily to his confessions and proposals, smiling deep within herself and thinking that in spite of all she could not become that which her companions became. Their mode of life aroused a deep aversion in her for she felt a truly organic revulsion to all forms of filth. But these attentions of Wladek had at least this effect, that they awakened in her for the first time conscious thoughts of love.

She dreamed at moments of loving a man to whom she could give herself entirely and for all time; she dreamed of a united life full of ecstasy and love, such a love as poets presented in their plays; and then there would pass before her mind the figures of all the great lovers about whom she had read, passionate whispers, burning embraces, volcanic passions and that whole Titanic love life, the remembrance of which sent a tremor of delight through her.

Janina did not know whence these dreams came, but they would visit her ever more frequently in spite of the poverty which again began to grow more distressing, and the frequent hunger that gripped her as it were in bony embrace. Her bracelet again went to the pawnshop, for she continually had to buy some new article of wear for the stage, so that often she was forced to deny herself food only to be able to buy what she needed. New plays were continually presented to draw the public but success was as far off as ever.

Such a situation harassed and tormented Janina dreadfully, robbing her of her strength, but it also awakened a rebellion which began to seethe silently within her. She felt at first an indefinable animosity toward everybody. She regarded with a fierce envy the women whom she met on the street.

Often, she would be seized with a mad desire to stop one of those well-dressed ladies and ask her whether she knew what poverty was. She observed intently their faces, their clothes, and their smiles and came to the painful conclusion that these ladies could not know that there were other people who suffered, wept, and were hungry. But later Janina began to reason that she herself was dressed in the same way as these other women; that there may be among them others in the same plight as she, and that perhaps unknowingly they passed her on the way, hungry and desperate, hurling the same glances at other passers-by that she did. She tried to distinguish the faces of such sufferers in the multitude, but could not. All appeared to be satisfied and happy.

Then, something like the triumph of her own ascendancy over this well-dressed and well-fed multitude lit up Janina's face. She felt herself to be far superior to this world of everyday mortals.

"I have an idea, an aim!" she thought. "What do they live for? What is their object in life?" she would often ask herself. And unable to answer that question, Janina would smile pityingly at the emptiness of their existence.

"A race of butterflies that knows not whence, nor why, nor to what end their life has been given them!"—she whispered, sating herself to her heart's content with that silent scorn of people that was growing to abnormal proportions in her.

Cabinska, Janina now hated with her whole soul, for although Pepa always treated her with a sugary affability, she never paid her for Yadzia's piano lessons, taking advantage of Janina's situation and abilities with a hypocritical smile of friendliness. Janina could not sever relations with her, for she felt distinctly that behind that mask of politeness that Pepa wore there was hidden a fury who would not forgive her that.

Furthermore, she hated Cabinska as a woman, a mother, and an actress. She had come to know her well, and moreover, in her present period of continual strain and struggle, she had either to love or hate someone immensely. Janina did not love anyone as yet, but already she hated.

"Do you know it is hardly believable that such an incompetent judge as the directress should herself assign the rôles for all our plays!" she once remarked to Wladek greatly embittered by the fact that she had been ignored in the selection of the cast for an old melodramatic caricature entitled *Martin, the Foundling*.

"It is too bad that you did not ask her for a rôle for, as you see, the director can do nothing," said Wladek.

"Quite true! That's a good idea! I'll try it to-morrow."

"Ask her for the rôle of 'Mary' in *Doctor Robin* which we are to present next week. Some amateur wishes to join our company and he is to make his début as 'Garrick.'"

"What sort of rôle is that of 'Mary?'"

"A splendid display rôle! I think that you would act it superbly. I can bring you the play, if you wish."

"Good! we can read it together."

On the morrow Janina received a solemn promise from Cabinska that she would be given the part.

In the afternoon Wladek brought *Doctor Robin*. This was his first visit to Janina's home, so he took care to appear particularly handsome, elegant, polite, and somewhat absent-minded. He acted love and respect for Janina with the skill of a virtuoso; he was very quiet, as though from an excess of happiness.

'For the first time I feel shy and happy!" he said, kissing Janina's hand.

"Why shy? You are alway so sure of yourself on the stage!" she answered, a bit confused.

"Yes, on the stage, where one only plays happiness, but not here . . . where I am really happy."

"Happy?" she repeated.

Wladek glanced at Janina with such passionate intensity, with such mastery of facial expression, accentuated by a rapturous smile, simulating the ecstasy and transport of love, that had he shown this on the stage he would have been warmly applauded.

Janina understood him excellently and something stirred in her as though some new string in her heart had been lightly plucked.

Wladek began to read the play. With each of "Mary's" words, Janina's enthusiastic nature burst forth anew. With bated breath, and eyes fixed on Wladek, she listened, not daring to mar, either by word or gesture, the impression that his reading made on her. She feared to dispel the charm that spoke through his eloquent voice and in the velvety softness of his black eyes.

When he had finished reading, the girl cried out in rapture: "What a splendid rôle!"

"I am willing to wager that you will make a furore in it," remarked Wladek.

"Yes . . . I feel that I could play it fairly well. 'Garrick, that creator of souls, so mighty in *Coriolanus!*'" she whispered, repeating a remembered line of the play.

And Janina's face glowed with such fervor, so radiant did she become with her deep inner joy, that Wladek scarcely recognized her.

"You are an enthusiast," he said.

"Yes, because I love art! Give all for art and everything is contained in art! . . . that is my motto. Beyond art I see almost nothing," answered Janina suddenly kindling anew with ardor.

"Even love?" asked Wladek.

"But art appears to me to be a greater and completer expression of the ideal than love . . . " answered Janina.

"But it is more alien to human beings and not so necessary to life as is love. Without art the world could exist, but without love . . . never! Moreover, art causes more painful disappointments than love."

"But it also gives greater joys. Love is an individual emotion; art is a social emotion, a synthesis. One loves it with one's humanity, one suffers for it, but only through art does one sometimes become immortal!"

"Those are dreams. Thousands have given their lives to become convinced of that and thousands have cursed that unattainable mirage."

"But those thousands had their lives filled with that mirage and felt more than one can feel, who dreams about nothing."

"But since they were not happy, what is it all worth?'

"And are most people happy?"

"A thousandfold more so than we!"

189

Wladek emphasized that "we" significantly.

"Never!" cried Janina, "for our happiness lies in pain as it does in joy, in dejection as well as ecstasy. Even this in itself is happiness: to be able to develop one's self spiritually; to reach far out into infinity with the arms of desire; to create new worlds in our mind, larger and more beautiful than those surrounding us; to chant, even through tears and pain, hymns to beauty and immortality; to dream, but to dream so intensely as to forget about life entirely and to live in dreams alone!"

Janina felt so great a flood of happiness and inspiration flowing into her soul that she spoke, as it were, only in periods of her thought, so that she might express herself at least in part. She spoke, entirely forgetful of the fact that some one was listening to her and spun out aloud ever grander and ever more evanescent dreams.

Wladek at first listened attentively, but later grew impatient.

"A comédienne!" he thought with irony. And he was sure that Janina was unfurling before him the peacock feathers of fervor and enthusiasm merely to fascinate and conquer him. He did not answer or interrupt her, for it finally began to bore him.

"That rôle of 'Mary' is a trifle too sentimental . . . " added Janina after a longer silence.

"To me it seemed merely lyrical," answered Wladek.

"I should like some time to play 'Ophelia.'"

"Are you familiar with *Hamlet?*" asked Wladek, somewhat surprised.

"During the last two years I have read nothing but dramas and dreamed of the stage," she answered simply.

"Truly it is worth bending the knee before such enthusiasm!"

"Why? All that is necessary is to help it, to give it a field, an opportunity. . . . "

"If I only could. . . . Believe me when I say, that with my whole heart I desire to see you reach the heights of art."

"I believe you," Janina answered in a quieter tone. "And I thank you very much for *Doctor Robin.*"

"May I copy out the rôle for you?"

"I will copy it myself; it will give me a certain pleasure."

"While you are learning it, I could act as a prompter for you, if you like."

"Oh, I should not want to take up any of your time . . ."

"Exclude a few hours each day for the performance and the rest of my time is yours to dispose of as you will," he said with fervor.

They gazed at each other a moment.

Janina gave Wladek her hand; he held and kissed it for a long time.

"Beginning with to-morrow I shall start to learn the part for I have a day off," said Janina.

"I also do not appear on the stage to-morrow."

Wladek went out a little angry at himself, for although he called Janina a "comédienne" she had made him feel abashed with her simplicity and enthusiasm. Moreover, he felt in her a certain intellectual and artistic superiority.

Janina feverishly applied herself to the study of *Doctor Robin*. In a few days she knew not only the rôle of "Mary," but had memorized the entire play. So intensely eager was she to play the rôle, that it seemed as though she were staking her whole life on this performance. Her former dreams that had been subdued a bit by poverty and the feverish life of the theater now again burst forth with a flaming intensity that dazzled and hypnotized her. The theater again took so powerful a hold on Janina that there was no room in her consciousness for anything else. In her hours of ecstasy it appeared to her like a mystic altar suspended high above the gray vale of everyday life and glowing with flames like a second burning bush of Moses; it seemed to her like a miracle that endured eternally.

Wladek came to see Janina each day in the interval between the rehearsal and the performance, although he was already beginning to be immensely bored by her endlessly repeated raptures and was growing impatient over the fact that in her mad absorption in art she did not pay much attention to him. He could not penetrate her morbid enthusiasm, as he called it, with his love, but he nevertheless continued to go to her.

He began to desire Janina's love ever more strongly. He was invited by her naïveté and by the talent which he felt she possessed. Moreover, he had long since desired just such an elegant and educated mistress. He wanted by all means to possess this refined and genteel girl, who was so different from his former mistresses and who captivated him by the charm of her superiority. His triumph would be all the greater, he told himself, because of the fact that she seemed to him one of those ladies of the fashionable world upon whom he would often cast covetous glances in the Ujazdowskie Allées.

Janina had not told Wladek that she loved him, but he already saw it in her eyes and spun an ever stronger web about her made up of smiles, passionate words, sighs, and exaggerated respect.

For Janina this was the most beautiful period that she had known in her life. Poverty she treated with scorn, as though it were only a temporary thing that would soon pass away.

Sowinska, after Wladek's frequent visits, became more intimate and friendly with Janina and advised her to sell those parts of her wardrobe which she did not need, even offering to do it for her.

And so life went on for Janina who was oblivious to everything else but that performance of *Doctor Robin* which she awaited with the greatest impatience. She lived, as it were, in a troubled dream. Through the prism of dreams the world again appeared brighter to her, and people kind. She forgot about everything, even about Glogowski, whose recent letter she laid away only half read, for she now lived entirely in the future. She fortified herself against the present with dreams of what was to come.

Furthermore, Janina loved Wladek. She did not know how it had come about, but she now knew that she could not do without him. She felt very happy and peaceful, when, leaning on his arm, she walked along the streets and listened to his low, melodious voice. The soft velvety glances of his dark eyes made her glow with passion and a sweet helplessness. . . .

Everything about him attracted her. He appeared so beautiful upon the stage! He acted with such fervor and lyricism the parts of unhappy lovers in the melodramas! He spoke, moved about and posed with such charming simplicity. He was the favorite of the public; even the press bestowed frequent praises upon him and predicted a brilliant artistic future for him.

It pleased Janina to see him applauded on the stage. And so skillfully did he know how to exhibit the resources of his brain, that he was generally taken for an educated man, while in reality he possessed only cleverness and the brazenness of a Warsaw loafer and trickster. Moreover, for Janina he was the first and only man to whom she had ever surrendered herself. It seemed to her that this bound them for all time and indissolubly.

It happened, as it were, of itself, after one of the rehearsals of *Doctor Robin* in which Wladek acted as a substitute in the rôle of "Garrick." When they had left the theater he spoke or rather declaimed to her about love with a volcanic outburst of passion and accentuated his emotion with such pathos that he stirred her to the very depths of her soul. She felt sudden tears of tenderness welling up in her eyes; and a desire for tremendous happiness through life and death remained in her dreaming heart. Her whole soul was absorbed in the desire for love.

Janina did not even know what was happening to her, for she could not resist the fascination of his voice. That musical pleading of love, those burning kisses, and those passionate glances flooded her entire being with an overwhelming and mad desire for joy. She abandoned herself to him with the passiveness of a fascinated creature, without a word of protest or resistance, but also without a consciousness of what she was doing; in a word, she was hypnotized.

She did not even know what it was in him that she loved: the actor masterfully playing upon her emotions and enthusiasm, or the man. Janina did not think of this. She loved him because she loved him and because he personified the theater and art for her.

It seemed to Janina that through his eyes she saw farther and deeper. Her soul was growing (as the peasants describe certain stages in the development of youth), so besides her distant plans of fame in the future, she needed something for herself alone, she needed to strengthen herself and support herself on some loving heart which would at the same time serve as a stepping-stone for her own elevation. She no longer felt lonely, for she could now reveal to Wladek her most secret thoughts, dreams, and projects for the future and go over various heroic rôles together with him. He was a sort of physical complement of her, and outlet for her excessive energy and dreams.

Janina did not submerge and lose herself in Wladek's being, but rather absorbed him into herself. And not for one moment did she think that she had surrendered herself to him, that he was henceforth her lover and lord and that she belonged to him! She did not even consider whether he had a soul or not. It sufficed her to know that he was handsome, popular, that he loved her and that she needed him. Even in her most intimate confidences and whispers of love there was a tone of unconscious superiority. She spoke with him continually but almost never asked him for his opinion and very seldom listened to his replies.

Wladek could not understand this, but he was conscious of it and it acted as an unpleasant restraint upon him, for in spite of their intimate relation, he could not feel at ease with her in his own way. It wounded his self-love, but he had no way of remedying it. He possessed her body, but not her soul—that mysterious something, that love that gives itself for life and eternity and makes of itself a footstool for the lover. This attitude of Janina's irritated him, but nevertheless attracted him so irresistibly that he doubled his pretenses of love, thinking that by a larger dose of sentimental falsehood, and a better acting of emotion he would at last captivate and conquer her completely. However, he did not succeed in doing so.

Janina, aside from this love, gradually renounced everything, yet in spite of that she felt content. She often suffered hunger, but it was enough for her to have Wladek at her side and to become absorbed in her rôle, to forget about the whole world.

The performance of *Doctor Robin* was postponed from day to day, for the amateur who was to make his début in it became ill. In the meanwhile, other plays had to be given; so Janina was forced to content herself with waiting. She was consumed by impatience and the ambition to rise at once above the throng of her companions and was also impelled by the hope of ending her poverty by this means and finally, by the need of her own soul which had formed its own conception of the character of "Mary" and had to give it forth.

Janina did not even pay attention to what was brewing behind the scenes where every day schemes and projects for new companies were formed, only to be abandoned after a few days. Krzykiewicz had already delicately suggested to Janina on a few occasions that, if she wished, she could secure an engagement with Ciepieszewski. She declined, for she remembered Topolski's project and wished to wait for its realization, knowing that he was counting on her for sure.

Topolski was in reality organizing a company. It was meant to be a secret as yet, but everyone knew about it. It was openly said that Mimi, Wawrzecki, Piesh with his wife, and a few of the younger forces had already signed a contract and that Topolski had quietly closed a deal for the Lubelsk Theater, a new building that had just been opened. It was known for certain that Kotlicki and others had advanced him the necessary capital.

Cabinski, of course, knew all about this and loudly ridiculed these projects. He knew very well that he could win back all those who had joined Topolski by merely giving them larger advances on their salaries. He predicted that Topolski would not hold out for one season and would go to smash, for he did not believe that anyone was willing to loan him money for organizing a new company.

"There are no longer any such fools!" he said aloud with conviction. What amused him most was Topolski's proposed reform of the theater which he unceremoniously termed an idiocy. Cabinski knew the public well and knew what it wanted.

Topolski held frequent *soirées* at his home to which he invited all those whom he might need. But he did not yet speak openly about his company, leaving that to Wawrzecki who treated the matter enthusiastically as though it were his own and used it to taunt Cabinski with and to create more frequent rumpuses about his overdue salary.

Janina was present at a few of these evenings at Topolski's house, but was bored by them, for the men would usually play cards, while the women, if they were not gossiping or complaining, would enclose themselves within a narrow circle for secret whispering from which they barred Janina, fearing that she might betray something to Cabinski, to whose home she went daily to give piano lessons.

At the last of these evenings, while they were having tea, Majkowska quietly begged Janina to stay a little longer, promising that she and Topolski would accompany her home.

Wladek never appeared at these affairs, for he was an open and stanch supporter of Cabinski.

After all the rest had gone Topolski sat opposite Janina and began to tell her about the company he was organizing.

"It will be an exemplary theater for true art! I have a splendid ensemble of actors; I have made a contract for one of the best theaters, the library is ready to be sent away and the costumes are already half completed, hence we have almost all that is needed."

"What are you still lacking?" asked Janina, determining immediately to ask for an engagement.

"A little money ... a mere trifle of about a thousand rubles as a working capital for the first month," answered Topolski.

"Couldn't you borrow it?"

"Yes . . . and that is precisely what I want to talk over with you in a friendly way, for we already count you as one of us. I will give you a good salary and alternating rôles with Mela for I know that you are a capable actress. You have the appearance, the voice and the temperament, and, aside from intelligence, that is just what is required to make an excellent actress."

"Oh thank you, thank you sincerely!" cried Janina beaming with joy. And so elated was she that she kissed Majkowska, who, as was her habit, was almost lying on the table and gazing absently at the lamp.

"But you must help us!" said Topolski after a short pause.

"I? What can I do? " she asked in surprise.

"A great deal! If you only want to . . ." he answered.

"Well! if you say that I can, then, of course I shall be glad to help, for it is not only my duty, but also in my own interest! But I'm very curious to know what I can do."

"It's a question of that one thousand rubles. The money is already assured, only there is one little condition . . . "

"What is it?" Janina asked curiously.

Topolski drew closer to her, took hold of her hands in a friendly way and only then answered:

"Miss Janina—not only our theater, but your entire artistic future depends on this, so I will tell you frankly that there is someone who is ready to give even two thousand rubles, but he said that he would give them only to you personally, otherwise not at all."

"Who is that person?" she asked uneasily.

"Kotlicki!"

Janina dropped her head and for a while a deep silence reigned in the room. Topolski gazed at her uneasily, while Majkowska had upon her face an indescribably derisive smile.

Janina almost cried out with pain, so repulsive did that name and proposal strike her and after a moment she arose from her chair and said in a determined voice: "No! I will not go to Kotlicki ... and that which you have proposed to me is insulting and outrageous! Only in the theater can people lose so entirely their moral sense as to persuade others to base acts and purposely push them into the mire of degradation, so that they themselves may profit. You have miscalculated this time, my dear sir! I have not fallen so low as that. What hurts me is that you could think even for a moment that I would agree to go to Kotlicki, to Kotlicki, who is more repulsive to me than the basest reptile!" she cried, carried away by passion.

"Miss Janina! Let us speak it over calmly and sensibly, without getting excited."

"You dare to tell me not to get excited?"

"I must, for you are simply inexperienced; consequently that which I ask of you appears to you as something monstrous, something that will immediately sink you in the mud, dishonor you, and shame you."

"For God's sake, what is it then, if not just that!" Janina cried in amazement.

"Let us stop playing a comedy, let us drop this game of hide-and-seek and look at things as they are and we shall see that I am not proposing anything out of the ordinary to you. What am I asking of you? Merely that you go to Kotlicki for the money which is to be the foundation of our common future, the money which will create our theater for us and without which none of us can budge from Warsaw. So what is there wrong in this? What wrong can there be in that which will make almost all of us happy?"

"What? Is it possible that you do not see any wrong in the fact that I, a woman should go alone to the home of a man? And for what will he give me that one thousand or two thousand rubles?"

"When you lived with Glogowski no one regarded it as wrong. Now, when you are living with Wladek who blames you for it? After all, what is there so dreadfully dishonorable about it? We all live that way; and are we thereby committing anything base? . . . No! for that is a secondary thing, for we have something more important in our minds: art!"

"No, I will not go!" answered Janina quietly, depressed by the discovery that they all knew about her relation with Wladek.

She continued to listen to Topolski without hearing or understanding his words. He began to expostulate with her, to beg, and to explain that they were all sacrificing their very lives for the theater, something more than the mere whim of a woman. He pointed out to her that by her refusal she would deal a mortal blow to the newly organized company; that they were all counting on her and would be grateful to her until death, for by her sacrifice she would insure the welfare of dozens of people; that the new theater would be connected with her name. He wished by all means to break down her opposition which he could not understand, but Janina remained unmoved.

"If my life itself depended on it, I would not go; I would prefer to die!" said Janina with final determination.

"Well then, good-bye!" answered Topolski angrily.

Janina kept looking at him and still wanted to explain herself more fully, but Majkowska threw her cloak over her shoulders for her, brutally placed her hat on her head, and showering her with insults, opened the door widely before her.

Janina like an automaton, permitted her to do what she wanted with her and, like an automaton she walked down the stairs and along the streets to her home.

She felt sorry for the new company and regretted the prospect that she was losing by breaking with Topolski but at the same time she felt an unbearable shame consuming her at the thought that these people should take her for such a degraded being by daring to make such proposals to her and expecting that she would fulfill them.

Janina could not calm herself. That night she dreamed now of Kotlicki, now of Wladek, then again of the theater. She heard how all were cursing and reviling her, she saw as it were, a band of people covered with rags and with hatred glowing in their eyes, pursuing her with curses and trying to beat her. In those vaguely outlined faces she recognized Mela, Topolski, Mimi, and Wawrzecki. Again, she dreamed that she was walking along the street and that everybody was staring at her so strangely and so horribly that she felt like sinking into the earth to avoid their glances; but she had no strength to move and that multitude slowly filed by her while Topolski stood pointing at her and crying in a loud and derisive voice: "Behold! she lived with Glogowski and is now the mistress of Wladek!"

Janina could not bear that; she screamed wildly in her sleep for she saw, as it were, her father approaching her with Krenska at his side, pointing at her and calling: "She lived with Glogowski and now is the mistress of Wladek!"

"God, oh God!" she moaned, writhing with the torment of that dream.

And the throng of familiar faces continued to grow. There appeared the priest from Bukowiec, the teachers of her boarding school, her former companions and Grzesikiewicz. All, all passed by her hastily and stared at her with such a dreadful, horrible smile that it pierced her like a dagger and scourged her like a whip.

Janina awoke with tear-streaming eyes and utterly exhausted.

Before the rehearsal Wladek came to see her. For the first time she threw herself into his arms of her own accord.

"They all know!" she whispered, hiding her face upon his breast.

Wladek immediately surmised what she meant and answered: "Well, what of it? Is it a crime?"

He sat down in an ill humor, began to rub his knee and tossed about angrily in his chair.

Janina noticed his mood and, forgetting about herself, inquired: "What is the matter with you? Are you ill?"

"There is nothing the matter with me, only I owe someone a few rubles and am unable to pay them back. I can't ask my mother for the money, for she is sick again and it would only finish her! Cabinski will not give it to me either, and I am at my wit's end!"

He was, of course, lying, for he had been playing cards the whole night long and had lost all he had. Janina remembered the help she had received from Glogowski, so without hesitation she took off her gold watch and chain and laid it before Wladek.

"I have no money. Take this and pawn it and pay your debt and what you have left over bring me back, for I also have nothing," she said heartily.

"No, I shall not take it! What do you want to do that for? I really don't need it. . . . My dear child! . . ." remonstrated Wladek in his first impulse of honesty.

"Please take it. . . . If you love me you will take it."

Wladek demurred a little while yet, but the thought struck him that with the money he might play again to win back what he had lost.

"No! What would that look like!" he whispered, his resistance growing ever weaker.

"Go right away and on your way back stop in for me and we shall have breakfast together," urged Janina.

Wladek kissed her, as though he were embarrassed, muttered something about gratitude, but finally took the watch and went to pawn it.

He returned quickly with thirty rubles. He immediately borrowed twenty from Janina and wanted even to give her a receipt for them, but she became so angry that he had to apologize to her. Then they went out to breakfast.

Thenceforward they lived together. At the theater everyone knew about their relation, but it was such a usual thing, that no one paid attention to it. Only Sowinska would sometimes taunt Janina on the score and slight her and, whereas not so long ago she had done nothing but praise Wladek, she now told the vilest sort of tales about him. She delighted in tormenting Janina in this manner, and avenged herself in this way for the loss of her son's love.

At last it was announced that stage rehearsals of *Doctor Robin* were to begin. Wladek brought this information to Janina, because for a few days she had been very weak and had not left her home at all. She felt an oppressive drowsiness and exhaustion and an unbearable pain in her back. Then again such a feeling of helplessness and discouragement would possess her that she wanted to cry and had no desire to stir from her bed, but lay for whole days, gazing blankly at the ceiling. The humming sensation in her head returned and she suffered such a burning thirst that nothing could quench it. However, on hearing that she was to take part in the play, Janina immediately felt well and strong again.

She went to the rehearsal, trembling with fear, but on seeing the person who was to play "Garrick," she quickly mastered herself. This amateur was hardly more than a boy, skinny, awkward, and simple-minded. He lisped and waddled about like a duck, but since he was the cousin of one of the influential journalists who backed him, he regarded everybody at the theater with a haughty expression and· treated them with an air of condescension. The members of the company delicately ridiculed him to his face and laughed loudly at him behind his back.

Everybody was present at the rehearsal, as though they had all agreed upon it beforehand.

No sooner did Janina enter upon the stage than Majkowska ostentatiously withdrew behind the scenes, while Topolski did not so much as nod his head to her in greeting. Janina realized that relations with them were severed for good, but she had no time to think about it, for the rehearsal began immediately. Despite the fact that she had at first intended merely to recite her rôle, Janina could not now refrain from marking it, at least in its broad outlines.

She was irritated by the fact that everyone was looking at her and that from all directions numerous eyes were fixed upon her. It seemed to her that she saw ridicule in their glances and derision on all those lips, so at moments she would start nervously and break out with all the force of her temperament, or again, she would speak too softly.

Majkowska stood there hissing and laughing together with Zarnecka and loudly voicing her opinion of Janina's acting. Topolski, the stage-manager, made her leave and reënter the stage several times, for in her excitement, she did not enter properly.

Janina knew what they were doing, so she did not take very much to heart Mela's ridicule or Topolski's pedantic instructions. She played on and rendered her rôle forcibly, if a little unevenly.

There followed a characteristic silence; nobody laughed nor jested loudly.

The stage-director walked up and down behind the scenes contentedly rubbing his hands and grunting: "Good, good, but she does not yet put enough pathos into it!"

"Why, don't you hear she is already shouting, not speaking!" Majkowska jeered at him.

"My dear madame! You go into convulsions on the stage, and none of us, out of politeness, blames you for it," answered Stanislawski for his friend.

"Not that way! Who waves his arms in that manner? Are you trying to make a windmill of yourself?" cried Topolski.

"Don't discourage her, remember it is her first rehearsal!" cried Cabinska from the seats.

"You walk about the stage like a goose!" again remarked the irritated Topolski to Janina.

"She wouldn't be at all bad as a washerwoman!" hissed Mela.

In spite of all, although she felt tears of wrath rising to her eyes, Janina played on, without letting herself be confused and never for a moment losing her presence of mind.

When she had finished, Cabinska ostentatiously kissed her and began to praise her aloud so that Majkowska could hear: "I congratulate you and have no doubt that you will play the part excellently!"

"Work out the details a little better," Stanislawski advised her.

"Why, this is merely a rehearsal! I already have the entire character worked out in my head."

"We shall now have a real heroine, for one that is beautiful and talented at the same time!" cried Rosinska in a very loud voice.

Majkowska glared at her furiously, but did not reply.

Janina felt so happy that she had a desire to kiss everybody.

In two days the performance was to take place. That interval was like one immense vista of light in which Janina seemed eagerly absorbed. It seemed to her that she was entirely satisfied.

"At last! At last! Now, all my poverty and humiliation will end!" Janina whispered rapturously to herself. She thought that a repertory of rôles would immediately be assigned to her. She gave free reign to her imagination and already saw herself upon some pinnacle. She was already in that promised land of powerful emotions about which she dreamed every day—in that realm that swarmed before her eyes with a stately throng of heroic figures, superhuman passions, and dazzling beauty, a realm in which there reigned a perfect harmony between dreams and reality.

Janina smiled with pity at those days of want and poverty, as though she were bidding farewell to them forever. Everything that surrounded her, even Wladek, paled into insignificance before her fascinated eyes.

A thousand times she repeated the rôle of "Mary." She sat for hours at a time before the mirror, practicing the appropriate facial expression and became feverish with impatience while awaiting the arrival of the momentous day. At night, Janina would sit half asleep in her bed and gaze before her. It seemed to her that she saw the crowded theater and the representatives of the press, that she heard the quiet murmurs of the public, saw their enraptured glances, and that she entered the stage and played. . . . Half unconsciously she would repeat the words of her rôle, kindle with ardor, declaim them with exaltation. Then, overcome by drowsiness again, she would smile through tears of happiness for she heard most distinctly that well-known and thrilling thunder of applause and cries of: "Orlowska! Orlowska!" And with that smile on her face she would fall asleep and wake again to continue her dreams.

Janina sold whatever she could to buy the appropriate costume for her part. With a smile of contentment she would drive away Wladek so that he might not interfere with her.

On that day which was to be for her so important and decisive, Cabinski, before the general rehearsal, took away her part and gave it to Majkowska.

Intrigue and envy had gained their end. Cabinski was forced to yield, for Topolski had threatened to leave the company immediately unless he took away the rôle from Janina and gave it to Majkowska. It was the way he chose to avenge himself because of Janina's refusal to go to Kotlicki.

Struck to the very heart, Janina almost lost her reason under this blow. She began to stagger on her feet and felt that the whole theater was whirling about her and that everything was sinking with her into a bottomless darkness. She cast a glance of unspeakable grief at all those about her, as though seeking for help, but on the faces of most of the members of the company there was an expression of merriment over what they thought was a splendid joke, and the beastly joy of cretins at the suppression of talent. They mocked the defeated aspirant with their glances; burning taunts and jibes began to fall from all sides like stones upon her soul crushed by an unexpected blow. Brutal laughs arose, scourging her as with a whip and all the baseness of human delight in the pain of others found its object and outlet.

And Janina stood there without a word or motion, with that dreadful pain in her heart in which it seemed as though all the arteries had been torn open and were flooding it with the blood of despair.

She collected enough strength to ask: "Why may I not play the part?"

"Because you may not and that settles it!" answered Cabinski curtly. And he immediately left the theater, because he dreaded a scene and felt a trifle sorry for Janina.

She remained standing behind the scenes with that overwhelming and sharp pain of disappointment tearing at her soul. She felt such an emptiness and loneliness that at moments it seemed to her as though she were all alone in the world and that something had pinned her to the earth with an immense weight and was crushing her down, that she was falling with lightning speed to the bottom of some deep abyss where a grayish-green whirlpool was dimly roaring.

Her thoughts and feelings were breaking and snapping under the tremendous strain and tears of hopeless abandonment flooded her eyes. She went to the dressing-room and sat down in the darkest corner.

Her dreams were crumbling to pieces: those wonderful realms were vanishing and sinking away in the misty distance, those enchanting visions were waving like torn rags in her brain and soul.

The dull grayness of the dirty walls and decorations about her and the throng of shabby, jeering beggars seemed to saturate and oppress her whole being.

She felt so utterly weary, broken, sick, and helpless that she went out into the hall to look for Wladek to take her home, but she could not find him. He had cautiously disappeared, so Janina went back to the dressing-room and sat there in a daze.

"Beware of dreams! Beware of water!" she repeated to herself, remembering with difficulty who had told her that. And suddenly, Janina became pale and reeled back for such a chaos began to whirl in her brain that she thought she would go mad. . . .

For a long time she sat in a senseless torpor and wept without being able to restrain herself, for after partly regaining her consciousness the memory of all her sufferings and disappointments came back to her again. At last utterly worn out, and, lulled by the silence that enveloped the theater after the rehearsal, she fell asleep.

She was awakened by Rosinska who on that day had come earlier to the dressing-room, for she was to begin the play. When she saw the sleeping girl, the older actress was moved to pity. The remaining shreds of her womanhood covered by the artificiality of theatrical life, awoke in her at the sight of that pale face, worn by poverty and dejection.

"Miss Janina—" whispered Rosinska tenderly.

Janina arose and began nervously to wipe away the traces of tears from her face.

"Have you not seen Mr. Niedzielski?" she asked Rosinska.

"No. My poor child, so that is what they have done to you!—But you must not take it so much to heart. If you want to be an artist you must bear a great deal, suffer a great deal. My dear, if you only knew what I had to go through and still have to. If you wanted to grieve over all the afflictions that come to you, become irritated over all the gossip they spread about you or weep over every intrigue in which they try to entangle you, you would have neither any tears, nor eyes, nor strength left! There's no use crying over it, for things can't be any different in the theater! Moreover, you haven't lost anything by it! That one disappointment makes you richer by one more experience."

"Perhaps they are right, after all. I must have no talent whatever, if Cabinski took away the rôle from me. ..."

"It is just because you have a talent that they played this trick on you. I heard what the cousin of that amateur said at the first rehearsal."

"What good will all that do me, when I can't play and have nothing to live on."

"That is all the doing of Majkowska. She forced Cabinski to take the rôle away from you."

"I know she bears me a grudge, but I can't conceive why she should revenge herself in such an inhuman way!"

"You don't know her yet. ... I don't know what you two quarreled about, but I do know that when she saw you on the stage at the first rehearsal she became so greatly afraid that you might eclipse her that she immediately began to lay plans for your undoing. I saw how she hung about that amateur, how she fawned upon his cousin and Cabinski, how she kissed the hands of the directress! I saw with my own eyes! Did you ever hear of anyone degrading one's self in that manner? But she attained her end. She has already done away with many another in the same way. You probably do not know what I, an actress of long standing and with so large a repertory, have to suffer on her account. You could not notice what was being schemed, for it was all done so quickly that besides myself, probably no one else knew about it. Such a creature as she always has luck! But wait I will fix her to-day! I'll pay her back for the both of us!"

The dressing-room slowly began to fill with actresses, their noisy chatter and the smell of powder and pigments that were being warmed over the candles. They were beginning to dress.

At last Majkowska came in, stately and triumphant, with a bouquet in her hands and roses in her corsage. Seeing Janina sitting alongside of Rosinska she frowned and cried angrily: "If I am not mistaken, this is not the dressing-room of the chorus girls."

"You *are* mistaken, you pantomime artist!" retorted Rosinska.

"I am not speaking to you."

"But I am answering you. Please stay here," she said, turning to Janina who wanted to leave.

"Don't you begin with me! Do you think I'm going to dress together with novices, eh?"

"Wait, you'll get a separate cell with a strait-jacket of your own. You can't miss it."

"Shut your mouth! You forty-year-old simp."

"My age is none of your business, you ruined heroine!"

"She looks like a drenched hen on the stage and yet dares to raise her voice here."

Everybody in the dressing-room was shaking with laughter, while Rosinska and Majkowska began to quarrel ever more vulgarly, without however interrupting for a moment their make-up and hasty dressing.

Janina listened to the quarrel in silence. She hardly felt any grievance toward Majkowska for depriving her of the rôle, but only a physical aversion to her person. Majkowska now appeared to her so filthy, brazen, and base that even her voice sounded disgusting.

Only when they began to play *Doctor Robin*, Janina stood behind the scenes to see what would be done with her rôle. It is impossible to describe that subtle, excruciating pain that rent her soul when she saw Majkowska as "Mary" on the stage. She felt that that other woman was tearing out piecemeal from her brain and heart every word, every gesture, every pose and accent.

"They are mine, mine!" she breathed, unable to help herself. "Mine!" And she devoured Mela with her eyes and then closed them so that she might not behold any more of it, nor torment herself with remembering the rôle as she had conceived it. "The thief!" she finally whispered so loudly that Majkowska trembled on the stage.

Rosinska sat behind the scenes on the other side of the stage. As soon as Majkowska entered there began a scene upon the stage for she repeated each word after Mela in an undertone and in a false intonation, laughed aloud at her acting, ridiculed and mimicked her gestures.

At first Majkowska paid no attention to this, but finally she could no longer refrain from looking behind the scenes and could not help hearing that raillery and mimicry of herself. She could not catch the prompter's words and stopped short in the middle of a sentence, while Rosinska continued to crowd her ever more mercilessly.

Majkowska grew furious with impotent rage, but her playing was becoming worse all the time and she felt it, and began to throw herself about the stage as though she were obsessed. Behind every scene she saw faces laughing at her; even Dobek in his box stopped his mouth with his hand so heartily amused was he by what was going on. That deprived Majkowksa of the rest of her self-control.

As soon as she left the stage she threw herself at Rosinska with her fists. There arose such a rumpus that the men had to part the two actresses, for they had begun pulling the hair out of each other's wigs. Majkowska was forcibly led to the dressing-room. She raged like a mad woman and got an attack of hysteria. She smashed mirrors, tore up costumes, and tossed about so violently that they had to call a doctor and tie her hands and feet.

Cabinska pulled out the rest of his hair in despair, but the actors laughed in their dressing-rooms and enjoyed themselves immensely.

The curtain had to be lowered in the middle of the play, and Topolski, almost pale with anger announced to the audience: "Ladies and Gentlemen! Because of the sudden and serious indisposition of Miss Majkowska, *Doctor Robin* cannot be concluded. The following play on the program will immediately begin."

Janina despite the satisfaction that she felt at the fiasco of her enemy, began to feel sorry for Majkowska when she saw her senseless and suffering. She was not yet enough of an actress to feel indifferent to it, so she went to her, but seeing in the room the doctor, and Cabinski, who was quarreling with Rosinska she hastily retreated.

Rosinska, Wolska, and Mirowska declared outright to Cabinski that if Majkowska remained in the company they would leave it the very next day.

Cabinski fled, but he next ran into Stanislawski and Krzykiewicz who told him the same with the addition that they would not remain a day longer with him for they were ashamed to be in a company where such public scandals occurred.

The director almost went crazy, for he was not prepared for such a thing. He tried to squirm out of it as best as he could, made promises, gave orders on the treasurer to all who wanted them and, spying Janina called aloud to her with the object of mollifying somewhat his previous conduct: "If you want something from the treasurer, I will give you an order, for I must leave right away."

Janina asked for five rubles. He did not even so much as make a wry face but gave it to her and immediately ran off to Pepa, but on the way he was again tackled by that amateur and his cousin and things began to grow so noisy behind the scenes that the public listened uneasily, wondering what was the matter.

The performance was concluded amid the silence of the audience; not one handclap sounded.

Janina, on leaving the box office with the money, met Niedzielska hobbling slowly along.

She stopped and wanted to greet her, but Niedzielska looked at her threateningly and barked: "What do you want, you! you!" She coughed violently, threatened Janina with her cane with which she supported herself, and dragged herself on.

Janina unconsciously looked about her, to see if she could spy Wladek anywhere, but he had already vanished. She had not seen him since that morning.

Wladek purposely avoided her, for he had reached the decisive conclusion that it was better to have intercourse only with ordinary women, for with them it was not necessary to restrain one's self, to pretend, and to be continually forced to take everything into account. Moreover, Janina had made a fiasco as an actress and continued to be nothing but a chorus girl, and his mother had threatened to disinherit him because of her.

Janina gazed for a long time after the old woman, who, no doubt, was going to seek her son, and then she went slowly home.

# CHAPTER X

 JANINA lay sick in bed.

It seemed to her as though she were at the bottom of a well and, from those depths into which they had shoved her she could see only the pale, distant blue of the sky, sometimes complete darkness, sometimes the twinkling of the stars, then again some wings, flying past, would cast a shadow over her eyes so that she lost knowledge of everything. She only felt that those eddies of life without, its voices, noises, cries, fears, and despair oozed down the smooth sides of the well and flowed into her soul as into a reservoir, penetrating her whole soul with an unconscious pain which she, however, felt with every fiber of her being.

The days dragged on as slowly as though they were strung on the chain of ages, as slowly as they drag on for those who have lost everything, even hope.

Janina sent word to the director that she was sick, but no one came to see her. Cabinska merely sent Wicek to say that Yadzia was longing for her piano lessons, and nothing more.

There, they were playing, learning, creating something and living! Here, she lay sunken in a complete apathy, like a crushed soul that hardly dares at moments to think that it still exists and then again sinks into an agony which cannot, however, end in the oblivion of death.

Janina was not really physically ill, for nothing pained her, but was dying from inner exhaustion. It seemed to her as though she had spent the whole store of her strength in those three months of theatrical life and that she was now dying from the hunger of her soul that had nothing left with which to keep it alive.

Throughout those long days, throughout that endless agony of silent nights she slowly pondered the nature of everyone whom she had met here; and that slow, but entirely one-sided, cognizance of her environment filled her with bitter sadness.

"There is no happiness on earth . . ." Janina whispered to herself, and it seemed to her that hitherto she had had a cataract blinding her eyes which fate had now brutally torn off. She now saw, but there were moments in which she yearned for her former blindness and groping in the dark.

"There is no happiness!" she repeated bitterly, and rebellious pessimism mastered her soul entirely.

Everywhere Janina saw only evil and baseness. There passed before her the forms of all her acquaintances and she scornfully thrust them all down into one pit, not excluding Wladek. He had dropped in only once to see her and began to excuse himself for his absence, but she impatiently interrupted him and asked him to go away.

She already knew him well enough and wondered as the thought occurred to her that she had ever loved him.

"Why? Why?" Janina asked herself.

Shame and regret began to fill her at the thought that she had fallen so low and for him. He now appeared to her miserable and common. She could not forgive herself.

"What fatality placed him in my path of life?" Janina asked herself further. In her own eyes she felt deeply humiliated.

"I did not love him," she pondered and a shudder of disgust shook her. He began to grow hateful to her.

And the theater also, lost a great deal of its glamor for Janina in those hours of reflection. She now looked at it through the prism of those continual quarrels and behind-the-scenes intrigues, through the vanity of its priests and through her own disappointments.

"It is not as I used to see it formerly!" she lamented.

Everything became increasingly smaller and grayer to Janina's inner vision. Everywhere she began to discover rags, sham, and falsehood. People obscured everything for her with their baseness and pettiness. She no longer desired to reign as a queen upon the stage.

"What is that? What is that?" she whispered to herself and saw a motley, heterogeneous public that was indifferent to the quality of a play. It came to the theater to amuse itself and laugh; it hankered for clownishness and the circus.

"What is that? Comedianism for profit and for the amusement of the multitude," Janina answered herself. The stage now appeared to her as a real arena for the feats of clowns and trained monkeys.

"I wanted to be an entertainer of the mob! And where does art come in? What is pure art, the ideal, for which hundreds of people sacrifice their lives?

"What is it and where is it to be found?" she asked herself uneasily, beginning to see that everything is rather an amusement than an aim in itself.

Literature, poetry, music, painting, and all the fine arts passed before Janina's mind. She could not separate their utilitarian aspect from their purely artistic one. She saw that all artists played, sang, and created only to amuse that vast, brutal, mob. For it they sacrificed their lives, their strength, and their dreams; for it they struggled and suffered, lived and died.

To Janina that vast multitude of Grzesikiewiczs, Kotlickis, and counselors, appeared in its ignorance and low instincts like a cruel master who, with a half-mocking, half-favoring smile, looked down upon that entire human throng of artists that painted, played, recited, created, and begged with a nervous look for his favor and recognition.

And she saw one immense wave of human beings spreading over the wide plains of earth, swaying slowly and going nowhere; and on the other side all those artists who were passing through the mob in all directions, loudly proclaiming something, singing with inspired voices, pointing to the expanse of heaven, calling attention to the stars, trying to bring about some order in this disorderly, teeming multitude, opening paths among it, imploring it in deep tones. But the multitude either laughed or merely nodded its assent, but did not budge from its place. It surged and pushed about and trampled the artists underfoot.

"What is that? Why?" Janina asked herself, greatly terrified. "If they do not need us then we ought to let them alone, keeping ourselves apart from them and living only for ourselves and with ourselves." But again everything became confused in her mind and she could not conceive how it would be possible to live apart from the rest of humanity and concluded that it would not be worth living at all in that way. Her thoughts whirled in confusion through her brain.

Sowinska, who now took care of her with motherly solicitude, came in and interrupted her frenzied thoughts.

"Why don't you go home?" she advised Janina sincerely.

"Never!" answered Janina.

"Why should you wear yourself out in that way? You will rest a little, gain new strength, and return again to the theater."

"No," answered Janina quietly.

"I forgot to tell you that old Mrs. Niedzielska was here to see me yesterday."

"Do you know her?" asked the younger woman.

"Not at all, but she had some business with me. Oh, she is a sly fox, that old hag!" added Sowinska.

"Perhaps she is a bit too miserly, but otherwise she is a rather honest woman."

"Honest? You'll find out yet for yourself how honest she is."

"Why?" asked Janina, but without curiosity, for it didn't at all interest her now.

"I will only say this much . . . that she does not love you in the least, not in the least!"

"That's strange, for I never did her any wrong," answered Janina.

Sowinska's demeanor suddenly changed, for she glanced angrily at Janina and wanted to say something sharp, but seeing that Janina's face wore an expression of complete indifference, she refrained and left the room.

Janina thought about Bukowiec.

"I have no home," she thought, even without bitterness. "The whole wide world is my home," she added, but suddenly remembered what Grzesikiewicz had told her about her father and stirred as though some hidden pain had awakened in her. An uneasiness, not such as besets one on the eve of some event, but such as one feels on remembering some good that one has lost forever, filled Janina's heart. It was the pain of the past like the quiet remembrance of the dead.

But those memories of Bukowiec and those lonely nights when she dreamed, forgetting about everything, and created for herself such wondrous worlds, now flashed upon her mind in all their vividness. Only the memory of that exuberant and majestic nature, those vast fields, and those silent glens full of murmurs and bird songs, verdure, and wild grandeur swathed Janina in melancholy and lulled her weary soul with its charms.

The woods in which she was reared, those dim depths full of unspeakable wonders, those gigantic trees to which she was united by a thousand affinities, outlined themselves in her mind ever more powerfully. Janina longed for them now and listened through the nights, for it seemed to her that she heard the grave autumnal murmur of the forest, the somnolent rustling of its branches. It seemed that she felt within herself the slow, endless swaying of those giant trees, the soft motions of the verdure bathed in golden sunlight, the joyous cry of the birds, the fragrance of the young pine saplings and juniper bushes— the whole leisurely life of nature.

Janina lay for whole hours at a time, without a word, thought, or motion, for her soul was there in those verdant woods. She wandered over the meadows covered with wild raspberries and waving grass, strayed across the fields where the rye grew high like a wood, swaying and murmuring in the breeze and gleaming with dew in the sunlight, penetrated the groves full of the pungent smell of the resin. She followed each road, each boundary, each wood path, greeted everything that lived there and cried out to the fields, woods, the hills, and the sky: "I have come! I have come!" smiling as though she had found a lost happiness.

These invigorating memories restored Janina's health almost entirely. On the eighth day she felt strong enough for a walk. She was longing for the fresh air, the verdure unsoiled by city dust, the sunlight, and the vast open spaces. She felt that the city was stifling her, that here, at every step, she had to limit her own ego and continually struggle against all the barriers of custom and dependence.

Janina passed through the Place of Arms and, going beyond the Citadel, she walked along the damp sand dunes to Bielany.

An unbroken silence enveloped her on all sides. The sun shone brightly and warmly, but from the water there blew a brisk, invigorating breeze.

She gazed at the quiet river flecked with spots of white foam and at the indistinct silhouettes of boats trailing along in midstream. She breathed in deeply the calm that surrounded her and felt a resurgence of her wasted strength.

Janina lay down upon the yellowish sand of the bank and, gazing at the gleaming expanse of waters, forgot everything. It seemed to her as though she were flowing on with the current of the river, passing the shores, houses, and woods and hurrying on continually into a blue and boundless distance like the illimitable expanse of heaven that hung over her. It seemed to her as though she no longer remembered anything, but felt only the ineffable delight of rocking with the waves.

Janina suddenly awoke from that half dream, for there passed near her an old man with a fishing rod in his hand. He looked at her in passing, sat down almost beside her on the very edge of the river, cast his line into the water and waited.

He had so honest a face that she felt a desire to speak to him and was thinking how to begin, when he addressed her first: "Would you like to take a trip over to the other side?"

Janina glanced at him questiongly.

"Aha! I see that we don't understand each other. I thought that you wanted to drown yourself," he said.

"I wasn't even thinking about death," she replied quietly.

"Ha! ha! It would be an unexpected honor for the river."

He adjusted his fishing tackle and became silent, centering all his attention on the fish that had begun to circle about the bait and the hook.

A deeper silence, as it were, diffused itself about and began to fill Janina's soul with a blissful calm. She felt that an immense goodness was pervading her, that the majesty of that expanse of heaven, of the waters and the verdure was uplifting her and drawing from her breast a hymn of thanksgiving and the pure joy of living, free from all earthly things.

The old man cast a sidelong glance at her and on his narrow lips there hovered an unfathomable smile.

Janina felt that look and in turn glanced at him. Their eyes met in a long and friendly gaze.

She felt a sudden and irresistible impulse to reveal the depths of her soul to him.

She moved closer to him and said quietly: "I was not thinking about death."

"Then you were seeking calm?"

"Yes, I wanted to take a look at nature and to forget."

"Forget about what?"

"About life!" Janina whispered hoarsely and tears of violent grief filled her eyes.

"You are a child. It must have been some disappointment in love, some thwarted ambition, or perhaps the lack of a dinner that put you in such a tragic mood."

"All that taken together is not enough to make one feel very, very unhappy," answered Janina.

"All that taken together is one big zero, for according to my way of thinking there is nothing that can make wholly unhappy an individual who knows himself," he said.

"Who are you . . . that is, what do you do?" he asked, after pausing a while.

"I am in the theater," answered the girl.

"Aha! the world of comedy! Simulation which you afterwards take for reality. Chimeras! All that warps the human soul. The greatest actors are merely phonographs wound up sometimes by sages, sometimes by geniuses, but most often by fools. And they speak to even greater fools. Actors, artists, creators are merely blind instruments of nature which uses them to reveal itself and for ends known to itself alone! To them it seems that they are something real, but that is a sad deception, for they are merely instruments which are thrown into the discard when they are no longer needed or have lost their usefulness."

"Who are you?" Janina asked, almost unknowingly, stirred by his words.

"An old man as you see, who fishes and likes to chat. Oh yes, I am very old. I come here for a few hours every day in the summertime, if the weather is fair, and catch fish, if they let themselves be caught. What good will it do you to know who I am? My name will tell you nothing. In the sum total of humanity I am merely a pawn which is given a certain number upon entrance into this world and retains the same at the time of its exit. I am a cell of feeling long ago registered and classified by my fellow-beings as a 'ne'er-do-well,'" he said, smiling.

"I had no intention of offending you by my question."

"I never get angry about anything. Only foolish people anger themselves or rejoice. A man ought merely to look on, observe, and go his own way," he added, drawing a gudgeon from his hook.

Janina was a bit chilled by his gravity and by his decisive way of speaking which admitted of no discussion.

"Are you from the Warsaw Theater?" he asked, throwing out his line again.

"No, I am in Cabinski's company. No doubt you know him."

"I don't know him, nor have I heard about him."

"Is it possible that you have never heard anything about Cabinski, nor read about the Tivoli?" asked Janina greatly surprised that there could be anyone in Warsaw who did not know and was not interested in the theater.

"I do not go to the theater at all and I do not read the papers," he answered.

"Impossible!"

"One can see right away that you must not be more than twenty years old, for you cry out in amazement, 'Impossible!' and look at me as though I were a lunatic or a barbarian."

"But after talking with you, it was impossible for me to assume even for a moment that . . . "

"That I am not interested in the theater, yes, that I do not read the papers," he concluded for her.

"I can't even understand why."

"Well, because that does not interest me at all," he answered simply.

"Are you not at all interested in what is going on in the world, in how people are living, what they are doing, what they are thinking?"

"No. To you that doubtless appears monstrous; nevertheless it is entirely natural. Do our peasants interest themselves in the theater or in world affairs? They do not. Isn't that true?"

"Yes, but they are peasants and that is entirely different."

"It is the same thing, merely with this addition; that for them your famous and great men do not exist at all and it doesn't make the slightest difference to them whether Newton or Shakespeare ever lived or not. And they are just as well off with their ignorance, just as well."

Janina became silent, for what he had said appeared to her paradoxical and not very true.

"What will I learn from your newspapers and your theaters? Merely that people love, hate, and fight one another the same as ever; that evil and brute force continue to reign as they always have done; that the world and life are merely a big mill in which brains and consciences are ground to dust. It is more comfortable to know nothing rather than that," he continued.

"But is it right for anyone to seclude himself so egoistically from all that is going on in the world?" asked Janina.

"Precisely in that lies wisdom. To desire nothing for ourselves, care for nothing, and be indifferent—that is what we ought to aim at."

"Is it possible to attain such a state of complete apathy?"

"It is attained through the experience of life and through thinking. Remember that the smallest pleasure, a mere momentary satisfaction, always costs us more dearly than it is really worth. The average man will not, for instance, pay a thousand rubles for a pear, for he knows that would be an insane absurdity, and moreover, he knows the relative value of a thousand rubles and of a pear. But out of the capital of his life he is ready to squander thousands for mere trifles—for a light love affair that lasts only as long as it takes a two cent pear to ripen, for he has never considered the almost priceless value of his own vital energy and becomes blind to all, like a bull when the toreador flashes a red rag before his eyes, and pays for that blindness with a part of his life. The majority of human beings die, not from natural necessity, like a lamp when its oil has burned out, but from bankruptcy, from squandering their powers and strength on foolish things that are worth a thousand times less than one day of life."

"I would not want to live such a cold and calculated life without frenzies, dreams, and love."

"The world would not come to an end, if people did not love."

"It would be better to kill one's self than to live and dry up like a tree."

"Suicide is the vulgar cry of the animal who suffers; it is the rebellion of the atom against the laws of the universe. One must allow the candle of one's life to burn out slowly and calmly to the very end—in that lies happiness."

"So that is happiness?" asked Janina, feeling a sudden chill penetrating her soul.

"Yes. Peace is happiness. To negate everything, to kill one's desires and passions, to tear out of oneself illusions and whims—that is the way to attain it. It means to hold fast your soul in the grip of self-knowledge and prevent it from dissipating itself in foolish things."

"Who would want to live under such a yoke? What soul could endure it?"

"The soul is knowledge."

"So you advocate nothing but stony indifference and peace! Never to know or feel anything else but this! No, I prefer the ordinary trend of life."

"There is still another way: the best remedy for our mental sufferings is to expand our hearts, to become one with nature."

"Let us drop that. I don't like to speak about it, for it stirs me too strongly."

They both remained silent for a long while. The old man gazed into the water and mumbled something to himself, while Janina was rapt in thought.

"All is foolishness," he began anew. "Behold and wonder at the water, if nothing more; it will suffice you for a long time. Observe the birds, the stars, and the elements; trace the growth of the trees, listen to the wind, drink in perfumes and hues and everywhere you will find unparalleled, everlasting miracles. It will replace for you entirely life among people. Only do not gaze at nature with the eyes of the vulgar, for then the most beautiful bird songs will sound to you like a mere screeching; the most majestic forest will seem nothing but so much kindling wood; in animals you will see nothing but meat for food; the meadows will appear to you as so much hay; for then, instead of feeling, you will be calculating."

"All human beings are like that."

"There are a few who can read from the book of nature and find in it sustenance for their life."

Again they became silent.

The sun began to sink behind the hills on the opposite shore and to shine ever more coldly as though it were burnt out, dyeing the water blood red with its parting rays. The thickets seemed to shrink, for they appeared to grow lower and wider at their bases. The yellowish sands on the river bank became shrouded by the gray dusk. The distant horizon seemed to sink away in the mists which rose up as though they were the smoke of the burnt-out, smoldering sun. An even deeper silence descended and enveloped the earth in sleep, as though it were weary of the labors of the day.

Janina pondered over the words of the old man and a quiet, gloomy sadness filled her heart and cast a vague and shadowy fear over her mind. A feeling of passive submission and torpor overcame her.

She arose to go, for it was already growing dark.

"Are you going?" she asked the old man.

"Yes, it is already time and it is quite a way to Warsaw."

"Then we shall go together."

He put away his fishing tackle in his cane, deposited the fish in a small can and began to walk along with Janina at a swift enough pace.

"I do not know your name," he began to say slowly, "and I'm not at all interested in that, but I see that you must not be very happy in life. I am a crazy old man, as my neighbors call me, and an old mason, as the town gossips like to add; I'm alone and, reconciled to my fate, I am awaiting the end. Some time ago I knew a little of what it means to suffer and love, but that is past long ago, long ago," he whispered, gazing as it were, into a distant past, with a faint smile of remembrance on his face. "The greatest boon that man possesses is his ability to forget, otherwise he could not live at all. But all this does not interest you in the least, does it? I sometimes chatter nonsense, catch myself talking to myself, and often forget things, for I'm just an old man, you see. You have an honest-looking face, so I will give you this bit of advice; whenever you suffer, when everything disappoints you and life becomes unbearable—flee from the city, go into the open country, breathe in the fresh air, bathe in the sunlight, gaze at the sky, think about eternity and pray . . . and you will forget all your troubles. You will feel better and stronger. The misery of the people of to-day arises from their estrangement from nature and from God, from loneliness of the soul. And I will tell you one more thing; forgive everything and be merciful to all. People are bad only through their ignorance, therefore you be good. The greatest wisdom is in the greatest kindness. I am here every day while it is warm. Perhaps we shall meet again sometime. Good-bye, and may you be happy." He nodded his head kindly in farewell.

She gazed a long time after him until he vanished from her sight near the church of St. Mary. Janina rubbed her eyes, for it seemed to her that this meeting had been merely a hallucination.

"No, that cannot be," she whispered to herself, for she still felt upon her face the pure gaze of his peaceful old eyes and heard his voice saying: "Be good! Pray! Forgive!" She repeated the words to herself as she walked along the street.

"Forgive!" and she saw her father and afterwards the theater, Cabinski, Majkowska, Kotlicki, Mme. Anna, and Sowinska and remembered those days of suffering, abuse, and insult.

"Be good!" and she saw again Mirowska, who bore the most painful wrongs with a smile, who never did anyone any harm, and yet was the laughing stock of the entire company. Then, there was Wolska, who at the expense of her own life saved her child from death and who was cheated and forced into poverty. There was Cabinska's nurse sacrificing herself for a stranger's children. There was, too, the old stage-director, slighted by everybody; there were the peasants in the country, treated like animals, and the exploited workmen in the cities. There were all the swindles, cheatings, and crimes which were going on continually. Janina felt that something within her was trembling, breaking, and crying out in protest; that the suffering of all humanity was pouring into her soul; that all the injustice, all the wrongs, all the suffering and tears stood before her, and a grave voice from above was saying: "Be good, forgive, pray," while round about her a jeering laughter arose, as though in response to it.

She arrived at her home and for a long time could not calm herself. She pressed her hands to her head as though trying to still those tumultuous thoughts that were whirling through her brain in such confusion that she could not distinguish truth from falsehood. For in a moment of clairvoyant vision she had seen that both the good and the bad suffered equally, that all were struggling, all were clamoring for salvation and protesting against life.

"I shall go mad! I shall go mad!" Janina whispered to herself.

On the next morning Wladek came to see her. He seemed to be so good and kissed her hand so tenderly that she could not help noticing his devotion. He complained about Cabinski and aired at length his grievances against his mother.

Janina regarded him with a cold look, for she understood almost at once that he wished to borrow money from her.

"Go and buy me some powder, for I must go to the theater to-day," she said to him.

Wladek rose eagerly to fulfill her behest.

"Close the door after you, for I am going to dress."

He closed the door with the latch to which he had his own key, and departed.

On the street, almost at the very door Wladek spied the counselor. A sudden idea flashed through his mind, for he smiled and cordially approached the old man.

"Good morning, esteemed counselor."

"Good morning, how are you feeling, eh?"

"Thank you, I am entirely well, only Miss Orlowska is ill. The directress has just asked me to see how she was getting along."

"What? Miss Janina is ill? They told me so behind the scenes, but I did not believe it, for I thought . . . "

"Yes, she is sick. I am just now going for some medicine."

"Is she dangerously ill?"

"Oh no, but would you like to convince yourself personally?"

The counselor started violently, but then, adjusting his glasses, he said: "Indeed, I would like to. I wished to do so many times before, but she is so inaccessible."

"I will smooth the way for you."

"You are joking. How can that be done? Although, considering my friendly attitude toward her ..."

"You can see her. Here is the latchkey to her room. She will receive you; she even told me that she would be pleased to have her friends visit her, for she spends entire days all alone."

"But if ..."

"Go. If she received me, she will receive you all the more readily. I will be back in about an hour and then we can have a chat." So saying, Wladek left hurriedly.

The counselor wiped his glasses, fidgeted about nervously, and had not yet made up his mind whether to enter or not, when Wladek turned back and called:

"My dear counselor! Lend me four rubles, will you? I would first have to look for Cabinski to get the money and the medicine is needed here right away. I have taken an unpleasant task upon myself, but what is one going to do when companionship demands it? I will return the money to you this evening, only please don't say anything about this. And pardon my boldness."

The counselor willingly reached for his pocket book and, handing Wladek ten rubles said: "I am glad I can help you. If any more is needed, tell Miss Janina to mention only a word to me and she can have it."

Wladek went off with the money, whistling merrily.

The counselor entered the house, quietly opened the door to Janina's apartment, took off his hat and coat and walked into the room.

Janina was combing her hair and paid no attention to the opening of the door, for she thought that Wladek had returned.

The counselor coughed a few times and approached her with extended hand.

Janina sprang up hastily and threw a scarf over her naked shoulders.

"Mr. Wladyslaw has just told me that you were ill, so I thought it would be a sin not to come to see you," said the counselor, speaking rapidly, adjusting his glasses and smiling a colorless, banal smile.

Janina stared at him in amazement, for a moment, but when she felt the touch of his cold, clammy hand in her own, she grew red with anger, sprang toward the door so violently that the scarf fell to the floor, revealing the stately lines of her shoulders, and opening the door with an energetic gesture, cried: "Leave the room!"

"But I give you my word of honor that I hadn't even the slightest intention of offending you. As a well-wishing friend I came here merely to offer you my sympathy. Mr. Wladyslaw . . . "

"Is a scoundrel!"

"To that I'll agree, but you needn't get angry at me and express your indignation in such a drastic manner; that is a trifle too …"

"Please leave the room immediately!" cried Janina, trembling with anger.

"A comédienne! A comédienne, upon my word!" whispered the counselor to himself, hastily putting on his overcoat, for he was irritated and offended. He hurried out, angrily slamming the door after him.

"Oh, what a scoundrel! What a scoundrel! and I belong to such a man ... I! They are jackals, not human beings, jackals! Wherever one turns there is mud and filth!"

And so great grew Janina's indignation, that she cried almost aloud through her tears: "Base wretches! wretches! wretches!"

Soon afterwards, Wladek returned bringing with him the powder, a bottle of whisky and a package of sandwiches. He eyed Janina curiously and looked about the room.

"The counselor was here!" she flung at him harshly.

The actor laughed cynically and exclaimed in a barroom jargon, "I cornered him. Now we can have a little feast."

Janina was about to tell him how base he was, but suddenly there rang in her ears those words: "Be good! Forgive!"

She restrained herself and began to laugh, but so harshly and so long that she fell upon the bed and, tossing about on it, began to repeat amid that dreadful, hysterical laughter: "Be good! Forgive!"

.    .    .    .    .    .    .

After a week's intermission there began again for Janina her former hard life and an even harder battle, because now it had become a struggle for mere daily bread.

She sang, as before, in the chorus, dressed as a chorus girl, peered through the curtain at the public, whose attendance at the theater was decreasing every day, strayed about the stage and the dressing-rooms during the intermissions, and listened to the whispered conversations, the music, and the quarrels. But how different now were her thoughts and her feelings, how different now and unlike her former self was Janina!

She no longer sought in the eyes of the public enthusiasm and love of art, nor did she cast challenging glances at the front rows of seats, for poverty had taught her how to estimate from the stage the size of the audience and from it to draw deductions as to the proportionate size of her salary. Poverty taught her to take covertly from the storeroom the bread that was often used on the stage and to eat it on the way home; frequently this was her entire daily sustenance. No one admired her now, or escorted her home; nor did she contend with anyone about art.

Kotlicki had completely vanished, the counselor was angry at Janina and kept away from the theater, while Wladek spoke with her only at times and visited her ever more rarely, offering as his excuse his mother's growing weakness and the need of being with her. Janina knew that he was lying, but she did not contradict him, for he was entirely indifferent to her. She felt a deep contempt for him, but could not break with him entirely because there still lingered deep down in her consciousness a memory of the happy hours they had spent together. She treated him coldly and did not let him kiss her, but she could not tell him outright that he was a scoundrel, for he was, in a way, the last link uniting her strange soul with the world.

Janina had grown frightfully thin. Her complexion became pale and unhealthy, and from her enlarged glassy eyes there looked forth a dreadful and constant hunger! She walked about the theater like a shadow, apparently quiet and calm, but with that feeling of unceasing hunger mercilessly tearing her within and with despair in her face.

There were whole days when she had not a bite of food, when she felt a painful emptiness in her head and heard only one thing echoing through her brain: "If I could only get something to eat! Something to eat!" Aside from that one desire, everything vanished from her mind and had no importance.

A similar poverty existed throughout the whole company. The women shifted as best they could, but the men, particularly the more honest ones, sold everything they possessed, even their wigs, to save themselves.

With what terror they awaited each evening! "Are we going to play to-night?" This whisper could be heard all over the theater: in the dressing-rooms, behind the scenes, in the restaurant-garden where the autumn wind frolicked, and on the deserted veranda, where the waiters, vainly waiting for guests, repeated it. It was also repeated by Gold, who sat huddled in his box office, shivering with cold.

An oppressive silence reigned in the dressing-rooms. The funniest jokes of Glas could not chase the clouds of worry from the brows of the actors. They became careless in their make-up and none of them learned their rôles, for everybody was waiting in dread suspense for the performance and every now and then going to the box office and asking in a whisper: "Are we going to play to-night?"

Cabinski presented a new play every day, but he could not draw the public. He gave *The Trip Around Warsaw* and *The Robbers*, and still the house was empty. They played such curtain-raisers as *Don Cæsar de Bazan*, *The Statue of the Commander*, and *The Fortune Teller of La Voisin*, but the theater remained as deserted as ever.

"For goodness' sake, what do you want?" the director cried to the public from behind the curtain.

"Do you think they themselves know what they want? If there were three hundred people present, then another three hundred would appear, but when there are only fifty with the addition of cold and rain, then only twenty remain," the editor explained to Cabinski, for of all those numerous acquaintances who used to come behind the scenes he alone remained, the rest having dispersed with the first rains.

"The public is a herd that does not know where it is going to graze on the following day," said Mr. Peter, with animosity.

Oh yes, they hated that public, and yet prayed to it. They cursed it, called it "a herd" and "cattle," threatened it with their fists and spat upon it, but only let that public appear in larger numbers, and they fell upon their faces before it and felt a deep gratitude toward that capricious lady, who had a different humor each day and each day bestowed her favors upon someone else.

"The public is a harlot! a harlot!" whispered Topolski threateningly. "To-day she is with a monarch, to-morrow with a clown!"

"You have told the truth, but it will not give you even a ruble," answered Wawrzecki, whose humor still survived, but had already become sharp and bitter, for Mimi had left the company and gone to join another one at Posen.

Several members of the company had already left, although there still remained a whole week till the end of the season. Especially the choruses had almost entirely dispersed, for they suffered the most from poverty.

The rains continued to fall in the morning, the afternoon, and the evening. The atmosphere at the theater became unbearable. There were draughts in the dressing-rooms, and mud covered the floors, for the roof leaked everywhere. The cold was intense.

To Janina it seemed that this theater was slowly falling apart and burying everyone among its ruins, while that other one on Theatrical Place stood strong and invincible. Its ponderous walls had grown black from the rains and it appeared even sterner and mightier than before and filled Janina with a pious, unexplainable awe whenever she gazed at it. It sometimes seemed to her that this vast edifice rested its columns on piles of corpses and that it drank the blood, the lives, and the brains of the actors in the smaller theaters and throve and grew mighty on them.

"I shall go mad! I shall go mad!" often whispered Janina, pressing her burning head with her hands, for dreams and hallucinations tormented her even more than hunger.

There was still another thing which made her deathly silent, so that she would sit for whole hours listening within herself, and thinking of those strange, indefinable impressions and feelings which prevaded her ever more frequently. Janina felt that something dreadful was happening within her, that those sudden fits of trembling and weeping which would seize her without any explainable cause, those violently changing moods to which she gave way and those strange sufferings were somehow unnatural and resulted from something about which she feared to think. She had no mother, nor anyone in whom she could confide and who would enlighten her, but there came a moment when with womanly instinct she knew that she was about to become a mother.

Janina wept for a long time after that discovery, but her tears were not tears of despair, but only of tender pity, sensitiveness and shame at the same time. She felt then that death had crouched behind her and was standing so close that it sent a shudder of frenzy through her entire being and cast her into an apathetic indifference. She ceased to think and surrendered herself passively, with the fatalism of people who have suffered long or who have been crushed by some overwhelming misfortune, to the wave that bore her on and did not even ask whither it was taking her.

One day, unable to endure any longer the sharp pangs of hunger, Janina began to look around her room for something which she might sell. She began feverishly to rummage in her trunks. She had only a few light theatrical costumes.

Sowinska was again reminding her almost every day about her overdue rent and that daily nagging was an unbearable torment. Janina could not ask her to sell those costumes, for she knew that Sowinska would unscrupulously keep the money, so she decided to sell them herself.

She wrapped one of the costumes in a piece of paper and went to the door to wait for a buyer of old clothes, but the porter was walking about the yard, servant girls were going to and fro, and in the windows of the houses she saw the faces of women who had often cast scornful glances at her. No, she could not sell here, for in a moment the whole house would know about her poverty. She went to one of the adjoining houses and waited a short while.

"Any old things to buy! Any old things to buy!" came the hoarse voice of an old Jew.

Janina called him. The Jew turned his head and came to her. He was as dirty as he was old. She went with him to the stoop of some house.

"Do you want to sell anything?" asked the Jew, laying his bag and stick on the stairs and bending his thin face and red eyes over the package.

"Yes," answered Janina, unwrapping the paper.

The Jew took the costume in his dirty hands, spread it out in the sunlight, looked over it a few times, smiled imperceptibly, put it back in the paper, wrapped it up, picked up his bag and stick and said, "Such fineries are not for me." He began to descend the stairway, derisively smacking his lips.

"I will sell it cheap," Janina called after him, thinking with fear that perhaps she might get at least a ruble or a half-ruble for it.

"If you have some old shoes or pillow-slips, I will buy them, but such a thing is of no use to me. Who will buy it? Rubbish!"

"I will sell it cheap," she whispered.

"Well, how much do you want for it?"

"A ruble."

"May I fall down dead, if that is worth more than twenty kopecks. What is it worth, who will buy it?" and he came back, unwrapped the costume, and again examined it indifferently.

"The ribbons alone cost me a few rubles," said Janina, and she became silent, deciding that she would take the twenty kopecks.

"Ribbons! What's that ... all pieces!" chattered the Jew, glancing over the costume hastily. "Well, I will give you thirty kopecks. Do you want it? As I'm an honest man, I can't give you more ... I have a good heart, but I can't! Well, do you want it?"

This barter filled Janina with such disgust, shame, and grief, that she felt like throwing down everything and running away.

The Jew counted out the money to her, took the costume and went away. From the window of her room Janina saw how in the full light of the yard he examined the dress once more.

"What shall I do with this?" she whispered helplessly, pressing in her hand the dirty and sticky kopecks.

Janina owed money to Mme. Anna for the rent of her room, to the tender of the theater-buffet, and to a few of her companions of the chorus, but she no longer thought of this, only took the thirty kopecks and went out to the store to buy herself something to eat.

She returned home, and having eaten, she wished to take a little nap, but Sowinska entered and told her that someone was waiting for her for the last half-hour and immediately there entered Niedzielska's servant girl with eyes all red from crying.

"Please Miss, come along with me, for my mistress is very sick and wants to see you without fail," she said.

"Is Madame Niedzielska so seriously ill?" cried Janina, springing up from the bed and hurriedly putting on her hat.

"The priest has already been there this afternoon with the sacrament and she has only a few hours to live," whispered the faithful old servant with tears in her eyes. "She can scarcely draw her breath and all I understood her to say was that I should run to you and tell you that she wants to see you right away. And where is Mr. Wladyslaw?"

"How can I know? He ought to be with his mother," answered Janina.

"He ought to, but he is a worthless son," whispered the servant in hollow tones. "Already for a week he has not been at home, for he had an awful quarrel with his mother. My God! My God! how he swore at her and abused her and even wanted to strike her. O merciful Lord, that is the way he repaid her for loving him so dearly that she even denied herself food to supply him with money. She was such a miser that she did not want to spend money for a doctor or any medicines and he ... oh! oh, God will punish him severely for his mother's tears! I know that you are not to blame for it, miss ... I can guess that ...but ..." she whispered quietly, hobbling alongside of Janina and every now and then wiping her eyes, all red from crying and loss of sleep.

Janina hardly heard a word of what she was saying for the noise and the din in the street and the splashing of water flowing from the drainpipes to the sidewalk drowned out everything else. She went along only because the dying woman had summoned her.

The first room of Niedzielska's home was almost filled with people and Janina greeted them as she passed through it, but no one answered her and all eyes followed her with a peculiar curiosity.

In the room where Niedzielska lay, there were also a few persons seated about her bed. Janina went straight to the sick woman. She was lying flat on her back, but fixed her eyes upon Janina as soon as she had crossed the threshold.

On Janina's entrance the persons in the room stopped talking so abruptly that the sudden silence sent a strange thrill through her. She met Niedzielska's gaze and could not tear her eyes away from it. She sat down alongside of the bed, greeting her in a subdued voice.

The old woman grasped her hand tightly and in a quiet voice with a very strong accent asked: "Where is Wladek?"

Her brows knit themselves in an expression of severity and something like hatred gleamed in the yellowish whites of her eyes.

"I don't know. How am I to know?" answered Janina almost frightened by her question.

"You don't know, you thief! You have stolen my son and yet, you dare tell me that you don't know!" gasped Niedzielska, striving to raise her voice a little, but it sounded hollow and wild. Her eyes opened ever wider and gleamed with hatred and menace, her pale lips quivered nervously, and her thin, yellow face twitched continually. She raised herself a bit on her bed and in a hoarse voice, as though rallying her remaining strength cried: "You streetwalker! You thief! You . . ." and she fell back exhausted, with a hollow groan.

Janina sprang up, as though an electric shock had passed through her, but the old woman gripped her wrist so tightly that she fell back again on her chair, unable to free her hand. She glanced about desperately at everybody, in the room, but their faces were stern. She closed her eyes for a moment to shut out the sight of the yellowish wrinkled faces of those women who stood facing her like specters glaring at her with their skeleton-like faces in the shadowy twilight of the room.

"So that is she! So young and already ..."

"A base serpent."

"I would kill her like a dog, if she tried to do the same with my son."

"I would have her locked up and sent to the workhouse."

"In my days such women as that were put into the pillory as a punishment. I remember well."

"Be quiet! quiet!" whispered an old man trying to pacify the women.

"And for her he ran away to the comedians, for her he squandered so much money, for such a low-down thing as she, he beat his mother! May you perish, you base serpent!"

Such were the voices full of hatred and scorn that hissed all about Janina and the poisonous malignity that dripped from their words and glances flooded her heart with an ocean of pain and shame. She wanted to cry out: "Mercy, people! I am innocent," but her head bent ever lower on her breast and she had an ever dimmer consciousness of where she was and what was happening to her. Janina's soul had already been weakened too much by misery to resist this blow. An immense wave of fear began to shake her, for it seemed to her that the hand of the old woman which held her so tightly and those dreadful eyes bulging from their sockets were drawing her down into a dark abyss and that this was death and the end of everything.

Later, Janina no longer heard anything that was being said and saw no one but the dying woman. At moments, she still felt a desire to spring up and run away from there but it was a mere flicker of will that passed through her nerves without reaching her consciousness.

So many previous sufferings, and now this blow at her very heart, benumbed her brain with a quiet madness. She grew frightfully pale and sat as though dead, gazing at the face of the dying woman. Those same fragments of thoughts and visions now swarmed through her brain that had done so once before: that same vast mass of greenish waters seemed to submerge her consciousness. She was not even aware that they had torn her away from Niedzielska and shoved her into a corner where she stood immovable and bereft of her senses.

Niedzielska was dying. It seemed as though she had only been waiting for Janina before giving herself up to death, for anger and hatred kept her alive a few hours longer. Now, there followed a general dissolution. She lay there rigid and straight, with her hands upon the coverlet, which they tugged at automatically, and with her sad eyes gazing upward as though into the eternity into which she was entering.

The consecrated candle shed a yellowish light upon her face impearled with the sweat of her last struggle and death agony. Her gray hair, scattered in a disheveled mass upon the pillow, formed a sort of background upon which appeared in sharper relief her withered head, shaking with the unconscious and frightful convulsions of death. She breathed heavily and slowly and gasped with effort, catching the air with her pale lips. At moments her face would writhe and her mouth twitch with a dreadful spasm of pain and she would raise her hands as though she wanted to tear apart her throat to get more air. Her white and fever-coated tongue slipped spasmodically from her mouth and so tense did her body become in the struggle with death that the veins stood out like black whip cords on her temples and throat.

The silence was full of weeping and sobbing of those kneeling about and the awful groans of the dying woman. Feverishly whispered prayers, tear-streaming eyes, the sobbing of the servant and the children filled the room with an atmosphere of dreadful and overwhelming tragedy. The dark shadows at the farther end of the room trembled as though engulfing it all. The candles diffused a yellowish, ghastly light that seemed to steep everything in boundless grief.

The room filled up completely with kneeling people and only she, who lay there rigid, unconscious, and dying, reigned from the throne of death over that bowed throng begging for mercy.

An old man with silvery gray hair made his way to the bed, knelt down, took a prayer book from his pocket and, by the light of the candle, began to read the Penitential Psalms. He had a clear and melodious voice and the words of the psalms, like a murmuring rainbow, or like flashes of lightning full of terror, tears, might, and heavenly grace, floated above the heads of all those present:

"Have mercy upon me, O Lord, for I am weak; O Lord, heal me, for my bones are vexed."

"Thou art my hiding place; Thou shalt preserve me from trouble . . . "

"Many sorrows shall be to the wicked, but he that trusteth in the Lord, mercy shall compass him about."

"My lovers and my friends stand aloof from my sore and my kinsmen stand afar off."

"They also that seek after my life lay snares for me; and they that seek for my hurt speak mischievous things and imagine deceits all day long."

The words rang out ever stronger and eddied through the air like the breath of a mighty power that bent low all foreheads and cast them down into the dust with tears of sorrow, penance, and supplication. All those present repeated them after the old man and that confused, tearful and monotonous murmur of voices awoke Janina from her torpor. She felt that she was still alive, so she knelt down on the threshold of the room and with fever-parched lips whispered those sweet words long since forgotten, and drew from them a deep comfort full of sadness and tenderness.

"Purge me with hyssop and I shall be clean; wash me and I shall be whiter than snow."

"Hide not thy face from me, lest I be like unto them that go down into the pit."

"And of thy mercy cut off mine enemies, and destroy all them that afflict my soul, for I am thy servant."

She repeated the words fervently and large tears rolled down her face, uniting with the tears of all the other mourners and purging her soul of all sorrows and memory of what had passed. But after a while those tears began to stream so freely and stifle her so that Janina quietly arose and left the place.

On the street she met Wladek running toward the house in haste and fear. He stopped to ask her about his mother, but she went on without even glancing at him.

Almost all feelings were dead within Janina, save that of a deathly weariness. She entered the lighted Church of St. Ann on the Cracow Suburb and, seating herself in one of the pews, gazed at the illuminated altar and the throng of kneeling worshipers. She heard the solemn tones of the organ and a wave of song rising above it. She saw looking at her from the walls and the altars the peaceful and happy faces of saints, but all this did not awaken a single emotion in her.

"Thou wilt cut off mine enemies and destroy all them that afflict my soul. Thou wilt destroy them ..." Janina repeated mechanically and left the church. No, no, she could not pray—she could not.

Janina slept after all this with a deep, stony sleep that was free from dreams.

On the following day Cabinski gave her a big rôle that used to be Mimi's. Janina accepted it with indifference. With the same indifference she went to Niedzielska's funeral. She walked at the end of the procession unnoticed by anyone and gazed indifferently at the thousands of graves in the cemetery and at the coffin and not a scintilla of feeling stirred in her even at the sound of the sobbing over the grave. Something had broken within her and she had lost all ability to feel what was going on about her.

In the evening Janina went to the theater for the performance. She dressed as usual and sat thoughtlessly gazing at the rows of candles pasted to the tables, at the scribbled walls and at the rows of actresses sitting before their mirrors.

Sowinska continually hung about the dressing-room and observed her curiously.

Her companions spoke to Janina, but she did not answer them. Every now and then, she fell into a state of torpor in which one beholds without seeing anything and lives without feeling, while deep within, at the very bottom of her consciousness, there was reflected the image of that dying woman and there swarmed and hissed those stinging and scornful whispers of her neighbors, mixed with the words of the Penitential Psalms.

Suddenly, a tremor ran through Janina, for a voice reached her from the stage which sounded like Grzesikiewicz's; so she arose and went out.

Wladek was standing on the stage, engaged in a lively conversation with Majkowska, whose naked shoulders he was kissing.

Janina paused behind one of the scenes, for some feeling without a name passed through her heart, like the sharp, cold edge of a dagger, but was swiftly gone again, awakening in her a certain knowledge.

"Mr. Niedzielski!" she called.

The actor threw back his shoulders, while across his clean-shaven face there passed a shadow of impatience and boredom. He whispered yet a few words into the ear of Mela, who smiled and departed, and then, without trying to disguise his ill humor, he approached Janina.

"Did you want anything?" he asked irascibly.

"Yes . . . "

In the despondency that filled her at that moment Janina wanted to tell him that she was unhappy and ill. She longed to hear a warm word of sympathy and felt an irresistible need of telling her troubles to someone and of weeping on some friendly breast, but on hearing the sharp tone of Wladek's voice, she suddenly remembered how much she had suffered through him and how base he was, so she suppressed those desires within herself.

"Are we going to play to-day?" she asked.

"We are. There are about a hundred rubles in the treasury."

"Ask them for some money for me."

"What do you think! Do you want me to make a fool of myself? Moreover, I'm going right home."

Janina glanced at him and said in a quiet, expressionless voice: "Take me home, for I feel so very miserable."

"I have no time, I must immediately run to my own home, for already they are all waiting for me there."

"Oh, how base you are! How base you are!" she whispered.

Wladek recoiled a few steps, not knowing whether he should smile, or pretend to be offended.

"Are you saying that to me, to me?" he asked. He did not dare to swear, for that girl with her proud face and glance of a lady imposed respect upon him and thrust back into his throat, as it were, the brutalities that he wanted to hurl at her.

"To you!" Janina answered. "You are base! You are the basest person in the world . . . do you hear! . . . the basest!"

"Janina!" he cried endearingly, as though he wanted to shield himself thereby from her accusation.

"I forbid you to address me in that manner, it insults me!"

"Have you gone crazy, or what has happened to you? What sort of farce do you call that!" he choked out in anger.

"I have found out what you are and I scorn you with my whole soul."

"Whew! So that is the kind of pathetic rôle you have chosen to play? Are you preparing it for your début at the Warsaw Theater?"

Janina answered him only with a look of scorn and walked away.

Sowinska came up to her and with a mysterious and cruel pity in her voice whispered: "It isn't good for you to get so irritated and also, you ought not lace yourself so tightly."

"Why?"

"It may harm you, because . . . because . . ." and she whispered the rest into Janina's ear.

The blood rushed to Janina's face with shame at the thought that Sowinska. had recognized her condition which she was seeking to conceal. She had no more strength left to reply to her, nor time either, for she had to go on the stage.

They were playing *The Peasant Emigration* and Janina appeared in the first act as a super.

In the men's dressing-room that evening, a storm broke out. In the intermission before the so-called "Christmas Eve" scene of the play, Topolski, who was acting the part of "Bartek Kozica," sent to Cabinski a letter, or a sort of ultimatum demanding fifty rubles for himself and Majkowska and, in case of a denial, refusing to play any further. While waiting for Cabinski's reply, he began slowly to remove his make-up.

Cabinski came running almost with tears in his eyes and cried: "I will give you twenty rubles. Oh, oh! you people have no mercy on me!"

"Give me fifty rubles and we shall continue to play; if you don't then . . . " Here he unglued one half of his mustache and began to take off his leggings.

"For God's sake man! there is only one hundred rubles in all in the treasury and that is hardly enough to cover the expenses."

"Let me have fifty rubles immediately, or else you can finish the play yourself or return the public its money," calmly said Topolski, pulling off his other legging.

"Up till now, I had thought that *you*, at least, were a man! Just think what you are doing to us all," pleaded Cabinski.

"Don't you see, Director ... I am undressing."

The intermission was being prolonged and the public outside was beginning to shout and stamp its feet with impatience.

"No, I should sooner have expected death than that! And you, who are my best friend, are you going to go back on me now?" continued Cabinski.

"My dear Director, there's no use talking any further. You can fool everyone else, but not me."

"But I haven't the money. If I give you thirty rubles now, I will have nothing left with which to pay the rent of the theater!" cried Cabinski in despair, running about the dressing-room.

"I have said: if you do not give us fifty rubles, we shall go straight home."

In the hall there began to rise a very pandemonium of shouts and catcalls.

"All right, here is fifty rubles, take them. You are robbing your own companions, but you don't care a rap about that, for you'll have something with which to organize your own company. Here, take them, but that ends all relations between us!"

"Don't worry about my company; I shall reserve the position of a stage-hand for you."

"Sooner will you check coats in my theater, before I join yours."

"Silence, you clown!"

"I'll call the police and they'll quiet you right away!" shouted the infuriated Cabinski.

"I'll silence you immediately, you circus performer!" cried Topolski, who had just finished dressing, and, taking Cabinski by the collar, he gave him a kick that sent him flying out of the dressing-room; then he himself went out on the stage.

The performance was concluded peacefully, but a new quarrel started around the box office. The actors and actresses stood there in a close group so that only their heads and faces, shining with the grease used to wash off the paint, were visible in the gaslight. They were all shouting for money and demanding their overdue salaries. They shook their fists threateningly at the cashier's window, their eyes flashed lightning, and their voices were hoarse from shouting.

Cabinski, still red and trembling from the abuse that had just met him, quarreled with everybody and swore and wanted to pay only the usual installments.

"Whoever isn't satisfied with what he gets, let him go to Topolski! It's all the same to me ..." he cried.

Janina approached the window and said: "Director, you promised to pay me to-day."

"I haven't the money!"

"But neither have I," she begged quietly.

"I am not paying the others either, and yet, they do not importune me as you do."

"Mr. Cabinski, I am almost dying from hunger," she answered straightforwardly.

"Then go and earn some money. All the others know how to help themselves. I like naïve women, but only on the stage. A comédienne! Go to Topolski, he will advance you the money."

"Oh, Topolski assuredly won't let the members of his company suffer poverty. He will pay each what is due him and will not cheat people!" cried Janina impulsively.

"Then you can go straight to him and don't show up here again!" shouted Cabinski, driven to fury by the mention of Topolski.

"Listen there, Director!" began Glas, but Janina listened no longer and, pushing her way through the crowd, left the theater.

"Go and earn it . . ." she repeated to herself.

She walked along the almost empty streets. The gas-lamps cast a ghastly, yellowish glare like that of funeral tapers on the silent and deserted thoroughfares and alleys. The dark-blue vault of the sky hung over the city like a huge canopy embroidered with brightly scintillating stars. A cool breeze swept down the streets and chilled Janina to the marrow.

"Go and earn it!" she again repeated to herself, passing before the Grand Theater. She had come here without being aware of it.

Janina glanced at the building and turned back. An unbearable pain racked her head, as though there was a burning iron ring about it. She was so utterly weak and worn-out that at moments she could scarcely resist the desire to sit down on the curbstone and remain there. Then again, so desperate a realization of her poverty filled her that she was almost ready to give herself to anyone who might ask, if she could only relieve that agonized trembling within herself, that almost deathly weakness and exhaustion.

She dragged herself heavily along the streets, for she no longer knew what to do, and the chill night air, the silence, and that deathly weariness gave her a sort of painful ecstasy. Before her eyes there hovered only phantom forms and fiery spots, so that she knew not where she was or what was happening to her. She felt only one thing and that was that she would no longer be able to endure it.

"What am I going to do further?" Janina asked thoughtlessly, looking before herself.

The silence of the sleeping city and the silence of the dark heavens seemed to be the only answer to her question.

Janina felt as though she were falling swiftly down a steep incline and that there, at the very bottom, lay the outstretched corpse of Niedzielska.

"Death!" she answered herself. "Death!" and she gazed fixedly at that dead face with the congealed tears on its cheeks, and not fear, but an immense silence enveloped her soul.

She looked all about her as though she were seeking for the cause of that deep silence at her side.

Then, she began thinking of her father, of the theater, and of herself, but as though they were things which she had only seen or read about.

"What am I going to do?" Janina asked herself aloud after she had returned home. It was impossible for her to see or even to imagine what the morrow would be like.

"In this condition I can't go to the theater, I can't go anywhere. But what am I going to do? " That question smote her now and then, as with a club.

Day began to dawn and flood the room with its drab and gray light, but Janina still sat on the same spot, gazing blankly out of the window, with deeply sunken eyes and whispering with lips blackened by fever: "What am I going to do? What am I going to do?"

# CHAPTER XI

THE season ended. Cabinski was leaving for Plock with an entirely new company, for Topolski had taken away his best forces and the rest had scattered among various companies.

In the pastry shop on Nowy Swiat, Krzykiewicz, who had broken with Ciepieszewski, was organizing a company of his own. Stanislawski was also starting a small company on a profit-sharing basis. Topolski was already preparing his company for its trip to Lublin.

The local garden-theaters were all closed for the season and a deathly silence reigned over them. The stages were boarded up and the dressing-rooms and entrances locked. The verandas were strewn with broken chairs and rubbish. The autumn leaves fluttered from the trees and torn scraps of programs of the last performances rustled about sadly in the breeze. The season was over.

Nobody visited the theater any more, for the migratory birds were preparing for their flight, only Janina from force of habit, still would come here, gaze a moment at the deserted haunts and return again.

Cabinska wrote her a very cordial letter, inviting her to her home. Janina went there and found that they were already packing up for their journey. Immense trunks and baskets stood in the middle of the rooms, a large pile of various stage paraphernalia together with mattresses and bedding lay on the floor—the entire outfit of a nomadic life.

In Cabinska's room, Janina no longer found either the wreaths or the furniture, or the canopied bed; there shone only the bare walls with the plaster broken here and there by the hasty removal of pictures and the pulling out of hooks. A long basket stood in the middle of the room and the nurse, perspiring from her exertion, was packing into it Pepa's wardrobe. Cabinska, with a cigarette in her mouth, directed the packing and continually scolded the children, who were tumbling in great glee over the mattresses and the straw strewn about the packages.

She greeted Janina with exaggerated cordiality and said: "There is such a dust in here that it is unbearable. Nurse, be careful how you pack, so that you don't crush my dresses. Let us go out on the street," she said to Janina, putting on her coat and hat.

She pulled Janina along to her pastry shop and there, over a cup of chocolate, began to apologize to her for the discourtesy that Cabinski had shown her at the box office.

"Believe me, the director was so excited that he really did not know what he was saying. And can you wonder at it? He was giving his best efforts and even pawning his personal effects, only that the company might lack nothing and, in the meanwhile, along comes Topolski, creates a rumpus and breaks up his company. Even a saint would lose patience in those circumstances and, moreover, Topolski told my husband that you were going to join his company."

Janina answered nothing, for she was now entirely indifferent toward the whole matter, but when Cabinska told her that on that very afternoon they were leaving for Plock and that she should immediately pack her things, for the expressman would call for them directly, she answered with decision: "Thank you for your kindness, Mrs. Directress, but I shall not go."

Cabinska could scarcely believe her ears and cried out in amazement: "Have you already secured an engagement and where?"

"Nowhere, nor do I intend to," answered the girl.

"How is that! Are you going to abandon the stage? You who have a big future before you!"

"I have had more than enough of acting," answered Janina with bitterness.

"Come now, don't reproach me with it, you know it's your first year on the stage and they wouldn't give you big rôles at once, anywhere."

"Oh, I am no longer going to try for them."

"And I had already been planning that in Plock you would live together with us and that would not only make it easier for you, but my daughter also could derive more benefit from it. Please think it over and I, on my part, assure you that you will also get rôles."

"No, no! I have enough of poverty and have absolutely no more strength left to bear it any further and, moreover, I cannot,

I cannot . . . " answered Janina quietly, with tears in her eyes, for that proposal flashed before her mind like the dawn of a better future and awakened for a moment her old enthusiasm and dreams of artistic triumph. But immediately she thought of her present condition and the sufferings that she would have to endure on that account, so she added with even greater emphasis: "No, I cannot! I cannot!"

But she could not hold back the tears which continued to stream quietly down her face until even Cabinska was touched and, drawing nearer to her, whispered with sincere sympathy, "For God's sake what is the matter with you? Tell me, perhaps I shall be able to help you."

In reply Janina blushed faintly, warmly clasped Cabinska's hand, and hastily left the pastry shop.

Tears were stifling her; life was stifling her.

Immediately afterward Stanislawski came to Janina and urged her to leave with him for the small provincial towns. He was organizing a company of from eight to nine persons in which each was to hold a share. He offered Janina leading rôles and spoke in glowing terms of the certain success that awaited them in the provincial towns. He enumerated all those whom he was engaging: all young people and novices, full of energy, zeal, and talent. And he promised himself that he would lead them along the path of true art, that his company would be in the nature of a school for drama and that he would be a real teacher and father, who would make of these people true artists worthy of the theater and its traditions.

Janina refused Stanislawski briefly. She thanked him heartily for the kindness he had shown her during the summer and took leave of him cordially, as though forever.

When he had gone, she determined finally to end it all. She had not yet told herself decisively: "I will die!" So far, if someone had told her that she was contemplating suicide she would have denied it sincerely, but already that thought and desire were lurking in the subconscious depths of her mind.

Janina knew when the Cabinskis were leaving, so she went down to the steamboat landing. She stood upon the bridge and watched them steam away. She gazed at the gray waves of the Wisla splashing against the sides of the pier and at the distant horizon veiled in autumn mists, and such an intense sadness and grief overwhelmed her that she could not move from the spot, or tear her eyes away from the water.

Night fell and Janina still stood there, gazing before her. The rows of lights on the river banks sprang up from the darkness like golden flowers and dotted the rocking, greenish surface of the water with quivering gleams. The din and hum of the city echoed dimly behind her, the hacks sped with noisy clatter across the bridge, the bells of the tramcars clanged incessantly, crowds of people passed by with laughter; sometimes the echo of a song reached Janina, or the merry tones of a hand organ, then again, a warm breath of wind, saturated with the raw odor of the river, fanned her feverish face. All these sights and sounds beat against her as against a lifeless statue and rebounded again without making any impression on her.

The water in its depths began to pass through ever stranger transformations: it turned black, but that blackness was interwoven with gleams of light, flames of red, streaks of violet, and rays of yellow, like the glowing flame of pain. There, in those silent depths, there seemed to be a better and fuller life, for the waves murmured so joyously, broke against the piers and stone bulwarks and, as though with frenzied laughter, united again, blended, tumbled over one another and flowed on. Janina seemed almost to hear their care free laughter, their calling to one another and their voice of mighty joy.

"What are you doing here?" suddenly said a voice behind her.

Janina trembled and turned around slowly. Wolska was standing before her and curiously and uneasily watching her.

"Oh, nothing, I was just gazing about."

"Come with me, the air here isn't healthy," said Wolska, taking Janina by the arm, for she read in her dimmed eyes a suicidal intent.

Janina allowed herself to be led away and only after they had gone some distance, she asked quietly, "So you have not left with Cabinski?"

"I couldn't. You see, my Johnnie's health is again worse. The doctor has forbidden me to move him from bed and I believe that it would kill him," whispered Wolska sadly. "I had to stay, for, of course, I can't send him to the hospital. If it comes to the worst, we shall die together, but I will not forsake him. The doctor still gives me some hope that he will recover."

Janina gazed with a strange feeling at the face of Wolska which, though worn and faded, beamed with a deep motherly love. She looked like a beggar woman in her dark, stained cloak and gray dress, frayed at the bottom; she wore a straw hat and black mended gloves and carried a parasol which was rusty from continual use. But through all this poverty there shone, as bright as the sun, her love for her child. She saw and heeded nothing else, for all that did not concern her child had no meaning for her.

Janina walked alongside of her, gazing with admiration at this woman. She knew her story. Wolska was the daughter of a rich and intelligent family. She fell in love with an actor, or else with the theater itself, and went on the stage and, although later her lover abandoned her and she suffered poverty and humiliation, she could not tear herself away from the theater and now, she centered all her love and all her hopes upon her child that had been seriously ill since the spring.

"Where does she get all her strength?" thought Janina and then, turning to Wolska, she asked: "What are you doing now?"

Wolska shuddered, a faint blush flitted over her worn face and her lips quivered with a painful expression as she answered: "I sing . . . What else could I do? I must live and must earn enough to pay Johnnie's doctor bills. I must. Although it fills me with shame to do it, I must. Alas, such is my fate, such is my fate!" she moaned complainingly.

"But I don't know what you mean," said Janina, who could not understand why Wolska should feel ashamed to earn a living by singing.

"Because, you see, Miss Janina, I don't want anybody to know about it. . . . You will keep it to yourself, won't you?" she begged with tears in her eyes.

"Certainly I give you my word. Moreover, whom would I tell …? I am all alone in the world."

"I sing in a restaurant on Podwal St.," said Wolska in a low and hurried voice.

"In a restaurant!" whispered Janina, standing stock-still in amazement.

"What else could I do? Tell me, what else could I do? I need money for food and rent. How else could I earn it, when I don't even know how to sew? At home I knew how to play on the piano a bit and could speak a little French, but of course, that would not bring me a penny now. I saw an advertisement in the *Courier* for a singer, so I went there and got the position.

They pay me a ruble a day together with meals and . . . " but tears choked her voice and she grasped Janina's hand and pressed it feverishly. Janina returned the hand-clasp with a similar one and they walked on in silence.

"Come along with me, won't you? It will make me feel a little more at ease," said Wolska.

Janina willingly agreed.

They entered the restaurant "Under the Bridge" on Podwal St. It was a long and narrow garden with a few miserable trees. At the very entrance there was a well. A whitewashed fence on the left side of the garden divided it from the neighboring property which must have been a lumberyard, for piles of beams and boards could be seen looming above the fence. A few kerosene lanterns illuminated the place. A number of little white tables with varnished tops and around them three times that number of rough-hewn chairs constituted the entire furnishings of that summer restaurant. A small office on the ground floor and the top of the neighboring house enclosed the right side of the garden, while at the back there arose a high, rough brick wall with small, dirty, and barred windows; it was the rear of the former Kochanowski Palace, standing on the corner of Miodowa and Kapitulna Streets.

Near the fence, a small stage shaded by a canvas roof with its two open sides facing toward the audience, formed a sort of niche, the walls of which were covered with a cheap, blue paper dotted with silver stars. The smoking kerosene footlights on one side of the stage cast a drab light upon a musician with a disheveled gray beard and grease-stained coat, who was pounding away at the keyboard of a wretched piano with an automatic motion of his arms and head.

The garden was filled with a public of working-class people and those from the poorer section of the city.

Janina and Wolska pushed their way through the crowd to that little office building in which there was a dressing-room for the performers, divided into a men's and women's compartment by a red cretonne curtain.

"I am already waiting!" came a hoarse, drunken voice from behind the curtain.

"You can begin your part, I will come right away!" answered Wolska, dressing herself in feverish haste in a grotesque, red costume.

In a few minutes she was all ready for her appearance. Janina followed her out and took a seat facing the stage. Wolska, all flushed with hurrying and still closing the last buttons and hooks of her costume, appeared on the stage, greeting the public with a long bow. The musician struck the yellow keys and at the same moment there arose the tones of a song:

> Once upon a stump among the hills,
> Between the oaks there sat two turtle-doves,
> And I know not for what sport of love's
> They kissed each other with their bills.

The strains of the old, sentimental song from *The Cracovians and the Mountaineers* floated on, interrupted only by frequent bursts of applause, the banging of beer glasses against the tables, the clatter of plates, the slamming of doors and the reports or rifles in the shooting galleries. The lanterns diffused a hazy and muddy light; girls in white aprons and with their hands full of beer glasses, passed in and out among the tables, flirted with the drinking men and flung cynical remarks and answers at those who accosted them. Ribald laughter and coarse jokes flew around like fire-works and were immediately answered by broad, thoughtless merriment.

The public expressed its satisfaction with the singing by shouting, beating time with their canes, and banging their beer glasses. At moments the wind would entirely drown out the singing, or bend the few wretched trees with a rustling sound and scatter the leaves over the stage and the heads of the public.

Wolska continued to sing. Her red vaudeville costume, with low-cut front, gleamed like a gaudy spot against the blue background of the stage and excellently accentuated her thin, thickly painted face, her sunken and pale eyes, and her sharp features which looked like the skeleton-like face of a starving man. She swayed from side to side with a heavy motion to the measure of the song:

> Such ardent love took hold of me,
> I embraced Stach most tenderly.

Her voice floated through the garden with a hollow, rasping sound and added to the din made by that noisy and drunken crowd. Brutal laughs broke out in sharp, penetrating scales, and those bravos emitted by the drunken threats of a Sunday public and interrupted by hiccoughs, beat against the stage with a hoarse and hollow roar together with the biting jibes that were not spared the singer. But she heard nothing and sang on, indifferent and cold to all that surrounded her. She flung forth tones, words, and mimicry with the automatism of a hypnotized woman, only at moments, her eyes would seek Janina's as though they were begging for pity.

Janina grew pale and red by turns, unable to endure any longer that alcohol-saturated atmosphere and that drunken din which filled her with aversion and disgust.

"I would rather die!" she thought. Oh, no, she would never be able to amuse such a public. She would spit in its eyes and scorn herself and then ... if there were no other way out ... drown herself in the Wisla!

Wolska finished her song and her partner, dressed in a Cracovian costume, went about among the drinking crowd with his notes in his hand, collecting money. Remarks that froze one with their cynicism and brutal frankness, were hurled into his face, but he only smiled with the dull smile of a habitual drunkard, nervously twitched his lips and humbly bowed his thanks for those ten-copeck pieces that were thrown on his notes.

Wolska, with closed eyes, stood beside the piano, nervously tugged at the golden lace of her waist and, groaning with painful anxiety, counted in her mind the number of copecks which her partner placed together with the notes beside her. The pianist again struck the keys and Wolska and her partner began to sing together some comic couplets, interwoven with a kind of "Krakowiak" which they danced in a half dreamy manner.

Janina could hardly wait for the end of the performance and, without saying anything about the impression that that drinking den had made on her, she took leave of Wolska and fairly ran away from that garden, that public, and that degradation.

During the entire day following, she did not leave her home. She ate nothing and hardly thought at all, but lay in bed and gazed blankly at the ceiling, following with her eyes, the last fly that crept drowsily and half dead over it.

In the evening, Sowinska came in, sat down on a trunk and, without any introduction, said harshly: "The room is already rented to another tenant, so to-morrow you can clear out of here.

And since you owe us fifteen rubles, I will keep all your duds and give them back to you only when you pay me the money."

"Very well," answered Janina and she looked at Sowinska indifferently, as though nothing out of the ordinary were at stake. "Very well, I shall go!" she added in a quieter tone and arose from the bed.

"You will doubtlessly manage to help yourself in some way, won't you? You will yet come to see me in a carriage, eh?" said Sowinska and an ugly, hostile light gleamed in her owlish eyes.

"Very well," repeated Janina in the same mechanical way and began to pace up and down the room.

Sowinska, growing tired of waiting for some kind of reply, left the room.

"So all is ended!" whispered Janina in a hollow voice and the thought of death became a conscious reality in her mind and shone alluringly.

"What is death? A forgetting, a forgetting!" she answered herself aloud, standing still and sinking her eyes in those murky deeps that opened up before her soul.

"Yes, a forgetting, a forgetting!" she repeated slowly and for a long time sat motionless, gazing at the flame of the lamp.

The night dragged on slowly, the house became quiet, the lights were gradually extinguished in the long rows of windows and an ever deeper silence spread itself about, until everything became steeped in this drowsy silence.

The gray light of dawn was already beginning to streak the horizon and to illumine the faint outlines of the housetops when Janina awoke from her torpor and gazed about the room. She felt fully determined, so she sprang up from her chair and, driven on by some thought that lit up her eyes with a strange fire, walked quietly to the door and opened it. But the noisy click of the latch which she closed after her penetrated her with such a strange, sharp fear that she reeled back against the frame of the door and breathed heavily for a few moments. Finally, she quietly pulled off her shoes and boldly, but with the utmost caution, passed through the hall and entered a large room adjoining the kitchen which was used as a dining room and a workroom in the day time and as a sleeping room for Mme. Anna's apprentices at night. The close and heavy air of the room almost suffocated Janina. With outstretched hands and bated breath, she stole toward the kitchen so slowly that those minutes seemed an eternity to her. At moments, she paused and, overcoming her trembling—that awful trembling—listened to the loud breathing and snoring of those sleeping there and then went on again, setting her teeth with a desperate strength. Large drops of perspiration rolled down her forehead from exertion and fear and her heart beat so slowly and painfully that she almost felt the pulsation of it in her throat. The kitchen door was open and Janina passed through it like a shadow, but she stumbled against the bed of the servant-girl, which stood very near the door. She grew numb with fear and for a long time stood motionless and breathless, almost in a state of suspended animation, gazing with terrified eyes at the bed whose dim outlines she could scarcely make out in the darkness. But finally, rallying all her strength and courage, she walked boldly to the shelf upon which stood various kitchen utensils and supplies and felt one after another with the greatest caution, until finally, her hand rested upon a flat oblong bottle containing essence of vinegar. She had seen it here a few hours ago and now, having found it, she snatched it up so violently from among the other articles that a tin cover fell with a crash upon the floor. Janina unconsciously bent her head in terror, for the clash of the falling cover resounded with such a tremendous echo in her brain that it seemed as though the whole world were crashing down on her.

"Who's there?" called the servant, awakened by the noise. "Who's there?" she repeated in a louder voice.

"It is I . . . I came for a drink of water," answered Janina with a choking voice, after a long while, nervously pressing the bottle to her breast. The servant indistinctly mumbled something and did not speak again.

Janina ran to her room, as though pursued by the furies of madness, no longer caring whether anyone heard her or might awaken and, having reached it, locked the door and only then collapsed, half dead from exhaustion and trembled so violently that she thought she would fall to pieces. The tears, which she did not even feel, began to stream down her face. They gave her so great a relief that she fell asleep. In the morning Sowinska again reminded her that it was time to move and, brutally opening the door before her, told her to get out. Janina dressed hastily and, without answering a word, left the house.

She walked along the streets, feeling nothing but her homelessness and that dizziness in her head which was engulfing all her thoughts. She passed through Nowy Swiat and the Ujazdowskie Allées and did not stop until she reached the lake in Lazienki Park.

The trees stood dying and their yellow leaves spread a golden carpet over the paths. The tranquillity of an autumn day hung in the air and only now and then a flock of sparrows flew by with a noisy twitter, or the swans upon the lake cried out mournfully and beat with their wings the muddy-green water that looked like worn velvet. All around could be seen the destruction wrought by the hand of golden autumn. Wherever it touched the trees, there the leaves withered and fell to the ground, the grass dried up and the last autumn asters bent their lifeless heads and dripped with dew, as though weeping tears after death.

"Death!" whispered Janina, pressing in her hands the bottle that she had secured on the previous night and she sat down, perhaps on the same bench on which she had sat that spring. It seemed to her that she was slowly drowsing away and that her thoughts were fading, for her consciousness had begun to disintegrate and she was already ceasing to feel and to know. Everything was falling away from her and dying, like the nature about her that also seemed to be burning out and drawing its last breath.

A rapturous feeling, full of peace and calm, filled Janina's heart, for the entire past was vanishing from her memory; all her miseries, all her disappointments, and all her struggles faded away, paled and dispersed, as though absorbed by that pale autumn sun that hung over the park. It seemed to her that she had never passed through them, never felt anything, never suffered anything. It seemed to her that she was curling up within herself, growing smaller and shrinking, like that withered leaf that hung upon the barbed wire of the fence, all ready to drop and be hurled down into the abyss of death by that light breath of wind. Then again it seemed to her that she was ripping to pieces, like that spider web that tangled itself about the grass and floated in glistening filaments through the air; that she was unwinding into such gossamer strands, into ever finer and finer filaments, until she had vanished away into infinity and lost all consciousness of herself. This feeling moved her strongly and a strange tenderness and pity for herself filled her heart with sorrow.

"Poor girl! How unhappy she is!" whispered Janina, as though she was speaking of some other person.

Janina's soul was so rapidly disintegrating in its agony that she no longer had a full and clear conception of what the miseries were that had vanquished her, what misfortunes had broken her, nor did she know why she was weeping or who she was.

"Death!" she repeated mechanically and that word found a deep and unconscious echo in her brain and nerves and pressed only a few tears from her eyes.

She stopped, without knowing why, before the marble figure of the dancing Faun. The rains had darkened his stony body and rusted the locks of his hair that curled like hyacinths, and his face, furrowed by streams of water, seemed to have grown longer since the spring, but in his eyes there gleamed and burned that same mockery and his crooked legs continued their mad dance. "Io! Io! Io!" he seemed to sing, shaking his flute, laughing and jeering at everything, and raising boldly to the sun his head which was crowned as though with a bacchantic wreath by the withered leaves that had fallen on it.

Janina gazed at him, but being unable to remember or understand anything, she passed on.

On Nowy Swiat, in one of the *chambres garnies*, she asked for a room, ink, letter-paper, and envelopes. When everything had been supplied, Janina locked herself up in the room and wrote two letters: one brief, dry, and painfully ironical letter to her father and another longer and entirely calm one to Glogowski. She notified them both of her suicide. She addressed the letters with the greatest accuracy and laid them in a conspicuous place.

Afterwards Janina calmly took from her pocket the bottle with the poison, uncorked it, held the liquid up to the light and then, without thinking or hesitating any longer—drank it to the very dregs.

Suddenly, she stretched out her arms, a gleam of terror shot across her face, her eyes closed, as though blinded by some measureless void that opened before, and she fell prone upon the floor, in dreadful convulsions of pain.

A few days later, Kotlicki, having returned from Lublin where he had installed Topolski's company, was sitting in a coffee-house, looking over the newspapers, and by some strange chance his eye fell upon the following item among the local accidents of the day:

"THE SUICIDE OF AN ACTRESS

"On Tuesday, in the *chambres garnies* on Nowy Swiat, the servants were aroused by moans issuing from one of the rooms which an hour ago had been engaged by an unknown woman. They broke open the door and a dreadful sight met their eyes. Upon the floor lay writhing in pain a young and beautiful woman. Two letters left behind by her revealed that she was a certain Janina Orlowska, a former chorus girl who appeared last season in the N. N. Theater under Cabinski's management.

"A physician was called and the unconscious woman was taken to the Hospital of the Infant Jesus. Her condition is serious but it still holds forth some hope. Miss Orlowska poisoned herself with essence of vinegar, as is attested by the bottle that was found in her room. The cause of her desperate act is unknown, but an investigation is being made. . . . "

Kotlicki read this over several times, knitted his brows, tugged at his mustache, read it again and, finally, crumpled up *The Courier* and threw it in anger upon the floor.

"A comédienne! A comédienne!" he whispered scornfully, biting his lips.

# THE END

# For the Love of Children

"Witek! My dearest Witek!"

The boy stopped the young stallion that he was riding and glanced back to reply in an irritated voice, "What?.. Whoa, you devils! Don't think I'll let you make mess again, you swines."

He slapped the horse to get in advance of a herd of colts, which were scattered along the road and across the meadow, and drive them all together. Having done so, he approached the garden fence, near which a girl, aged ten or so, was standing.

"My dear Witek, help me climb over the fence, will you? Oh please, dear! I'm afraid lest I fall!" she prattled sweetly, clinging to the sharp-pointed stakes that composed the fence.

"No way I can get there."

He rolled the legs of his trousers down off his knees quite indifferently.

"Just come closer!"

"How should I cross the ditch?"

"Indeed," the little thing cast a glance of disappointment at the deep ditch that paralleled the fence.

"Just hold a stake firmly, Miss, and get down on all fours."

"What's on all fours?"

"What's the point of talking to women? You can't understand anything! Can you hold the stake with your legs and let yourself slip down?"

"I understand, I do!" She recalled the way Ewka had slipped down from the mow. "Turn away while I'm getting down!"

"Why?"

"Because I told you to!"—she shouted indignantly, and her face blushed with anger at him because he would not understand.

The boy snorted but obeyed to turn away. She dropped the book she had been holding onto the footpath and slipped down the fence just the way Witek recommended. She stepped across the ditch with a cheerful shout, "Will you bring your horse here? I want to ride with you!"

This made the boy give his head a scratch of anxiety.

"Give me your hand, now! I want to have a ride with you!"

251

"Somebody can see us riding and tell noble Mistress," Witek grumbled in a sour voice.

"Nobody will know. We'll go to the woods or to the meadows. Please, Witek, darling!.."

"I dare not, Miss! Noble Master said, if they caught me riding with you, he'd get me whipped…"

"Dad won't find out. Give me your hand, won't you? Don't you want me to give you a scarlet ribbon to wear on your shirt?"

That appeared compelling. The boy stretched out his bare foot, which the girl used as a stirrup, and held her by the hand as she jumped onto the horse in front on Witek, clinging to the stallion's mane, and began to kick his flanks with her shoes on unstockinged feet. The horse tender drew her closer with one hand, slapping the the horse on the neck with the other to turn round; he whistled and spurred the horse, detting him on a wild gallop.

They rushed along the road to the bottomland lying in between the estate park and the forest. The girl was smiling happily with both her lips and her eyes, seized by a wild daring, a passionate need to rush on and on, to get a chestful of fresh air, to shout; she was jumping and pricking the horse forward. Her cheeks were glowing; her hair was fluttering in the wind; the vast fields were flashing before her eyes. She felt very lightheaded at times and could hardly catch her breath, but she kept pricking the horse, shouting in a boisterous voice, "Hop! Hop!" And they arrowed on. Witek held her tightly, battering the stallion's flanks with his heels with increasing frequency, and, fascinated to be racing so madly, also cried loudly, "Hop! Hop!"

"Hop! Hop!" the girl echoed cheerfully and galloped on, as if glued to the horse's back, heated, delighted, her eyes half closed. They shot across the bottomland without noticing the haymakers, crossed the river in a shallow spot, and galloped over the fields with crops already eared, across grasslands, where herds were grazing and shepherds were shouting merrily to each other.

They rode unconsciously on and on, breathless, until a high wall of the woods blocked their way. Exhausted, the horse slowed down and began to balk. Having stopped on the forest fringe, Witek jumped off onto the ground; the girl did the same. She took his hand, while he used his free one to hold the horse's mane, and they went into the woods.

Gloom and a solemn silence reigned there. The children chose a small mossy glade to have a rest. Lying on his stomach, Witek sniffed and panted, while the girl wiped her face covered with perspiration. Hearing a noise in the woods, she felt anxious and moved closer to her defender. Golden pine trunks stood still like thousands of pillars supporting a green dome, below which lay a carpet of rust colored moss as soft as silk, and every once in a while fans of fern swayed gently in a sudden waft of wind. Hardly poking through a mass of branches, the sun was drawing fancy golden arabesques on the moss and on light green hazel leaves.

The children drank the tarry forest aroma. The silence made them feel eerie, and they sat for a long time without saying a word, listening to a woodpecker chiseling on a pine restlessly and an occasional crow croaking on its way over the trees. A faint echo of the haymakers' songs sometimes reached them from the fields; somewhere in the woods, people called out cheerfully to each other. Then everything grew so silent that the children could hear long golden pine needles murmur as they fell onto the ground. A tiding of magpies appeared; they fought and made enough chatter to make the woods boil with noise, and then flew away. Bugs chirped; a bee flew by in search of flowers, buzzing. Sometimes they could hear a squirrel crunch on last year's cones, or wind flutter among treetops, shattering the calm of giant pines, which swayed for a while afterward, exchanging whispers of indignation. Sun glints sank in the green covert, and amber colored tree trunks glowed like cloth of gold. But then a shadow crept over the forest, soaking into it, and the forest grew dark; everything seemed to disappear out of sight; vague plaintive moans reached them through the noise of the woods, and the cold breath of the thicket flushed a piercing cold in the children's faces.

Suddenly the horse, who had been nibbling on young shrub leaves, neighed anxiously, and the children felt joyful again, fatigue forgotten. Witek spotted a crow's nest on a pine and tried to get it but could not climb that high. The girl made an attempt of her own to no avail but a torn dress and scratches on her legs. They raced, hiding from each other behind trees, and tumbled. The girl was desperate to learn to stand upside down, but she walloped down every time in spite of Witek's holding her legs, and the two of them broke into merry laughter. Witek cut two hazel sticks and taught the girl to play another game. They made the woods reverberate with laughter, and the young colt echoed it, neighing and running after them like a dog. The girl was having great fun and forgot everything else. When they were tired of games, it occurred to them that it was time to return. They rode at a slow pace.

Witek seemed to be concerned—he fidgeted all the time, casting glances towards the place where he had left his herd.

"I'm thirsty," the girl said as they were crossing the river, and the horse stopped to draw in some muddy water through his teeth. Witek bent down to get some water in his straw hat and gave it to her. She gulped it. "Why is it so muddy?" "They've opened water locks in Kotliny. Look, you can see it overflow!" River waves, covered in yellowish foam, roared by, flooding the banks.

"Where's Finka?" the girl asked. "How should I know? She must be running about. She wasn't with me as I was grazing horses yesterday." "Has she got puppies yet?" "No, she hasn't." "Bring me one, will you? I love puppies! It will sleep in a bed with my doll. "Oh yes! They'll never let it. Noble Master will get it drowned in a swamp. Oh, Miss, let's ride faster!" Witek added, thinking of the landowner. "Wait a little! Just look how beautiful it is!" "I left the colts on the road…If they didn't go to the fold but got into the rye—it's a trouble!" he kicked the horse to make him pick up the pace. "How beautiful! Look, look, Witek!" she pointed at the setting sun. "Indeed! Red as fire…"

The girl was lost in contemplation of the sky, and Witek kept speeding the horse, terrified by the thought of the colts.

In the west, the grey blue sky seemed to be covered in gold-emroidered scarlet scales. The sun hung low above the ground like a gigantic lashless eye, unbearably radiant, and a long copper colored strip flashed crimson stretched above it. Seized by the sunset flame, barley spikes looked an opalescent greenish gold, and the rye was the shade of steel. The sanguine carpet of clover blossom, spangled with lilac anemone specks, was very distinct against the grayish oat fields. Sunlight falling straight on trees produced long shadows, making them look like mythical giants. Leaves were golden on one side and black on the other. The sun lavished streams of light on leaves and branches, turning roadside grass into a golden background for shadow patterns, like artists did in the ancient Byzantine Empire.

Time passed by. Darkness crawled out from unknown coverts to spread in widening circles. The sun waned, and gloom grew thicker in burrows, ravines, under wide pear branches; the moon was silvery with dew, and a purple haze was creeping over it. Silence was descending to embrace the world.

Witek noticed nothing of that; he kept saying ever and again, "Quick, Miss, for God's sake, quick!" "Don't you be afraid. I'll ask Dad not to beat you. Riding with you is so much fun! I don't understand—why should Mommy forbid me to?" "Because you are not expected to mix with me." "Why, Witek?" "You're the daughter of a landowner, and I'm a colt tender." "So what? Riding with you is more fun than learning silly French words." "It doesn't matter. You're noble, and I'm a peasant." "But Madam says all people are the same." "How come? The nobles have plenty of land, they are learned; their clothes and ways are not like peasants'." "Witek, why won't your mother send you to school?" "She's got no money. I think I'll always be an unlettered peasant." "If you had money, Witek, what would you do?" "If I had money, Miss, I'd learn whatever the noble are taught... and get decent clothes... If I had enough money, I'd buy some land from Klemb or Gulbas, breed horses and cows... I'd be a good landowner, and the peasant would appoint me their *wójt*[*]... I'd carry the baldachin over the priest on holidays..." Witek smiled wistfully.

"Madam is always getting a pony saddled for me; it's as slow as a calf, isn't it?" "It is, Miss." "When I'm a grown up, I'll only ride my father's horses. You don't believe me, Witek, do you?" "Those are studhorses, flyers. You can't cope with them, Miss." "Well, you can ride with me. Will you, Witek?" "Maybe I will, if I become a coachman." "We'll dress the horses like they do in Kraków, lots of ribbons, and ride in the new carriage, the one my Daddy bought... Fast, very fast! Won't we, Witek?" "We will, Miss." "Witek, where's my book?" "How should I know? Is it the one with pictures?"

---

[*] The mayor of a village.

"No, that's another one. French Grammar. I brought it to the park to learn my lesson. God, where did I put it? Oh, Mother will be so angry! Let's go there, - maybe I left it when I climbed the fence…"

They galloped until they reached the estate. The girl jumped off the horse and soon found her book. The poor grammar was lying on the ground, its pages in a mess, still bearing a hoof print. The girl was terrified to see it; she tried to wipe it with her dress, but it did not help.

"Give me a lift." Witek bent down, and she jumped onto his shoulders, got onto the fence, slipped down in a moment, and disappeared into the park.

Witek went on search of the colts, looking round with anxiety. In the meanwhile, the girl opened the book and began to prepare her lesson hurriedly, reading out the words. "J'aime, il aime, tu aimes, vous aimez, nous aimons, ils aiment," she repeated the rule with such zealousness that she did not hear the voice calling her at first. "Tosia! Tosia!" Tosia startled and ran towards the house, conjugating the French words even more hastily. She was scared. In spite of the hurry, she noticed that her teacher was standing on the terrace that overlooked the garden. Tosia ran even faster; she rounded the house and walked across the yard to the main entrance, whispering with exasperation, "J'aime, il aime, tu aimes, vous aimez, nous aimons…" She failed to recall what came next and suddenly broke off, seeing her mother on the porch, looking at the girl intently from the distance.

The mistress could easily guess that her daughter had been horseriding—Tosia's hair was disheveled, her dress wrinkled and torn, pieces of peaty soil from the ditch stuck to her yellow shoes. Her mother just asked in a snappy tone, "Where is Madam?" "I don't know, Mommy. I… I was in the park… preparing my lessons… I haven't seen her," Tosia muttered apologetically, shaking with fear and sidling bashful, suppliant glances at her mother.

"Show me the book!" The girl went pale and began to conjugate the French verb feverishly again. "What is your assignment?" Tosia showed the page. "Tell. And watch yourself!.." Scared to hear her mother speak so harshly, Tosia blabbered. "Speak slowly and distinctly!" hissed her mother; it took her a great effort to keep down her irritation. "J'aime, il aime… j'aime… j'aime…" the girl muttered unconsciously with dismay. "Repeat it!" the mother ordered, gripping harder on the whip that she had been hiding behind her back.

Tosia noticed the move foreboding a punishment; she stood stupefied, unable to utter a word, merely gazing at her mother, her eyes wide and dull with terror. "So this is how you learned your lessons! It must be for you to remain ignorant why I pay the teacher, indeed! Have you been in the park?" "Yes, Mommy," said Tonya in a tearful whisper, which was barely audible. "Don't you lie!" the mother lashed her across her back. Hysterical, the girl fell on her knees in front of her mother, crying loudly, shaking with pain and panic. "Mother! Mommy!" she kept repeating madly. "Will you mix with horse tenders, you worthless child? I shall teach you a lesson! I shall flog out your love for them savages! A girl of ten years! To know not a single word in French! To spend two years playing scales! You bloody bastard, you care for nothing but servant girls and horseriding with that Witek of yours! I can show you what is what, you monster!" speaking so, she kept whipping her daughter as heavily as she could.

The girl writhed with pain, trying to catch her mother's hands, clinging to her legs, grasping at her dress, and then trying to shield herself from the blows, groaning, "Mommy! Mommy!" Her mommy grew even more frantic, whipping her on and on.

The teacher put an end to the torture by tearing the girl, mad with pain, from her mother's hands.

The landlady collapsed onto a bench, red in the face with rage; panting, she was tearing her bodice clasps. Seeing a worker walk by the porch, she struggled to wheeze, "I want Witek here!" She still needed somebody to shout at and to beat until her nerves could calm down.

"What a punishment of a daughter!" she spoke after a long pause, and her thin face with high cheekbones was contorted with anger again. "No matter how much I do for her—I go out of my way, I pay for her teachers—for nothing! Mrs Zielinska comes to tell me, oh, so spitefully, that she has seen Tosia and Witek riding across the fields. I was so ashamed that I wished the ground could swallow me up! Zielinska has two daughters, true dolls of daughters. Perfect manners, fluent French, piano concerts for guests. This disgraceful girl has brought nothing but shame on me! I order to call for her, telling my guests that Tosia is preparing her lessons in the park, but the filthy woman just has to persuade me that she has seen Tosia riding bareback, Witek holding her by the waist. What a scandal! What will she grow to be? She will only ride about with shag rags, nothing more. What can one expect if she is never told a thing and is allowed to do whatever she fancies?" "I do not interfere with her upbringing or order her about, for this is what we agreed upon in the very beginning. The girl's upbringing has been very poor. She is not naturally gifted, and constant nagging and reprimanding have made her downtrodden." "How dare you tell me this! My daughter's upbringing—poor! She is not gifted! I am a bad mother, I treat my own child badly! Have you ever heard such a thing? I pay you for teaching her—why else should you be here? Instead, you're always making eyes at men if not devouring yet another book Darwin! Idling around in peasants' huts—look at this benefactress, this do-gooder! You prefer to take care of them dogs, while the girl is left to herself and can do what she wants to! No wonder, given your example..." "I do not want to reply to your insults, because you are merely an insane woman! I can leave tomorrow; I have had enough of your noble bread!" She banged the door closed at leaving. The landlady dashed about the porch, hissing through clenched teeth, "Oh, that viper, that Warsaw whore! Oh, scum!.."

"Don't you dare leave!" she shouted at Tosia, who was going to steal away. The girl sat down on a bench, and, covering her glowing face, swollen from crying, with her hands, tried to control her convulsive sobbing but could not cope with it.

"We pay her a hundred rubles and treat her like an equal— so this is her gratitude! A shoemaker's daughter—pah!—dares make fuss and give me sermons! Please do leave and break your neck! I can get a dozen teachers like you at my whistle!.. Aha!"

"Get him closer!"—she shouted to the worker, who was dragging along protesting Witek.

"Let me go, Kuba! Let go, you devil! Come on, let me go, for God's sake!" "Oh yeah! She'd tear my head off!"

Grabbing him firmly by the collar, Kuba put Witek up and placed him standing on the porch. The landlady darted towards him, caught his hair, and, for a start, battered his round-cheeked childish face with her fist. "You bloody bastard! Did I told you not to ride with my daughter? Did I? You dare disobey, you son of a bitch! You dare hold my daughter with your savage claws! Take her for a ride! So this is how you obey your masters, huh?" She thrashed the whip violently across his body. "Oh, Mistress, I won't, I'll never do it again! For God's sake! Oh, dear! Jesus! Oh dear! I won't!"

"Mommy, dear! Mommy, it was me who wanted it; it's not Witek's fault!" Tosia screamed, shielding Witek with her body and clinging to her mother's legs; but she got her hands lashed, pulled away and ran inside, waving them and crying.

At last, the noble mistress calmed down; Witek could hardly breathe by that time. She kicked him off the porch and left.

The boy tumbled down the steps, hitting his face against the gravel of the parkway. "She beat me, Mommy, she beat me so badly!" he wailed and howled, but soon got onto his feet and wobbled into the kitchen, feeling his cheeks, and shoulders, and head, constantly whining, "They beat my, Mommy, they beat me!"

"Witek, do come here!" The boy rushed to his mother, who was mashing potatoes by the door. "Mommy, it hurts!" She gave up her work, patted his hair down, and wiped his face, cut across with livid bruises, with her apron. "What a witch, damn you! To beat a child like this! Pest on you, beast! To treat human beings worse than dogs!" She entered the kitchen and brought a piece of bread and half a cup of buttermilk for the boy. "Here, eat this, and don't you cry! God sees everything, even though his punishment may not be quick…May you see no good, bitch!.. There, there, don't you cry!"

The boy gradually quietened; he ate his bread with buttermilk, brushing his sleeve against his eyes to wipe away the tears that still welled from time to time. His mother stood near, stroking him gently over the head, and said when he had finished, "Go to bed. I'll come later and bring you some of the dinner leftovers. Hurry up lest the pest comes and beats you again!" "Please get something for Finka, too, Mommy."

Witek left. He whistled from time to time on his way, calling for the dog in a soft voice, "Finka! Finka!" He sought in every corner of the yard, but the dog was nowhere to be seen. All of a sudden, he heard a noise and shouts from where the mill was—and he ran in that direction.

The road led from the estate past utilities and then over a mount forming a half-ring around a large pond with dams to keep the water high. Leading farther past the mill, across fields, it crossed the water locks and reached a village stretched in a long irregular line. The mill stood in the bottomland, its roofs level with the pond water.

In spite of thickening darkness, Witek could see a crowd gathered on the dam before the mill. For some reason, people were running in all directions, climbing trees and fences, and inarticulate disturbing screams were piercing the air. The lock was open; water was roaring down through the gates from a height of about four meters, smashing flat waves against the banks, splashing foam onto the road. When the narrow bed could not hold it anymore, the river overflew its banks, flooding them.

Witek kept looking around, and, seeing a dog running towards him, shouted, "Finka! Get here!"

People were shouting to him from trees and fences, but he could not hear a thing amid the noise of the water and continued to call up Finka, unstirred. The dog stopped for a moment and rushed to him wildly. Having got to him, she squeezed up against his feet and yelped brokenly. Her face was covered in lather, her eyes bloodshot.

"Finka!"

The dog sprang to his chest, snapping at his canvas pants with a wild clatter of her teeth, rolling in the sand, running away to return with desperate yelps.

Somehow it scared Witek. He could not understand why she was bellowing and thrashing about, and he ran to the mill. The dog ran ahead of him, down the mound, and splashed into the water. For some time, she swam towards a small island that lay at the end of a triangle formed by flows running from under the mill wheels and the water lock to merge into a roaring river. However, she was soon drifted by the powerful stream and finally washed out onto a meadow. She dashed around for a short while and eventually rushed back to the mound, rounded the mill, and lay down above the foamy water, howling and yelping terribly.

Hearing people shout the dog to be rabid, Witek climbed a high fence. The landowner, whom fear had driven to climb a tree, sent a laborer of his to get a gun from the house. Witek felt so sorry for the dog that he called for her in a sweet voice. Finka ran up to him and began gnawing on fence stakes, digging the sand with her hind legs, whirling, and yelping. She was running up to trees with people on them, yipping, scratching off tree bark with her claws, rolling on the ground, dashing to the water every once in a while, panting, exhausted, and dirty, crawling up to the edge of the mound to cast a glance of her bloodshot eyes at the haze over the roaring water. Her yelping was convulsive was anguish. Sometimes she ran to people again, thrashing even more heavily. Her entire body was wriggling, and then she lay dead still, curled up. Finally, she was too weak to even yawl, and only her wheezing could be discerned against the noise of water, which was getting higher and higher. Only the middle part of the tiny island, which was the tallest one, still showed its white sand above it. Gulls leaving their nests squalled above the fields, and a thick fog covered everything.

The gun was brought. It took the landowner long to aim at the dog's head. At long last, he shot, and Finka fell off the dam into the water; she was fighting the waves for a couple of minutes, but then she managed to get out. Wheezing heavily, she ran towards the fields.

Witek got off the fence and watched her disappear into the dark sadly. "She was so good at driving colts and pigs," he thought, disappointed to lose his helper. "What's the matter with her? If only she could have puppies!" As he meditated, he could feel tears well in his eyes. But somebody cried out for him to help—they had to close the gate, for the water pressure was getting lower.

It was a moonlit night when he left the dam. Silence and gloom had descended onto the fields silvery with water. Only the mill was roaring and gates were squeaking in the estate; horses were neighing in their stables every once in a while; the village was awake with vibrant pipe music and occasional conversation.

Witek looked around the fields again but could not make out a thing. His pity for Finka was growing painful; he felt like crying. So he went to the shed, where old carts and tools out of use were kept. It was his shelter; here, in an old rotten wagon, he used to sleep together with Finka.

His mother came soon to bring him soup. "Here you are, eat. There's even a little meat in it." "You know, Mommy, Finka got rabid. Master shot her." "That's a pity! I called her at noon, but she didn't come." "And she didn't come to graze horses with me yesterday!" "She might have puppies. Maybe she was watching them." "And today she got rabid!" "Does it still hurt?" "Sure it does!" "That bitch turned the house into a babel. She beat Jewka and sent the governess away. And she hit Iontek on the head with a jug; he's got a huge goose egg above his eye. Rabid witch! What can you do to her? A dog has more mercy for us people…"

When Witek had finished his meal, she covered him with her coat and left.

The boy fell asleep, but the sleep was feverish—he shouted at the dog and then at the colts; he cried and tried to run away, and then he shouted merrily, murmuring repeatedly "Miss," smacking his lips to speed the horse, and woke up many times to relapse into sleep.

At dawn, when the air was getting gray, revealing silhouettes now clear, and cocks were crowing, Witek woke up at hearing the dog yelp quietly as she was licking his face. "Get off!" he muttered sleepily and was about to push her away, but the feel of her wet hair made him pull his hand back at once and sit up, now totally awake.

"Finka!" he exclaimed in a scared whisper. "Good God, Finka!"

The dog lay stretched, moaning quietly and licking him on the face, neck, chest… Two pied puppies, smeared with blood and dirt, had rolled themselves into tiny balls and were now sucking at her breasts.

"So she wanted to get to her puppies! And they thought she was rabid!" Witek muttered, moved deeply, as he stroked Finka on her wet head, which the dog had put on his chest and was stretching higher and higher, panting. "Finka! Doggy, my poor doggy! Finka!" the boy murmured in a tearful voice, wiping her blood-stained side with his sleeve and shirttail and trying to cover her with the coat. The dog was staring at him with her dull yellowish eyes, and her wheezing was getting heavier and quieter. Her body stretched in an agonic spasm, she kicked her hind legs, trying to catch her puppies and then Witek's hand with her lips, which were growing numb, and whimpered feebly. At last, she gave the boy and her puppies another lick, produced a plangent snarl, and ceased to breathe, her body contorted.

Witek could not fall back asleep. Trying to warm the freezing puppies with his body, he kept whispering to them, "You poor things! You little orphans! She brought you to me all across the river… A dog, but how much better than some of us men…"

In the morning, as Witek was driving the colts to the pasture, he put the puppies carefully in his bosom and spoke to them with a paternal affection, "Don't you be afraid; I'll bring you up all right so you can herd in colts and pigs…"

*1897*

# NOTES

We *greatly* appreciate when our readers take time to submit *good reviews* for our books.*
* www.amazon.com/dp/1530484367
www.amazon.co.uk/dp/1530484367
When readers take the time to leave a little note of thanks or that they liked your book, it means the world.

Please feel free *to share the link**
to this book on social networking sites (Facebook, Twitter, etc) or with your friends and colleagues.
* www.createspace.com/6130907
www.amazon.com/dp/1530484367
www.amazon.co.uk/dp/1530484367

The latest version of the book in a *hard* copy can be found at the following locations:

in UK & other European countries:
www.createspace.com/6130907    www.amazon.co.uk/dp/15304843

in the United States & Canada:
www.createspace.com/6130907    www.amazon.com/dp/15304843

The latest version of the book in *electronic* form can be found at the following locations:

in Poland: www.amazon.co.uk/dp/B01I2D6VU4

in the United States: www.amazon.com/dp/B01I2D6VU4

in UK: www.amazon.co.uk/gp/product/B01I2D6VU4

in Canada: www.amazon.ca/dp/B01I2D6VU4

in France: www.amazon.fr/dp/B01I2D6VU4

in Spain: www.amazon.es/dp/B01I2D6VU4

in Japan: www.amazon.co.jp/dp/B01I2D6VU4

in Brazil: www.amazon.com.br/dp/B01I2D6VU4

in Mexico: ww.amazon.com.mx/dp/B01I2D6VU4

in Australia: www.amazon.com.au/dp/B01I2D6VU4

in India: www.amazon.in/dp/B01I2D6VU4

in Germany: www.amazon.de/dp/B01I2D6VU4

Made in the USA
Lexington, KY
17 April 2018